D0240166

The Sloping
Experience

SCEPTRE

Also by Ursula Bentley

The Natural Order
Private Accounts
The Angel of Twickenham

The Sloping Experience

URSULA BENTLEY

SCEPTRE

First published in 1999 by Hodder and Stoughton
A division of Hodder Headline PLC
A Sceptre Book

British Library C.I.P.
A CIP catalogue record for this title is available
from the British Library

ISBN 0 340 68584 0

Typeset by Palimpsest Book Production Limited,
Polmont, Stirlingshire
Printed and bound in Great Britain by
Mackays of Chatham PLC, Chatham, Kent

Hodder and Stoughton
A division of Hodder Headline PLC
338 Euston Road
London NW1 3BH

For Margaret and Sarah

ſ

'Oh, *God*. Death makes life so *complicated*.' Arden occupied herself by placing hymn books under her black patent shoes, to avoid scuffing the toes. She was crossly aware that expostulations about inconvenience were no substitute for grief. Her brother Tim, angled like a lamp between the kneeler and the pew, shushed her. For a moment they bowed their heads in silence. Their father's catafalque, as Arden insisted on calling it, rested on trestles a few feet in front of them, tastefully draped in purple and surmounted by blood red carnations. The proximity of his remains disturbed Arden, and distracted her from the incense-filled Gothic gloom in which she would have revelled in normal circumstances.

The priest who had received the coffin and, among other things, sprayed it with a kind of perforated pestle, had discreetly withdrawn. Arden assumed the church was empty. A shaft of sunlight slanted across the carnations on to a padlocked candle tin under the statue of some Herbert she did not recognize. The statue showed a monk, in flawless make-up, holding a sheaf of lilies in one hand and struggling with a large book and baby Jesus in the other. Some sort of medieval New Man perhaps. Arden's enthusiasm for the Middle Ages did not extend to its hagiography.

'How long are we supposed to stay here?' she whispered. Tall, and only partially collapsible like her brother, she was concerned that her pins and needles would turn into gangrene.

Tim shrugged and said, 'Shhh.'

'Why? There's no one here. Honestly, why did Humph have to convert? This is so *barbaric*.'

'Right up your street then.'
'Bollocks. This is anally retentive Victorian—'
'Arden, *please.*'
'Sorry.' Again they bowed their heads. 'I just can't believe Dad's in that box. Sixty-nine is no age these days.'
'He couldn't face another Labour government.'
'Bit drastic, though.'
'Shhh.'
'No, *you* shhh.'
They managed to remain quiet for some moments. Arden covered her face with her hands and tried to concentrate. Her mind sifted through a lifetime's memories of her father for something appropriately positive for the occasion. Their childhood had been almost idyllic, thanks largely to his absence in the merchant navy. When he was at home his presence seemed obtrusive. Not from any character fault so much as his determination to cram as much fathering as he could into the time available, and to correct the lackadaisical habits they got into when he was away. Out went demand feeding, skipping baths, TV dinners and hanging round the bus stop till all hours. In came flash cards, family councils and regular bedtimes. They all needed to lie down in a darkened room after he went back to sea.

The last twenty years yielded few pickings. Since her divorce, and her decision to leave her son with his father, they had seen very little of Humph. Particularly after he'd moved to Suffolk and got hooked on fungi. At least he had always encouraged in her the habit of independence, even if he'd been unwilling to pay for it. She recalled the moment immediately after her successful driving test when he'd asked her to go and fetch a car from a friend of his in Aberdeen, impressing on her the degree of trust, esteem and respect this demonstrated. It was years before Arden came to wonder what kind of cheapskate would ask someone who had had their licence for two days to drive a strange car hundreds of miles in order to save the cost of proper transport.

On the other hand he had not over-reacted when she moved in with Tim. A more attentive parent might have queried the double bed and notable absence of other love interests. But then Humph had been so cross about her divorce, his irritation had used up the meagre store of attention he reserved for her affairs.

Not that she or Tim had spelled it out to anyone. It was no one's business. It went without saying they would not have children. Anyway, one was quite enough. Fond though she was of her son, of all the things that made life complicated children were the worst. They got one so het up. Arden liked to think of her emotions neatly stacked and labelled like pickles in a larder, rarely opened and used. There were accidents, naturally.

She was distracted from her thoughts by the sound of footsteps coming down the aisle. By a heroic effort of will she resisted turning round and instead peered through her fingers as the stranger approached the coffin. It was a woman.

Arden glared. The woman was about thirty-five and somewhat heavy above elegantly tapered legs. Her blonde hair suggested an unsuccessful argument with Sun In and she wore an electric blue jacket that was too big for her. Arden nudged her brother, who had nodded off. They watched, incredulous, as the woman walked boldly up to the coffin, placed an envelope on it, bowed her head and then, with downcast eyes and one hand over her mouth, walked back down the aisle and out of the church. She had been crying.

They both frowned at the spot where she had stood. Then Tim resumed his prayerful sag over the pew. Arden studied him in disbelief. 'Aren't you going to get it?' she hissed.

'What? No – no.' He shuddered, rather than shook, his head.

'Why not?'

'It's nothing to do with us.'

'Don't be stupid. Of course it is. Go *on*.'

'No! Oh . . . all right.' They looked round to make sure they were alone. Then, with an embarrassed shuffle and head down, Tim whipped the envelope off the coffin and handed it to Arden.

'It's not stuck down.' She studied the writing. 'It just says "To Humph". Well, it can't be delivered, can it?' She began to open the envelope.

'Arden, no! It's private.'

'Don't be such a wimp. What's the harm?'

Tim made the muted gurgle of frustration that always heralded immediate capitulation. He hated to be called a wimp and his being an accountant did not help. He could not resist a challenge to his manhood. 'Go on, then.' They settled back into the pew.

'It's a card,' said Arden. 'Very tasteful. Fog Over Windermere.'

'Hurry up. I feel like a grave robber.'

'"My darling Humph, no words can express how much I'll miss you. My dearest friend, you were the best. Your ever loving, Thalia". *Thalia!* Who the fu—I mean, who is this?'

'Let me look.' Tim studied the words, but could not improve on Arden's reading. 'Some girlfriend. Does it matter now?'

'*Matter?* That's not the point. If you're right, why didn't we . . . Surely it couldn't be a girlfriend – with Mum still alive?'

'Only just, love. Be fair. Perhaps she didn't mind. Or even know. Look, I don't think this is the best place to discuss it, do you? That lady from the undertaker's is probably here by now. We've vigilated long enough.'

Arden tapped the card thoughtfully against her teeth as they walked up the aisle.

The assistant director of Rattle & Son was waiting in the porch, engrossed in a pamphlet she had taken from a rack of spiritual mini-guides. She was picking her nose, as one does when absorbed in fine literature. Arden experienced a flush of anger and contempt for the woman, which surprised her. Considering her own supposed detachment from her father, she could not immediately understand why this indignity offered to him made her feel like ripping the piscina from the wall and braining the woman with it.

'There's a bin outside,' she said, in what she hoped was an icy tone.

The woman jumped, and blushed a deep magenta that blended surprisingly well with the discreet navy blue ensemble. She did not follow Arden's suggestion, if she had understood it.

'Ah – Mrs Fairbrother. Mr Mason.' She quickly put the pamphlet back on the rack. 'I got rather carried away there. All about a saint called Uncumber. She grew a beard to stop her father marrying her off. Fancy.'

'Did it work?' asked Tim.

'Yes and no. He crucified her instead.'

Arden pulled a face. *'Fathers!* Honestly.' She turned to Tim. 'There's always someone worse off than oneself.'

'Oh, I'm sorry. That was tactless – with your father—'

'Not at all.' Tim elbowed Arden aside.

'And I trust the arrangements were satisfactory?'

'Yes, thank you, Mrs Body. I'm sure the funeral will be – even better.'

'Brady. Not Body. Mrs Brady.'

'Did I say . . . ? Oh, dear, I'm so sorry.'

'Not at all, sir. Our old friend the Freudian slip.' Her smile gave Arden to understand that the faux pas with the bogey was now history. 'Happens all the time. It's very hard conducting such sensitive arrangements with strangers.'

'You're very understanding, Mrs Brady.'

Arden felt like offering to wait in the car, as Tim and Mrs Brady beamed at one another.

'There are one or two delicate matters to discuss, if you and your sister are ready?'

'Certainly. All right, Ard?'

'Fine.'

'Shall we step outside, sir? It's still pleasantly warm.'

The path to the lych gate was lined with standard roses that lurched southwards from their beds of tatty forget-me-nots. The church, a red brick mishap, had been built in the last century on a hill at the edge of the town. Mrs Brady invited them to admire the excellent view of rape and corn fields that spread out towards the distant village of Sloping St Wilfrid, with its castle on a tree-covered plateau beyond. It was in the grounds of this castle that their father had lived.

Despite the pleasantly warm temperature, Arden felt cold and trembly. She put it down to delayed shock. The drama of death and its imperative hustle of arrangements. And the trees of Sloping Castle shrouded the site of her last real encounter with Humph, when she had instinctively sought his moral support for her decision to leave her husband. It had not been forthcoming. From having opposed the marriage in the first place, her father reacted as though the divorce involved the loss of a hefty deposit on his part. He blamed their mother's indulgent child-rearing practices for Arden's inability to get past the first hurdle. In vain did she point out that her husband Garth had taken a vow of celibacy – an obstacle to marriage that at least bore comparison with Bechers Brook. Not to mention his insistence that she stay at home and recycle her tights, and spend every weekend with the Woodland Folk. In retrospect, Arden realized that she had only married him because they both thought England had gone steadily down the drain since the death of Simon de Montfort.

Following her troubled gaze, Tim took her hand and gave it a squeeze. Mrs Brady was in full throttle about the need for a bypass as a couple of HGVs full of petrified chickens thundered into the narrow streets.

'You said there were some matters to discuss, Mrs Brady?'

'Yes, sir.' She lowered her voice. 'One in particular. We haven't received any instructions as to whether you wished to place any mementoes in the coffin. It's rather late in the day, but it could be arranged. I understand your father had been a merchant seaman? Perhaps some instrument he particularly valued? A nautical octant, for example, or a favourite mushroom.'

Tim and Arden looked blank. 'Um, the thing is, Mrs Brady, my sister and I haven't been able to see much of our father since he's been up here. I don't think we could say, with any confidence—'

'Don't worry. It's just such a pity when people think of it too late. We have followed the solicitor's directions about the box of letters, of course.'

'Letters?' Arden swivelled to face her. 'What letters?'

'Why, the ones your father left instructions were to be buried with him, Mrs Fairbrother. You didn't know, I take it? That's not unusual, I'm afraid, in such personal—'

'Can we see them?'

'I'm afraid not. They're already in the coffin.'

'So? If you can open it to put something in, you could do so to take something out.'

Mrs Brady gasped as politey as she could and looked at Tim for assistance.

'No, Ard, of course we can't. I'm sorry. My sister's upset.'

'And I don't mind telling you why, Mrs Brady.' She took the card out of her coat pocket. 'This was put on our father's coffin by some woman we'd never heard of, implying they had had an intimate relationship. Of course I'm upset. Perhaps the letters would tell us more.'

Mrs Brady took a step backwards and stumbled on a Coke can. She was deeply flustered. 'With respect, Mrs Fairbrother, if the deceased wishes to take an item with him to the grave, it usually means he doesn't want anyone else to see it.'

'Did you get a look at them?'

'No, I did not.'

'How do you know they were letters, then?'

'Because they were so described by the solicitor, Mrs Fairbrother. I wouldn't dream of doing such a thing.'

Tim put an arm around Arden to prevent her from assaulting the undertaker. 'Please excuse my sister. This has been an added shock, you see, on top of everything else—'

But Mrs Brady did not look mollified. In fact she looked at Arden as though she had stepped beyond all known pales of funerary behaviour. 'Anyway, the tin was locked, as you would expect.'

'Tin? I thought it was a box.'

'All right – a *tin* box. An old cash box type of thing.'

'No jewelled casket, then?'

'Calm down, love. I think we'd better be going, Mrs Brady. Was there anything else?'

'Only the flowers, sir. What would you like done with them?' Mrs Brady was on autopilot now, her face a mask.

'I've no idea. What usually happens to them?'

'Some people like to take them home. Others send them to a local hospital.'

Arden snorted. 'I'd think that was the last place that would need reminding of mortality. Just leave them.'

'Whatever my sister wants, Mrs Brady. We'll just leave them.'

'Very well. Shall I arrange for their disposal after – a week, say?'

'Yes. Good.'

'It's not really a waste, you know,' said Arden. Mrs Brady clearly thought they would be depriving the sick of their statutory right to nearly new flower arrangements. 'The gesture is in the waste, isn't it? If they were recycled as mattress stuffing it wouldn't be quite the same, would it?'

'I never said it would, Mrs Fairbrother. It was only a routine enquiry, I assure you.'

'Fine.' Tim steered Arden towards the gate. 'We'll see you tomorrow, Mrs Brady.'

'Yes, sir. And may I say again how sorry I am for your loss.'

'Thank you. Come on, love. Let's go and see if Bos has arrived yet.'

'Let's drive round for a while, Tim. I love this landscape. You half expect Piers Plowman to be hitching a lift back to his hovel.'

'If you say so, Ard. Look, there's a chap hitching back to his. Shall we?'

'Certainly not.'

Fearing for his wing mirrors, Tim turned into a narrow road, down which an incontinent tractor had recently passed. 'You were a bit hard on Mrs Brady, Ard. You can't go around accusing people of professional misconduct.'

'I didn't. I only asked. What do you suppose they were – the letters?'

'Who knows? One always thinks of love letters in this sort of situation, I suppose.'

'*Dad* writing love letters? Or receiving them!'

'We didn't know him when he was young. The most obvious candidate is – well, you know. Who's the one person he never talks – talked – about?'

Arden thought hard. 'Ah, I know. Your mother.'

'Exactly. Makes sense, doesn't it?'

'Perfect sense. Self-centred to the last. It never occurred to him that you might like to have them after he'd gone. You know so little about her. Aren't you curious?'

'Let's not jump the gun, Ard. It's only a possibility.'

'Still, letters apart, you never *were* curious. I haven't thought about it before.'

'I didn't need to be, did I? To be honest, I don't think I liked the idea of having a different mother from you. Mattie did a good job. If I'd gone banging on about my mother it would have – well – spoiled things, wouldn't it?'

'Yes, I see what you mean. Did you think of that at the time, or just now?'

'At the time. I'm the sensitive, caring one, remember.'

'True. But that wasn't the reason. It just means you had strong – and subtle – survival instincts. You evolved to suit the prevailing conditions.'

'Flatterer.'

'Was I very horrid to Mrs Brady?'

'Unnecessarily so, yes.'

'Sorry. I'll praise her lock-knit jumper suit next time, to make up for it.'

'Ard—'

'Did you think she was attractive?'

'For pity's sake, I don't notice things like that at a time like this.'

'Or any other time. I worry about you.'

'Put a sock in it, Ard.' Tim fidgeted and flushed whenever his relationships with other women were touched on. He had once been married – to a small, neat girl Arden had never liked who subsequently went to the very top in garden furniture. He had never got used to trailing round DIY stores in the name of love and did not take much persuading to resume where he and Arden had left off when she was twelve and began to worry that any babies they produced might have three heads. As his mother had run off to Canada with a pilot when he was two he had early on received the impression that women, apart from Arden, were all unreliable.

'Squirm away, darling, but I must say this. If you did meet someone else, you mustn't worry about me. Being lonely and destitute and whatnot.'

'No, I wouldn't. Do shut up, Ard.'

'Oh, I've got such a headache. I thought this was all going to be so straightforward. Painful but definitive, as it were. Now there's all this *crap* with mystery blondes and buried letters. Honestly, why did Dad have to make his life so *complicated*?'

Tim laughed. 'I've told you before, if you want an uncomplicated life you'd better be an uncomplicated person. You always talk as if people happen to life. It's the other way round, surely? As for the mystery blonde – so Dad had a mistress. It's hardly a talking point these days.'

'No. What gets under my skin is that, to judge by her mushy

sentiments, he was closer to her than he ever was to us. I think
I'd like to thump her.'

'That's one way of making life complicated.'

'Let's go back. There's a nasty smell of the midden coming off
these fields.'

'The smell of the Middle Ages. I'm surprised you don't wear
it behind your ears.'

'That's not so fanciful. Healthy human turds smell of violets.
Can you hurry up, darling. You're right, Bos might be here
by now.'

Bos was Arden's son. She had come to regret calling him
Bosworth. While pregnant she had got carried away by *The
Daughter of Time*, a persuasive vindication of Richard III. These
days she would probably have chosen something more conventional – like Sigismund.

Against her will, Arden was deeply moved by the funeral, a
standard menu for the use of relatives like herself and Tim who
were not at hand to organize a personalized tribute. Afterwards
she rationalized that her detachment from her father, which
had functioned smoothly, with occasional *engagements*, for most
of her life, was undermined by the grossly unfair weight and
solemnity of public ritual. Ritual arising from and answering
the needs of the collective unconscious, which entirely ignored
her own lack of need for it. She protested to Tim that she
would probably have got just as upset at her boss's funeral.
Or anybody's. 'I mean, you're *massaged* by all those minor keys
and gut-wrenching poems. It positively forces your emotions up
like toothpaste. It's so *unfair*.'

Tim did not say anything. He, too, had experienced an unwelcome tendency to remember only the good things about his
father as the ceremony progressed. But it was no good trying
to explain to Arden that she was grieving for what might have
been. She had an absolute horror of psycho-babble.

Bos, at least, seemed unaffected by grief obtained by deception.
After the last mourners had departed from the Bishop's Hat – the
Blonde was not among them – he flopped into an armchair in the
Mitre Lounge and quenched the thirst brought on by red wine
and anchovies with a pint of bitter. Bos did not take after his tall,

raven-haired mother, although Arden was far from disappointed by his appearance. He was of average height, muscular build, and had a broad face with large, guileless grey eyes and a hammer-head nose that made him look positively medieval, especially now that his straw-coloured hair was down to his shoulders. She could imagine him training at tilt and mace, chasing boar with a group of rowdy young squires, freed from the unnatural demands laid on modern youth to sit at a desk all day and gain qualifications in the use of Windows or Leisure and Tourism.

Fortunately Bos was unaware of his disadvantages in this respect, and was quite cheerfully doing Welsh Women's Studies at the University of Newton le Willows. Arden had anxiously followed his development under his father's influence, always on the lookout for signs that he would fulfil Garth's ambition to retire from the world and live in a tepee with a self-sufficient commune on disputed land. For despite her enthusiasm for all things between 1066 and the Reformation, Arden shared with her medieval role models a sharp eye for the main chance. If Bos were to have an uncomplicated ride he must be equipped for today's world. She had therefore kept him well supplied with computer games and Adidas trainers and encouraged him to consider financial services as a career.

Despite longing to go to her room and loosen her waistband, Arden knew it was appropriate that she talked to her son instead. It was not that she did not want to talk to him, but it was always difficult to re-engage their gears in the short periods they were together, particularly so in a hotel lounge. As she sat down opposite him she was rewarded by the shameless glow of gratification on his face. She wondered how his features would cope with depression. They were designed for optimism, foolish or otherwise.

'Thank you for coming, Bos. Especially as you didn't know Humph very well. At all, that is. I appreciate it.'

'That's all right. I s'pose I should've come when he was alive, really.'

Arden sighed. 'We could all say that. On the other hand, he could have come to see you, but he never did. The fact is, there are some people it's a helluva lot easier to say goodbye to than hello. Humph was one of them, I'm afraid.'

'Why was it you didn't get on? I mean, it's cool you sitting there talking like that, but it's weird too. He didn't, like, abuse you or anything?'

'*Of course not!*' Arden pulled herself into an upright position. '*Really*, is that the first thing people think about these days? Do you *honestly* think I'm the sort of person – even as a *child*, who would—' She stopped with her mouth open. With a slight prickling of the neck she was reminded that, in view of her relationship with Tim, the uninformed might well think she *was* such a person. She was unsure how much Bos knew. Not that she minded him knowing. It just made things less complicated if he did not. Of course, she and Tim were almost of an age when they would rather watch *Gardener's World* than have sex anyway. And being only half siblings, like Lord Byron and Whatsername, it hardly counted. But most people were too obtuse to understand that. Not that it was anybody's business. Arden still occasionally boiled with indignation at the thought that complete strangers, given the opportunity, might have an opinion on the subject.

'Anyway,' she continued, 'the truth is far less titillating. Humph simply wasn't interested in us. He barged in and tried to control us from time to time, but his heart wasn't in it. Children know. And we didn't need him. Mum was perfectly adequate, so we resented his interference. I did try. Particularly as a teenager, when girls suddenly realize their father's a man, but it didn't work. I hope you don't feel that about me, Bos? Just because I left you.'

'Perish the thought, Mum!'

'Bos, don't tease.'

'Sorry. How was he round Gran, then?'

'Much the same. He was away so often it didn't matter. But he's been very good to her since she's been – deteriorating. Quite surprised us, actually. You did know he was married before, to Tim's mother? We always assumed she was the love of his life and poor Mum didn't quite cut the mustard. By the way, we'll go and see her while we're here. Can you come or do you have to get back?'

'Yeah, I do. Tonight, if that's okay. Can you give me a lift to Diss?'

'Er – all right. How's it going?'

'Okay. Well, I reckon I won't get thrown out, though . . .'

'I should think not.'

'Only – Mum?'

'What?'

'You couldn't spare some cash, could you? There's this geezer I owe—'

Arden tensed. She was reluctant to believe that Bos had come to his grandfather's funeral purely in order to ask her for money. But there was no denying she had felt much more cheerful the moment before.

'What geezer? I thought you had a student loan, besides what I give you.'

'Yeah, I do. And I'm very grateful and all that, but it doesn't go very far, Mum. And there's this Russian bloke in Feminist Approaches to the Cottage Industry who offered to lend me some money when I was short, and now he's getting heavy about it. He wants it back before we go down. I'd pay you back, Mum. I'll get a job in the vac.'

'Why can't he wait, then?'

'Well, I had a visit from some of his friends. And I think they're, like, drug dealers? I was a bit – naive, you could say.'

'Oh, my *God*! Bos! How much is it?'

'About three grand.'

'*What?* How can you *possibly* have got through so much? This is *appalling*.'

'Yeah, don't overdo it, Mum. Call it a failed business venture. Me and some mates organized a gig and – well – nobody came, in a nutshell. We had to pay up front. They probably wouldn't actually do anything. I don't have a car, so they can't split me tyres—'

'Oh, Bos, how could you be so foolish? Why didn't you ask me?'

'Come off it, Mum. What do you know about gigs? It looked like a sure thing. We didn't realize you had to advertise. Plus there was no transport to it. But it was a good experience, Mum. If I could just get this wanker off my back—'

'Bos, you take my breath away. I think I'm going to faint. My only child pursued by gangsters. Did you have to spring it on me like this?' Arden slumped back in her chair and fanned herself with a beer mat.

'I thought it was best to come straight out with it. Look, don't get fussed. It's probably not *that* bad. They haven't actually threatened me yet.'

'Oh, good. Great. But why *you*, Bos? What about your fellow entrepreneurs?'

'They're up to their eyeballs in debt anyhow. And this bloke only wanted to lend it to me. He said I had an honest face.'

'You have. Unfortunately it's more likely he knew it would be easier to pursue one person than half a dozen. Oh, I can't deal with this now. I'll have to discuss it with Uncle Tim. He's the accountant.'

'Sure. No problem. I've got till the end of term.'

'You seem to assume we can raise the money just like that.'

'No, I don't. But s'posing I did get stuffed, you'd only say I should've asked you, wouldn't you? Wouldn't you?'

'I suppose so. Oh, *God*.'

2 ∫

At the earliest opportunity Arden complained to Tim that this crisis was precisely the sort of thing she had in mind when she maintained that children made life complicated. It was all so *unnecessary*. Why could Bos and his friends not simply attend lectures, go out for a beer occasionally and stick to their budgets? Momentarily forgetting that she would rather have had Bos boar hunting or manning a siege engine, she complained in querulous tones that it was not too much to ask of young people that they reached adulthood without causing their parents heart failure or bankruptcy. Tim pointed out that these fates were standard practice for parents and she might as well expect young men to stay in on Saturday night. Arden was exasperated with this facetious response, and came close to pointing out that, as he had no children of his own, such complacency was only to be expected. However, as Tim's co-operation would be needed to get Bos out of the mess, she stopped herself in time.

Sloping Castle (remains of) was concealed from the surrounding approaches by a curtain wall, crumbling towers of ancient flints, and stately old trees. The chestnuts were heavy with their thick, phallic fluorescence – to Arden's eyes like jumbo candelabra set about a shrine.

The licence to crenellate Sloping had been granted to Sir Tomas de Slupynge in 1368, as a reward for curing the Black Prince's heartburn after the great feast at Saint-Jean-Pied-du-Port. The rebuilding had resulted in much spreading of tail feathers by Sir Tomas and his family at the time, but its situation was too out of the way to make it practical even to pillage the herring route from Great Yarmouth, so its life as a working fortress was brief. The demesne was sold off to local farmers, and domestic housing established within the baileys. The gatehouse still stood, its arrow slits home to cooing collared doves and elder bushes. The driveway beneath was barred by a bright new metal gate with a large notice on it warning visitors to Keep Out.

Tim pulled the car on to the grass verge by the curtain wall, mainly to avoid a thundering DAF that emerged from a concealed entrance further down the road. Arden was non-plussed by the Keep Out sign. 'How do we get in, then? I'm sure that wasn't there last time I came.'

'It was twelve years ago, love. Things move on. We'll leave the car here and walk.'

She approached the gatehouse racked – for her – with powerful emotions. The sombre consideration that they were to visit the cottage where their father had died was powerfully at odds with the thrill of approaching an edifice that had been home to genuine medieval folk. They were not smelly midgets, as she liked to inform people in queues at the supermarket, but on average only two centimetres shorter than modern man, and people who liked nothing better than to share a hot bath with their friends. She had often brought dinner parties to a standstill with such amazing anecdotes, including the fact that the Battle of Evesham was lost thanks to hot tubs, as Simon de Montfort's son had taken his men to bathe in the village so that they would be fresh for the battle, thus allowing the enemy to surprise them while armed only with a sponge. The idea that twelfth-century soldiers liked to be fragrant before fighting never failed to stop spoonfuls of avacado mousse in their tracks.

Tim carefully closed the gate while Arden took their bearings. The driveway ran between wide lawns dotted with trees, and forked just beyond an unidentifiable pile of flint masonry with a door sagging off it. Swifts sucked in rolling drifts over the tower in the curtain wall, their wings sharp as the daggers the inhabitants below had once used to eat their breakfast. Arden felt faint with awe and took Tim's arm to steady her step.

The main drive led round to the Hall belonging to their father's friend Harry Jermigan. The smaller, scruffier one went to the cottage, and beyond to a terrace of agricultural cottages that were rented out to Jermigan's workers. It occurred to Arden that they should have confirmed that they were to inherit the cottage before coming to inspect it, but it was too late now. She made a mental note to call the solicitor, who was also the executor of the will, and ask him to send them a copy. Odd that Humph had not asked Harry Jermigan to be the executor, as they were such old friends. Sad, she supposed, that he had had to employ a professional, but as they were the only children she did not foresee a problem.

It was a strange thing that Humph had made up for all his failings by leaving them a gift which Arden, at least, would have died for, although she would have preferred the whole thing. She doubted that the present lord of Sloping appreciated his possession. Jermigan had been a childhood friend of Humph's, the son of a plumber, and he and Humph had joined the Merchant Navy together. His wife, who had died when a giant teacup had gone out of control at a funfair, had been extremely wealthy. He was not an obvious candidate to be a guardian of the national heritage.

They separated at the masonry pile. A slice of varnished redwood was nailed to it, inscribed Sloping Hall, and underneath were smaller but matching slices with the names Jermigan, Tree and Makepeace. Arden looked searchingly at the Hall for signs of Jermigan's unworthiness to possess it. They were not immediately apparent. No tilt-'n'-turn windows, no satellite dish hinted at an interior resembling an Argos living room. In her mind's eye she blotted out the later additions and saw the original long house, with a porch in the middle and stumpy wings to either end. It would probably have been thatched, which would have softened the outlines of the starkly dressed flint. Dreading yet longing to see a hideous three-piece suite in front of the inglenook, they approached the front door and rang the bell. At least it did not play 'Danny Boy'.

The door was opened a crack by a pale teenage girl, represented by a hank of thick mousy hair and one large eye. Arden peered past her and was disappointed to see a well-worn Knole sofa, some decent portraits, banqueting chairs and a pulpit. She switched on the reassuring smile she trained on new clients at the estate agency where she worked.

'Sorry to disturb you. We've come for the keys to Barnacle Cottage. Mr Mason's. We're his children. I believe you were expecting us. Is Mr Jermigan at home?'

'No. Wait.' She pushed the door to and left them there.

'*Honestly!*' tutted Arden. 'Manners. Mum would have died if I'd been so rude.'

'Perhaps she hasn't got a mum.'

'That's true. I never heard that Jermigan had any children.'

While they waited, Arden was reflecting on the blessed quietness of the place – a quietness so stressfully denied to modern man – when the ground shook with the vibrations of some diesel-powered behemoth starting up beyond the surrounding copse. Simultaneously a trio of yapping black hell-hounds bounded out of the trees towards them. Tim clutched her arm. He had been petrified of dogs since a traumatic incident with a West Highland White when he was three. Arden swiftly pushed the door open and pulled him inside.

An upright older woman in an apron was approaching them with an expression of helpful enquiry. She stopped, and continued to dry her hands on a tea towel with a more wary expression. This must be Miss Tree, of whom Arden had heard but never met. The cardigan and skullcap haircut did nothing to flatter her skinny frame, but Arden noted the delicate features and flashy rings and was not surprised when the woman spoke in the distinctive tones of the squirearchy. It took a certain class of person to wear four eternity rings while doing the housework. Why on earth she was skivvying for Harry Jermigan was a question that momentarily distracted Arden from the business in hand.

'Mrs Fairbrother? Lottie said you had come for the keys.'

'What? Oh, yes. Sorry to crash in like that. The dogs.' She indicated the front door, where the mighty oak was yielding as to a battering ram.

'Oh, dear. They're supposed to be in the kennel while Mr Jermigan's away. One of the men must have let them out. They can be a bit naughty. Sorry about that. Did they blood you?'

'No, we're fine. Aren't we, Tim? This is my brother, Timothy Mason.'

'Miss Tree.' They shook hands. 'How d'you do? You'd better

come in and have a coffee or something while I look for the keys. Mind how you go on the rugs, the flags have just been polished.'

'Are they Qum? The rugs,' said Arden, her fingers crossed.

Miss Tree smiled and perceptibly relaxed. 'Yes, they are. The one you're standing on is a Boteh, of course.'

'Of course.'

'I keep telling Mr Jermigan to hang them but he says the dogs would get rheumatism on the bare stone. They will anyway, but there we are.'

'What you need in here is medieval matting. It's all the rage in Chiswick.'

'Really? Well, come through.'

Tim smiled at Arden, to comfort her for the way her pleasantry had landed at Miss Tree's feet like a shot partridge. Arden shrugged. She was quite willing to eat humble pie prepared by such well-qualified hands.

Miss Tree led them through several wonderfully gloomy rooms, sparsely furnished with blackened oak, tapestries, and the occasional well-placed wooden angel. Tim had to drag Arden out of the dining room, where the bull's blood colourwash had been carefully applied to allow the image of a naked man being boiled in a cauldron to stand revealed.

In the kitchen Miss Tree seated them at the table and Arden looked around with blatant delight. In many ways it was the *pièce de résistance* – a square, beamed room not seven feet high, with a sooty inglenook large enough to park an ambulance. In the outside wall were two small shuttered windows, the mullions so dark that a light was needed even on the sunniest day. Arden was particularly relieved that Smallbone of Devizes had not been let loose on the room. A Belfast sink and Rayburn were the only modern touches. Food and utensils were crammed into worm-eaten cupboards. She commented to Miss Tree on the impressive drive for authenticity she had observed so far. Miss Tree remained thin-lipped.

'Mr Jermigan would have liked me to take the washing down to the stream but I drew the line there.'

'I had no idea he was so keen on the Middle Ages. Mind you, buying a place like this should have been a clue. It must be terribly expensive to run. How does he manage it?'

'You will excuse me if I don't discuss my employer's affairs, Mrs Fairbrother. Milk?'

'Yes, please. Tim has three sugars.'

'You can help yourselves. Now, where did I put those keys?'

As Miss Tree started to search the drawers, Arden signalled to Tim to take over the conversation while she recovered from her gaffe. It was one of many discreet semaphors they had developed to communicate with each other when they were in company and diversionary tactics were called for. As when Arden had been innocently boasting of her Campbell ancestors to a Macdonald.

Tim opened with a query about crop rotation. Miss Tree was adjusting to the change of tack when there was a knock at the back door and a young man in overalls came in, with some urgency.

'Oh – sorry, Miss Tree. Didn't know you had visitors. Can you come to the office? Darren's on the phone from Spoleto. Wankers at the warehouse won't let 'im unload and if 'e hangs around too long 'e'll miss out on the tomatoes at Casirighi or something.'

'Can't Vera handle it?'

'She's just gone off to the mobile breast unit.'

'All right. I'll take it in the study. Wait here, Jake. Excuse me a moment.'

'Of course.' Arden was intrigued. It was clear that the trees from which the dogs had emerged concealed the site of a sizeable haulage business. Not the kind of occupation she would have expected from a man supposedly steeped in medieval values. Miss Tree went off, calmly confident, to deal with the crisis. Was there anything she did not do for Harry Jermigan?

Tim dusted off his query about crop rotation, but Jake was from Kennington and was happiest talking about HGVs. So while Tim discussed the case for eight-wheeler rigids as opposed to artics, Arden cocked an ear to Miss Tree on the phone to Spoleto.

'Darren? It's Miss Tree. What's the problem? Yes. Yes, I see. Don't worry, Darren, Ted had exactly the same trouble with them. Yes. Won't they? But surely the equipment is there? No, that's not a good idea, Darren, there are too many of them. Calm down, dear. Have you tried talking to them? I see. Yes.

Have you got a pencil? Go on. All right. Sono kee dah n po di tempo. Got that? Chay la possibilita chay ill meeo camion venga skarikahto ogeee. All right? Yes. Just a moment. Here we are. Ill kareecho devay esseray portahto in a altro magazeeno. Let me know how it goes. What? Oh, dear, the splitter box. Yes, that's very worrying. Yes, I know, Darren. Let's put it this way: better the splitter box than the contract. Are you with me? All right. Vera will be back by then. Goodbye, dear.'

As Miss Tree came back into the room Tim gave the signal that they should be going – three tugs on the left earlobe. Arden ignored him. An opportunity to talk to Miss Tree might not come again. She boldly drained coffee from the percolator. Tim sat down.

'I don't want to rush you,' said Miss Tree, 'but you'll have to excuse me if I get on with the men's lunch. It's just soup. They bring their own sandwiches. But Mr Jermigan likes those that are here to sit down together – with him, usually. However, we carry on.'

'You have a pretty varied brief, Miss Tree. Mr Jermigan's away on business, I presume?'

'Not exactly. He's hunting elk in Canada. Or moose, as I believe they're called over there.' She stirred onions with unnecessary force. No breath of criticism would pass her lips, but she obviously did not approve.

'That explains why he wasn't at the funeral. We did rather expect him. He and my father were such old friends, weren't they?'

'He was informed, naturally. He was deeply sorry, but unfortunately it wasn't possible for him to get away. It was a terrible shock for all of us. Your father was very special. Very special.'

'Thank you.' What did that ever mean? thought Arden. It was an irritating catchphrase that covered everyone. 'Did you come to the funeral, Miss Tree? I'm afraid I don't remember.'

'Of course. But I had to go straight home after the service. Lottie came too. Charlotte. She was very fond of your father.'

'Was she?' Arden wanted to add 'Why?' 'She's Mr Jermigan's niece, I gather?'

Miss Tree sighed. 'Yes. He adopted her when his sister died.'

'There seems to be a high mortality rate in his family. His wife, his sister—'

'They died together. It was terrible.'

'What in that same – teacup, wasn't it?'

'Adjacant teacups. It was a family outing for Lottie's birthday.'

'Poor *child*. How *appalling*. No wonder she's . . . It was good of him to look after her. Was it – you know – guilt? A sense of responsibility?'

'I really couldn't say. But he has never regretted it. Lottie's got a father somewhere. New Zealand, I think. He never bothers to get in touch with her. No doubt he'll turn up to see her get a double first at Oxford.' A swede bore the brunt of Miss Tree's indignation.

'Is that likely?'

'Perfectly. If she doesn't go off the rails to save the planet, or the poor, or whatever nonsense young people get up to these days. I don't know what's going on in her head sometimes. She has more rapport with animals than people. Especially her family. That cat's her principle confidant.' She pointed to a white puffball with eyes, which stood by his empty bowl swishing his tail with the rhythmic menace of a nuclear countdown. 'Mr Jermigan worships Lottie. It's very hurtful for him. Very hurtful.'

It must be, thought Arden, for Miss Tree to wax so blunt about relations within her revered employer's family. Her indignation had overcome the reticence of loyalty. 'Still, adolescents are notoriously self-centred, aren't they? They have such contempt for their parents they would have no trouble at all finding a cat superior. It's just a phase.'

'Possibly. She could read when she was two, you know. And hasn't stopped since.'

'That's nice.' Arden was unimpressed. The world had got on perfectly well before every Tom, Dick and Harry could read. Bos had not started until he was nine, and stopped shortly afterwards, and it had not done him any harm. 'Miss Tree, did you know my father well?'

Tim tapped his watch. 'Ard, we should be—'

'Shhh. Did you, Miss Tree?'

'Pretty well. He was in and out a lot. One of the family, as it were. I wouldn't say we were intimate, but – oh dear, we will miss him.'

'Would you be aware if he had any personal relationships?'

'Ard!'

'Shhh. Let me be frank – I mean girlfriends. It won't upset me, or anything, but I would really like to know.'

'Well . . .' Miss Tree looked genuinely puzzled. 'No, I don't think he did. Mind you, we can't see the cottage from here. He could have concealed them from public view. Not that he would have done. It would be completely out of character, with your mother still alive. Surely you don't need me to tell you that? I can't imagine why you ask.' Miss Tree had frosted over.

'It's not just prurience on my part. You see, I have evidence that someone called Thalia was very important to him. And we have no idea who she is. Have you ever heard the name? Or seen him with a blonde woman in her thirties?'

Tim groaned and began to walk about.

'No, I haven't. I know nothing about it.'

'I don't mean to offend you, Miss Tree. But it seems that this Thalia was very close to him and I can't help being curious.'

'Perhaps not. If she was that close, she might be mentioned in the will. I presume he made one.'

'The will . . . Good thinking.'

'You may find some more evidence at the cottage.' Miss Tree's tone was disdainful.

'That's true. I should have thought of that. Come on, Tim.'

'I've been ready for hours.'

'Here are the keys. I'll show you out.'

Lottie was curled up on the Knole sofa with the white cat in the Great Room. She was reading a large textbook, and muttered a monosyllable when Arden said goodbye. Miss Tree shook her head by way of mitigation for her manners, reluctanctly realigning with Arden as a put-upon adult. She came outside with them. Arden breathed deeply of the softly sprouting thyme in the box-edged beds in front of the Hall. They were interplanted with Kaufmannii tulips, brought on by the warm spring. A pity. Tulips were a glaring anachronism.

'Oh, look, Tim – doves. Are they turtles?'

'Collared, I think. Same thing, really.'

Arden followed the doves' flight up to the tower, where a bored guard in a leather cap would have stood in more exciting times, on the lookout for raiding parties from Beccles. She felt the weight of a mulberry worsted gown on her limbs, saw the peasants dragging their wooden ploughs through the pure, organic soil, smelt the wholesome steam of bacon and pease pottage. It was all too much.

Miss Tree handed Tim the keys. 'I'm really very sorry about your father.'

'Oh, that's all right,' said Arden. Miss Tree looked confused, possibly affronted. 'We'll bring these back as soon as we've finished.'

'I presume you plan to sell the cottage.' She meant 'hope' as Tim, at least, was well aware.

'We haven't thought about it yet.' Tim took Arden's arm and joggled it a bit, recognizing the glazed look that overcame her in the presence of medieval rubble. 'But I expect we will.'

'Mr Jermigan might be interested. Perhaps you could give him a ring when you decide. He should be – back in a month or so.'

'Certainly. That might simplify matters. Save agents' fees, eh, 'Ard?'

'What? I don't know that I want to sell it.' The mention of Jermigan's interest in the property had raised her hackles. Did he not have enough seigneurial acreage already? He had probably been waiting for Humph to die in order to close that gap in the demesne. The cottage was as isolated in enemy territory as West Berlin under the communists.

'Perhaps I spoke out of turn,' said Miss Tree. 'Forget I said anything.'

'Now don't give me the third degree for quizzing her about the blonde.' Tim was frog-marching Arden down the drive. 'I'm determined to get to the bottom of it. I'm not asking you to do anything. Anyway, as a man, perhaps the whole thing just raises Humph in your estimation?'

'Don't talk rubbish, woman. He's dead now. What's the point of pursuing it?'

'Would you still be so sanguine if he's left her everything?'

'Well . . .'

'Precisely.'

'But you don't even know she was his mistress.'

'What else could she have been – the cleaner? When nobody ever saw her? Even if it is all perfectly innocent, I just want to know.'

'I still don't see why it's so important.'

They arrived at Barnacle Cottage. It was not, sadly, medieval but circa 1780, double-fronted, the plaster painted a tasteful Almond Biscuit, now chipped and stained. An ancient wisteria grew across the front door. The area in front of the cottage was paved with large flagstones, and there were two tubs of rhododendrons choked with grass. Despite its relative newness it was a charming des. res., snuggled in the lea of the curtain wall now romantically obscured with ivies and lichen. Arden had imagined this would be a sticky moment, emotionally, but she was too flustered for reflection or sentiment.

'If you must know, I think it's because the idea made me so angry. He never had time for us – or Mum. And yet he could dance attendance on some woman. Perhaps I want to find out it isn't true? It's no wonder so many people go to shrinks when their parents die. They don't do anything to prepare us for it, do they?'

'I dread to think what a psychiatrist would make of your curiosity in this case. If he knew about us, anyway.'

'What do you mean?'

'Well, you know.'

'That I'm experiencing sexual jealousy? *Honestly*, Tim, don't be so *stupid*. You know perfectly well we got together because we couldn't be bothered to look for anyone else.'

'Did we?'

'*Of course*. Did you think we'd got some keep-it-in-the-family gene or something? Well, that's not all there was to it, you know that.' She gave his arm a reassuring squeeze. 'Oh, no, there's no soakaway out here. And the gutters are cracked, too. Dad must have been poorly for some time or he'd have had that fixed.'

The door led straight into the living room. There was a gate-legged table with chairs at one end and an old sofa and rocking chair at the other. Knocked through, thought Arden, noting the two fireplaces. Would fetch £95,000, possibly £105,000, if it was decorated. There was a longcase clock with a picture of Windsor Castle on the face and a 'fine' secretary, but apart from old photographs of ships and new ones of mushrooms there was little to personalize the room. Arden experienced no intimations of cosmic loss. The air was not plangent with the anger of their last encounter. And Humph had not taken her advice to Unibond the plaster before painting, as it was now bubbling and damaged. She led the way through the glazed door into the kitchen-cum-family room. Tim walked over to the sink.

'Look. His mug is still unwashed.'

'There's no one else to do it. That's our job now, I suppose.'

'Lot of stuff to clear up in here.'

'Not really. It's mostly magazines.' Yellowing piles of the *Mycologist* and *Radio Times* were stacked by the wood-burning stove. Piles of books supported shelves of more books. Old trainers and green, rubber boots were neatly arranged on a shoe rack by the back door. Tim gazed thoughtfully, into the garden. It was paved, like the front, with more shaggy evergreens in tubs. Arden hugged him.

'It's frightfully romantic. You could put a water feature in the middle there, and have a pergola round the outside. You know, gothic arches. Look, there's a door in the wall. Do you think there was a moat outside? Shall we go and look? I don't remember any of this.'

'I don't give a sod about the moat, Ard.'

'No. All right, dear.' She left him to his mysterious manly thoughts and went into the study, which was a single-storey extension to the family room.

It was a pity Tim had mentioned clearing up. There was a month's worth in the study. It was packed with filing cabinets and lined with shelves on which were piled labelled shoe boxes, wicker baskets, glass phials, sieves and more books. A glazed cupboard contained bottles of potassium hydroxide, ammonia, ferrous sulphate and vanilla. There were slews of photographs of fungi and spore patterns, two microscopes, a computer, and an old fridge under the bench. A withered mushroom, originally a foot in diameter, lay on a pile of bills on the desk.

Arden tiptoed back to the door to check that Tim was still

deep in thought and then, as quietly as she could, rifled through the papers and drawers. There was an old address book but, of course, no Thalia under 'T'. She slipped it into her handbag. No diary. That was strange. It was possible that the woman had a key and had already removed evidence of her part in his life. But then, why would she want to? And there was an organic asymmetry to the disorder that made it difficult to believe it had been tampered with.

Once the search was completed Arden began to feel uncomfortable in the confined space where Humph had spent so many happy hours not thinking about them. He must indeed have been lost to the fungal kingdom – a dusty calendar stood at 3 September and it was now April.

Tim came to the door. 'We'll have to get a skip for this lot.'

'Yes. But have you thought when?'

'Have to come at the weekends. There's Mum to be considered as well. We'll have to visit her now Humph's gone.'

'Tim, we can't drive four hours and back every weekend. She may not even recognize us by now.'

'You can't mean we should abandon her?'

'*Of course not.* Perhaps she could be moved nearer to us?'

'Oh, Lord, I don't know. Do you want to look upstairs?'

'Not particularly. But I suppose we should.'

There was certainly no evidence of a woman's presence in the bedrooms. No spare clothes in the wardrobes, no Quickies on the window ledge in the bathroom. Neither was there any trace of their mother except for some family photographs taken when Tim and Arden were in primary school. Their father's bed had been casually made, and they tidied it up before leaving.

'Change is in the air,' said Arden as they drove back into town. The streets were festive with the red and yellow standards of Labour and its catchily named candidate, Mr Blizzard.

'I doubt it,' said Tim. 'Not if they don't have the bottle to raise taxes. That's probably why they put the yellow in.'

'Do you know, I met a woman the other day who said she was looking forward to having a government for which one need not blush. Isn't that extraordinary? Fancy being so interested in politics that you actually have feelings about it.'

'Nothing wrong with that. Just because you live in the past.'

'*I do not* live in the past.' Tim braked suddenly and a copy of *The Paston Letters*, which Arden kept in the glove box, shot out. 'It's just that it's more interesting.' She picked up the book. 'Like this, for instance, in 1449. This is Margaret Paston writing to her husband to send more crossbows and quarrels to defend the manor from their enemies, and at the end of the letter she reminds him about the sugar and almonds, and sends detailed instructions for broadcloth for the children. What a woman! People just don't live like that anymore.'

'Yes, we're the living dead all right.'

'She was burned out of the manor in the end, but did that stop her complaining that she only had glass beads to wear for Margaret of Anjou's At Home? Not a bit of it.'

'Poor Ard. You're wasted in a democracy.'

'I know. Still there's one thing to be said for the twentieth century. If we'd lived in the Middle Ages we'd probably have been burned at the stake.' She kissed him on the cheek, in gratitude for his willingness to indulge her fantasies. 'What was that woman's name?'

'Mrs Brady.'

Rattle & Sons, Funeral Directors, stood in a quiet side street away from the milling crowd. The fine weather had drawn at least twenty people into the town, many of them old ladies. The funeral parlour had been brought up to date with the life-enhancing tendency of today's obsequies by fresh pistachio paint, blow-ups of daffodils and the Conquest of Everest, thickets of potted palms and a sofa in living green. Mrs Brady came round the desk to shake hands. She wore yet another smart lock-knit ensemble, this time in charcoal grey with revers that matched the sofa.

They exchanged cliches about the funeral and Arden asked if they might have the cards from the floral tributes. Mrs Brady disappeared into the back through a kasbah curtain. Tim sat down and opened his jacket. He looked paler than ever. Arden assumed the strain of the last few days was taking its toll and put a comforting hand on his shoulder. Mrs Brady came back with the cards in an envelope.

'And the account?'

'We'll be posting that to the solicitor shortly, but perhaps you'd like to have some idea?'

'That would be most helpful.'

'Of course. Won't be a moment.'

Tim stood up. 'I think I'll get some fresh air, Ard.'

'Are you all right?'

'Yes. I'm not used to a fried breakfast, that's all. I'll wait outside.'

When Mrs Brady returned with the folder she went through the items with such an insouciant air that they were made to seem quite inexpensive. She handed Arden the list.

'Are you staying in the area long, Mrs Fairbrother?'

'No. We're going back tomorrow, unfortunately. After we've visited our mother. She's a bit – you know. A stroke.'

'How sad. You're virtually an orphan then. We see so many people in your situation, and it doesn't matter how old they are, when their parents go they suddenly feel all alone in the world. Like little children again. But it passes.'

'Really?' Arden had a ghastly feeling she might cry. The idea of being an orphan was one of those emotive bludgeons that could get to you if you were not prepared. They smiled at one another, woman to woman, both wondering how to get out of the charmed circle of the personal touch without being rude.

'Look, Mrs Brady, I'm sorry if I was a bit – short – at first. You know. To be quite honest, I didn't know how to cope.'

'That's all right, Mrs Fairbrother. I took no notice. We're used to the fact that grief takes people in different ways.'

'Quite so. I must say, you seem to be awfully good at your job.'

'Well, thank you. It's very rewarding. Would you like a coffee? Do you have time?'

'My brother's waiting. Hang on a minute.' She went to the door and looked for Tim. The street was deserted. He had probably gone for a walk round the shops. 'All right. Thanks.'

Arden made herself comfortable on the sofa, feeling a bit odd. She was only accustomed to accepting refreshments at the hairdresser or the occasional rare book shop. She encouraged Mrs Brady to talk about the rewards of her profession, compared and contrasted them with the frustrations of her own. Mrs Brady looked rueful, and confessed that talking about her work gave her a conscience as she was thinking of giving it up.

'What a shame. Why is that?'

'Strictly between ourselves, it's the money. My husband left me a few months ago and I've two children to bring up.' She lowered her voice and glanced over her shoulder. There must be a Rattle or Son in the back room. 'I've been selling these clothes in my spare time. What I wear for work. You probably didn't notice.'

'Indeed I did. They're very – versatile.'

'Exactly. That's their big selling point. Anyway, I'm actually rather good at it. But it's very time-consuming, with a full-time job as well. My area manager wants me to go full-time on the clothes. And, you know, the sky's the limit if you're good. She earned more than £40,000 last year.'

'*What?*'

'It's true.' Mrs Brady sucked in her cheeks and nodded, aware that she had hit the bell on the register of amazement. '*And* she could have done even better if so many of her ladies hadn't got pregnant. She reckons I could be a senior co-ordinator in six months.'

'I don't know what to say.'

'The risk, though. That's the problem. The usual dilemma – low pay and security, or risk and rewards. And I do enjoy this job. I feel responsible for the clients. They need a sympathetic professional. I'm not sure it's right to work only for money.'

'Then you're a very rare bird, Mrs Brady. But, speaking as a mother, I would say you have to put the interests of your children first.' Arden could say this without blushing as she had no doubt that was what she had done by leaving Bos with Garth. 'You do enjoy selling the clothes?'

'Oh, yes. I love it. And it's so flexible, with the children.'

'Well, then. If you don't go, you won't settle back into your present job as if nothing had happened, you know. I understand how you feel. I'd love to do something different for a change. There's nothing worse than feeling one will only leave one's present job in a coffin. Oops! Sorry.'

'No matter. Is that really how you feel?' Mrs Brady looked

Arden straight in the eye then fetched her handbag and gave her a card. '*Suitables*. That's our trade name. And we're launching a de luxe range for evening called *Highly Suitables* in the autumn.'

'How about a range of lingerie called *Unsuitables?*'

Mrs Brady laughed. 'I can see you're a kindred spririt. Perhaps if you're up here again you could come to one of my presentations? See how it's done. You'd be good at it. You have a very forceful personality, if you don't mind my saying so.'

'Not at all. But I wasn't thinking of myself—'

'Come to the presentation anyway. You won't regret it. All the clothes are non-iron and machine washable. You could test drive them round Brands Hatch and still wear them for a cocktail party in the evening!'

Tim was hurrying down the street towards Arden.

'There you are. Feeling better?'

'Yes, fine. Just the hip playing up. I went and sat down in the market and watched the traffic warden hunting for prey. Pleasant little town.'

'You'd better go to the doctor when we get home.'

'Nonsense. Musn't bother the doctor with every twinge.'

'Don't be so typically *male*, Tim. I insist.'

'It's all right for you to say. You haven't been to a doctor in twenty years.'

'Yes, I have. I had the coil out. Do you want to come with me to the florist?'

'No. I'll go back to the hotel.'

'Won't be long.'

Arden bought a bunch of green parrot tulips to ease her way into the florist's confidence. She was surprised to find designer flowers in such a remote spot, and more so when the assistant told her they were normally sold out in a couple of hours. Arden tried to look self-deprecating. 'I have the usual townie's preconceptions, I'm afraid. Don't tell me the greengrocer sells cardoons?'

'No. But you might get them at Waitrose in Norwich.'

'*Waitrose?*' Arden's incredulity was genuine. She had assumed the sun-dried tomato set would be dependent on mail order in this area.

'You're not from round here, madam? Neither am I. Reading, originally.'

'Is there anyone from round here round here?'

The assistant smiled. 'One or two. Are you on holiday?'

'No. My brother and I came up for our father's funeral. It was at St Polycarp's on Wednesday. Perhaps you knew him? Humphrey Mason. He lived up at Sloping Castle.'

'No, I'm sorry, I didn't. I did a lot of the flowers, though.'

'That reminds me – I want to write and thank everyone who sent them, but there are quite a few I don't know personally. I wonder if you have a record of who sent what?'

'Yes, I do. But I'm afraid that information is confidential, madam.'

'What? You mean you can't tell me? Why not?'

'It's the customer's privilege, madam. If they want to remain anonymous they're entitled to. I'm sorry.'

'I see.' Arden sniffed. This was a real disappointment. She had thought it would be so easy. 'But actually the one I'm thinking of in particular wasn't anonymous. It had a name on it – Thalia. And it was so . . . well, expensive-looking, I'd hate the person to think we didn't appreciate it.' Her aggrieved expression and watery eyes gave the kindly florist the erroneous impression that Arden was tormented by the idea of hurting another's feelings.

'What was it like?' She took out a large record book from under the counter.

'Um – a huge bouquet. Blue irises, those narcissi with the orange cup, pink tulips with a green streak down the petal, those greyish things – I think they're eucalyptus – and a few pink gerberas.'

'You're very observant.' A couple of women who were waiting to be served started chatting pointedly about missing the bus. 'Look, I really shouldn't do this but I'll tell you which area it was sent from. Then perhaps you'll be able to guess who it was.'

'Thank you very much.'

'Let me see . . . Here we are. Great Yarmouth.'

'Great Yarmouth? Are you sure?'

'Yes. Does that help?'

'I'm not sure. Which florist in Great Yarmouth?'

'Sorry, I really can't say anymore than that. They wouldn't give you any information either. Perhaps you should ask some of your father's friends?'

'Yes, I will. Well, thanks for your help anyway.'

'Not at all.'

Arden strolled, disheartened, from one antique shop to another, staring blindly in at the windows. It was not just that the great detective had been so swiftly cut off at the knees, though that did make her feel somewhat foolish. What really rankled was the fact that her well-meant and surely natural desire to find out more about the unknown Thalia could be thwarted by something as mundane as retail etiquette. Such rigidity simply did not work for the general good. It was so unfair. If only she had had her wits about her she could surely have devised some distraction for the florist and looked in the records herself. The more she thought about it, the more convinced she was that this intimate friend of her father's would be overjoyed to make the acquaintance of his daughter.

3 ∫

It was tea-time at The Ashes. Some of the more sprightly residents sat at tables on the terrace, enjoying views of the well-kept grounds and trying to protect their biscuits from a hooligan blackbird. The building was mock-William and Mary, disfigured by fire escapes and clapboard extensions but retaining enough echoes of gracious living to soothe the consciences of concerned relatives. Arden and Tim spoke to the senior nurse before seeing their mother. He was a handsome, camp young man who threw himself into a discussion of their mother's care as though normally starved of human contact. He consulted his notes ostentatiously.

'Doctor's *very* pleased with Mattie. For a moment we thought she'd be up for the posy baskets but –' he gave a tender sigh '– we decided not to push her.'

'Is she on medication?'

'Is the sky blue! Let's see . . . There's the Catopril for her blood pressure, that's twice a day. Then she gets some Temazepam for the night and – what else – ah, yes, waterworks. That's a spot of Frusamide. Lovely name, isn't it? Frusamide. Does you good just to get your tongue round it. The main problem right now is the depression. Doctor's trying her on Prozac, which *personally* I think is a bit dodgy when you haven't got much to be cheerful about, but there you go.'

'Does she really need all those pills?' Arden was distressed at the idea of Glaxo and the Wellcome Corporation slugging it out over her mother's symptoms.

'That's nothing, love. Some of them take so many pills they're too full to eat. But we have to treat them, don't we? Your mum's on a pretty standard slate, I would say. There's only the ones I've mentioned, plus a spot of Aspirin for the thrombosis and Fibogel, of course, to keep her regular.'

'Please. Spare me the details.'

'Don't upset yourself. Mattie's a very happy little person when she's herself. Such a sweetheart. And that smile! Ooh, I'd love to wake up to that smile, wouldn't you? Well, I suppose you did. She should be in a good mood today. Flo – that's her room-mate – she's gone for a liver biopsy for a few days. They don't get on, I'm afraid. Poor Flo's a bit – strident. Used to be a headmistress. She's always telling Mattie she's useless at papercraft.'

'Can't you separate them?'

'We will as soon as we can. Strictly *entre nous* we're expecting a vacancy on the first floor shortly. We'll pop your mum in there.'

'Do you think she'll recognize us?'

'Umm. On a good day, yes. Unless it's a long time since she last saw you. Don't think me rude, but *I* don't recognize you and I've been here three years.'

Tim chortled with embarrassment. 'We have kept in touch, you know. But we live in London. It's difficult to get away.'

'Oh, I see.'

'And until our father died we knew she was visited regularly.'

'Yes, Mr Mason was very regular. And there have been one or two others. Forgive me, I didn't mean to sound judgmental.'

'That's all right. By the way, have you told her? About our father.'

'Doctor thought better not. At least until she can see how your mum's responding to the Prozac. But if you think we should you could have a word with Doctor?'

'What do you think, Ard?'

'There's no need to upset her for nothing.'

The young nurse beamed his approval. 'I'll show you through to the terrace, then, shall I? Not too long, now. We like to bring them in before they get dew on them.'

Fortunately the warm weather meant the doors and windows were open and a light breeze almost wafted away the dreaded fumes of embrocation, sanitary knickers and lunch that hangs about old people's homes when the double glazing is closed. Arden and Tim tried not to notice the comatose residents in the lounge who were too frail to go outside. The young man pointed to where their mother sat smiling at her biscuit. They thanked him.

'There is just one more thing,' said Arden.

'What's that, love?'

'Well – who's paying for all this? Is it the council or did our father pay?'

A quiver passed over his pleasant features. 'That's not my area of responsibility, Mrs Fairbrother. Ask the manager. I'm sure she'd be happy to help.'

He excused himself and left them at the door to the lounge.

'That could have waited, Ard.'

'Oh, stop *patrolling* my behaviour, Tim. I'm fed up with it. We have to know. Supposing they want to throw her out now Dad's dead. Or sell the cottage to pay the fees. Were they joint owners?'

'How should I know? It isn't as simple as that, anyway. If they're beneficial joint tenants Mum will inherit, but if they're tenants in—'

'Yes, all right, don't get carried away.'

'It's important, woman. If it's Mum's it'll probably have to be sold to pay the fees. If it's ours, it won't.'

'Oh. I hope we don't have to sell it. It's not the money I'm worried about, I just don't want Jermigan to have it.'

'Why not?'

'I don't know. He's got enough. And I'm sure Dad would have wanted us to enjoy it.'

'That's totally illogical. You spend the rest of the time complaining he didn't give a toss about us.'

'Don't exaggerate! But I don't see why we couldn't retire there. It wouldn't matter to you where we lived, and surely you can see how fulfilling it would be for me? Something to look forward to.'

'Well, thanks very much. I know you don't rate democracy that highly but don't I even get a say in where I spend my twilight years?'

'You've never had an opinion about it before. Look, don't

let's argue here. It's years before we retire anyway. Come on. They'll be taking them in before we've had a chance to talk to her.'

They threaded their way among the tables. Mattie was sitting with her back to them, immobilized by a thick mohair dressing gown and cellular blankets tucked tightly round her legs. Arden placed a hand on her shoulder and gave her the parrot tulips. 'Hello, Mum. Remember me? Arden. And Tim.'

Mattie looked up, startled, her pale blue eyes still clear, face as pretty as it could be considering her age and hair loss. They kissed her.

'Emily?' Then she burst into tears and groped for her hankie.

Arden sat down and took her mother's lifeless, wrinkled hand, 'No, Mum. Not Emily. Arden. And Tim is here, see? Your children. Don't you remember us?'

'How are the children, dear?' Mattie immediately brightened up. She leaned towards Arden conspiratorially. 'I'm going to get out of here. I'm not staying here. Horrid place!' More tears. Arden wondered what she would be like without the Prozac. 'Harry said so. He'll get me out.'

'Harry Jermigan? Has he been to see you?'

'No, he never comes to see me. Never. Not once.'

'Don't cry, Mum. You mean Humphrey, don't you? Humphrey came – comes – to see you a lot, doesn't he?'

'Oh, yes.' With a sudden movement Mattie clasped Arden's arm and whispered, 'I never had an affair with him, you know. Never. Not me.'

'Who – Harry Jermigan? Of course you didn't, Mum. No one's saying you did.'

Mattie raised her voice to a shout. 'Never! I didn't.'

'All right, Mum. Shhh. People are looking at us.'

'Doesn't matter. They're silly old fools.'

This logical sequence relaxed them all. Tim drew his chair closer. 'When was the last time Dad came, Mum? Did Humphrey come last week?'

'No. He never comes. Nobody ever comes.'

'Oh, dear.' Arden decided it was time for associative memory, or whatever it was called. 'I've still got those wings you made me, Mum. When I was a firefly in the school play. Do you remember? You used all that clingfilm Mrs Baker brought back from America. And wire hangers from the dry cleaner.'

'America? *I* never went to America.'

'I know you didn't, Mum. Mrs Baker did. You know, our neighbour who had the first Whirlybird on the street. She went to America the same year Dad was made first mate on the *City of Leeds*. He brought you a kimono from Manila to celebrate. Don't you remember? You gave it to me when I went on a school trip to France.'

Mattie looked browbeaten under this barrage of geographical data. 'France? Humph doesn't like France. Won't set foot in the place.'

This was encouragingly coherent. 'Why not, Mum? Why does he hate France?'

'Dirty whore! Dirty whore!'

'Mum, please – shhh.' Tim signalled to Arden to stop this line of questioning, and she signalled back that of course she would and to stop treating her as if she did not know how to behave. He sometimes wondered if flags would be quicker. But there was no chance to pursue the matter anyway as Mattie had decided to eat her biscuit and was now concentrating on it intently.

'What's the food like here, Mum? Is it good?'

'Very good. Did you pick up the order from the greengrocer?'

Arden sighed. 'Yes, Mum.'

They did not linger after their mother had been wheeled back into the lounge. She seemed blissfully indifferent to their departure.

The manager was a tall, faded Irish woman who took her responsibilities seriously, not to say solemnly. She had the financial situation itemized in her head. Yes, the council had been paying so far, as their father had been resident locally. 'Now – sadly, but it's so – if the cottage is in Mrs Mason's name they will expect it to be sold to recover the fees.'

'We have no say in the matter?'

'The only alternative would be if you could come up with another source of funding. I imagine that would be acceptable. Would you like the address to write to? Most people can't nearly afford it. It's a wicked thing but there you are.

We'll be taking in insurance plans with our mother's milk before long.'

'Perhaps if Labour get in they'll insist the council pays?'

'Now I know you're joking, Mrs Fairbrother. More handouts? I doubt it. Sure, politicians are like those pigs in *Animal Farm*, are they not? Before they get elected they make out everything's going to be better with them in charge, and afterwards there's even more going to the knacker's yard than previously.'

'Goodness, I thought *I* was a sceptic.'

'My own mother's with the nuns, Mrs Fairbrother, thank God. But we do our best here. Mrs Mason's well cared for, you need have no fear of that.'

'We're sure she is. And we're very grateful. She just seems more depressed than we were prepared for. She used to be so – so much fun. So easy to please.'

The woman shrugged. 'It'll come to us all, no doubt.'

'She didn't recognize us, Tim. It just wasn't *her*.'

'I know. Shall we take the A12 or the M11?'

'Obviously she can't be moved. It would finish her off.'

'We'll just have to come as often as we can. The staff seem very pleasant.'

'There's not much stimulation, though, is there. Posy baskets. Huh! Surely they can do better than that?'

'She's beyond the reach of basket-weaving, Ard.'

'What do you suppose she meant by that "dirty whore" business? Not like Mum to break into metaphor.'

'It's no worse than "perfidious Albion".'

'No, she must have been thinking of a real person. Such vehemence, though. I never saw Mum spit anything more lethal than a cherry stone, did you?'

'No. I can't even remember her raising her voice.' Tim kept a white-knuckled grip on the steering wheel. 'That stroke was meant to be the *coup de grâce*, you know. Good old NHS. They bring her round then wash their hands of her. Well, yes, she is a crazy old vegetable who shoves biscuits up her nose, but quality of life is relative, isn't it?'

'Come on, Tim. Calm down. She doesn't realize what she's like.'

'But I do.'

Seeing their mother so debilitated was worse for Arden and Tim than the death of Humph. The combined experience left Arden in particular disoriented and unable to concentrate. As she had observed to Mrs Brady, it was not possible to settle into one's job again after mentally leaving it behind. Back in Chiswick, the shades of Sloping Castle, the cottage with tremendous potential for the discerning buyer, the intriguing Miss Tree, the empire of the HGVs – even the air, kept constantly fresh with reinforcements from Siberia – seemed to have loosened her ties with Cramp Blaze, Estate Agents.

The sales rate had stepped up in her absence. Half the population appeared to be on the move, desperate to tie up fixed interest mortgages before the election. Gazumping had taken over from gazundering. Hysterical buyers threatening to bomb the premises were a regular feature. There was a new girl in the office with a degree in Law and Soft Furnishings, according to the typist, who was clearly being groomed for management. As this young woman was too young to remember the Beatles, let alone Simon de Montfort, she and Arden did not get on.

In her imagination, Arden began to renovate the cottage and thought how thrilling, yet how restful, it would be to return there after work instead of to a house within fifty yards of a four-lane flyover. The house was charming enough in itself: a Victorian terrace with hard standing – done up to the nines with paint-effect wallpapers and coir carpet. Friends had wondered why she had not turned it into a Gothic fantasy, considering what can be achieved with MDF and a jigsaw, but Arden's soul was stern for authenticity. She was not seduced by the fake and the fanciful. Although she did allow a fleur-de-lys towel hook in the downstairs lavatory after a colleague at work reminded her that Gothic Revival was authentic Victorian.

The doctor sent Tim for a bone scan, under protest. He thought all contact with diagnostic procedures was likely to be self-fulfilling. But Arden insisted. It was one of the small ways in which she exercised her limited maternal instincts. Tim was adamant throughout that he felt as fit as a fighting cock. It was a rather fateful pronouncement. The following morning, when he went to his office in the gleaming black obelisk that was the headquarters of House of Waffles UK, he had a very funny turn. Security guards were waiting to usher him, with unnecessary force, into the visitors' reception suite, where more guards were on duty to prevent his escape. Several of his colleagues were already there, pale-faced, some pacing the floor, others illicitly smoking next to a potted plant.

'What the hell's happening?'

A chirpy graduate trainee brought him a coffee. 'Takeover. The ones who've got the chop are just clearing their desks. They've got an hour to get out. Still, we're all right.'

'For the moment,' added another older colleague with five children. 'I'm walking. Soon as I get the chance.'

There were murmurs of solidarity. Tim sat down, speechless, and listened to a bitter discussion as to what part the imminent change of government might have played in the timing of the takeover. Just after ten the young graduate gleefully called them over to the window, from where they could see their ex-colleagues being escorted from the building. Most of the women, all of child-bearing age, were in tears. The only representative of House of Waffles UK there to see them go was a junior personnel manager who looked as though he was wetting himself.

Arden was apopleptic with indignation, not at first realizing how the upheaval fitted in with her scheme for change. It was at least an hour before it occurred to her that Tim could be more easily persuaded to leave his job and become independent if the threat of redundancy was ruining his working life anyway. Of course, it would be a bit of a comedown for him to help shopkeepers fill in their tax returns after handling millions of pounds worth of salary accounts for a multi-national company. But with the introduction of self-assessment there should be plenty of work, and their expenses were modest.

There was one major obstacle besides Tim to be overcome: money. It seemed to Arden that the need for money, rather than the love of it, was the root of all evil. She had no illusions about the Good Life and the romance of getting up at five o'clock in the morning to lug hay bales to the livestock in Arctic blizzards. In the Middle Ages people were used to that sort of thing, but she had nothing but scorn for those who imagined their soft twentieth-century bodies could be thrown into mortal combat with nature and win.

Assuming that the cottage had been left to them, they could live there rent free, but they would need a financial safety net until Tim got established. And there was still council tax, bills and moving expenses. It would be as well to rent out the house in Chiswick as back-up if the scheme did not work. Arden had read enough blurbs on paperbacks to know that things do not always turn out as one expects. But the rent received would not leave much to live on once agent's fees, water rates, insurance, maintenance, tax on a secondary residence and the mortgage had been deducted. In fact, they might end up paying the tenants. She would have to get a job, and postpone the moment when she could immerse herself in medieval matters. For consolation she drew up a plan for a physic garden with turf seat and bought a very expensive book on fish ponds and stews in fourteenth-century Scotland.

But if Arden knew she could not afford to busy herself full-time with bread trough and beehive, she was equally sure that she did not want to continue in the property business. As an outsider she would be at a disadvantage anyway.

As when a woman is pregnant she notices other pregnant women as never before, Arden began to notice women in lock-knit co-ordinates wherever she went. The tell-tale blends of Charcoal and Olde Rose, Victoria Plum and Racing Green, revealed a network of *Suitables* fans on a hitherto unimagined scale. She said as much to a woman client to whom she was showing an immaculate two-bedroomed maisonette. The client was a bank manager who was about to get divorced and her outfit was a particularly pleasing combination of Parchment and Mocha. She had the kind of confidence that made the scenario she embodied – in which the world was taken over by divorced women in machine washable jersey – wholly convincing. Not to be part of this vanguard was already a source of shame. The bank manager was delighted to treat her as an aspirant. Swift as a lizard's tongue the business card was produced from the handbag, and the name of the nearest *Suitables* co-ordinator inscribed on it.

The next presentation was to be held on election night. The hostess had been informed of Arden's aspirations, and was forthcoming with inside information. It was important to utilize seasonal events to promote the range and the election was a godsend as the ladies would be encouraged to come in party mood – and easily removable clothes – and be given the opportunity to try on different combinations until the sun rose over New Britain.

Just as Arden was about to leave the house Bos rang, wanting to know if she had come to a decision about the money. Arden explained that their plans were up in the air at the moment, but if and when the house was sold she might be able to help.

'I have to tell you, Bos, that Uncle Tim takes a rather dim view of baling you out. It's not as if it's anything to do with your studies.'

'I'm not asking Uncle Tim. Haven't you got any money?'

'Not much. And what I have got is all tied up in PEPS, Bos. I can't get my hands on it just like that. And there's your grandmother to think of. We may end up paying for her as well.'

'Why are you giving up your job, then? Don't you think you're being a bit selfish, Mum?'

'*Selfish!* You think I should work to pay off your debts and you call *me* selfish!'

'All right. Sorry. Do you think you could let me have a few hundred to fob 'im off? I'll get a job in the vac and pay you back. Honest.'

'We'll see. I've got to go, Bos. Love you.'

Arden had never been comfortable in huddles of women, or huddles of any kind. Her domestic arrangements made the sharing of intimate details inadvisable. But her reluctance to do so would have held good even were she stuck in a lift at a convention of women who had had sex with their half-brothers. In her opinion the arrangement gave her no more in common with other people than it had Hatshepsut and Tuthmosis.

She was at a loss to understand what was wrong with her relationship with Tim anyway. It had arisen from their personal circumstances, which was hardly surprising. He was a male, she was a female. They knew each other intimately and were very fond of each other. If they had not had to share a bedroom when young it might never have happened, but it had. They would never have children, of course. It had been simply a matter of maximizing their resources when they both found themselves single again. Marrying relative strangers was an incredibly high-risk policy after all. This arrangement was not. It was as unique as the flavour of rhubarb to the earth it grows in, and as natural in Arden's view. And it spared them both the excruciating rituals of courtship. There was nothing lurid or titillating about it, but try telling that to a generation raised on tabloids and soap opera. Arden was therefore grateful to be assisting at the *Suitables* presentation, rather than watching, which minimized the opportunity for personal enquiries.

She arrived early to help the hostess arrange the room, and pick up tips. Jeanetta took a long look at Arden's figure and picked out some outfits from a crowded rail of garments.

'You're lucky, you won't need a model. Nice and tall – that shows off the draping quality of the fabric. And that dark hair . . . excellent. Goes with everything. Are you Autumn? Here, try this.' She held up a russet bathrobe. Arden was surprised to be told that it was in fact a reversible floor-length patio-cum-beach lounger that doubled as a sleeping bag. Jeanetta whipped it away. 'No, you're Winter. This is you.' A pure white version replaced it. Arden saw at once that her skin lit up like a searchlight.

'Always study the client's colourway. Don't let them try on anything that will make them look like cat's vomit. It's a waste of time, and we all know what time is. Likewise the weight. Most of these garments would look good on the Albert Hall but some of the pants definitely wouldn't. Remember, this is all about making stressed-out British doormats feel good about themselves. Forget about the money – until they try to leave, anyhow. Think Fairy Godmother. You're about to change their lives forever.

'And it *does*. You'd be amazed how many women turn to their *Suitables* co-ordinator in a life crisis rather than their GP. The more they buy, the better they feel about themselves. It's so thrilling to be able to spread happiness because you know you're doing them a good turn. It's the co-ordination, you see. Gives them a feeling of power and control. Just a few basic items can give you hundreds of variations. Like tonight, I'm going to pretend to be Cherie Blair. I'll show them how they could have got through the entire election campaign on ten reversible garments and some chunky jewellery.'

It all came to pass exactly as Jeanetta said. At the end of the evening she had taken cheques and credit card payments for £1,985 – £300 of which was Arden's.

As she explained to Tim the following day, it was her own susceptibility that had convinced her of the money-making potential of *Suitables*. She spoke as though some out-of-body experience had occurred, which was the only way she could explain to herself why she had spent £300 on clothes she did not need when it could have been used to prevent Russian gangsters from carving up her son. Arden considered herself to be the last bastion of consumer resistance. If she could be brought down by a volley of mix-'n'-match, anyone could. She was now fully persuaded that the possession of garments in which one could skateboard and/or host a charity ball, and which could easily be converted into a tote bag for the beach, was indeed a liberating experience.

This conviction gave her the extra measure of confidence needed to bully Tim into agreeing to a complete change of lifestyle. Their removal to the cottage at Sloping Castle was not only possible, it was essential, she argued. They had to be near their mother. Tim's hip trouble and the threat of redundancy at work meant he must reduce his stress levels. Arden herself felt the pressure of ambitious youth nudging her towards the exit, and was getting too old to be an employee anyway. It would not be long before she was taken off client interaction and assigned to mortgage and insurance liaison in the back office. If she were to be her own boss and have time to spare for her real interest in life, it was now or never.

'It's one of those tides in the affairs of men, Tim.'

'Tides go out as well as in. Ever heard of a beached whale?'

'We're not talking O Level Biology here. You know what I

mean. Why shouldn't we make a success of it? We don't need a lot of money and we're not proposing to make it from patchwork tea cosies or goat's cheese. You're at the top of your profession. You'll be beating off clients once the word gets round. Harry Jermigan might employ you. I'm sure he has lots of books that need fiddling. If he doesn't, I'm certain he knows lots of the right people. And I'm determined to make a success of this clothes thing. It's a piece of cake. They sell themselves. With so many women getting divorced and starting second careers there couldn't be a better moment. Besides, you'll have much more time to write your book.' Tim was compiling a history of the weathervane in England. His main hobby was implementing Arden's wishes, but occasionally he got up before dawn to make notes and trawl the Internet for the latest weathervane sightings.

But the more reasonable the venture sounded, the more angry and resistant he became. This was a good sign. It showed he felt the net closing in. Arden withdrew and let him rant for a while. It was his time of the month. Although men did not menstruate, she had noticed that Tim, at least, had a lunar cycle which caused him to errupt in irrational and uncharacteristic spleen when the moon was full.

Meanwhile Arden rang the solicitor and asked him to send a copy of the will as soon as possible. From her experience of conveyancing she knew this could be anything up to six months, so she asked if he could confirm that Barnacle Cottage had been left to her and Tim. The solicitor, Mr Abel Gordon, could not be sure but thought that it had. Arden then asked if there were any other outstanding bequests. She thought he hesitated before saying that there were but he could not remember the details. He excused himself and rang off before she could ask if the name Thalia rang any bells.

4

It was a hot, sunless, steaming day at Sloping Castle. The giant hollyhocks, which had seeded themselves between the flagstones in front of the cottage, sagged to the ground.

Arden loved the heat. It stimulated her imagination more than any other season. She pictured herself with long skirt hitched up, wearing floppy linen headgear and swigging ale from a leather jug under an oak tree during a break from harvest – and, all right, local warfare, plague and the occasional famine. At least one would never have been bored. People had too much life these days – and what did they do with it? Watch television for six hours a day. What was that but an entire nation feeding on its entrails? It was really annoying that there was so much of interest to watch.

Arden had got up early to finish the unpacking. Like every good *Suitables* co-ordinator she had wasted no time in organizing presentations and was anxious to get the cottage in order so that she could devote her energies to work. The area supervisor in Chiswick had given her some contacts to start with and she had swiftly added to them, starting with the helpful florist and the headmistress of the local primary school whom Arden had sat next to at the hairdresser. Every outing, however humble, was now a *Suitables* opportunity. Sloping Castle would be an invaluable backdrop for *Suitables* promotions. There would be lots of ladies who would come out of curiosity to see beyond the Keep Out sign and have a legitimate reason to view the premises of Harry Jermigan. Whenever his name was mentioned Arden had come to expect knowing looks and smiles but a reluctance to say why, which gave her the same feeling as if she had been walking round all day unaware that a boiled sweet was stuck to her forehead.

Since they had moved in two weeks previously there had been no sign of him. Miss Tree had been mildly courteous at their arrival and assured them that Mr Jermigan would call as soon as he got back. Whenever someone approached the cottage Arden half expected it to be him, but when at last he did she knew him at once. A man of baronial appearance and indeterminate age strode up the driveway, carrying a letter. Arden jumped up and whipped on some lipstick. His lordly gait smacked perhaps more of the jungle than the manor, for he was powerfully built and his tattooed arms swayed with simian ease. Even at a distance she could see that the eyes were shrewd as a rat's and the lips were set in a sardonic smile that Arden imagined he slept in. She went out to meet him, and he crunched her hand.

'So you're Humph's daughter. I wouldna known you.'

'Thanks. It has been a long time. Won't you come in?'

'I've not got long. There's an Iveco Eurostar come this morning.'

'Ah, yes, the haulage empire. We didn't know about that.'

'The noise bother you, do it?'

Arden laughed. Nervously, to her irritation. 'Would it matter if it did?'

Jermigan looked surprised, but the smile stayed put. 'No. I just thought you might be one of them poncey incomers who complains to the council about birdsong an' that.'

Well, this was a good start. Arden had been bracing herself for condolences. She reminded herself she liked people who were direct.

'Would you like some coffee?'

Jermigan settled himself in her rocking chair.

'I'll have a beer if you got one.'

'At this hour in the morning? How wonderful. An ale man. I'm afraid we don't. Tim's allergic to it.'

'He about?'

'No, he's just gone into Norwich to get some office supplies. He's an accountant, you know.'

'I know.'

'Of course. I expect you heard a lot about us from Dad.' Not too much, hopefully. She paused, as it seemed like a suitable moment for Jermigan to sympathize with them in their loss. But no uncomfortable shifting in his seat occurred to suggest the dam that held back his manly feelings was about to break. 'Tim's hoping to start up on his own. I don't suppose you could put any work his way?' There was no harm in applying *Suitables*-style opportunism to Tim's line of business.

Jermigan chuckled. 'You his agent? Don't waste your breath, does you?'

'That rather depends on the reply.'

'How long I got?'

'Ooh – at least until the kettle boils.'

'And how long's your kettle take to boil then?'

From his expression it was clear that sexual innuendo was intended. Arden was appalled. This was cod liver oil and malt to her, puckering the mouth and the mind equally. Apart from the fact that her maturity should protect her, she was his best friend's daughter and that friend scarcely cold in his grave. She could not compromise herself by laughing it off, even for Tim's advancement. Incest apart, Arden had distinctly old-fashioned ideas on appropriate behaviour. 'Please don't. You know what I mean. Actually, Tim hasn't been very well. That's one of the reasons we moved out here. He needs less stress.'

'Startin' his own business ain't going to fix that, is it?'

'Well, I've my own business too. We'll manage. And – don't ever tell him this – but I simply couldn't resist the temptation. I'm *desperately* interested in the Middle Ages, you see. Couldn't turn up the chance to live over a medieval midden. It's odd, because I don't think Dad was in the least. I often wondered why he came to live here. I should have asked, I suppose.'

'He not tell you how he came by it then?'

'No. He was from this area originally, wasn't he? He just fancied it, I suppose.'

'Is that a fact? This is for you.' He handed her a letter. 'It came to the Hall by mistake.'

'Thank you. I'll have a word with the postman.'

'Don't bother. It's taken care of. Won't happen no more.'

'That sounds ominous. What did you threaten him with – boiling pitch?'

'Look here – Arden, isn't it? Funny name.'

'What would you call normal – Noleen? And, please, spare me the jokes about being a bit thicket. I've heard them all. I was named after a ship, as it happens.'

'Whatever. I reckon we won't be socializing much, whatever yer name is. We keep out of each other's way, I reckon we'll get on fine.'

'Is that what you came to say?'

'No. I just thought of it. I'll be on my way. Give my regards to Tim.'

'Does he come under the exclusion order as well?'

'Howzat?'

'I mean, is he to keep out of your way as well?'

'That's up to him. If he got a mind of his own anyhow. What I hear, he's in your pocket like.' This was accompanied by – yes, a wink.

'What do you mean by that?' Surely – *surely* – Humph had not told him about her and Tim?

Jermigan merely smiled and put a finger to his lips. '*Honi soit.* Be seein' you. Or rather not.' He let himself out and strode off as confidently, or more so, as he had come. Then he stopped and looked back. 'Doesn't you want to know how he come by this place then?' He indicated the cottage.

'I'm listening.' By now Arden was so steeped in shock she was prepared to hear that Humph had swapped his first wife for it.

'I give it to 'im. 'Bye now.' He waved as he disappeared behind the tower of rubble.

Arden was so agitated by the encounter that she forgot to open the letter and instead stormed round the house swatting flies with it. The fact that her own misplaced pertness about the postman had opened hostilities was the greatest torment and she toyed with the idea of stabbing herself with a dessert fork. It was her misfortune that in Jermigan she had met someone who spoke his mind at the time, rather than saving it up for a counsellor in the future. Someone whose reactions were not filtered through the wadding of convention that enveloped most people. Someone, in that respect – she hoped – like herself.

It was a short step from this to admitting that it fell to her to make peace with him. On reflection the agression had been mostly on her side, and in practical terms it did not make sense to be at daggers drawn with the person who controlled the water supply, sewage and electricity sub-station. It was just as well she had not dwelt on the fantasy in which Jermigan rushed to fill the role of father figure out of his great regard for Humph and a corresponding need to offer Tim and herself employment, help with the decorating, regular meals while they settled in and an instant social life. She had to admit he was different. Perhaps in time they would have one of those cult film-type relationships between unlikely friends which demonstrate the Family of Man thing.

With her mind on this prospect she skimmed over the contents of the letter which was from the solicitor. It included a copy of the will. There were several minor bequests of mycological specimens and papers to a professor in Cambridge. The cottage, with contents, went to herself and Tim. Nothing to Mattie. The remainder of the estate, including shares, an endowment policy for £30,000, a signet ring and a silver gilt statue thought to be of St Louis at present in a bank vault in Ipswich, was to be shared by the deceased's friend Mrs Thalia Sewell and her son Gavin.

Arden read this clause several times, went to the lavatory and came back, but it was still there. It was an outrage. It could not be true. She felt faint and lay down on the floor. If Humph had been an inadequate father before, he was now the Pol Pot of inadequate fathers. How could he? He had ignored his wife, made minimal provision for his children and left a possibly huge sum to a blonde in Great Yarmouth. Arden knew nothing about silver gilt statues of St Louis but the bank vault spoke volumes. She could not imagine love on such a scale. Of course, the affair had never been put to the test of domesticity. It would hardly have survived if it had. And her *son*! Her *son*! Could there be any doubt at that price that he was also Humph's? A son! A brother for Arden and Timothy. No wonder he had not bothered to keep in touch with them. He had far more precious ties close to home. She got up and hurried down the drive to look out for Tim.

These revelations gave Arden two objectives in addition to spreading the gospel of *Suitables*. Thalia Sewell must be found and confronted – no, befriended. Or just met. At least once.

Arden would have no peace of mind until she had made the woman realize what damage the affair with her father had done to their family. Well, perhaps not damage exactly. In all honesty she could not believe that her father would have been any more attentive if Thalia Sewell had not existed. It was possible she did not even know of or expect the bequest. She might be an almost innocent party. She might not even know Arden and Tim existed. Knowing Humph, he might simply have forgotten to mention them. The money was nothing to do with it. Arden had not expected it and they could manage very well without. It all boiled down to the fact that she just wanted to get hold of Thalia Sewell and shake her till her head came off.

The other imperative was to pacify Harry Jermigan and find out if he knew anything about the affair. It would not look good to ring up the solicitor and demand to know the whereabouts of Thalia Sewell. The only thing she could do right away was consult the phone book. There were three Sewells listed in Great Yarmouth. Three times she was obliged to apologize for a wrong number.

Tim had been suitably shocked by the will and the suggestion that Jermigan had 'given' the cottage to Humph. But as, unlike Arden, he had never considered himself a full member of the family, his outrage was more subdued and evaporated almost immediately. He was besides far too preoccupied with the fraught business of persuading local taxpayers to use his services. Despite self-assessment he had not been bombarded with calls and was beginning to grow nervous. He spent a lot of time dusting his Simons Direct Tax Service and re-reading the Finance Act. Arden suggested that, as he had experience in tax, insurance and pensions, he should broaden his brief to that of Independent Financial Advisor. This brought on one of Tim's monthlies. He raved that the project was doomed. Their savings would not last long and they could not exist on the tiny margin between the mortgage on the house in Chiswick and the rental they achieved on it.

'Let's sell it, then,' said Arden cheerfully.

'Sell it? We haven't got enough equity in it to generate a decent income. We'd need about half a million.'

'Don't *worry*. My presentation diary is almost full for September. Well, I've got one a week so far, which isn't bad, considering.'

'And how many padded leisure suits have you sold this week, then?'

'Sneer if you want, darling. But I think I'd do rather better with support and encouragement.'

'So would I! I'm panicking.'

'I know. But we can't afford to. Look, why don't you go to Blythburgh and check out the weathervanes? The Autumn collection's arrived. I've got to give some serious thought to my combinations.'

Whenever Arden saw Jermigan she smiled boldly, in defiance of his ban on contact. He did not immediately try and run her down in his Vauxhall Frontera, which was encouraging. To get any closer was difficult. The only likely channel was Miss Tree. Arden thought up several thin excuses to call on her for advice, in the course of which she could not help noticing that Miss Tree badly needed to re-vamp her wardrobe, so she invited the dubious housekeeper to view the Autumn Collection.

'I don't have much need for business suits,' said Miss Tree, casting a grim look along the ranks of Medlar Crush, Pear Perfect and other colours reminiscent of cookery columns.

'Ah, that's the joy of this range. They can be adapted to absolutely *any* occasion. You must go out sometimes, surely?'

'Not much. There's plenty to occupy me here.'

'Yes, I'm sure there is. Don't worry if you don't want to buy anything. I thought you might like a change from manning the fort, that's all. But, you know, these colours would look absolutely *ravishing* with your silver hair. The thing is, you always look so elegant, I'm just *dying* to see you in them. Won't you try something on just so I can see what they look like? It's so helpful for me to practise, you see. Take these Cossack pants. They're ever so practical for housework, and you could dress them up with a slub silk tunic for the evening.'

'The parish council would think I'd got a fancy man.'

'Why not?' Arden plied her with *biscotti* and jasmine tea. 'Give them something to talk about.'

'They do too much of that already.'

Arden smiled over gritted teeth and laid the Cossack pants over the arm of the sofa in full view. 'By the way, what happened to that driver who was stuck in – Spoleto, wasn't it? Did he pick up the tomatoes?'

For the first time that afternoon Miss Tree's expression softened. 'Yes, he did in the end. Unfortunately he got stopped by the police on the way back. Overshot his hours. Can't say I blame him. The work's very unpredictable. And he thought his splitter box was damaged so he had to come home as soon as possible.'

'He didn't get into trouble, did he?'

'Mr Jermigan sorted it out.'

'Really? I wonder what that involved?'

'I don't.'

'No. Look, you get on awfully well with Mr Jermigan, don't you? I wonder, is there the smallest possibility you could ask him something for me?'

'What?'

'The thing is, every so often we have a big selling event to promote the new collections. For all the ladies in the scheme and their customers. It's terrific fun, honestly. Don't look like that, you'll make me laugh. Anyhow, this place is too small. I was wondering if Mr Jermigan would let me use the Hall.'

'Probably not. You would have to ask him yourself. I really couldn't do anything to jeopardize my own position.'

'No, of course not. The thing is, it would have to be with your co-operation. That's the only reason I suggested it. I couldn't go straight to Mr Jermigan over your head, could I? Especially if you weren't happy about it.'

'I suppose not.'

'And you would get the hostess credit. Not that you'd have to do anything – I'd arrange it all. Ten percent. Plus a garment of your choice.'

Miss Tree's eyes swivelled to the Cossack pants for a long moment. Arden gathered up the clothes.

'All right,' said Miss Tree. 'I'll speak to him.'

Some days later Miss Tree telephoned to say that Mr Jermigan could be approached on the subject of the presentation, but would appreciate it if Arden asked him herself.

'On my knees?'

'I beg your pardon?'

'Nothing. Thank you very much, Miss Tree. I'm really very grateful.'

So Jermigan wanted to see her crawl. Arden breathed in deeply. She had been hoping to put off the grisly business of pandering to him for a little longer, but it was best to get it over with. She went straight to the industrial park, as she called it. Deep-throated fartings and grumblings of diesel engines suggested a high level of activity.

The new Iveco Eurostar was in the maintenance shed. Its egg yolk-yellow cab was tipped forward as though partially decapitated. Jermigan stood beside it, in hot debate with one of the drivers. He looked at Arden without acknowledging her so she was obliged to stand aside and listen to an emotive exchange about the pros and cons of pneumatic actuation and whether the driver even knew what a clutch assembly was or, indeed, could count up to sixteen. He was a very young man with a spotty complexion, and did not look his best when close to tears. Jermigan eventually sent him off to the office, where he proceeded with much ineffectual tossing of his gelled crewcut.

'He seems very upset.'

'Huh. Only burnt 'is fuckin' clutch out in the fuckin' Ardennes, didn' 'e? Drives like a black dog, that 'un.'

'Shouldn't you fire him then?'

'Think so? You're 'ard.'

'Not really.' Misfired again. Arden had only thought to impress him with a bit of macho swagger. 'But I imagine reckless drivers can get expensive?'

'Too right. He's just a young 'un. I'll give 'm another chance. Look at 'm. Spit on a stick, in' 'e?'

'He does look rather malnourished. I'm surprised he can handle these trucks. They're so – monumental.'

'Want to go up?'

'What?'

'In the cab, like.'

'Well, not this particular one.'

'Follow me. I'll show you round.'

Arden was amazed by his affability. He seemed to have completely forgotten the injunction. She followed him across the yard and duly admired the DAFs and ERFs lined up there. 'How many do you have altogether?'

'Twenny. Twenny-one with the Iveco. The lads fancied a change. Here you go.'

He opened the door of a DAF XF and sprung-loaded her into it. Arden marvelled at the commanding view, the steering wheel like an inter-galactic frisbee, the handy fridge under the seat. She took instruction in loading a tacho disk and just stopped herself in time from remarking that the cosy bunk would be an ideal spot for hanky-panky. For one thing, the imprint of Jermigan's hand was still warm on her ankle. For another, she noticed Lottie lolling against the shed looking around for someone with an air of feigned cool. It was a hint to be decorous. Arden had not seen the girl since the weather turned hot. The sight of her fragile arms and neck bones against an unrevealing skinny-rib top was very touching. She was surprised to see Lottie there. She assumed the girl spent most of her time indoors studying, or reading novels where people have thoughts the colour of celery or find the shape of their lover's nostril oddly moving. Not one for the *Suitables* camp unfortunately.

Jermigan frowned at his niece at first and then called to her in a jolly familial way. She moved her head slightly in what could have been a nod, and turned quickly back towards the Hall. His face was suffused with pride and fondness as he watched her go.

'She's the business, my Lottie, in' she?'

'Absolutely.' This was an unexpected confidence. Almost intimacy. Arden began to wish she was not stranded in his cab. 'You adopted her, I gather.'

'That's right. Miss Tree did most of the lookin' after an' that, but I get all the credit. She's gonna take off, that one. Bright as a bee's arse she is.'

'That's nice.' Arden flushed with maternal resentment at the existence of children cleverer than her own. At least Bos was good fun and could give the car an oil change. She patted the steering wheel. 'Right, I'll take it. Just wrap it up, please.'

'Fancy a trip in 'er?'

'No, thank you. I might get the bug and I've just started a new career.'

'So Miss Tree tells me. She says you sell clothes an' that.'

'Just clothes. I really came over here to ask you if I could possibly use the Hall—'

''Course you can. No problem. I'd like to see you in operation.' That dreaded wink again.

'Oh. Oh, dear. I don't think it would work if you were there. Damn, I didn't think of that.'

'Why not?'

'There'd be lots of ladies running around in their underwear. They'd be embarrassed. I'm sorry, forget it. I couldn't banish you from your own house.' This insurmountable obstacle to the plan was galling, especially as Jermigan was being so co-operative.

'I could go down the pub, I s'pose.'

'No. Why should you do that?' She did not mean to sound suspicious, but she was. When benign despots like Jermigan started being too helpful it felt like a spider offering the fly an extension ladder. But then perhaps his still unexpressed feelings for Humph were sufficient explanation.

'Come on down. I got summat else to show you.'

Oh, no, thought Arden. Don't tell me he restores Sopwith Camels in his spare time. It was not only that she had used up her stock of phoney wonder at mechanical masterpieces. That was no different from praising toddlers' art works. It was more that Jermigan appeared to have forgotten his embargo on her company so thoroughly it was almost insulting. Consistency would have injected a more personal note into their fledging relationship. This complete change of attitude to her was confusing. It was as if she were an object that occasionally appeared on his radar screen and which he dealt with as the mood took him.

He led the way behind the huge sheds and through a spinney to a place where the ground rose slightly to a plateau before dipping gradually down to the now-familiar landscape of undulating fields and stands of tree. Set square on the plateau were the foundations of a large, rectangular building of perfectly hewn marzipan sandstone. Blocks of the stone stood about on pallets among the detritus of construction. Their symmetry and pallor reminded Arden of the fantasies of the arch faker Viollet le Duc. It was an awful premonition.

'What exactly is this, Mr Jermigan?'

'This goin' to be my mead hall, gal. I ain't got no facilities for banquets and that just at the minute. You any good at sewin'? I'm goin' to need thirty, forty banners, like, for decoration.'

'Have you tried the Women's Institute? I'm afraid I'm too busy.' Arden was torn between horror at the whole cod medieval project and awe at the financial resources Jermigan must have at his disposal. Those were solid stones, it was no breeze-block and cladding job. 'Was it hard to get a mortgage?'

Jermigan laughed. 'What's that when it's at 'ome?' He patted the low walls. 'Beauties, ain't they? Guess where they come from?'

'Give up.'

'Normandy.'

'Goodness. How was that?'

'Remember that jumbo crashed over there a couple o' years back? Place called Bonjol. Summat like that.'

'Yes, I think so.'

'Came straight down on their whatsit – town hall, like.'

'The *Hôtel de Ville*.'

'That's the one. That's where this lot was goin'.'

'How did they end up here then?'

Jermigan laughed and shrugged. 'They went walkabout, didn' they?'

'Now wait a minute. Are you saying they're – *stolen?*'

'Nah. They's all paid for, like. Other bloke gets it off the insurance. Everybody's happy.'

'You're kidding me?'

'Nope.'

'But you must be. Why would you tell me all this? I could inform on you.'

'Reckon I's a better judge o' character than that. You like people as minds their own business, doesn't ya? I saw that right off. Wouldn't even 'ave to put the frighteners onya.'

'Cheers. But I still don't believe it. How could anyone smuggle stuff of this size? It would take ages to load and you'd have to have special equipment.'

'Smugglin' don't come into it. Took it out in broad day-light, didna? Nobody don't wanna know, do they? At a price, naturally.'

Arden felt faint. 'Hush money?'

'If y'like. My lads did a good job. They were lookin' out for me, like. Knows what I wanted. And they knows how mad I gets when they come home empty.' He chortled.

She walked away from him, ostensibly to inspect the foundations, actually to get her breath back. Jermigan obviously loved to shock, particularly women perhaps? Was she supposed to scream and tremble? Perhaps it gave him a thrill and this whole thing was a wind-up. The alternative was that he was a serious, unapologetic law-breaker. Arden had never knowingly met one. It was a bit like meeting God. One had heard rumours but . . . Why he had chosen to put himself in her power was inexplicable. Either he had an agenda, as yet unrevealed, or he simply manipulated people as a hobby. He leaned against the scaffolding watching her.

'Why isn't there anyone working on it?'

'They comes and goes when they can fit it in, like. For the time being. What d'you think then?'

'I think it could look like a de luxe garage if you're not careful. What is it going to be used for?'

'Banquets, o' course. It's goin' to be the centrepiece of the whole show, like. I got plans for this place.'

'But – mead hall. That sounds rather out of period. Shades of Beowulf. What period is it exactly?'

'Same as the castle – thirteen sommat. What d'you think?'

Arden thought he should be arrested by English Heritage and force fed on roasted skylarks before being dumped in the sea with a hogshead of frumenty tied to his ankle. 'I should like to see the architects' drawings before committing myself.'

'It's goin' to be fantastic. Inside, like, they'd be the dais up that far end there with all banners o' Jermigans dead and gone all down the 'all, and the walls all covered with huntin' scenes and that. Then your minstrels' gallery, o' course. I'm 'aving me own throne made from a old yew tree as fell down up Sloping Church.'

'Are you sure it wasn't pushed?'

He chuckled. 'You're gettin' there. The kitchen and buttery and what have you be down the other end, and the solar and that over the porch so's the guests can 'ave their noggin o' posset before they're led in.'

'You can't have the solar over the porch. It would be behind the dais end.'

'Don't matter.'

'Seems a shame not to be authentic in the design when you're going to so much trouble. I suppose you'll have lavabos built in?'

''Course. Two at each end.'

'Can't wait. I'll give you an engraved aquamanile as a hall-warming present.' His eyes flickered with doubt, to Arden's satisfaction. She might not know an axle hop from a day at the races but Jermigan would have to bow to her superior knowledge of fourteenth-century clobber. 'And will your guests have to crap through a hole over the moat?'

'They would if I had my way, but the fuckin' Health and Safety Herberts'd shut me down, wouldn't they?'

'You mean, this is going to be a commercial venture?'

''Course. Like I said, this be just the centrepiece.'

'Of what? A total experience? A total *heritage* experience . . .'

'Sort of. But not like that theme park crap. More like them livin' museums, only folks can do it themselves 'stead o' watching, like. No gas, no electric, sleep on straw pallets, all that. Games – Shove-Groat, Hot Cockles – all that. Them that can ride'll take the 'awks out and in the evening the full monty banquet in 'ere. See 'ow they go eating custard wi' a dagger.'

'But where will you get – I don't know – two hundred Puddings de Swan Neck round here?'

'Make them, o' course. The guests can pitch in wi' that an' all. What's the matter? You look like you swallowed a bus.'

'It's just – you *can't* be serious. You say it won't be a theme park, but it *will*. You'll have to have a Gifte Shoppe and exhibitions of local crafts made in China, and homemade teas and things. The place will be ruined. And it's so perfect as it is. Even if there's not much of it. And I can't believe it will be commercial. Schemes like that collapse all the time. You'd never recover the capital fast enough even if you did get people to come.'

'Don't you doubt it. There's a place over Wymondham way – Hempknott House it's called – people pays to take part for the day, pretendin' to be brewsters and pantlers an' that. Pay for their training, the lot. I'll take you there next time they 'ave one o' them days. Packed out it is.'

'For the day, perhaps.' Arden shook her head in despair. She could see a vision of Hell: people wearing trainers under their houppelandes and using their mobile phones while waiting for a go on the quintain.

'Besides, it won't be all work, y'know. There'll be dancing and that. Ale house, bath house . . .'

'Don't tell me – communal baths?' How often had she envied those naked lovers with their hats on, squashed into sawn-off beer barrels. But not, Good Lord deliver us, for kinky business-men playing away from home. Or, worse, romantic twats like her ex-husband. 'Wait a minute. What about the trucks? Wooden wheels, perhaps?'

'Sarky cow.' This was said without malice. 'They'll be movin'. Got a site over Beccles.'

'What about us? The cottage will be right in the middle of it.'

'A few fake beams and a bit o' thatch'll soon fix that.'

'Now I know you're joking.'

'I'd give you a decent price for it. Make life a lot easier for both on us.'

'Over my dead body! What makes you think I'd let it be turned into a half-timbered tea cosy?'

'That ain't fair. Everything'd be done dead authentic-looking.'

'Sorry, you can't count on us. Never. And I'm sure Tim would agree with me.'

'Always do, don' 'e? Pity. He could've helped wi' the books.'

'Oh, nice try. I don't think laundering invoices is quite his style.'

'Wouldn't come to that. It's all straight up. I've 'ad this planned for years.'

'Then you've been mad for years. I'm sorry, but I think it's a ghastly idea. And it will never work.'

'Now look 'ere, this 'ere's a fuckin' job creation scheme! Fuckin' incomers, you're all the same. This 'ere's a designated European backwater, y'know. There's thousands o' young lads round 'ere won't ever get a decent job if somebody don't do sommat.'

'And that's your motivation, is it? To help the unemployed? *Please*. You want to do this because you think you can make money from it, and satisfy some primal instinct to ponce about in tights at the same time.'

Jermigan looked at her with unmasked distaste. 'I wish you 'adn't said that. And you will too. And what's more, I'll tell Miss Tree you did.'

'Oh, *wow*. She's not my *nanny*, you know.'

He pointed a threatening finger at her. 'You show respect for Miss Tree, mind, or you'll be sorry. Now get off my property.'

5 ʃ

The weeks after the election brought Tim several clients. As the trend towards moral and financial self-sufficiency was spelled out by the new government in terms of long-term care insurance, university fees and the abolition of tax relief on private pensions, a healthy proportion of the population turned their thoughts to dodges and deviation. Careful liaison with Arden was essential, as there had been a few occasions when ladies in their underwear had overlapped with anxious taxpayers.

She had not told Tim how disastrously the meeting with Jermigan had ended. Try though she might to shrug it off as an amusing throw-back to baronial spats, she could not dispel an uneasy feeling that she had been humiliated. Being thrown off someone's property *was* humiliating, however righteous the victim. In fact, being a victim was humiliating, innocent or not. But Arden could not countenance the idea of victimhood, and therefore must wipe the whole episode from her mind as far as she could. She did tell Tim about Jermigan's plans to turn the castle complex into a farts-and-all immersion experience, and transform their cottage into a thatched bath house called, no doubt, the Way Inn. She sought confirmation from him that the finances of the venture were rubbish, in the hope that he would go and put Jermigan right on that score. But Tim did not know enough about venture capital to pose as an authority. Not that he would have done anyway. From what he had seen of Jermigan Tim had every intention of avoiding him as he would a rabid dog. Especially since Jermigan had recently started taking his hell-hounds, Rocky, Sperm and Malice, around with him everywhere.

One night Tim was dreaming that these beasts had cornered him in a lift in Debenham's and someone was rattling on the door demanding to know if they used holy water. He woke up, relieved, to find Arden asking the same question. She was leaning across from her bed, thwacking him with a paperback.

'Did she use holy water, Tim? Do you remember? Did she cross herself? Wake up!'

'Stop it. What are you talking about? What time is it?'

'Thalia Sewell. It just occurred to me that if she's a Catholic that would be one way of getting access without a direct approach. I could ingratiate myself at coffee mornings. Perhaps he converted because of her.'

'Don't be daft. If they were having an affair he wouldn't exactly have religion on his mind, would he?'

'I suppose not. But still, do you remember if she crossed herself?'

'No. Anyway, High Anglicans cross themselves. And Formula One racing drivers.'

'That's true. Holy water, use of, would be more of a giveaway. Do you remember?'

'Of course not. We were in the church. We wouldn't have seen if she used it anyway. What time is it? I can't believe you woke me up just for that. I'll have my own room if there's any more of this.'

'*Miaow.* Sorry. There's no pen on my side table otherwise I would have written a note and asked you in the morning. It's only one o'clock. Plenty of time to get back to sleep.' But Arden was no longer in the mood to sleep, and after some time spent glaring at his immobile form she gently lobbed the paperback at it to see if he was still awake.

One convenience of an itinerant job was that Arden could go anywhere without having to account to Tim for her movements. And Mr Gordon, the solicitor, having met Arden before, did not question the fact that she spoke for both of them. He looked distinctly defensive as she took her seat. She had trumped up some queries about the probate application, but there was no dodging the real reason for her presence.

'Mr Gordon, I think, possibly, you were a bit reluctant to talk about the contents of the will at first. I mean, this bequest to Mrs Sewell.'

He shuffled his papers defensively. 'It's not really any of my concern, Mrs Fairbrother.'

'No, of course not. I just wanted to reassure you that we knew all about it. We're not going to make a fuss or anything.'

'Ah.' He relaxed. 'Nothing was further from my mind. Coffee?'

'No, thank you. But could you just let me have her address? I'm afraid I've left my address book in London and I wanted to write and thank her for the lovely flowers she sent.'

'Of course. No trouble. I'll just go and look in the file. Will you excuse me a moment?'

Arden smiled her gratitude as Mr Gordon hurried out, buoyed by the prospect of concluding the interview so painlessly.

Shortly after getting the address from Mr Gordon, Arden achieved a *Suitables* presentation in Gorleston, hard by Great Yarmouth. As she would be in the area on legitimate business, it would be possible to reconnoitre 24 Rosemount Avenue without feeling like a paparazzo. The death of the Princess of Wales had given her a moment's unease about the ethics of persuing Thalia Sewell. Another moment had been enough to decide that there was no comparison. She had no intention of pestering the living daylights out of Thalia. Her curiosity, particularly in view of the bequest, was only human.

Arden had been totally engrossed by the princess's funeral. Tim had stayed in bed. Never one for displays of emotion, she could nonetheless sympathize with those who claimed they were more upset by this loss than they had been by the death of a spouse or parent. And Earl Spencer's challenge to the Royal Family from the pulpit had her on the edge of her seat, nerve ends a-quiver. She half expected him to chuck a gauntlet on to the sanctuary carpet. Not since Henry III had accused Simon de Montfort of seducing his sister, at the queen's churching feast, had there been such high drama on the public stage. On that occasion Simon and his wife had escaped in a small boat – an option the present royals might well contemplate with envy.

The hostess for the presentation was a satisfied client from the headmistress's circle. Arden went through the guest list with her beforehand, to memorize names and target the likely spenders. She was impressed. There was a lawyer, a marine engineer, a garage owner and the wives of businessmen with interests in chip shops and steel tubes among other things. Arden's preconceptions about rural backwaters took further readjustment. The house was a large Victorian semi, with swags and sofas that would be perfectly at home in Chiswick.

The mood among the ladies was at first subdued, in line with the nation's. A glass of Frascati and a respectful gossip about the sad event eased the communal conscience and provided a useful bonding exercise. Arden had by now enough experience to enjoy demonstrating the range. She had discovered a performance gene she never knew she had, one which put clients at their ease. There was nothing worse than a salesperson who was clearly in need of a stiff drink. A couple of the wives, who had come together, were the most attentive. Arden identified them easily as Autumn and Spring and when the others went off into the dining room with bundles of garments to try on, they stayed behind and poured out their hearts about their bottoms and short waists. She was in her element matching their problems with *Suitables* solutions, fascinating them with the trompe l'oeil effects of bias cutting and personalized colourways. They were an odd couple, one tall and one short, with matching pageboy haircuts and fringes. So serious was their enthusiasm for the *Suitables* philosophy that they stripped down to their La Senza underwear right in front of her. The tall Spring one looked sensational in a five-piece powder-blue cruise costume. Autumn hardly recognized herself in a sludge-green boiler suit with matching tank top. Arden discreetly deployed her order forms. It was always difficult at this stage to know whether to go for the sales and leave it at that, or seize the opportunity for recruitment. Like the universe, *Suitables* owed its existence to expansion and it dared not stop.

The first move was to establish the client's current commit-ments. Arden concentrated on the tall Spring – Helen – as the clothes would look better on her. Helen was a receptionist in a veterinary practice, which was partly why she chose a colour that did not show up dog hairs. Yes, she did love her work, although it was emotionally very draining. She also had three children, so the hours suited her. The smaller friend, Becky, caught Arden's drift at once.

'You're looking for recruits, I suppose?'

'In principle, yes. Do you think you might be interested?'

'Don't know. I got fed up with selling. I've done the lot – plastic kitchen ware, aromatherapy, Avon Calling. I was Salesperson of the Month once on the kitchen ware. It was that year Delia Smith demonstrated the perforated pie top roller. D'you remember, Hell? I had people ringing me up in the middle of the night for one.'

'Oh, yes. It was like those – whatdyacallums? Cabbage Patch dolls. Mass hysteria.'

The Cabbage Patch outbreak had passed Arden by, but her view of Becky's potential had changed. If she had the nous, perhaps she could use Helen as the model. She passed Becky her card with the order form.

'Think it over. There's no hurry. We don't have mobs baying for the stuff, but sales are doing really, really well. And it's fun, don't you think? Have you enjoyed this evening?'

'Oh, *yes*,' they choroused.

'But then, I always enjoy getting away from the old man, don't you, Beck?'

'I'll say.'

Arden thought it rather sad. She always looked forward to going home to Tim, whereas ninety per cent of her *Suitables* clients behaved like puppies let off the leash for a few hours.

'Are you married, Arden?'

'What? No. I share a home with my brother. We're both divorced.'

'You don't know how lucky you are.' More giggles.

'I'm beginning to.'

Becky studied Arden's card. 'Sloping Castle . . . That rings a bell.' She passed it to Helen. 'Isn't that where that bloke Harry Jermigan lives?' At this they both spluttered with laughter again.

'Yes. Do you know him?'

'Do *you*? I'd get your locks changed double quick!'

'Sorry, I don't follow? Lots of people seem to know of him, but I haven't been here long so I'm not in on the joke.'

When Becky had brought her paroxysms under control, she said, 'He's got a reputation as a ladies' man, as you might say. I've got a friend in Loddon – she says they call him Lord of the Flies.' This had them both clutching their stomachs.

'Oh, is that all? I did rather get that impression. But I'm afraid Mr Jermigan and I don't hit it off. In fact, I think he's trying to get rid of us. Or he'd like to anyway.'

Helen sobered up. 'You want to be careful then. He's a real sweetheart with his women but you don't want to get on the wrong side of him.'

'He doesn't scare me.'

'No kidding, Arden, he put a bloke in hospital. That's why he went to prison'

'Prison? I don't think . . .'

'Honest! He only just got out.'

'But he was on a hunting trip in Canada.'

Helen and Becky exchanged amused looks. 'I don't know who told you that. It was in all the papers. He and some mates of his beat up this bloke really badly. Mind you, he asked for it. Jermigan was seeing his wife and the bloke kicked her in the – you know – down there.'

'Yes,' said Helen, 'the husband was a right bastard. No one would testify against Jermigan but the husband and his best friend. If there'd been more women on the jury it'd been thrown out for sure. Are you okay?'

'Yes. Yes, I'm just thinking . . . Are you absolutely sure about this?'

'Of course! I told you, it was in all the papers.'

Arden was thrown severely out of selling gear by this information. At first she had thought it could not possibly be true because Miss Tree had told her Jermigan was in Canada. Not only was it more difficult to believe Miss Tree would lie than that Jermigan could be a jail bird, but if it had been in the papers there would surely have been no point in her lying? Then she remembered that at that time they were living in London and Miss Tree had assumed they would sell the cottage. If that had happened there would have been every chance they would never find out the truth.

As a result of Arden's being off the ball takings were down –

a mere £842. But at least she had the prospect of a new recruit. Talk of there being no hurry was bollocks, of course. She would be on the phone to Becky in the morning.

Arden's keenness to check out 24 Rosemount Avenue was also dented. Lugging tons of clothes to and from the car was tiring, never mind sparkling all evening. Or failing to. But she managed to get lost on the way out of Gorleston anyway, and once she realized she was heading for Great Yarmouth it seemed silly not to have a quick look.

'Rosemount' was something of a misnomer. The street was a treeless terrace near the docks. Many of the tiny houses had been done up with PVC doors, the brick façades painted and the lintels picked out in a contrasting tone. The irrepressible home improvement instincts of the British householder were particularly noticeable on this challenging canvas. Number 24 was one of the smartest. It had mullioned replacement windows and a carriage lamp by the door. Arden could only cruise past as there were so many cars parked to either side. She drove round the block and came back past it. A man of perhaps sixty was at the window, drawing the curtains. Not Gavin, obviously. Perhaps Thalia Sewell's husband? Presumably they would move to a larger house when the bequest was paid out. They could afford a semi with a garage and front garden. But then, did they need it? She really must shake off the estate agent's assumption that the human race was primarily concerned with aspirations to grander premises.

She reminded herself that Humph must have been a frequent caller at this neat little done-up house. Or they might have had to meet in secret, though Thalia's boldness in leaving her tribute on his coffin did not suggest secrecy. But by then she would have had nothing to lose. It was all so ordinary, so cosy and domesticated in Rosemount Avenue. The front rooms glowed with the spectral light of television screens. Polystyrene milkbottle holders stood ready for the morning. If there had not been a man in the house, for two pins Arden would have knocked on the door and introduced herself. As it was she went home and shouted at Tim for not recording One Foot In The Past.

It was with fascinated horror that Arden read posters advertising the town's Festival Fun Day, as the main attraction was a jousting tournament by an outfit from Birmingham called the Roistering Rebels. She could just about stretch a point to condone genuine reconstructions based on meticulous research, but the prospect of a staged romp in melt-down medieval dress by amateurs, who clearly should get out more, was anathema. Besides, Saturday afternoons were reserved for admin – sending off order forms to headquarters, bringing the accounts up to date, and delivering orders to clients. She sat down to work in the study after lunch. The room still smelled mouldy. Arden was beginning to suspect rising damp as well as ancient fungal spores. Perhaps it would be a good idea to get a survey done after all. Not that it would make any difference to her wish to live here. The cottage felt more like her own home than anywhere she had lived since childhood, one good reason for that being that all the other residences had belonged to someone else.

Tim was having a nap, a habit he had got into since they had moved. Arden was afraid the pain in his hip was worse than he was prepared to admit. Manly endurance was all very well on the battlefield, but in the office it was downright silly. The sky was rolling with pewter-grey clouds. It was one of those September days that are too cold for bare legs but not cold enough for central heating. Processing the orders from the Gorleston presentation was a distracting business. The image of 24 Rosemount Avenue had been in her mind ever since her visit, along with several illegal schemes for calling there to read the meter or present herself as a council surveyor. It would be much more sensible simply to introduce herself. Thalia Sewell must not become an obsession. Arden did not want to end up like Victor Hugo's daughter, a crazed bag lady wandering the streets – of Great Yarmouth, in this case – in search of a long-forgotten object.

After that same evening she had confirmed with the invaluable Mrs Brady that Jermigan had indeed been to prison. It gave her the shivers.

Disgusted with her own weakness, she gave up the struggle with the paperwork and surrendered to curiosity. She would see the tournament. It had begun to rain so she disguised herself as the Queen on holiday – gum boots, mackintosh, headscarf and round sunglasses. She left a note for Tim on the kitchen counter.

The event was held on the meadows by the river. The jousting arena was surrounded by tented stalls selling the whole range of fête fare, predominantly furry toys in fluorescent green and pink. When Arden arrived there was a display of knot dancing by the Methodist Women's Guild on the arena, clear evidence that the Fun Day had no plans to knock the Edinburgh Tattoo off its perch. If Tim had been with her, Arden would have taken droll delight in such traditional entertainments but on her own it felt like strictly business. She queued up for a hot dog and two pieces of raisin fudge and settled herself on a hay bale to eat them. The dancing display came to an unexpected halt when the tape recorder broke down. An announcement over the Tannoy urged spectators to stay seated as the joust would commence shortly. An old man in a smart raincoat sat down on the other end of the hay bale. He smiled at her in a way that suggested small talk was to follow. Arden looked around and was relieved to see the headmistress of the primary school, who had been one of her first hostesses. She was with a teenage boy and they were eating ice creams smattered by rain drops. Arden hurried over to her.

'Hello, dear. Steeping yourself in local culture, I'm glad to see. This is my son, David.'

'Hello, David. I'm surprised you recognized me, Angela. I thought I was incognito.'

'Why should you be? You haven't come here to pick pockets, I presume?'

'No. It's just so *embarrassing* to be at a thing like this on one's own. Or *at all*, come to that.' David drifted off. 'I can't stand cod history numbers like this, really. I'm so weak.'

'Don't be such a snob.'

'I am *not* a snob. I'm a purist.'

'Well, I hope we can still be friends if I tell you I'm thinking of hiring this tournament lot for the school's anniversary day.'

'Angela, you're *not*?'

She laughed at Arden's horrified expression. 'Why not? The kids love it. Look at them all. Don't worry, it'll be backed up by pukka history lessons. And for science they can work out how much fuel would be needed to burn an average-sized male heretic at the stake.'

'You're winding me up.'

'Well, it's so easy.'

'No, seriously, Angela, this sort of thing's rather a sore point with me at the moment. My neighbour wants to turn Sloping Castle into a medieval theme park.'

'So I've heard. He'll take it right to the Department of the Environment if necessary. It's been in the pipeline for years, you know.'

'Has it? I hope it doesn't get that far. You know this government's populist agenda – the people's lottery, the people's princess, the people's millennium dome. I think they got their ideas from Caligula. It could be just the sort of project they'd go for.'

'It would employ a lot of people . . .'

'Don't you start. Why don't they employ people to build houses, for God's sake?

'All right, keep your headscarf on. Look, the fun's starting. Shall we find a seat?'

They hay bales cleared miraculously of small children as their headmistress approached, and they had a front-row view and the chance to be flattened by a frisky charger. Arden was seriously worried about the possibility as she could see that the ill-fitting crinets on the horses' necks could easily slip and cause temporary blindness. Nor was she convinced that the animals were used to performing in front of screaming children throwing leftover hamburgers. Was this what she had to look forward to at Sloping, while the smell of roast oxen permeated her soft furnishings?

Rabble-rousers in tabards bearing the cross of the Knights Templar preceded the horses. They took up position in front of the crowd where there were the most children, and with much name-calling of the 'loathsome churl' variety, set about whipping up partisan passion. The white knight, Sir Godwin de Selly Oak, was a large young man with a beer belly and a revolving horse. He also had difficulty controlling his lance which threatened to take the roof off the cake stall. His mortal enemy, Sir Osbert de Coventry, was a much more fetching figure, in black with gold spread-eagles. His mount was wisely reluctant to take part and had to be prodded by an assistant, whereupon he reared and whinnied before hurtling down the lists.

Arden covered her eyes as the two lumbering destriers charged at the revolving quintain. A roar greeted the successful thwacking thereof. Sir Osbert was unseated. Arden was forced to admire the unsuspected skill of Sir Godwin, in what had looked like an impossible task. The exercise was repeated several times so that Sir Osbert was allowed to threaten Sir Godwin's supremacy and bring the crowd to a state of feverish suspense. As the children, at least, had got the picture by then and were beginning to grow bored, the abuse of the rabble-rousers was stepped up, and one of them got into a real fight with some little boys who kept calling Sir Godwin a wanker and started a chant of '*Os*-bert, *Os*-bert'.

Angela, being a headmistress, was used to feigning enthusiasm for childish pursuits, but Arden had seen enough in the first few seconds. She would have liked to leave, but felt she had to demonstrate that she was no snob by staying and joining in with faint cries from time to time. When she saw Harry Jermigan coming towards her around the edge of the crowd it was with as much relief as apprehension. She had not seen him since learning of his prison record, and their last encounter had ended awkwardly, and yet Arden felt they had unfinished business. He seemed to be looking out for someone, and in case it was her she excused herself to Angela and went to meet him. There was no knowing what was on his mind, or how he would express it, and she did not want to be throttled with her own headscarf in front of her friend.

His expression, masked as ever by that enigmatic smile, was neutral. He reached for an envelope in his inside pocket and handed it to her.

'I went up the cottage. Tim told me you was here. This is for you.'

'Just me?'

'You both. I wanted to be sure you got him.'

'You're always bringing me letters, it's rather quaint,' said Arden, and wished she had not. 'What is it?'

'Just read it. Take your time.' He turned to go, then stopped and grinned. 'Crap this, ain't it?' He indicated the jousting knights, who were taking their bows. 'We'll show 'em.'

'People seem to like it.'

'I thought this sort of thing stuck in your gullet?'

'Yes, it does. A friend asked me to come.'

'Ah. See you.'

It was a weighty letter. On the back of the envelope was the Jermigan coat of arms, two cocks respectant on an azure field. Arden walked away towards the river as she tore it open. It was an official offer for the cottage. A very respectable offer – £120,000 cash. Undoubtedly more than it was worth. That was the final insult. Assuming that they had a price. Well, Jermigan would be told in no uncertain terms that they did not! The junket she had just witnessed confirmed all her prejudices. Arden rammed the letter in her pocket and hurried back to the car park. Spectators were leaving as the rain was coming down in piggins. Angela and her son waved as they ran towards their car. They started to get in, then Angela remembered something and ran over to Arden.

'I forgot to ask you – can you and Tim come to a quiz night in a couple of weeks? Topham St Peter. A friend of mine is making up a team. It's for the school trip to Alton Towers.'

'Oh, yes, all right. I think we can.' There was actually no question about it. Angela was too useful a contact. Headmistresses had to look smart and Arden had hopes that Angela would host many more *Suitables* presentations in the future. Fortunately Tim was brilliant at quizzes. He shone at matching pop songs with Bible quotations and was a consistently high scorer on Sporting Tackle.

Arden felt like a thwacked quintain herself when Tim declared in favour of accepting Jermigan's offer. He did so with much pre-emptive bluff, anticipating a struggle. His argument, on financial grounds, was irrefutable. They had been mad to become self-employed at the same time. Even if he could not get his old job back there would be greater opportunities as an independent in London, and it would be the same for Arden. While it was true that her earning potential, in particular, was good, it would take too long to realize, by which time the Sloping Experience might be a *fait accompli*. And if it were, they could never hope to sell the cottage to anyone other than Jermigan if it was going to be surrounded by hoi-polloi enjoying a fourteenth-century knees-up, of which carousing into the small hours would be the principal feature.

'It's not certain he'll get planning permission,' objected Arden, but without her customary conviction. It was not just Tim's arguments that swayed her. More persuasive was the realization that, if that was how he felt, it was neither fair nor practical to force him to stay. She sat slumped before her untouched omelette and chips. Tim topped up her wine glass. Arden in an attitude of capitulation was as rare a sight as a flock of ospreys.

'I know it's a disappointment, Ard, but I'm only thinking of the future. We've got to keep up the pension contributions, and they'll be going up.'

'Yes, of course.'

'And it's better to cut our losses before it's too late.'

'Have we made losses?'

'Well, no, not yet. But – well, there are just far too many variables in the situation. If we sell this place we'll be in a very good position.'

'I suppose so.'

'Look, tell you what, you know you've always wanted to walk to Compostela? We could do that, if you like. If we had some money in the bank, I could afford to take a few weeks off.'

Arden could not help smiling. 'You would walk to Compostela for me?'

'I'd walk to the Mir space station for you, Ard. You know that.'

'But you wouldn't stay here?'

'I would if it weren't so risky. Possibly. I just feel if we don't take this opportunity, we'll regret it. And if we leave it too long and the housing market picks up we'd only have to pay capital gains tax on the differential. There are so many things we could do with the money, Ard. The crusader castles, for instance. That's something else you've always wanted to do, isn't it? Krak des Chevaliers. You could see Saladin's bathroom. Think of that.'

Arden was too depressed to point out that Saladin was on the other side. It had been such a gallant attempt to cheer her. But now Tim, too, was on the other side. They had never had a serious difference of opinion before. From his point of view, of course, the whole relocation plan was hare-brained and selfish. She *should* be grateful that he had even agreed to give it a chance. Happy those whose most hare-brained ambition is the perfect with-profits endowment trust. But with this gulf between them she could not tell Tim that on that first visit to Sloping in April she had recognized her spiritual home. How much kinder fate would have been if it had not offered her this taste of homecoming, only to snatch it away.

The phone rang. Tim got up to answer it and pressed the secrecy button. 'It's Bos, Ard. Do you want to speak to him?'

'Not just now. He'd only worry if I didn't have the energy to argue with him. Tell him I'll call tomorrow. I know what he wants, anyway.' Bos's financial problems were, of course, another good reason to sell the cottage.

Tim told his nephew that Arden was at Weightwatchers, a tease that roused her briefly from her torpor. When he put the phone down, she got up. 'I'll do it now. Get it over with.'

'It can wait till the morning, Ard.'

'No. I must start getting used to the idea right away.' With her head held high, even managing a smile and a reassuring touch on Tim's shoulder, she went to the study and set out her writing paper.

She had not had much time for Mary, Queen of Scots until this moment. The woman's choice of men, for starters, suggested a deeply frivolous nature. Now she thought of Mary's last night on earth, penning valedictory letters to loyal supporters. As she wrote the date, Arden was somewhat consoled by a frisson of martyrdom.

It was sickening the way the news transformed Harry Jermigan into a neighbour who could have come out of *Scouting for Boys*. Suddenly nothing was too much trouble. It was anticipated that the paperwork on the sale might take up to two months, but in the meantime all the resources of Sloping Hall and Jermigan Haulage were put at their disposal. He offered to organize a sale of contents if they wished. Rocky, Sperm and Malice were kept off their premises and he sent Jake to remove the stains of their deposits from the flagstones in front of the cottage. This blatant admission of previous intimidation annoyed Arden so much she almost cancelled the sale. She was slightly mollified by his offer of the Hall for her presentations although there was not much point in taking it up as she would have to run down the *Suitables* operation rather than build it up. Jermigan even invited them to dinner – an offer which Arden also declined. There was no point in meeting new people if they were moving. Tim was disappointed. He missed their modest social life in Chiswick.

On the day they were to go to the Topham St Peter quiz night, Arden and Tim visited their mother at The Ashes in the afternoon. Mattie was relatively coherent. The residents had been dragooned into making corn dollies for harvest festival, and she had always been good with her hands. The clingfilm fireflies had been one of many fancy dress triumphs, and Arden and Tim's costumes for school plays had been displayed at assembly as an example to which other parents should be encouraged to aspire. Alas, Mattie's skills had deteriorated sadly by now. Her corn dolly looked like a deranged bundle of faggots but the effort had activated memories.

'You've dyed your hair, darling,' she greeted Arden, in the fond tones they remembered from when she had marvelled at every achievement from mastering shoe-laces to passing A Levels. 'It *does* look nice.'

'Thanks, Mum. It's only a rinse, you know. I'm not going grey.'

'Of course you're not. You've got lovely hair. Just like your father.'

'Humph had – has – ginger hair, Mum.'

'Oh, yes, of course he does. Silly old me. I meant my father.'

'You seem well today, Mum,' said Tim. 'Do you fancy a run in the car? We could take you out for tea.'

'Ooh, lovely. Can we go to the Bun in the Oven?'

'No, Mum. That's in Chiswick. But we could go down to Walberswick. The seaside. You like the seaside, don't you?'

'I do. It's a bit far though. Why don't we go there when your father gets back from Rangoon?'

'Tim, you know what, don't you?'

'Yes.' They had left Mattie happily disassembling a Viennese whirl. 'I forgot about Mum.'

'In a nutshell.'

'How could I?'

'Don't be hard on yourself. We're just not used to being

responsible for her, that's all.' Arden knew it was not nice to use Mattie's senility as the answer to her prayers, but in her head ran through some suitably low-key reactions if Tim came round to the idea of staying at Sloping.

'She seemed a lot better today. And she remembered the Bun in the Oven. Perhaps if we did move her back to Chiswick she might remember a lot more.'

'Possibly. On the other hand it would be a big responsibility if she hated it and we had to bring her back here. She's confused enough as it is.'

'I know, I know.'

'Would the council in Chiswick pay the fees? She hasn't lived there for almost twenty years.'

'God, I don't know. Why do all these things have to be organized by the local authority? It would be much simpler if it was centralized.'

'There must be some rules, otherwise they'd all want to be in Bournemouth.'

'Perhaps they'll go back to whipping the homeless for straying over parish boundaries? Just like your beloved Middle Ages.'

'That was under the Tudors, I think. In the Middle Ages tending the poor was seen as a God-given opportunity for people to save their own souls. My, how times change.'

'Would you put me in a home, Ard?'

'Never. I'd have you humanely destroyed.'

6

Topham St Peter lay almost ten miles to the south-west of Sloping, deep in the notorious district of The Saints where, as the guidebook warns, no one ventures without good reason. Legend has it that during the war signposts were removed, in the certain knowledge that if the enemy strayed into the area they would never find their way out. Arden was amused by this Doone Country gloss on a workaday landscape, now gilded with the evening sun. She had 'ventured' into the Saints several times on *Suitables* business and, yes, a compass helped, but the supposed air of menace was a silly myth. What she had seen were pretty-ish villages with active Brownie packs and satellite dishes. There *was* a rather strange, cheerful old fellow who wheeled his perfectly healthy dog around in a pram all day, but the thing was, such people were simply more noticeable in the country than in town.

The primary school was a new building of reclaimed brick, timber and solar panels, already sporting a peace garden with disabled access by the entrance. It inspired confidence that inside would be found the traditional hamsters and bright colours alongside the whole range of modern hi-tech equipment, barring only a particle accelerator. And a few well-attended Auctions of Promises would soon fix that.

The quiz was held in the lower school hall as the upper school hall was set out for an in-the-round production of *Where the Wind Blows*. The headmaster, Mr Cragg, apologized for the fact that they had to sit on little chairs at little tables. Arden and Tim had particular difficulty deciding where to put their knees. Fortunately they had brought several bottles of wine, which eased the pain. Arden's mood was rueful as she absorbed the atmosphere of parental *esprit de corps*. The mural collage of the sea bed reminded her of the days when she had saved sweet wrappers herself for Bos's projects, and her garden-on-a-plate had won him a bag of crocuses and promotion to class monitor.

The crowded hall was buzzing with friendly chat and nervous anticipation. The other members of their team were Angela and her husband, Chris, and a young couple called Simon and Tina. Simon had just returned from servicing an electricity supply station in Gabon and his globe-trotting experience was thought to give the team a competitive edge. Tina was a nurse and Angela's husband a builder, so they were confident that between them they must have ninety per cent of human experience covered. Arden was pleased to see that Tim was entering into the spirit of the event, and had happily fallen into the joshing mode set by Simon and Chris. It made her realize that he had been starved of male company since they'd moved and that she should have made some provision for it. Tim was not a bloke's bloke, but, as with the body's need for vitamins, the total absence of blokeship caused damage quite disproportionate to the amount needed.

Mr Cragg's welcoming speech was interrupted by the swaggering entrance of four shifty-looking men with their collars turned up. Their poise faltered a moment as a hush fell over the hall and some people started whispering to their neighbours behind their hands, but once the men had each paid their two pounds and received a ticket they boldly set up a nest of tables for themselves in a vacant space in the corner. Arden had a good view of them.

'Are they taking a break from badger baiting? What on earth are they doing here? They're not parents, I bet.'

Angela pulled a face. 'I'm afraid you're right. They're semipros. They'll be a team from a pub somewhere who go round all the local quizzes scooping up the prizes. They were here last year.'

'How *mean*. Can't they be banned?'

'Yes. They could also come back and break all the windows. It's a free country.'

'You can't ban people from a public event,' said Tim. 'Not unless you want the European Court of Human Rights on your back.'

'But it's so *unfair.*'

'Lighten up, Ard. It's only a quiz.'

Arden recognized the hint not to spoil the party, but to judge by the subdued atmosphere in the hall she was not the only one to feel that the men were as welcome as the SS at Rick's Bar in Casablanca. It did nothing to raise spirits that they had given their team name as the Sheep Worriers. 'Are they really good? Do you think we can beat them?'

'England expects,' said Chris with mock solemnity. Tina made the sign of the cross, at which even Arden giggled.

The first round was *What Year?*, a general category to warm everyone up. Mr Cragg explained that he had set all the questions himself, under the supervision of his ten-year-old daughter. Impatient laughter. He apologized for any mistakes in advance and started to read out the questions in the jolly, well-enunciated manner which made his assemblies such inspiring occasions. Arden and Tim's team, the Holey Jumpers, had little trouble with this round, apart from, *In which year did Elizabeth Taylor marry Richard Burton for the second time?*

'Who cares?' said Arden, crossly, as they er'd and aah'd.

They scored eight out of ten, the same as the Sheep Worriers, which made them joint leaders. Chris urged them not to get over-confident as the papers were handed out for *Wars of the World*. The surprise boffin in this round was Tina, who knew not only the participants at the Yalta Conference, but Monty's real name. She explained, modestly, that she did a lot of reading on night duty, and resisted attempts to sign her up there and then for next year's contest. After *How Does Your Garden Grow?* and a round about *East Anglian Murders*, the Sheep Worriers had pulled ahead to thirty-four points to the Jumpers' joint second with thirty-one. Arden kept a hostile eye on the Worriers, who were hunched in deadly earnest over their tiny tables, never looking round. She was still fulminating with indignation at their intrusion into family fun, not to mention their superior general knowledge. She had, however, every hope that the *Books and Things* round would see the intruders humiliated and they could all break for the buffet with honour intact. Sure enough Angela careered through the literature questions like an Intercity 125. There was only one which floored her *What was the name of*

Emily Brontë's dog? Chris loyally objected to the headmaster that this was not a proper literature question. Tim calmed him down by pointing out that it could come under 'and Things'. There was a stunned silence when the Sheep Worriers scored full marks.

Tim kept close by Arden's side as they joined the scrum for the buffet. Her eye, by now malevolent, was fixed on the enemy as the intruders piled their plates with sausage rolls and filo parcels. Pigging out on the *entrées* was another anti-social offence, although she would have been almost disappointed if they had not. Tim was seriously concerned that she would harangue the men about their greed before they could snaffle all the best puddings.

'Perhaps there'll be a round about medieval underwear, Ard. You'd see them off all right then.'

'Not if they're cheating. They *must* be cheating. How else would they know about Emily Brontë's dog?'

'Don't be silly, Ard. If they were cheating they'd have had to break into the headmaster's house and steal the papers. And all for a bottle of Kanoonga Hills 1996 between the four of them? I don't think so.'

'They're fanatics. Fanatics will stop at nothing. Shall I cut you some broccoli quiche?'

'No, thanks. I'll stick to bread and cheese.'

'You're not feeling queasy again, are you?'

'A bit. I expect it's your fault. You give me anxiety attacks.'

'Not deliberately.'

'That's no consolation, Ard. Just lighten *up*, will you? The others will think you're being cared for in the community.'

'All *right*.'

In the second half she did as she was bidden and made no more barbed remarks about the Sheep Worriers. In fact she became so quiet and serious that Tim was racked with guilt that he had spoiled her evening. That was the trouble when one loved someone for the very qualities that caused public embarrassment. It was a constant struggle to tone her down without warping her nature.

He need not have worried. Arden had only gone quiet so that she could eavesdrop on the neighbouring tables. This proved particularly useful in the music round when she correctly identified

the key of the opening bars of *Das Heldenleben*. She avoided Tim's
eye. By the penultimate round they had drawn level with the
Worriers, leaving the field behind but far from unaware of the
head to head contest for the Kanoonga Hills. The atmosphere
was charged with incredulous hope as Mr Cragg explained
the rules for the last round which, as if the suspense was not
life-threatening enough already, involved a test of nerve as well
as knowledge. It was a cumulative clue round. Ten points if they
guessed the answer after one clue, nine after two and so on.
Chairs were pushed back so as to be ready for the dash to the
adjudicator with the answer paper. Mr Cragg cleared his throat
as attentive silence gripped the crowd.

'*His father was known as the Scourge of the Albigenses.*'

Arden yelped, grabbed the paper, scribbled the answer and
ran up to hand it in. Her table was in disarray, pleading with
her not to risk ruin. There were gasps of admiration from the
hall, but best of all the Worriers looked up at last, incredulous,
gutted. Arden resumed her seat, panting with excitment.

'Anyone else want to risk it before I give the next clue?' asked
Mr Cragg, looking directly, defiant and proud, at the Worriers.
They hastily consulted their leader, a bald man with a handlebar
moustache. He gave the nod and one of the others wrote down
the answer and gave it in. They resumed their huddle, anxiety
for once breaking through the confident mien.

Arden was downcast. If the Worriers knew whose father was
the Scourge of the Albigenses her life had been lived in vain.
Then she was pierced with doubt. Supposing there were others
whose fathers had been so described? She listened, tense with
fear, as the second clue was read out. '*He always wore a hair shirt.*'
That fitted. A couple of punters gave in their papers after this, but
the majority waited until the last, decisive clue: '*Killed at the Battle
of Evesham in 1265.*' Arden relaxed. But it was still to be revealed
whether the Worriers had got it right. They could not share a
bottle of Kanoonga Hills. She felt faint at the prospect of a sudden
death play-off. As the count went on Mr Cragg announced that
the mystery man was, of course, Simon de Montfort and Arden
received the congratulations of her table. She tried to join in
their banter but her teeth were chattering.

One of the lady adjudicators took a paper over to Mr Cragg and appeared to ask for guidance. There was much urgent discussion and shaking of heads and the adjudicator returned to her seat with what looked like a suppressed smirk on her face. Finally the results were brought to Mr Cragg. He looked serious, even nervous, as he addressed the impatient crowd.

'I'm afraid it is my somewhat painful duty to say a few words about the result before it is announced.' He loosened his tie. 'Now I know this has only been a game but you have all played it in a spirit of good humour and fair play. Games are very important in life. Through them we develop competitiveness, yes, but also humility and respect for each other. So it's only right and proper that we should stick to the rules, isn't it?'

A wag at the back murmured 'Yes, sir.' Mr Cragg laughed and continued.

'Now you will remember that at the beginning I did point out several times that entries would be disqualified if the name of the team was not on the paper. It makes life very difficult for our volunteers here if they have to go round trying to identify the team. It's a question of consideration for others, which is also very important. So, although there was a tie for the top prize on the result of the last round, I'm sorry to say that one of the answers was not attributed and is therefore disallowed.' Arden felt sick. Had she been in such a hurry that she had forgotten to fill in the team name? 'However I have every faith that the runners-up will accept the decision with good grace and join us all in offering our heartiest congratulations to this year's winners, the Holey Jumpers.'

As the cheers and applause broke out the moustachioed Worrier leaped to his feet. 'That's a fucking fix, you wanker! You saw it was us.'

Mr Cragg blushed and held up his hand as if to ward off a blow. 'Now, please, let's all be reasonable about this. The papers are open to inspection.'

Arden clutched Angela's arm. 'I don't remember filling in the name either.'

'Don't worry, I did.'

'Thank *God*.'

'I'll fucking report you,' said the Worriers' leader, jabbing a finger towards Mr Cragg. 'And this fucking shit hole. Come on, lads.' As the others got up he kicked over his little chair with utter contempt. The others did the same. One of them upturned a little table. They slammed out of the door, cursing.

There was uproar in the hall. Some called for the police to be sent for. Others consoled the more tremulous ladies who were in shock. A group of men came over to the Holey Jumpers to offer protection if necessary. Arden laughed. 'Surely that won't be necessary? They'll get over it when the drink's worn off.'

Angela shrugged. 'Let's hope so. They're obviously not used to losing. I wonder if their mothers hugged them enough?'

Chris was agitated. 'Was it worth it for a bottle of plonk, Arden?'

'*What?* Are you suggesting it's all my fault for not letting them win?'

'I'm just saying . . .'

'How was I to know they'd get violent? We're new round here.'

'Oh. Not used to our Normal For Norwich ways, is that it?'

'Hey, that's enough, Chris. Of course it's not Arden's fault.'

'If you go into hiding for six months it'll all blow over,' said Simon pleasantly.

'Well, we *are* moving, if you must know.' As she spoke Arden knew she was reacting as a mad monarch quick to punish and that she would be the one to suffer, but her sense of injustice had a life of its own. 'We've had quite enough of this bovine culture, thank you very much.'

Tim groaned. Angela, Simon and Tina looked shocked, then pitying and embarrassed. Chris was relieved of guilt for upping the ante. 'Nice of you to give it a try. We normally just get anthropologists.'

Seeing Angela's mortified expression, Arden, as usual, felt instant repentance, but was not going to admit it in front of Chris. 'Well, until you opened your mouth we were having a very nice time. Thanks for asking us, Angela.'

'That's all right. Thanks for coming.'

They tidied the tables and prepared to leave in silence. By the time they were in the car park Arden was tormented not only by remorse, but the thought of all the *Suitables* opportunities she had blown by offending Angela. 'Wait here a minute, Tim. I won't be long.' She fought her way upstream of departing parents to the hall, receiving their support and congratulations. Simon and Chris were among the few still helping Mr Cragg to clear up. Angela and Tina were probably in the staff toilet. She met them coming out.

'Look, I feel bad, Angela. I didn't mean it, you know. I'm sorry. I'm always blowing a gasket and having to clear up my own mess.'

Angela, who had been surprised at how hurt she'd felt by Arden's insult, was happy to have the barb removed. 'Don't worry. I'm getting used to you.'

'Oh, dear. That makes me sound like traffic noise.'

'That's not a bad comparison.'

'At least it's a necessary evil. Anyway, I didn't want you to think I was secretly despising you all. I love it here, really.'

'Then why are you moving?'

'That was just pique talking. I'm not sure we are now, because of Mum. But we've told Harry Jermigan he can have the cottage. We're in a bit of a corner about it. Tim thinks it's sensible to sell up and go back. So do I, but I don't want to.'

'I don't envy you if you have to tell Mr Jermigan you're withdrawing from the sale.'

'Oh, I'm not scared of him. He couldn't do anything illegal. It would be so obvious who it was, wouldn't it?'

'Yes. But unfortunately the law only puts off people like you and me, not the Harry Jermigans of this world.'

'He isn't so bad.'

Angela and she parted on terms of incipient intimacy. Arden was gratified. There was nothing like self-flagellation for bringing out the best in onlookers.

An autumn squall had ripped through the gilded landscape while they were inside, drawing night and dustbin lids in its wake. The wind was beating itself into an epic tempest. Bullets of rain began to fall as they drew away from the school. Before long they appeared to have driven into a car wash, so heavily did slews of water deluge the windscreen, drowning the frantic gyrations of the wipers. Tim caught only glimpses of the narrow roads, flanked with low hedges if they were lucky, more often dissolving into infinite, featureless darkness. They had headed off confidently the way they had come. In the dark the roads looked different, all the same – when they could see them. They came to a crossroads offering them a choice of St James or St Lawrence. Arden was sure they had come through St James so they turned left. After a tense ten minutes churning through small lakes the headlights revealed a settlement rising up from the plain like Carcassone. 'Where the hell is this?' said Arden.

'How should I know? I'm driving, you've got to navigate.'

'Where's the map then?'

'Oh. Damn. I took it out to check the location of a weathervane. Sorry.'

'Great. Well, it seems we can go to Harleston or Halesworth. Try Halesworth. If we keep going left from there we'll end up – more or less where we started.'

They followed the road to Halesworth, then saw a sign to Beccles and thought that would be quicker, but came to another crossroads that went right to St Lawrence and left to St Michael.

'You must have missed the turning, Tim. This is ridiculous. Do pay attention.'

'It's all right for you. There's a bastard behind us with his beams on, not that I can see a thing anyway.'

'That's funny. There was someone behind us when we set out. Is it the same one?'

'What a stupid question. All headlights look the same. Do you want to drive?'

'Not likely.'

'Well, shut up then. Now make your mind up. Left or right?'

'You decide, if you're going to be so nasty.'

'For fuck's sake—'

He turned left, as St Lawrence at least had the advantage of familiarity. The headlights followed them. Arden kept an eye on them in the wing mirror. Despite her defiant words at the time, she now admitted the possibility that it might be the Sheep Worriers, bent on vengeance. Lost, in the dark, on a lonely road in the howling rain, the minute chance that it might be them was multiplied by the potentially gruesome outcome if it were. She wished she were not such an addict of Crime Watch. Its reconstructions habitually showed victims setting off from some innocent entertainment before running into senseless killers. Of course, the idea was preposterous. Arden personally had done nothing to offend the Worriers. They should be pursuing Mr Cragg. But it was curious how night paralysed one's logical faculties.

'Quick, turn left here, Tim. Let's get rid of them.'

'But it says St Margaret.'

'Quick – just do it.' She grabbed the wheel to help him make up his mind. They careered round the corner and thumped to a halt as the front wheel skewed into a ditch.

'Now look what you've done, you stupid woman!'

'Don't talk to me like that, it's not my fault it's raining.'

'I'm not saying it's your fault it's *raining*, I'm saying it's your fault we turned off the fucking road.'

'Well, why did you do it, then? You're at the wheel, you're ultimately responsible.'

'Fuck. *Fuck!* I could strangle you, Ard.'

'That's gratitude. We've got rid of that car that was following us anyway. I might have saved your life.'

'Don't be so fucking ridiculous. Of course it wasn't following us. How are we going to get home?'

'Call the AA, of course. Didn't you bring your mobile?'

'The batteries are flat. I seem to remember asking you to get some last week.'

'Why should I have to do all the shopping?'

'You *don't*. But if you're not *going to* you should give me some advance warning so that we don't end up in a fucking ditch in the sodding countryside. Why are we here, Ard? Why? Just tell me.'

'Oh, *God*. Are you going to sit there crying in the wilderness or are we going to try and shift this bloody car?'

'*Fuck.*'

Arden got out and went to assess the problem. She made a token attempt to push the car back on the road. Tim joined her, cursing as they slithered about on the bank.

'It's no good. We'll have to walk. Brilliant.'

'There's bound to be somewhere we can phone from. It's only half-past eleven.'

'People go to bed early in the country.'

'Tim, don't be so *facile*. You know perfectly well most people round here don't have to get up at dawn to do the milking. There's bound to be some crack merchants still up. There are loads of redundant farmhouses in this area.'

'Crack merchants? Perhaps you can book them up for a *Suitables* presentation.'

'Very funny. Look, could we save the recriminations till we get home? We can have a full jury trial if you like, but it won't help now, will it?'

'This is a fine time for you to get rational. Pity it didn't hit you earlier this evening.'

'All *right*.'

Arden began to walk. It was hard not to defend herself with her customary vigour but she was actually worried about Tim's stress levels. He was showing all the signs of one of his monthlies, but she was sure it had only been two weeks since his last one. Technically, of course, it was her fault that they were now trudging carless and freezing, their faces flayed by the wind, shoes saturated, and the whole occasionally drenched in a tidal wave from a passing vehicle. But that was life, wasn't it? One just had to get on with things. She could see that Tim was building up to use the incident as some sort of jumbo last straw in their lifestyle experiment. She rehearsed in her head the counter argument about not giving up at the first obstacle and accepting that success would be meaningless without tribulation, and realized that she would sound exactly like their father. She stopped and waited for Tim, and took his arm.

After a mile or so a bulk of greater darkness loomed out of the night. It was a pair of large semi-detached brick cottages. A white plastic urn rolled about on the rough grass outside. The houses were both in darkness. Several old cars were parked on a rutted gravel area to one side. 'Dare we knock?' said Arden. 'The curtains aren't drawn on this side. Let's have a look.'

Tim took shelter under a tree while she peered in at the windows. The rain had become more fitful and the scudding clouds allowed faint glimmers of moonlight to penetrate the darkness. The front room was predictably decorated, although Arden could never understand the fashion for grey and maroon suedette furnishings in the home. Car showrooms, perhaps. It looked too tidy to have been recently occupied.

She went round the side of the house, groping her way as the clouds moved across the moon. Her hand found the edge of a window frame and as further shafts of cold light emerged through the cloud they fell upon a room in which every flat surface was covered with dolls' heads: bald, grinning and beady-eyed. Arden gasped. This was late-night movie land. She half expected to be hit over the head with a shovel.

'Tim! Come and look.' He came furtively across the grass to join her. 'This is weird. Why are dolls so sinister?'

'They'd look more friendly with bodies. God, I'm cold. I think there may be somebody in next door. There's a faint glow in the front room. I'll show you.'

They crept up to the front window of the other cottage. Heavy wooden shutters were closed on the inside but one of the slats was broken and Tim was tall enough to see through the gap. 'Eh?' he whispered. 'I don't get this.'

'What is it?'

'There are two pairs of feet up-ended on the wall. I think they may be a sculpture.'

'Let me look.' He lifted her up. 'Don't be daft. Oh, my God!'

'What?'

'They don't hold with underwear.' Tim let her down and they moved away from the window. 'They must be meditating. What on earth shall we do? We can't knock. They might get a shock and fall over.'

'Well, we can't loiter. I'm freezing. Either we knock or we go on.'

'Perhaps they don't hold with telephones, either.'

'There are wires going to the house. Come on. At least we'll get out of this sodding weather for a minute.'

The doorstep was cluttered with potted herbs in improvised containers of which chipped chamber pots were the most numerous. There was a message in oriental characters painted over the door. It might mean 'Tradesmen Please Use Rear Entrance', but Arden had hopes it was more auspicious.

There was a long wait before a light went on in the hall and the door was opened by a thirty-something young man doing up his jeans. He was naked to the waist, had a well-trimmed beard and an unblinking stare that disguised any alarm he might have felt at opening the door to strangers late at night. He waited for them to explain themselves.

'Sorry to disturb you,' said Arden, 'but our car's gone into a ditch and we were wondering if you could possibly let us use the phone?'

'I hope we didn't get you up?' said Tim, thinking this rather cleverly put the man off the scent that they had been spying.

'No. Down, as it happens. We were just meditating before we went to bed. Come in.'

'Thank you.' They fell gratefully into the hall and while the man went to speak to his partner Arden assessed the interior decorations. The walls were streaked with ochre limewash and hung with unframed pictures of purplish-brown splodges, the floorboards were bare, and someone had distressed the paintwork with a blow torch. An outsize coffee plant took up half the space in the hall and was working its way upstairs. There was besides a strong smell of marijuana and cats.

'Artists,' Arden warned Tim in a whisper. She was uncomfortable around artists, always expecting to be derided for her pension plan and polished shoes, which raised the concomitant question of whether she should deride herself for them.

The man called them into the living room. The glow they had observed from outside came from a wood-burning stove and they both rushed towards it with outstretched hands. The man's partner sat cross-legged on a sofa covered with a knitted blanket and laughed in a friendly way as she tossed her greying tresses away from a strongly chiselled face. A tube dress and chunky sweater hid whatever she was not wearing underneath. Arden thought how wonderful she would look in *Suitables'* season's trouser suit with the Beau Brummel jacket, and then of the futility of even mentioning it. That was another annoying thing about artists: they looked good in jumble.

The couple introduced themselves as Laurence and Shara. Laurence showed Tim the phone and Shara pushed three cats off the sofa so that Arden could sit beside her. Arden explained that they had lost their way in the Saints. Shara sympathized and brought them some wine. 'The Saints must have been a happy hunting ground for muggers in the old days,' she said.

'Actually, I think people would have had more sense of

direction when they went everywhere on foot,' Arden reflected. They'd have been able to read the landscape better, like which side lichen grows on a tree. That tells you where north is.'

'That's interesting. You mean, lichen always grows on the north side?'

'I can't remember. But if I could, it would be very useful, wouldn't it?'

'Perhaps Laurence knows. He's a palaeontologist.'

'*Is* he? Good Lord. Sorry, I don't mean to be *occupationist* but I could have sworn you were both artists.'

'We are, sort of. He gave it up. We've got our own business now, making thatched dovecotes. You don't need one, do you?'

'*Well* – I don't personally. But I know someone who might need several in the near future. Do you know Harry Jermigan?'

'Huh! I should say so. Who doesn't?' Shara reacted as though a bucket of water had been emptied over her, actually shuddering as if to shake off the drops. 'How do you know him?'

'We're his neighbours at Sloping Castle.'

'Jesus!' said Laurence.

Arden was starting to feel relatively uninhibited, encouraged by the warmth, the relief, the wine – on a stomach long since vacated by broccoli quiche and cheese footballs – and the company of free thinkers. She addressed Laurence directly. 'Now look, don't take this personally, but I am totally pissed off with this nod-wink reaction whenever I mention Harry Jermigan. People either giggle or turn pale and change the subject. He's a difficult customer, all right, and I know he's been to prison and all that, but it's as if there's some dark secret about him that nobody's telling us and it's really pissing me off.'

Tim looked up from his conversation with the fourth emergency service and gave Arden the signal for, *Why are you swearing and behaving like a prat?* She ignored him and fixed Laurence with an expectant stare.

'There's no mystery. He's a thug and a swine and an extortionist, that's all.' Laurence drained his glass, his grim expression leaving no room for any misinterpretation of his remarks.

Shara put a hand on Arden's arm. 'It's a sore point with Laurence. Jermigan once offered us a forty per cent discount on shipping the dovecotes to Germany if I'd sleep with him. He was quite open about it.'

'Forty per cent!' Laurence was reliving the trauma. 'The fucker wouldn't even go the whole hog and offer to do it for nothing.'

'Would that have made it all right?' said Arden.

'No, of course not. It's just typical of his peculiar blend of meanness and carnality.'

'They'll be here in forty minutes,' said Tim.

'Carnality isn't necessarily linked with largesse,' said Arden.

'Never said it was. But it might have put a gloss of sincerity on the transaction. We used to be quite thick with Jermigan and his cronies at one time. Got the false impression he'd look out for our interests. Couldn't quite square that with him fucking my woman.'

'No, indeed. He won't be buying your dovecotes, then.'

'I'd rather go out of business.'

'Which,' sighed Shara, 'is quite likely anyway. Someone like Jermigan could easily arrange that. By the way, Tim, stay by the phone. They always get lost and have to be talked in on their mobiles.'

'How do you mean, put you out of business?'

'Well – he could start a rival outfit. Undercut us for as long as it takes to get the bank baying for our assets. He's got the transport, hasn't he?'

'But surely he wouldn't? Why would he bother? He's got enough business interests already. Especially with this theme park he's got planned.'

'That's the point. He wouldn't bother just for the hell of it. But Laurence and I are involved with the protest against that shitty scheme. In fact, Laurence chairs the committee. If he wanted to get rid of us that would be one way of doing it.'

'Direct action's more his style,' said Laurence. 'He'd probably just burn the house down. *Pour encourager les autres*.'

'If we owned it he probably would. I'm relying on the fact that we're only tenants.'

'And I suppose your landlord is a friend of Jermigan's?'

'Probably. He's got his finger in more pies than Sweeney Todd.'

The conversation led by Tim moved on to route-finding gadgets and the possible effects of the European single currency on the devecote business. Laurence never quite recovered his steely composure after his outburst and Shara, attuned to his discomfort, was obviously distracted. Tim and Arden began to feel adrift in their conversational dinghy and strained intently for the sound of the AA man. Tim had already taken detailed directions so that they would not get lost again. They were no more than two miles from Sloping. Laurence went with him to the car and Shara and Arden relaxed into Home Front topics. Arden even found the courage to tell Shara about *Suitables*, with appropriately self-mocking delivery, and felt rather foolish when she expressed genuine admiration for her enterprise. They promised to keep in touch.

Tim was unexpectedly good-humoured as they finally set off for home using Laurence's masterful sketchmap of the district. From many points of view the evening could be described as a disaster, Arden admitted, but the joy of having the car back threw the disastrous bits into perspective.

'Nice couple,' said Tim. 'Why don't we have them to dinner? We should thank them somehow.'

'Good idea. But I wonder how they'd feel about walking into Jermigan's den? Do you think it's true about – you know – his offering them a discount to sleep with her?'

'Must be. They could hardly have misunderstood an offer like that.'

'But the nerve of the man! Still, that's him, I suppose. He'll come to a sticky end if he goes around upsetting people like Laurence.'

'He's cunning enough only to upset the law-abiding.'

'We still haven't decided what to do about Mum, Tim. Jermigan's solicitor wants to exchange contracts by the end of the month.'

'Ard, I really don't know what to do. Perhaps we should get on to the council and find out how far the planning application for this scheme of his has got? If there's an organized protest it might never happen.'

'And if it doesn't, does that mean you would think about staying?'

'I'm not making any promises, Ard. All I'm saying is that the idea of upping sticks again seems almost as much of a pain as staying on.'

Arden repressed a smile. Sloping was back on probation. She might not, often all, have to leave her medievel element.

The sight of the moon floating above the gatehouse was all she needed to calm her after the excitement of the evening. It was a quarter to two. She opened the gate as quietly as possible. Jermigan was deaf to HGVs rumbling on and off site in the wee hours but he complained that Miss Tree was sensitive to other types of disturbance after midnight. Arden had noticed that the workers in his cottages kept a strict curfew. The drive was awash with puddles. Jermigan would no doubt have someone out in the morning to fill in the holes. That was one thing they did not have to worry about. Another was security. It would be a bold burglar who ventured into Jermigan's domain. There was a lot to be said for the peace of mind that came from Mafia-style protection.

When she saw the heap of holdalls and loudspeakers on the doorstep Arden did wonder for a moment if her confidence had been misplaced. Someone had been there in their absence. She jumped out of the car and went to examine them. They were Bos's. Arden was appalled. He must have been thrown out of university. But why come to her? Perhaps his father had refused to have him back, although that would be out of character.

The note pushed through the letterbox was not, on the face of it, that of a desperate individual.

Hi, Mum. It's me. Could you please take my stuff in and put a hot water bottle in the spare bed? I'll be at the Hall till you get back. Don't forget! Bos.

7

It was out of the question to rouse the Hall at that hour in the morning. Arden spent a restless night, torn between fruitless speculation about Bos's fate and his awfulness in putting Jermigan to the inconvenience of accommodating him.

Jermigan's lads took it in turn to drive Miss Tree to church on Sunday mornings or if necessary he took her himself. Arden reckoned that if she went over at eleven there was a fair chance he would be out. There was no response to her knock at the front door, only the distant barking of the dogs in their kennel. Perhaps Bos was up but did not think it was his business to open the door to strangers. She went round to the back and peered in at the kitchen.

It was difficult to see through the greenish mullions, but it looked empty. The glow of smouldering logs in the inglenook created an ambience of primitive comfort. Forget the loaf of bread beneath the bough – a bowl of Fruit Bran and a cappuccino before such an ancestral hearth were Paradise enow. Arden knocked on the back door and, when no one came, gingerly opened it and went in.

There were breakfast dishes on a wooden rack by the sink. Miss Tree's and Jermigan's presumably. What did they talk about in such intimate moments? She went through to the Great Room. Bos's jacket was over the arm of the sofa. Upstairs a toilet flushed.

'Bos?' she called in a stage whisper, immediately realising the futility of trying to make herself heard over flushing water. If she nipped up and found him they could leave before Jermigan got back, and return later with formal thanks and a pot of marmalade for Miss Tree. Curiosity to see the upper floors would be satisfied at the same time. Quietly calling his name, she crept up the stairs.

From the top of the staircase a corridor of delicious crooked-ness led to right and left, propped up with crooked beams like an old mine shaft. Sunlight streamed through a stained glass medallion of the Slupynge coat of arms in a window at the far end, casting pools of blue and red on to the rush matting. The scene was such a paradigm of security, comfort and medieval building techniques that Arden had a sharp struggle to quell her pangs of envy.

Most of the small doors were closed. Arden stood outside the nearest one and listened for clues. She called his name again, softly. If she happened to wake Lottie it was no matter. It was unhealthy for young people to lie in bed until lunchtime.

By the time she had whispered Bos's name at all the closed doors she was beginning to feel uncomfortably like Goldilocks and decided it might be best to retreat. Just then a hand tapped her on the shoulder. Arden jumped and swung round to find Lottie, wearing knickers and a T-shirt and holding her imperious white cat, whose expression was indicative of a rough night. Arden's eyes travelled down the long skinny columns of Lottie's legs to the narrow feet – Celtic feet, as research had revealed, rather than the broad pads of the Teutonic invader. Lottie's big toes reminded her of Tim's. They protruded clear of the rest by a good half inch. Fortunately he had never wanted to be a ballerina and Arden was fairly confident that Lottie had not either.

'What the fuck are you creeping about here for?'

'Really, Lottie, there's no need to be rude. Does Mr Jermigan know you use such language?'

'I don't think it's any of your business.'

'Possibly not. I came to fetch Bos. There was no one about downstairs and I didn't want to wake anyone up. He left me a note. I was worried about him.'

'Why didn't you phone?'

'I've told you, I didn't want to wake anyone up.'

'Well, you woke me up.'

'Sorry. It is gone eleven. Oh, Bos, there you are.' A door at the far end of the corridor had opened and he stood peering out at them sleepily. He wore only his Calvin Klein underpants. Arden instinctively tried to obscure Lottie's view. 'I'm sorry I couldn't come over last night. We got home too late. Are you all right?'

'Yeah.' He sized up Lottie's legs approvingly and grinned at her. 'Hello, Lot.'

'Don't call me that.'

'Ah. You're not a morning person either, then?'

'She doesn't have to be, Bos. Hurry up and get dressed, darling. I'll go and start the breakfast.'

Lottie followed Arden down and let her out of the front door as Jermigan's Frontera turned into the drive. Arden cursed inwardly but smiled at Lottie. 'Don't say anything or the cat gets it.' Lottie appeared unaccustomed to waggish threats but, from the way she turned away as soon as she saw Jermigan, Arden guessed that she was not in the habit of volunteering information to him.

Jermigan was in a good mood and invited Arden back in for a drink. While declining, she could not help rueing the fact that his amiability would only last until they withdrew from the sale. It was much more agreeable to be under the wing of a vulture than in its sights. She thanked him effusively for putting Bos up for the night, and explained the drama that had delayed them. She thought it as well to inform him that they had made friendly contact with the enemy, but when Laurence and Shara were mentioned, Jermigan did not react.

'I know they're involved with this pressure group that's trying to stop your expansion plans, but I hope you won't shoot them if they come to dinner?'

'Wouldn't waste the bullet, would I? They can protest till the cows come 'ome, won't do them no good.'

'How can you be so sure?'

'When was the last time one of them groups got their way?'

'Er – I don't know. There must be a by-pass somewhere that's been shelved.'

'That's politics, ain't it? Saving public money. Private money – they don't give a toss, do they?'

'But even if you do get permission, the protestors could still make things very difficult – occupying trees and all that.'

He laughed. 'What is it in the Bible, like? "If thy eye offend thee, cut 'im out". Why you bothered, any how? Won't be your problem, will it?'

'No, of course not.' But of course it would, if they stood in his way. The scale of Jermigan's confidence was terrifying. Arden was tempted to tell him right away that they might not, after all, be clearing his path, just to get it over with. On the other hand, she had promised to cook Bos some breakfast and the urge to get on with it was suddenly overwhelming. She excused herself and, at the mention of Bos, Jermigan said he was a good lad and he had offered him work on the mead hall.

'That's very kind of you, but I'm sure Bos will be going back to college. I don't know yet why he's here, but I can't imagine it's permanent.'

'Why not? What good's a wanking degree in Women's Studies going to do 'im?'

Arden bristled. Bos had surpassed all expectations by getting into university. 'It requires the same amount of effort as any other degree. Anyway, the future is female, hadn't you heard?'

At this Jermigan roared with laughter. It gave her a glimpse of his piratical gold fillings. 'Dream on, my lovely.' He was still laughing as he let himself into the Hall.

Tim had the Sunday papers spread out on the kitchen table. He was in his pyjamas and dressing gown. Seeing him like that, Arden was suddenly thunderstruck at the thought the logistical problems that would arise with Bos living in the house. Whenever he had stayed with them in Chiswick she had moved into a spare room but in the cottage the third bedroom was Tim's study. 'What on earth shall we do?' she wailed.

'About what?'

'You know – the sleeping arrangements?'

Tim wriggled and shook the paper. He hated putting their situation into words. 'There's nothing *to* do. We've got twin beds. He won't think anything of it.'

'You think we should just bluff it out? A smokescreen of honesty? I think it would be kinder to give him some sort of explanation, so that he can maintain his illusions if he wants.'

'Tell him it's to save on the heating.'

'Then he'd feel guilty if he turned on his radiator. Oh, *God.* What did I *tell* you about children making life *complicated!*'

'Well, you take the spare room, then. Bos and I can share. He's not going to be here long, is he?'

'I don't know. Even so, the problem will recur, won't it? Oh, *God.* Perhaps we should tell him the truth? He's old enough.'

'*No.* It's not right to – muck up his mind with such matters.'

'Then I'll have to pretend I normally sleep in the spare room. Oh, *God.* I'll have to go and put my things in there before he comes. He'll be here any minute.' She screeched with frustration as she ran up the stairs, and then stopped suddenly. 'Put some bacon on, would you? I promised I'd have his breakfast ready.'

Tim humphed. 'You never cook me bacon.'

'For God's *sake.* You don't *want* it normally. Are you going to or not?'

He folded the paper with martyred resignation. 'So long as I'm not expected to make a habit of it.'

'Did I *say* that? What do you want – an OBE? Don't bother if it's too much trouble.'

'There's no need to be sarcastic. I said I'll do it.'

'*Urrrrrgh!*' Arden ran up the stairs three at a time.

Bos sauntered over almost an hour later, by which time the bacon was ruined but Arden had had a chance to transfer her clothes and knick-knacks to the spare room and spray it with Opium. She kissed his cheek. 'What kept you?'

'Jermigan. We was just chatting. He offered me work.'

'So he said. I told him you wouldn't be interested.'

'Why? I need the money, Mum.'

'But, darling . . . Look, sit down. I'll do you some scrambled eggs and you must tell me the truth. Is anything the matter at college?'

Bos did not sit down but wandered about the room, looking out of the window and feigning interest in the *objets.* 'Nothing new. It's just that geezer on my back again. It looked like a good idea to lie low for a bit. They'd never find me here, would they?'

'Are you saying you've been threatened?'

'Yeah. 'Spose I have.'

'Oh, Bos. Why don't you go to the police? All right, you

might owe him money, but that's not a crime. Threatening people is.'

'You don't understand, Mum. It wouldn't make any difference. If I went to the police he'd well do 'is nut. These wankers are outside the law.'

'Don't be ridiculous. No one is.' Arden spoke with less conviction than she would have done before she met Harry Jermigan. 'If it's serious enough that you have to go into hiding, you must tell the police, for, God's sake'

'*No*, Mum. I can't. Please shut up about it.' Bos's normally open, artless face was heavy with anxiety. 'Can I just stay here for a bit? If I earn enough money I can go back next year.'

'Next *year*? But what about your studies?'

'It'll delay things a bit but that won't matter. I didn't have a gap year because of the re-sits.'

'But, darling—'

'Don't you want me here?'

'Of *course* I do, Bos. It will be *wonderful*. But – won't you get bored? How about a job on a cruise liner?'

'Eh? If you don't want me around, Mum, just say so.'

Arden was confused. It always required a major adjustment to tune into Bos at first. And having a different Bos, a worried and unhappy one, to atune to would tax the skills of an experienced psychiatrist. 'Honestly, I'm only thinking of your best interests, darling. If you're going to take time off to earn money it should be to pay off your student loan, not the mob. I'll speak to Uncle Tim. He might think of some way we can come up with the money. Then you could go back and you won't have missed much.'

'I don't want your money, Mum. I've been thinking – I want to earn it. If you don't mind me staying, it's the best way to do it.'

'We'll see. Do you want ketchup on this?'

'Thanks, but I don't feel hungry now.'

Arden helped him carry his bags up to the spare room. She quickly turned on the radiator while his back was turned. 'I'll be sharing with Uncle Tim while you're here, Bos. We're a bit short of space in this house.'

'Won't he mind?'

'No, no. It'll be fun. Like when we were children. Honestly, don't worry about it.'

Bos chuckled. 'I hope he's had the operation.'

'*Bos!* Don't be so coarse.'

'Sorry. He's past it anyhow, I 'spose.'

'We both are.'

'*Ah*. Poor old Mum.' He hugged her. Arden was relieved to see his good humour restored, but a chestnut from 'O' level poetry came back to haunt her: '*Oh, what a tangled web we weave, When first we practise to deceive'*.

Bos went with them to see Mattie in the afternoon. She had not seen him for fifteen years so it was not surprising that she hotly denied he was her grandson. She decided he was her brother Arthur and they settled for that. Bos was somewhat in awe of this living relic, but in his own kindly way improvised reminiscences to please her.

The virtuous glow of helping the aged suited Bos. Tim and Arden were impressed and gratified by his response to their mum and suggested taking him out for a drink, which seemed a logical next step in the bonding process. They stopped at a pub with a promisingly decrepit exterior, and were rewarded by a soot-blackened parlour full of fishermen and their dogs, and decorated with sepia photographs of down-trodden farm workers and bits of old ploughs.

While Tim got the drinks Arden explained to Bos that she had not had a chance to ask his uncle about the money.

'I told you, Mum. Forget it. I'll earn it myself.'

'How much is Jermigan paying you?'

'Three pounds an hour.'

'Less tax and your stamp. Mind you, I wouldn't be surprised if he suggested keeping it strictly illegal.'

'Loosen up, Mum. It happens all the time.'

'You'll need spending money. And I don't want to be mean, Bos, but your staying with us will put up our household expenses a bit.'

'I know, Mum. I'll pay my way. How about twenty quid a week?'

'Fine. It's just that Uncle Tim and I are getting our businesses off the ground still, you know. We have to be careful.'

'It's okay. Did you find out about Gran's fees?'

'Yes, it's all right. The social services have asked for a copy of the will, and if they're satisfied it's genuine they'll go on paying.'

'Brilliant. It's good I can get to know her before she pops her clogs. Roots are important, aren't they, Mum? Especially for dysfunctional families like ours.'

'What *do* you mean? We're not dysfunctional.'

'All right – disassembled. Will you end up like Gran, do you think?'

'In what way?'

'You know – ga-ga.'

'*Honestly*, Bos, what a horrible idea. I don't know. I never thought about it. Thanks.'

'No, I'm not being nasty. I just meant, not to worry about it. I'll look after you. I can practise on Gran.'

'Oh, Bos. That's so sweet.' She squeezed his hand. After all, there was a lot to be said for reclaiming one's children when they were mature, caring adults. His failed business venture was a trivial fault when weighed in the balance with his good nature.

Tim joined them. He could not help noticing that even the dogs cast admiring glances towards Bos, and rather enjoyed the idea that people would assume he was the young man's father. Arden was worried that he had only brought mineral water for himself, but he assured her it was only because he was driving and that he felt perfectly all right. She told him that Bos was to start work on the mead hall in the morning.

'I see. Well done, Bos. Make sure you wear a hard hat. I trust this operation is properly supervised?'

'Yeah, 'course. Jermigan's got a team of builders coming in. He says he wants it finished by Christmas.'

'I bet he hasn't got planning permission,' said Arden. 'Perhaps the council will make him pull it down?'

'I don't think councils have got any spare cash to pursue cases like that.'

'We could bring a private action – I don't think!'

'Too right, Ard. And if this new law comes in about no legal aid for civil cases it'll be Christmas every day for people like Jermigan.'

'Terrific. You know, I've just had a ghastly thought. If we tell him we're withdrawing from the sale, he may decide he doesn't want Bos working for him.'

'Shit!' Bos looked crestfallen. 'But I've got nothing to do with it.'

'He may not. He's an odd man. Lawless, but strangely fair-minded in his own way. But we've got to tell him, Tim. Thank God Dad left the cottage to us. If it had gone to Mum, Jermigan would have found it much easier to get it off her.'

'He'd have had to take on social services. They'd have claimed it for her fees.'

'Huh! I'm sure Jermigan knows where the head of social services lives.'

Tim shifted uncomfortably. 'Actually, Ard, there's something I have to tell you about the cottage.'

'What?

'I had a phone call from the solicitor on Friday. I didn't want to mention it until I'd given the matter some thought. You know he's the executor? Has to draw up a list of Dad's assets for probate?'

'Yes, yes. Spit it out, Tim.'

'In short, there's a mortgage on the property. Not huge – about thirty thousand. Dad must have raised it about ten years ago. Naturally, at his age, the repayments were quite substantial and there's still a lot owing. So . . .'

'They're claiming it on the estate.'

'Precisely.'

Arden felt sick. This was a complication too far. And just when the gift of the cottage had begun to make her feel more well disposed towards her father than she had ever done when he was alive, it was revealed as a poisoned chalice. 'Well, isn't that typical? He leaves us the debts and all the money to his doxy.'

'Now hold on, Ard. It isn't as simple as that. For one thing, he probably expected to live a lot longer. We mustn't assume he intended to leave us in the soup. And there's the question of who has the responsibility for the debt. It could be taken out of the estate as a whole. At any rate, it looks as if we'll have to negotiate with this – this Thalia person.'

'I'd be delighted.'

'Oh, Ard . . . You'd better leave it to me. One thing's clear. Well, two things. We have to stay in this area to be near Mum. I wouldn't want the responsibility of moving her in her condition.'

'Hear! hear!' said Bos.

'But we either have to sell the cottage or the house in Chiswick.'

'We can't do that until the tenants leave.'

'That's right. We either sell the cottage to Jermigan – no one else would buy it with that planning application outstanding – or cash in our savings schemes to pay off the mortgage. We don't know how much it is yet, of course. That rather depends on this Thalia person.'

'Even if we did sell to Jermigan, if there's a mortgage outstanding it wouldn't leave us enough to put down on another house until we can sell the one in Chiswick. We couldn't borrow much on our present earnings.'

'No. Particularly not as we already have a mortgage.'

'*Shit*! What did Humph want with that money anyway? I thought Jermigan *gave* him the cottage. Why do things have to be so *complicated*?'

Tim looked at her with an air of condescending sympathy. 'I won't say it, Ard.'

'No, please don't.'

'Is this bad?' said Bos.

'It's only money, darling,' groaned Arden. Bang went any idea of paying off his debts. At least for the time being. 'We can't sell either place until the estate's settled, can we? But if we sell the Chiswick house, will there be enough equity to pay off this mortgage?'

'With the way the property market's going in London, yes – probably.'

'Then that's what we'll do. Tell Jermigan the sale's off and dig in here until we can sell the other house.'

'I'll make an appointment to see him in the morning.'

'We'll do it together.'

'No, Ard. You seem to rub him up the wrong way. If I see him on my own, man to man as it were, there'll be no histrionics.'

'You'd better have the last rites.'

*　　*　　*

Despite his reassuring words to Arden, Tim felt like a suicide bomber as he set off for his appointment with Jermigan the following Tuesday morning. A vision of his old office appeared before him: the team and its spirit, the regular hours and pay cheques, the becoming cloak of greatness that House of Waffles UK cast over its employees, the stimulating arguments about legitimate expenses. He did not blame Arden for initiating this madcap self-employment scheme. He should have put up more resistance. She might dominate their lives on everyday matters but he was confident of his influence over momentous decisions, and with luck they would scrape by. It would not be a disaster. But for someone with an avowed abhorrence of complications, Arden had an uncanny knack of attracting them.

Jermigan received Tim in his study. The flickering light from a log fire twinkled on the decanter and whisky glasses that were laid ready on a side table. Tim was shaken firmly by the hand and slapped on the back and settled opposite his host on one of the reproduction bishops' thrones to either side of the fireplace. He was quite uncomfortable enough without having a carved griffin stuck in his shoulder blade.

'Thank you for seeing me at short notice, Mr Jermigan. I know you're very busy.'

'Harry. Call me Harry, Tim.'

'Oh, very well – Harry.' This was getting worse. Jermigan sat at lordly ease, regarding his visitor with amused curiosity. Tim wondered whether he had a concealed alarm, like the Queen, to summon aid with a threatening or terminally boring subject. 'Look, Harry, I don't want to waste your time,' he began. 'The fact is, our financial affairs are in transition at the moment. There are problems regarding the distribution of my father's estate. It means we can't sell the cottage until it's sorted out. And even then – well, it will be difficult to persuade Arden to move out. She's developed some sort of sentimental attachment to the place. I don't share it actually but, you know, she's been through some hard times and I don't like to—'

'Shut it.'

'Right.'

Jermigan's face had closed down like a wicket. He got up and paced the room, spilling his whisky. Tim kept very still, afraid that any movement would trigger an outburst. After staring furiously out of the window for a few moments, Jermigan said, 'How much?'

'Sorry?'

'Don't fuck me about, lad. How much does you need to settle these – distribution problems? That's what you're on about, isn' it? You want more money.'

'No. No, truly, that never entered my head. Your offer was a very generous one.'

'Considering I gave the place to the bugger in the first place, I should say it was!'

'Did you really? I thought that might be some kind of euphemism for a good deal. That is, a different way of putting it—'

'I know what a sodding euphemism is, lad. Now what numbers we talking here – five thousand? Ten?'

'Rather more than that. There's a mortgage on the property. More like thirty thousand. We won't know the exact sum until we've discussed it with the other beneficiaries.'

'What did the stupid sod want to raise a mortgage for?'

'We thought you might be able to tell us, Mr Jermigan. And please don't refer to my father in those terms.'

'Hey,' He reared back in mock affront, like a Rottweiler threatened by kitten's paw, and chuckled. 'You don't want I should speak ill o' the dead, is that it?'

'He was my father.'

'Of course. Very right an' proper. You're your father's son in that, all right.'

'Thank you,' said Tim, although he was not sure it was meant as a compliment. Jermigan looked too amused. He resumed his seat.

'First off, there's no way you're gettin' another thirty thousand out o' me.'

'I never said—'

'Shut it, lad. Second, your sister can shove her sentimentality up her arse. I want that place and I mean to get it. Your *half*-sister, I should say. And that's a warning.'

'It sounds more like a threat to me.'

'As you like. I won't fuck around with you neither. Every day this application's delayed costs me money. Now you go 'ome and tell your *half*-sister what I said, and you talk 'er round. And don't think I don't know what you two is to each other. Pathetic, I call it, but there you go.'

Tim flushed. He was hyperventilating. 'How do you know? You can't possibly—'

'I can smell it, lad. Now, you wouldn't want a rumour like that to get about, would you?'

Tim was numb with horror. He had been prepared for Jermigan's fury and had rehearsed a dignified response. But matter-of-fact threats, issued without even the courtesy of a headless rabbit on the doorstep as an opening gambit, were beyond his powers to cope with. And the idea that Jermigan could deliberately make Tim's relationship with his sister a matter of public knowledge was a blow so low, so far beyond any norm of acceptable behaviour, that he began to wonder if Arden had put LSD in his porridge.

Jermigan helped him out of the bishop's throne and led him to the door. 'You're a poor thing, ain't you, lad? Should have been a monk, I reckon. It's not too late, you know.'

'A monk?'

'Aye. I can see you squintin' over a manuscript all day, takin' pride in your curlicues and sketchin' little rabbits in the margin – and leaving the business of the world to them that's suited to it.'

'You're probably right. Pity you weren't my careers master.' Tim clutched at the door handle to steady himself. He was white and sweating.

'By the way, you don't 'appen to know owt about satellite communications, I suppose?'

'What?'

'Only I'm thinkin' of investing in them Euteltrac systems for the fleet. The rep's comin' over later in the week. I could do with a clued-up boffin at me elbow.'

'I'm afraid I don't know what you're talking about.'

'No. Reckon that fits. No hard feelings, lad. On your way now.'

Arden was at the window anxiously watching out for Tim. She

had to go to Dereham to interview a potential recruit for *Suitables*, someone she had met while they were assisting a man who had a heart attack in the post office at Norwich. This was the way forward. If it worked out the woman would be the first stone in the pyramid of team workers under Arden's leadership, each contributing a percentage of their sales to her coffers. It was important on such an occasion to be both masterful and deeply caring – part glorious leader, part psychiatric social worker. She fought off thoughts of old dogs and new tricks, but it was difficult to think positive until she was sure that Tim had survived his interview with Jermigan. The signs were not good. He avoided looking at her when he came in and went straight to the lavatory. When he came out she sat him down next to her on the sofa and took his hand.

'You look awful, darling. Was it that bad?'

'Oh, it could have been worse. He could have just stuck me with a halberd.'

'He didn't *hit* you?'

'No, no. Actually, he was quite decent about it in the end. That was almost more confusing than if he had hit me. That and being called "lad" all the time. I kept checking to make sure I'd worn long trousers.'

'The patronizing git! I hate him.'

'He's not that keen on you either. And he means to have this place one way or another. He made that quite clear.'

'Well, he can't, can he? There's no way he could make us sell it.'

'Not legally. Or morally. But he's going to make life very unpleasant, Ard. For one thing, he – he knows about us. Don't ask me how. He actually threatened to spread it around. I couldn't believe it.'

'The *swine!* I'll kill him first. What business is it of his?'

'Don't be silly, Ard. He'll make it his business. I couldn't stand that. I really couldn't.'

'No, of course not. It won't come to that. There must be some dirt we can dig on him. In fact—' Was it too late to expose the affair of the *Hôtel de Ville*'s missing masonry? No proof, of course. Jermigan would have made sure of that. And he probably would not care. Arden, who had had more truck with him than Tim had, was prepared for him to react with an initial explosion followed by cool aggression. But she did not believe that he would put his threat of exposure into effect while there was any chance he could persuade them to sell.

'Darling, I've got to go now. You go and lie down. When I get back I'll book an appointment with the doctor for you. No, don't argue. You need a check-up. And don't worry. We'll sort this out somehow. The first thing is to settle the mortgage business. I'll get the solicitor to fix up a meeting with this Thalia person. Will you be all right till I get back?'

'Yes. Go on.'

'Bugger. You're supposed to be seeing that chimney sweep-cum-palm reader this morning. Shall I cancel for you?'

'No, thanks. It might take my mind off things.'

'That's the spirit. See you later.' She kissed him and set off for Dereham feeling strangely masterful.

Bos, after a ten-minute work training scheme, had been assigned to mix the cement. Unlike his mother, he did not object to the erection of faux-historic monuments or offering insults to piles of old stones, especially if work on them meant he could afford to go clubbing at the weekends. And pay off his debt. Debts. And contribute to the housekeeping. And get a proper CD system. The latter was the priority really. He asked Arden several times an hour how she could live without a music system but had failed to get a satisfactory answer. He started to work out the sums in his head but soon gave up.

It was a cold but brilliant sunny morning. Well liberating to be outdoors doing something useful. His dad would approve. Bos made a mental note to phone the old eco-prophet some time to let him know where he was. It was well different working with blokes after two years of Welsh Women's Studies. He expected some ribbing about the latter. But if you only got into college through the clearing system and were faced with choices between things like Cyber Technology and Philosophy With Textiles you had to get real. Bos felt he had got even more real of late.

The building team consisted of an old codger of a foreman who talked into a tape recorder or mobile phone a lot of the time, two jobbers, and Darren, one of Jermigan's drivers who was at a loose end because of the French hauliers' strike. Darren seemed less than gruntled, but the others were all right. In fact, very friendly and helpful.

Bos nearly dropped his hod when he saw Lottie, in overalls and hard hat, march puposefully towards the site and report to the foreman. The two of them had a bit of an argument, or at least Lottie shouted and waved her arms about, and it ended with much shrugging from the foreman and Lottie coming towards Bos with an expression which suggested a profound disgust with the human condition and him in particular.

'I'm supposed to help you.' She folded her arms and sneered, to convey what she thought of the idea.

'I don't need no help.'

'*Any* help. Don't they teach you to talk proper at university?'

'Shut it, you snotty cow. It's nothing to do with me.'

'Not much! You've just taken my job, that's all. That's why I'm late. Jermigan told me over breakfast so I had a go at him about it. I knew he was going to give you something to do, but I didn't think it would be *my* job. It's so fucking unfair.'

'Hey, watch it. This may be a building site but there's no need to talk like a navvy.'

'You sound like your bloody mother.'

'Well, that's not too surprising, is it? Anyhow, what's the problem? If Jermigan's paying us both. I reckon it's pretty decent of him.'

'The problem is, he promised *me* the job. A proper job. Not holding a screwdriver for some wanker from nowhere like you. He promised me ages ago. It's my half term. I don't want his fucking money for standing around doing nothing. It's so fucking typical! So fucking *patronizing*. I *hate* the fucker.' On the verge of tears, she turned away and threw herself head on at the cement mixer then sagged against it with her back to him.

The other men were watching them and Bos signalled as best he could that he was on top of the situation, whereas in fact he felt he was at the bottom of it. Not having a sister he had no experience of hysterical schoolgirls and would not have chosen this moment to start acquiring some. 'Is it your period?' he enquired, knowing this was the New Man-ish approach.

Lottie swung round and yelled, 'No, it is not my fucking period!'

'All right! You've got a well limited vocabulary, you know. You go on like that and you'll give these blokes the wrong idea.'

Lottie opened her mouth to release more expletives but glanced towards the other men and thought better of it. To Bos's amazement she blushed, the colour rippling over her freckles like a pink tide over pebbles. She raised one hand and wiggled her little finger at one of the men by way of acknowledging him. Bos turned to see who it was. Darren, the disgruntled driver, at present guiding the crane's load of stones, was waving back at her, but immediately fell prey to the limitations of his body language and turned back, embarrassed, to the load. Bos looked quizzically at Darren and began to think, slowly. He had not got very far when Lottie shook him roughly by the arm.

'Give me something to do then.'

'Oh. Are you sure you're all right?'

'Of course I am. Got to report to Jermigan tonight, haven't I? He'll want to know he's getting his money's worth.'

'Why do you call him that? What's he done to you?'

'Nothing. I just hate him. He's not even my real father. But he acts as if he is.'

'Sorry, mate, I don't get that. I'd have thought you'd be grateful.'

'Then thinking obviously isn't your strong suit.'

Bos sighed. 'Okay, so much for small talk. There's some bags of sand in that trailer over there. Bring them over in that wheelbarrow and pile them up by the mixer. That should shut you up for a bit.'

'Don't count on it.'

At the end of the day Bos was so hungry he ate ten pieces of toast and jam as soon as he got home. Arden's eyes widened as she tried to calculate how much of his twenty pounds would be left after seventy pieces of toast, but she did not say anything. She was too grateful that Jermigan had not turned Bos off the site in revenge against her and Tim. Her enquiries had revealed that unskilled jobs were indeed in very short supply in the area, and impossible to get to without a car – or lottery money if one went by bus. She asked her son how he had got on with the other workers.

'Great. Except Lottie's my assistant. Jesus, she's a bad-tempered little cow! Thank God it's only for a week.'

'Yes, she's a very angry young lady. Did you get any idea why?'

'No. Except that she hates Jermigan. She hates this place and everything in it apart from her mog and Miss Tree. She hates school too. Selfish bitch! Doesn't know when she's well off. It's well out of order the way she talks about Jermigan.'

'To be fair, he seems to take it like a lamb. She's his one weakness, I think. Ironic, isn't it?'

'Talking of weaknesses, I reckon our Lottie's got one for Darren. When she saw him she went bright red and started behaving herself. I dunno. I'm probably wrong.'

'Oh-oh. Poor Darren. I hope he doesn't have any ambitions in that direction.'

'What d'you mean?'

'Well, it would be tempting for him, wouldn't it? Whoever gets Lottie eventually gets Sloping. But if Jermigan didn't approve, Darren would be mincemeat.'

'Oh, right. That's a thought.'

'You don't fancy her as a future bride, then?'

'Eh? Come off it, Mum. She's a nutter.'

Arden had not meant it seriously. Nonetheless, if Bos were to marry Lottie all their problems would be solved. But she had no time to indulge herself in this particular fantasy. Her thoughts were elsewhere. Their solicitor had finally arranged a meeting with the mysterious Thalia Sewell.

8

They woke up feeling tetchy. The sight of the blanket of low, lumpy cloud that had stolen over the landscape overnight did not help. Arden stood by the bedroom window and fixed her eye on the castle keep to check if the clouds were even moving. They were not. It was typical of nature's obstreperous practises not to provide a background of suitably violent agitation to reflect her inner turmoil. By comparison, her first *Suitables* presentation was a sleepwalk. It was amazing how the wish to meet Thalia Sewell, which had once had her skulking round the backstreets of Great Yarmouth, receded when it was on the verge of being granted. There was no consolation in the fact that such was the fate of all wishes everywhere.

The more she thought about it, the less point there seemed in the meeting. Financial negotiations could be conducted via their solicitors. What Arden would really like to have known – that is, what Humph had told his lady friend about her and Tim, whether Humph was the father of her child and what he had seen in her in the first place – were not questions that were ever likely to be answered.

Where would they have met anyway? Arden mused. Perhaps Humph had advertised in the local paper: *Young 60-something fungi fanatic seeks cheap bonk and possibly more.* Arden no longer wanted to know. Even if one did not actively lay ghosts to rest they managed to do it themselves given time. She had heard enough encomiums to Humph from local sources to realize she had not known him at all. And no practical person would waste time and effort on trying to fathom a deceased.

Tim came down wearing a suit and tie.

'You're going to wear a suit and tie then?'

He looked at her as though she had addressed him in Swahili. 'Isn't it obvious? Why shouldn't I?'

'Nothing. I just wondered if we shouldn't look too well-heeled.'

'For God's sake, Ard, what elaborate meanness! Do you want her to think we're hard-luck cases so she'll hand over her share? We could turn up swigging meths, I suppose.'

'Don't be stupid. I didn't mean that. But she seemed rather hard-up herself. I thought we shouldn't look – you know – too different. Intimidating.'

'What kind of Byzantine reasoning is that! Don't you think it's rather patronizing to assume she'd be intimidated by a suit?'

'All *right. Sorry.* I thought I was being considerate.'

'This is not the moment to change the habit of a lifetime.'

'What do you mean? I'm very considerate. Just give me one case where I wasn't?'

'Don't change the subject.'

'Eh?'

'Look, this is a meeting with a solicitor. A professional person. And I am wearing a suit as a compliment to a fellow professional, all right?'

'Tim, just because you haven't got a proper job any more doesn't mean you have to use sartorial props to maintain your dignity. Dignity comes from within. Mr Gordon will respect you just as much in a sports jacket.'

'*Christ*, will you shut *up!*'

Arden complied, deeply resentful that her good intentions had been so wilfully misunderstood.

Mr Gordon leaped at every opportunity to get out of the office and had suggested they meet in the Bishop's Hat. As the funeral buffet had been held there Arden considered it quite appropriate. They drove into town in silence, far too early, and sat in reception staring in opposite directions. They had both almost forgotten why they were there.

The physical reality of Thalia Sewell and Mr Gordon was a shock. The solicitor had some experience of knock-down contests between rival beneficiaries. That was one reason he had suggested a public venue, where British reserve was more likely to be upheld than in private. In this case he did not know the parties well enough to be sure there would be no excitement, and was not encouraged by the murderous looks he caught on the faces of the deceased's progeny before they realized he was there. The next moment they were all conventional warmth and insincerity. Mr Gordon relaxed. He led them into a small side room and ordered coffee.

Arden, too, relaxed once the introductions were over. She could see that, of all of them, Thalia Sewell was the most nervous and ill at ease. She was no beauty but her broad face, with its monumental cheekbones, large pale blue eyes and loose red mouth, was arresting to say the least. Her skin was almost unnaturally fine and pellucid, without a trace of make-up. She wore a dark red suit that looked new and revealed most of her well-turned legs and effectively disguised her plumpish figure. Becoming highlights had replaced the Sun In and her hair was swept back in the swans' wing style that only lasts for a couple of hours after one leaves the hairdresser's. It was hard to tell what her habitual expression might be as the nervous smile was fixed and her eyes almost popped out of her head with apprehension, but Arden had no doubt that she was in the presence of a thoroughly harmless woman.

Mr Gordon got them chatting about Great Yarmouth, a subject that Tim took up with alacrity. Having established that Mrs Sewell knew nothing about Great Yarmouth in the Middle Ages, Arden's contribution was minimal. When they all knew as much about the town as the English Tourist Board she signalled to Mr Gordon to get down to business.

He began by distributing copies of the will, a manoeuvre which Arden thought lacked subtlety. She and Tim went through the motions of looking through it. Mrs Sewell blushed and left her copy on the coffee table.

'As you know,' said Mr Gordon, 'this is a very informal meeting to smoothe out any possible contentious areas of the legacy. I've drawn up a list of the assets here which you may like to glance at.' He passed them round.

'This is shaping up like a board meeting,' said Arden as she looked at the new list. 'Do you think we could skip to the crux

of the matter, Mr Gordon? We don't want to prolong the agony –
I mean, nothing personal, Mrs Sewell. I'm sure you're as anxious
as we are to get it over with.'

'Please call me Thalia. I've heard so much about you from
Humphie – Mr Mason.'

'Really?' *Humphie?* Humphie *Dumphie?* Arden froze. It was the
sort of insight into their intimacy that she had dreaded.

'Of course. He talked about you a lot.' She edged forward on
her chair. 'I just want to say, I don't want anything. Truly. Mr
Mason was very generous to me when he was alive. He was a
real friend. I don't deserve any of this. You should have it. That's
all I want to say.'

They looked at her in silence for a moment. This was something entirely new for Mr Gordon. He looked to Tim and Arden
for guidance.

'Out of the question,' said Tim. 'That's not why we're here –
Thalia. We didn't come to pressure you to give up your legal
rights. Not at all.'

'I don't feel pressured. It's entirely my idea.'

'But, Thalia,' said Arden, 'it wouldn't be what Dad would have
wanted, would it?' She indicated the will. 'Obviously.'

'No, I suppose not. But he never gave so much as a hint
about all of this. I wasn't expecting anything so I don't feel I'd
be missing anything either.'

'Mrs Sewell,' said the solicitor, 'I'm impartial here, naturally.
But I feel I should point out that your son is also a legatee. I'm not
sure you can legally disinherit him. Or, quite frankly, whether it
would be right to take that sort of decision on his behalf in any
case. He would be sure to resent it when he's older.'

Thalia looked crestfallen. She had never before encountered
the law as an implacable barrier to natural justice. 'There's no
reason he should know. He'll be all right. He'll have to fend for
himself like everybody else.'

'If it were my son I'd take the lot,' said Arden, to reassure her.
'His generation is going to have it much tougher than we did.'

'There's another thing,' said Tim. 'It's impertinent to ask,
I know, but have you thought about your pension arrangements? It could be that Dad was concerned you wouldn't be
provided for.'

'My pension arrangements? No, I haven't. I work as a care assistant part-time. I'm not sure if there are any.'

'No Personal Pension Plan?'

'No.'

Tim and Mr Gordon tutted in unison. 'It's just as well we met to discuss this, Thalia. I fear you might have rushed into a very generous but ultimately regrettable decision.'

'But so far as I understand it, I've been left with the money and you've been left with the mortgage. That's just unfair.'

'The will was made some time ago, Mrs Sewell. Before the mortgage was taken out. It was undoubtedly an oversight on Mr Mason's part that he didn't alter it accordingly. May I make a suggestion? It's quite simple, really. The debt is paid out of the combined assets of the estate, as it is bound to be. The residue is divided equally between the parties.'

'We would have to agree on the value of the assets.'

'Sounds all right to me,' said Arden.

'That rather depends on how much the residue amounts to.'

'Tim! You're changing your tune rather.'

'Not at all. I'm concerned that there won't be enough left for Thalia to have the sort of settlement Dad intended. If, for example, the cash is used to pay off the mortgage.'

'Does anyone know how much this silver gilt statue, thought to be of St Louis, is worth?' said Arden. Nobody did.

'We could sell the cottage and pay off the mortgage.'

'Tim—'

He held up a hand to silence her. 'But not until we can dispose of our house in London. And my sister doesn't want to sell. Therefore, I suggest we leave the will as it stands.'

'Tim dear, I don't want to appear grasping, but this statue thing might be worth half a million.'

Mr Gordon laughed. 'I seriously doubt it, Mrs Fairbrother. A few thousand, perhaps.' He then went into some detail about the progress of the probate application, which spun the meeting out until lunchtime. They agreed to go away and think about his suggestion and he promised to arrange a valuation of the silver gilt statue.

*   *   *

'We should have invited her to lunch.' Tim looked bothered, as though some grave error had been committed.

'We're not going out to lunch, are we?'

'Could have done. There's no point if there's just the two of us. Sardines on toast will be fine.'

'Will that be brown or white?'

'What are you still so crabby about? I thought the meeting went very well.'

'Yes, it did.'

'She's a charming woman, don't you think? Quite ordinary, I suppose. Nothing wrong with that, though. She seems to have thought the world of Dad.'

'Not a gold-digger, certainly. It's good to know he wasn't being used.'

'We owe her something for that.'

'We do?'

'The more I think about it ... what right do we have to renegotiate the terms of the will, Ard? Even when the mortgage on the cottage is paid off, it will leave a useful sum for us.'

'Only if we sell it to Jermigan. Besides, if we sell now we'd have to rent. More moving costs. We can't afford it. And do you really want to give in to his blackmail? I don't want to go. But if I do, it will be when I choose.'

'You, you, you! If Thalia were as selfish as you are we wouldn't even be having this conversation.'

'Is wanting something your definition of selfishness? That covers a lot of ground. I would have thought it was more the degree of ruthlessness with which one pursues something. And you can't say that about me because I agreed to go before. It was you who said you couldn't be bothered to move.'

'That was before Jermigan revealed his opinion on the subject. The game's not worth the candle now, Ard.'

'That's only *your* opinion. And, of course, the luscious curves of Thalia Sewell had no hand in forming it.'

'For pity's sake, Ard, I'm very touched that you are still so push-button jealous, but after all this time you should have grown out of it.'

'Now you're raving. I am *not* jealous. There are no scales on *my* eyes, that's all. I've told you before you're free to have another relationship if you want.'

'With my father's mistress? What is this – Bloomsbury? Ard, how did we get to this point – I only just met her for coffee.'

'It was long enough to decide that she deserved every penny – plus the statue of St Louis – even if we're the losers.'

'That's not far off the point. I do think she's deserving. She's a part-time care worker, for God's sake. Just the sort of person we'd want looking after Mum.'

'Oh. Well, how about – you marry Thalia, bring Mattie to live with you so that Thalia can look after her, and I'll just bugger off and join the Foreign Legion.'

'Thalia's married surely.'

'*What!* Is that your only objection?'

'Of course not. But it's a rational argument, which is what I'd prefer to be having.'

'There's nothing to stop you, if only you weren't so deluded about your motives.'

'Speak for yourself, my dear. My motives for wanting to be fair to Thalia Sewell are entirely philanthropic.' And to prove it he decided to go and see Thalia and persuade her to accept her proper dues.

What annoyed Arden most was being manoeuvred into an appearance of hostility to Thalia Sewell. If it could be managed to everyone's satisfaction Arden would not be averse to letting her scoop the jackpot. But it was only fair to Thalia not to burden her with the guilt of depriving her 'dearest friend's' family. No Judgment of Solomon was required. Common sense dictated that a fifty-fifty settlement was the obvious solution. She did not even mind that Tim was attracted to Thalia. The woman was – alluring – in a soft, nurturing style that had always eluded Arden despite her dutiful attempts to capture it. Her ex-husband, for example, would have adored Thalia. He would probably have made little clay models of her giving birth and sold them in aid of the Woodland Folk. Even Arden found her qualities therapeutic. So it was grossly unfair that she had been put in the position of arguing against Thalia's interests.

If she had not been so distracted by Tim's exercise in self-deception she would have made more of an effort to reassure Thalia that she was as philanthropic as he was, but with purer motives. Arden was not happy with the impression she had made. It felt like stepping on a ladybird. Olive branches were called for. The best thing would be to invite Thalia to the cottage. Arden could show her the new winter *Suitables* collection – always a sure-fire bonding opportunity. And then perhaps she could help Thalia understand why Arden was so attached to the place, why it answered so many of her primal needs.

By the end of Bos's first week the liberating effects of manual labour were wearing off. Only the prospect of a body to die for kept him cheerful. Where to find the women to make this ultimate sacrifice was a problem that occupied most of his waking thoughts. He had left a girlfriend, Nathalie from Newport, at college, and to spare her hassle from his creditor had deliberately given her to understand that he would be in Chiswick. This had cost him so much guilt and misery at the thought of her suffering that he borrowed the foreman's mobile phone and left a message at her hall of residence that he was sorry and would contact her when it was safe. He did not add that that might be next year.

Darren had taken him to the local pubs and introduced him to large numbers of under-age females. Bos assumed the over-eighteens were already married. The girls were friendly all right. He got the impression he could very well be the object of some in-depth market research if he cared to participate. Which only made him miss Nathalie all the more. She was quite a serious person, doing a thesis on 'The Glass Ceiling in the Light Industries of Gwent', and could not be easily replaced.

Bos told Lottie he had been out with Darren and could have sworn she blushed, so could not understand why she said she was less interested in Darren than in Nicholas Soames, whoever he was apart from he whom Lottie least wanted to shag. But she sent out confusing signals. No sooner had she bitten his head off about that than she invited him round to listen to the latest

Botulism CD. There was nothing else to do, so – liberally sploshed with Cerruti 1800 – Bos went.

Jermigan and Miss Tree were in the Great Room when he arrived, watching a programme about exploding cows on a television the size of a chest freezer. When he said Lottie had asked him round they looked at each other in disbelief, followed by cautious rapture. Miss Tree offered to call her, but Jermigan insisted on doing it himself, and gave Bos an encouraging slap on the back as he went up the stairs. Bos was again confused. He hoped they did not think he would sort Lottie out just because he was a normal bloke.

Lottie's room was huge. The double bed was on a dais partitioned off with rood screens, the ecclesiastical atmosphere heightened by a hammer-beam roof and vaulted window. It was offset by posters of Kermit Klein and hulks in G-strings. There were several hundred books on shelves that covered an entire wall. The sound system had been built into a medieval food cupboard. The white cat lay stretched out as in death in the middle of the floor, but the tip of its tail twitched a warning as Bos entered.

'Hi. Wow! Nice room.'

'I hate it.' Lottie was doing her homework at a large table under the window.

'How did I know you were going to say that? I suppose it is a bit dated. Gothic an' that.'

'Depends on your definition of time. Parallel universes obey their own rules, I imagine. That's not why I hate it.'

'Let me guess. You hate it because it's all your dad's idea and everything to do with him makes you puke?'

'He is *not* my dad. But apart from that, yes.'

'Jeez, you don't know when you're well off, you! My mum had to share a room with her brother till she was fourteen. They enjoyed it, she says.'

'Then that rather defeats your argument, doesn't it?'

'Eh?'

'Well, if they were perfectly content with the arrangement it just shows that having a large room to oneself is not a prerequisite for human happiness. How could you be so stupid as to think it would be? Sit down, for God's sake.'

Bos sighed. 'Force of habit.' Perhaps doing nothing would have been preferable. 'Where's the CD then?'

'In the machine. Put it on if you want.'

The volume was set so loud Bos was thrown back on to the sofa. He got up and turned it down. 'Don't them downstairs complain about the noise?'

'They can't hear it. Anyway, they wouldn't say anything in case it upset me. They're worried that I don't know how to enjoy myself because I'm still grieving for my mother.'

'You're cool. Some might say manipulative. Are you – you know – still grieving an' that?'

'Who knows? I don't really remember her. I don't want to talk about it. Spliff?'

'Pardon?'

'Do you want a spliff?'

'Right. Okay. Where d'you get the base?'

Lottie looked pitying. 'What planet are you from? Do you want to come to Norwich Friday night? I could take you round the clubs.'

'You mean, you want a ride.'

'Yes. I usually stay with a mate but I've got too much fucking course work. I'd rather come back.'

'Does Jermigan know you go clubbing?'

'Probably. I'm sixteen, for Christ's sake.'

'Oh, right.'

She joined him on the sofa and they lit up. Bos relaxed and waited for the sensations of grateful ease. They were a long time coming. He wondered if Lottie had been fleeced. The taste was a bit funny too, as though they had been spliced with cheese 'n' onion crisps. However, Lottie's eyeballs were dilating nicely. They were now fixed on the ceiling. 'Do you want to do me a favour, Bos?'

'You mean, apart from giving you a lift into Norwich?'

'Yes.'

'No.'

'It won't cost you anything. And I'll keep you supplied with stuff. I can afford it.'

'Twist my arm. What is it?'

'Just pretend we're going out. Only round here. You can do

what you like otherwise. It'll get Jermigan and Miss Tree off my back. They want to send me for counselling, for God's sake. If they think I've got a nice, thick boyfriend who'll look after me they'll stop worrying.'

'Shut it, you snotty cow! I'm going.'

'No – don't. All right, sorry. You're not thick exactly. But you know what I mean – non-threatening. They trust you. Jermigan thinks you're great.'

'Thanks. I don't know if you can get your head round this, Lottie, but that actually means I don't particularly want to cheat him.'

'Scared of him, are you?'

'No. Not at all.'

'Then what's the problem? I've worked it out. They won't expect us to see a lot of each other because I've got too much homework. All you have to do is come round here, say one evening a week, and get stoned out of your head. Then we can go out Friday nights and split up when we get there, but I'll come home with you. That's all, really.'

'What if something happens to you while I'm supposed to be with you? You can't go round the clubs by yourself.'

'I won't be. I'll be with my mates. That's what I usually do. I'll introduce you to them. Jermigan doesn't know what I'm up to when I'm out anyway.'

'I dunno. What if I want to – you know – stay with someone else?'

'There are six other nights of the week. Well, five. It doesn't have to be Friday, does it?'

''Spose not. I dunno, I don't like the sound of it. Why go to all that trouble just because you don't want counselling?'

'You don't know what it's like. They are so in my *face* about it. You must know what it means, being an only child? I feel like a fucking experimental animal. Like one of those kids who are brought up by gorillas or something. Please, Bos. If I don't do something I'm leaving. I can't stand them oozing over me any more.'

'Don't be stupid. Where could you go?'

'Plenty of places. A friend of mine has gone to Devon to work in a holiday camp.'

'They'd bring you back, you daft git.'

'Then I'd run away again. Oh, please, Bos. Give it a try. I don't *want* to leave. I just need some space.'

'It won't work.'

'Then you agree?'

'Oh, all right. You're a head case, Lottie. I'm only doing this because I feel sorry for you.'

'Don't bother. Thanks. There's only one thing – no shagging. Agreed?'

'You can count on it.'

'Great.'

Bos was mellowing at last. While uneasy about the plan – which smacked of sledge hammers and nuts – he had learned enough about female psychology in the course of his studies to know that you had to take it on trust. Managing women was a lot like being left in sole charge of a nuclear power station without the operations manual. 'Is that why you asked me round?'

'That's obvious, isn't it? Did you think I fancied you? Sorry.'

'I didn't. But, knowing you, I didn't think you was just being friendly.'

'Thanks. Look, I'm just going to take Lorca out for some fresh air, okay?'

'What?'

'The cat. I'm going to take him for a jog. I told you, I want some *space*. There's nothing to it, but it's just the kind of *symptom* that gets them into a frenzy of over-protection. I won't go far, don't worry. Here's the stuff. The TV's in that barrel. If they do come up – which they won't – say I'm in the loo.'

Bos knew he was not reacting fast enough. He stared at her. 'How are you going to get past them then?'

'Don't have to. There's another staircase through that door in the corner. See you. Won't be long.' She pulled a sweater on and turned to go.

'Hey!'

'What?'

'You forgot the cat.'

By the time Lottie returned Bos had fallen asleep. Botulism 3 was still on, presumably on repeat play. Woozily he wondered if that had not alerted the oldies. On the other hand, they probably thought all Lottie's music sounded the same. She shook him roughly. 'It's half-past eleven. You must go. Come on, I'll let you out the front door. Be quiet, they'll have gone to bed.'

But Jermigan was still downstairs. Lottie was cross. 'You didn't have to wait up, Harry.'

'Now you knows I always locks up, gal.'

'It's not necessary. I'm quite capable of shooting a bolt, you know.'

He grinned. 'She bosses me about something chronic. Women, eh, Bos!'

'Right. Yeah. Well, thanks for having me.'

'Y'right.'

Bos was not a happy bunny as he walked back to the cottage. He could not remember why he had agreed to Lottie's scheme. It stank. No one could jog with a cat for over two hours in the dark, even assuming Lorca's familiar-type relationship with his mistress would overcome his natural instinct to bugger off by himself. She was up to something, and Bos had a nasty idea what and with whom. He would have to tell her it was off. Counselling was exactly what Lottie needed, in his opinion. With a mallet. He would tell her after Friday night.

Patients at the surgery had spilled out of the waiting room and were squatting on the stairs. Posters reminding them that 'flu was best nursed at home had obviously misfired. Arden was indignant. She had come to pick up Tim but he was still waiting to be seen. He got up to give her his seat but she would not hear of it and forced the woman next to him to make room.

'This is ridiculous. Is there an emergency?'

'I don't think so. The last one to go in was pregnant. Perhaps she's having it.'

'They should have special maternity clinics. Do you want a magazine?'

'Yes, all right. I didn't want to lose my seat.'

'For heaven's sake!'

There had been a run on *Country Living*. Arden took a *Which Car?* for Tim and a *BBC Antiques* for herself then settled in for a long wait. Tim could not concentrate. Arden knew how he hated going to the doctor and squeezed his arm in sympathy. 'Don't worry,' she whispered, 'you won't have to give a sample on the spot.'

'What? You don't have to give samples for a hip replacement. Do shut up, Ard.'

'It'll be all right, honestly.' The pregnant woman came out and scuttled past the hostile stares. The Tannoy summoned the next patient, a woman with a noisy little boy who had been running round hitting people with an inflated hammer. When they had gone in a couple of older women started a righteous conversation about children today being out of control, and recalled the various tortures their own parents had used on them with blatant relish. Arden was burning to chip in with her opinion on the unnatural environment provided for boys in the twentieth century but heroically decided not to embarrass Tim. Besides, a surgery was no place to start a riot, as such an inflammatory topic was bound to do. She tried not to listen.

'I say, Tim, look at these prices. There's a china cow in here worth ten thousand pounds! That's about a hundred pounds per square millimetre. You couldn't even use it to scare crows. Look.'

'Umm.'

'Why on earth do people have ornaments? They're so useless.'

'Don't tell me they didn't have them in the Middle Ages?'

'They had useful objects that were also beautiful. Where do you think William Morris got his ideas from? That reminds me, I bet Mr Gordon hasn't done anything about that statue yet. I must give him a ring when we get home.'

Tim stood up abruptly. 'I'm going to the lav,' he muttered.

'Don't be long.'

'Well, I'm not going to drag it out, am I?'

'All right. Calm down.' Arden shook her head. Why were men so terrified of bodily corruption? No doubt because they could not be sure there would be a woman to do for them on the Other Side. Women, on the other hand, had a lot to look forward to.

Tim was in with the doctor for seventeen and a half minutes. His expression, when he came out, was inscrutable. Arden knew better than to question him. They were nearly home before he spoke.

'He reckons I've got to have an operation. Got to go for more bloody tests.'

Arden groped for his hand, but the car veered towards a ditch. 'Are you sure, darling?'

'No, I just said, I've got to have more tests. Terrific. Just as waiting lists go through the roof.'

Arden tried to think of a response that was not a cliché, but felt desperately up the creek, without an original thought. And try as she might, she could not avoid calculating the implications for their income. And the fact that if they had stayed in Chiswick he would be entitled to paid sick leave. 'You mustn't think about Humph, Tim. I mean, the fact that he died relatively young.'

'I wasn't!'

'Good. Because it doesn't mean you will. He had a heart attack. Your condition isn't life-threatening.'

'Is this your idea of cheering me up?'

'Darling, I wouldn't insult you by trying to cheer you up at the moment. I just don't want you to worry unnecessarily.'

'Then I suggest we don't talk about it at all.'

'Very well.' How like a man. It was common knowledge these days that talking about it, whatever 'it' was, could cure every ill. Not that she believed in the counselling culture. The idea of taking strangers into one's confidence was anathema to Arden's nature as well as her circumstances. Perhaps it might be better for Tim to write down his anxieties or put them in a poem? She was not averse to new ideas.

There was one more immediate problem. When they got home and Arden went to put the kettle on, the water trickled to a stop.

9

Arden stood riveted to the spot. Jermigan. It had to be. It had started. Did he not know Tim was unwell? Well, no, he did not. But still. How he had done it she could not begin to guess, but as he controlled all the utilities on the site there could be no doubt he was responsible. She ran upstairs, where Tim had gone to lie down.

'Jermigan's cut the water off. What are we going to do?'

He put an arm over his face. 'A midnight flit. How do you know it's him?'

'It has to be. He said he'd make life difficult, the bastard. Where is the stopcock anyway? We could sue him for creating a health hazard.'

'Ard, shut up. You're jumping to conclusions. It might be the Water Board. I'll ring them in a minute.'

'Are you sure you're up to it? I'd do it myself but I'm late for my appointment as it is.'

'Then I'll have to, won't I?'

'Oh, Tim. I'm so sorry.' She sat on the bed and stroked his hair. 'He's not going to get away with this childish intimidation. I'll – I'll go and tell Miss Tree what he's up to. She'll put a stop to it.'

'Ard, don't be stupid. You're always jumping to conclusions. You need evidence before you can accuse people. Like a plan of the plumbing system. Oh, Jeez.'

'Sshhh. Don't upset yourself, darling.'

'I'm not. *You're* upsetting me.'

'I quite understand that you don't want to take Jermigan on after the last time. Especially when you're a bit down. I suggest we don't do anything for the moment. When Bos gets home I'll ask him to go and reason with Jermigan. To be fair, the bugger hasn't taken his quarrel with us out on Bos.'

'Probably feels sorry for him, having a mother like you.'

Arden gasped. Just how much pain was he in? 'Tim! What a horrible thing to say. What's the matter with you?'

'You know what's the matter with me! Sorry. I didn't mean it.'

'Well. Good. You know, I'm very fond of Bos. He's turned into a really nice person.'

'Yes, he has.'

'If I'd stayed with Garth he would have been warped by the tension between us.'

'So you say.'

This was a less than hearty endorsement. Arden refrained from saying that this was a fine time to question that decision, and that his failure to do so before suggested he was engaging in the traditional ploy of rewriting history into a list of grievances. Anyone would think they were about to get divorced. But still, people did say silly things when they were in agony. After a couple of Neurofens and a nap he would no doubt be suitably penitent.

In the event Bos's diplomatic skills were not needed. The water had been restored during the afternoon. Relief was tempered by the confirmation that it must have been Jermigan's doing as the Water Board knew nothing about it. Arden did not say so, but she thought it was a sign that his preferred method of harassment would be psychological warfare. He would do just enough to bring on a nervous breakdown, without giving them grounds for legal action. Had Arden not felt empowered by an extremely successful presentation that afternoon her resolution might have wavered. The pre-Christmas *Suitables* offensive was well underway. Sales of scarlet tube dresses had rocketed. She felt ready for anything.

It was just as well. The water incident was followed by a half-hour power cut a few days later, while Tim was on the computer compiling a tax return for an organic turkey farmer. Rocky, Sperm and Malice resumed crapping on the forecourt.

Suitables deliveries were mysteriously diverted to the Hall. The driveway was blocked with traffic cones. Each day brought a fresh minor irritation. And that was only the first week. Arden moved the cones across the Hall's driveway and nervously awaited retaliation.

These developments put the statue of St Louis out of her mind for a while. When she got round to calling Mr Gordon about it, he was embarrassed that she had had to remind him and offered to take the statue up to Sotheby's himself as he had some business in London. It was Christmas shopping, but there was no reason for Arden to know that. Tim appeared disinterested in the St Louis saga. His offer to go and see Thalia Sewell in order to talk her out of her obstinate unselfishness was delivered as an heroic obligation. Arden was not fooled, but encouraged him with genuine enthusiasm. Anything to get him out of the house. And if he did hit it off with Thalia it might take his mind off his hip.

The prospect of Friday night with Lottie hung like a barrage-balloon over Bos's week. Deception was not in his nature. Guilt about not coming clean with Nathalie from Newport already made him feel like Atlas. He would have called off the phoney affair immediately but Lottie had Sky TV and there was a football match he wanted to see that week, so he went over to the Hall on the Wednesday and made out like a shy suitor for Jermigan and Miss Tree. They smiled at his eagerness to get out of the room.

Lottie was in her en suite bathroom putting on make-up when he went up. The stereo boomed. There was a six-pack of Tetley's on the coffee table. It looked ominous.

'Are you going somewhere?' He cast a leery eye over the jumble of discarded clothes, including microscopic underwear that she had presumably been trying on.

Lottie grinned. 'Just for a walk.'

'Come off it. I don't believe you. It's like some bleedin' fairy tale, you disappearing into the night all the time.'

Her mood soured at once. 'What do you mean "all the time"? It's only been twice.'

'Yeah, right. Blind me with science. What are you up to?'

'Mind your own business. I don't interrogate you about your private life, do I?'

'Why should you? I haven't asked you to be a stooge for it.'

'Well, that's gratitude. I supply you with all the dope and booze you can get your head round and all you have to do is sit here watching TV. What's the problem?'

'For one thing, it won't work. They'll find out. Then we'll both look like idiots.'

'You might. If they get heavy about it, I'm going.'

'So you'll just dump me in it? Thanks.'

'For God's sake! You're worse than they are. Don't you understand? They're stuck in a time warp. Do you know how long it is since they were my age? It was in the *war*. They just have no idea what's going on. Why should I suffer because I got dumped on a couple of old age pensioners? A girl in my class had sex when she was twelve!'

'That's disgusting.'

'Why? She made an informed decision. It wouldn't suit everyone, I know that. But it was right for her, and so what?'

'So what's that got to do with anything?'

'It hasn't. I'm just saying, kids today have set new standards. We're the ones who have to live with the consequences, so parents should just keep their noses out.'

'That's not most people's idea of standards, Lottie.'

'Christ! I knew you were a wanker. I didn't know you were a wanking bloody vicar!'

'Look, I don't give a toss what you get up to.'

'Then open a fucking beer and shut up.'

Bos was exasperated. Not least because it was almost half-time. He switched on the TV and threw himself with obvious disgruntlement on to the sofa.

'By the way,' said Lottie, 'I'm sorry I don't have any stuff today. I'll get some on Friday. You're still coming, aren't you?'

'Yeah. I'm really looking forward to it.'

'I told the OAPs. They were dead chuffed. Fell for it like two year olds. I can just see Jermigan proudly complaining about it to his mates. Yuk!'

'Most dads are like that with their daughters.'

'He is *not* my dad. How would you know, anyway? As far as I can see you're not a dad or a daughter.'

'Yeah, yeah.'

Bos felt like pointing out that such information was now available on the Internet, but he could not be bothered. He just wanted her to get lost. He would not have to put up with this sort of aggro after Friday. Lottie was ready. She was wearing a halter-neck top and mini skirt. Just the job for walking the cat in November. The dreaded Lorca was waiting by the door like an impatient husband.

'Don't worry about them coming up,' said Lottie. 'I asked them not to. Got the old nod-wink treatment. Gross.'

'I feel sorry for them.'

'Oh, shut up. You don't think I want things to be like this, do you? You don't know what it's like, living in this fucking dungeon. I have no choice.'

He was not up for a debate on free will. Lottie flounced off, saying she would be back by eleven. Bos glowered at the television. It was difficult to concentrate with Lottie's underwear giving him the glad eye.

The atmosphere that had descended on Barnacle Cottage was a new experience for Bos. When living with his father there had only been the two of them, so he always knew what was going on. Being in the pathway of telepathic communications was a dodgy business. Regular power cuts did not help, although they certainly generated friction between Arden and Tim. He decided that the real problem was his uncle's hip. As he must be in pain, it was likely that he did not want to share a room with Arden anymore. Bos considered the alternative combinations but, as they too involved sharing with a close relation, he eventually offered to sleep on the sofa. His mother was adamant against it. She could not bear the idea of unwashed bodies sweating and farting all night in the living areas. At least in the Middle Ages, when large retinues dossed down together in the great hall, the rooms were so draughty it was more like camping, really. She admitted that sharing with Uncle Tim was not an ideal arrangement and that they might have to consider a loft conversion if Bos was going to be around permanently. In the meantime he was not to worry. Uncle Tim was bound to be a bit tetchy until he had the operation. Bos must not take it personally. She did look seriously askance when he asked her if he could have the car to take Lottie out on the Friday.

'I thought you couldn't stand her, darling?'

'Oh – she's not so bad when you get to know her. She's just screwed up because of her parents and that.'

'That's just an excuse. You aren't, are you?'

'I dunno. Perhaps I'll have a delayed reaction and fail to establish stable relationships.'

'Bos, you're as stable as a paving slab. I'm sure you'll be a good influence on Lottie if you can put up with her. I wondered why you were going over to the Hall in the evenings.'

In fact, Arden was pleasantly intrigued by this development. It would do no harm for Bos to infiltrate the enemy camp. The fantasy of uniting their households through marriage was well under control. The price of having Lottie as a daughter-in-law was one she was not prepared to pay. But if the girl was keen on Bos, it might act as a restraint on Jermigan. His devotion to her was one of the great mysteries of the universe.

Tim's mission to Thalia Sewell did not quite accomplish its objective – she still insisted on giving up her share, but he persuaded her to transfer it to her son. In all other respects it appeared to have been a triumph. He came home from the meeting as cheerful as though he had just won a hefty rebate from the Inland Revenue. Arden had hoped the visit would raise his spirits; she had not expected them to levitate. She wondered why she was not jealous of Thalia with regard to Tim when she could have garotted her for carrying on with Humph. Perhaps because she was so sure of Tim, whereas with her father she felt that Thalia had been given the emotional family silver. The fact that Thalia had been their father's mistress was no great shakes. Arden was sure she had heard of a tribe in something-stan where it was a sacred custom for a son to take on his father's obligations in that line. The conventions of the West were so constipated. Besides, it was the most natural thing in the world for a father and son to share a taste in women. And, just to show how unthreatened she felt about the relationship, she carried out her intention of inviting Thalia to tea, so that they could all be friends together.

It had to be recognized that one factor which might be driving Tim into Thalia's arms was their pathetic social life. Arden's headmistress friend, Angela, had spoken of inviting them to dinner, but since the quiz night when Arden had, in the heat of passion, uttered the words 'bovine culture', things had cooled between them, despite Angela's gracious forgiveness at the time. Arden would in due course try and make it up with Angela, who must know they were natural associates. Laurence and Shara had agreed to come in principle, but could not fix a date. They were bogged down by worries about rising interest rates and a shortage of thatching reeds, never mind disrupting District Council meetings and organizing petitions to the Department of the Environment. Arden suspected they were leery of setting foot on Jermigan soil. They might even think Arden and Tim were tainted by association, which was totally unfair and the sort of counter-productive suspicion that was almost enough to make one rethink one's own position.

For herself, Arden was happy not to have to entertain. Success with *Suitables* was gratifying, but unbelievably hard work. The more underlings she recruited to her pyramid, the more paperwork and team leadership were required. A new respect for captains of industry inspired her efforts. Once her unit was complete she would also have to write a monthly News Flash. There was no letting up, especially with Tim underfunctioning. Her PC had to be paid for. It was getting difficult to find time to go and see Mattie. As she never remembered that they had been it was also frustrating. Perhaps, as Arden was so busy, Tim would agree to go on his own once or twice, or with Bos. The spirit was willing but the schedule was tyrannical. Arden could not really afford the time to see Thalia. It was not as if she were likely to buy any clothes.

Faced with approval on both sides for his dalliance with Lottie, Bos realized he would come in for quite a bit of stick if he gave up on her right away. The path of least resistance beckoned. Besides, somebody had to keep an eye on her. When they had gone out on the Friday, she had disappeared from the pub and told him she would be waiting for him outside Minto's, the club favoured by her mates, at two o'clock. She was, but worry had spoilt his evening. He would give it a month, or until he met a woman for whom it would be worth the trouble of dumping Lottie and incurring the disappointment of both families.

Bos lay exhausted on his bed after work as the darkness of the evening knitted seamlessly into the gloom of daytime, and wondered how the fuck he had got himself into this hole.

As expected, Tim did not go quietly when Arden asked him to leave her and Thalia alone for a womanly chat. He had exhausted the seam of weathervanes in the locality and was in no fit state to go shopping. Reluctantly he agreed to arrange a meeting with a client but on condition that he would come straight home afterwards.

As a test, Arden had not given Thalia directions to the cottage. Ears akimbo, she asked if it had been difficult to find.

'No. I've been here before.' Thalia, handing Arden her rain-coat, laughed and blushed. That in itself was not incriminating. She could just be embarrassed at what Arden might be thinking – that is, *exactly* what Arden was thinking. The red suit was the same one Thalia had worn when they met at the Bishop's Hat, as were the brimming eyes, nervous smile, the air of having been born to please. 'It was nice of you to invite me.'

'Not at all. I just hope you don't feel pestered by us.'

'How do you mean?'

'Well, I wouldn't want you to think it's because we had an agenda.' Thalia looked puzzled. 'About the will.'

'Oh, that. No. Anyway, no one could mind being pestered by Tim, he's so sweet.'

Arden took a while to digest this pronouncement. Such blatant directness must surely hide something. Was it a warning shot that Thalia meant to have Tim off her? Was it confirmation that Thalia was as guileless as a Teletubby? 'He certainly is. Do have a seat. I'll bring the tea.'

While they tucked in to crumpets and Bakewell Slices, Arden encouraged Thalia to talk about herself. Or, as it turned out, her family. Thalia dismissed herself in a sentence as not being worth discussing. Not so her father and young Gavin. Arden had brain fade after an hour's intensive coaching on the life and times of these two clearly beloveds. She gave up trying to interject complementary anecdotes about Bos's early life, and it was hard to empathize with someone who raved about their own father. Thalia's face glowed when she talked about him. He had had three nervous breakdowns and had not worked for thirty years but his character gave Father Christmas a run for his money and his carpentry skills were legendary. Thalia lovingly described the guinea pig hutch he had made for Gavin, the rocking horse, the bed in the shape of a space ship, the model castle complete with torture chamber. She stopped for a moment to bring her emotions under control.

Arden seized her chance. 'And what about Gavin's father?'

'He left me when Gavin was two. We'd been living in Coventry. I came down to stay at home for a couple of months as Mum was ill and when I phoned to say when I was coming home he said, Don't bother, I won't be here.'

'How *appalling*.' It was, of course. But Arden could not help wondering if Thalia's husband could ever have competed with her father for her loyalty.

'Naturally, I had no choice but to stay on at home. To tell you the truth it was a blessing in disguise. I never really liked being married. It's a lonely life, isn't it?'

'Well, that's one way of looking at it. Did your mother get better?'

'That time she did, yes. But she had to go into a home a few years ago. She died last September.'

'I'm sorry. And then Humph in April. What a sad time for you.'

'Yes. It was ironic really. Mum was in The Ashes – same place as your mother.'

'Oh, I *see*. Was that where you met him?'

'I'd always known him as a friend of the family. But, yes, I did get to know him better in those circumstances.'

Arden was pleased to note Thalia's look of confusion. Something stronger might be expected from a person who carried on with a man whose wife she saw in such a distressing condition. It was obvious how it had happened. Humph and Thalia would have started by exchanging pleasantries during gaps in the patients' coherence. They would find themselves leaving at the same time, lingering in the car park chatting about the dear ones' symptoms, which would inevitably lead to the nearest café as a regular fixture after their visits. She stopped short of wondering what had come between that and the zonking legacy. 'I suppose Dad was lonely. He doesn't seem to have had many close friends.'

'I wasn't aware of any. But then, I wouldn't know. I didn't, you know, keep track of him.'

'Of course not. What did you – er – I mean, did you see a lot of each other? This is awkward, Thalia, I don't want to pry, but I'm curious about Dad's last days, as it were. You probably knew him better than I did. We didn't have much contact over the last few years.'

Thalia looked unhappy. 'Is that why you invited me here? To talk about Humph?'

'No! Honestly, I only wanted to show you we had no hard feelings about the will.' It did sound unlikely. Arden knew she made an unconvincing altruist although she could never understand why.

'You must be very suspicious of me.'

Arden was taken aback by her mind-reading skills and unexpected astuteness in exposing the sub-text. This could be leading up to confession, or a declaration of innocence. 'Not at all. You mean, because Dad left you half his worldly goods? Should I be?' Thalia sighed and fiddled with her teaspoon. As she was about to reply Arden heard the car turn in at the drive. 'Damn. That'll be Tim.'

'Oh, good.' There was no mistaking the joy on Thalia's face.

Lottie's nocturnal walkabouts did not happen every time Bos went over to the Hall. He suspected that these occasions corresponded with Darren's absence on a long haul. Lottie was so grumpy that he suggested they go out for a drink rather than loll about getting stoned in hostile silence. She would sit on her own in the pub, chain smoking until it was time to go home. On the whole he preferred his lonely vigil in her bedroom. The OAPs, as he now thought of them himself, had never come up while he was there, even with mugs of tea, which Bos could have done with. But one night while he was slumped in front of The X Files he heard Jermigan's heavy tread on the stairs and gawped at the door as the footsteps approached.

There was a soft knock. 'Lottie?'

Bos panicked. Impressions were not his thing. There was no chance of imitating her antagonistic tone even if he had been in full control of his faculties. He hesitated and then opened the door a crack. 'Hi. Er – Lottie's in the shower.' He sniggered, realizing too late what interpretation this must be open to, and waited for Jermigan to punch him on the nose.

'Don't hear no water.'

'She's just finished, I think.'

Jermigan's smile was conspiratorial, so far as Bos could tell. An all-studs-together smile. Thank God they were not living in his mum's beloved Middle Ages. He would have been married off to Lottie at poleaxe-point on far less incriminating evidence.

'Don't matter. There's an urgent phone call for you. Y'r Uncle Tim called over. Could you go home right away?'

'Oh. It's not about my dad, is it?'

'No idea, lad.'

'Okay. Thanks. I'll – er – I'll just tell Lottie.'

'Right 'o. Apologize to 'er ladyship for disturbing you, like.'

'Okay.' Bos shut the door and waited until Jermigan's footsteps had receded. The television was loud enough to spare him the farce of talking to the shower hose. He waited a few moments, turned the lights and the TV off and went downstairs. Jermigan and Miss Tree were also watching The X Files. He grinned at them. 'Thanks, Mr Jermigan. Lottie's tired. She's gone to bed.'

Jermigan winked. 'Makes sense, don' it?'

'Ha – yes. Goodnight then.'

Bos ran towards home but instead of going in kept to the cover of the shrubbery and carried on to the terrace of workers' cottages where Darren lived with another driver. As he did not know which one it was he had to knock at the first cottage and ask. A woman came to the door and gave him the information through the letterbox, explaining that her husband was away. Bos wanted to point out that advertising his absence was a dumb idea in the circumstances but there was no time. He had to find Lottie before their cover was blown.

Darren's cottage was dark and nobody answered. Bos cursed and battered on the door. He threw some gravel at the first-floor windows. They might be in bed. Would Lottie have such bottle? Yes. He called Darren's name but there was no response. The next step would be to go down to the pub and look for them but by the time he had gone home and asked for the car it would be closing time and they might be on their way back. Should he creep back to the Hall and lurk around the entrance that led to Lottie's lair so that he could warn her? Shit. He'd known this would happen. Why had he let it?

Over at the lorry park the towering security lights, which together with the baying hounds reminded Bos of concentration camps, gave him a thought. Darren might be over there mucking out his cab. Perhaps Lottie would be innocently holding his wash leathers.

There were eight vehicles parked in a row, each the size of a village hall on wheels. It was an awesome sight. What red-blooded male would not want to be at the controls of forty-five tons of intimidation? Bos felt a reluctant twinge of respect for Darren's skills.

There were no lights on in the cabs. As Bos ran across the tarmac Rocky, Sperm and Malice lunged out of the shadows at full pelt, barking with hysterical fervour. They skidded to a halt in front of him, haunches braced in unmistakably threatening attitude. The barks alternated with deep-throated growls and twitches of the head, as when tearing off bits of raw flesh from a carcass. Bos wished he had paid more attention to Blue Peter. He was sure he had seen an item about dealing with dangerous dogs. He thought two fingers came into it. He made a hesitant V sign at them, then tried it the other way up, to no effect. The noise would soon have Jermigan out here with a shotgun but he dare not turn and run for it with the Beasts of Sloping at his heels. Desperate, Bos yelled Darren's name and after what seemed like half an hour Darren poked his head out of the window of one of the vehicles.

'What the fuck are you doing here? The boss'll do 'is nut.'

'Is Lottie with you? It's urgent.'

'Hang on.' Darren disappeared and was replaced by Lottie, brazenly buttoning up her shirt.

'Lottie, for Chrissakes, you must get back! I was called away. I told the OAPs you were in bed. What are you *doing?*'

'Playing Happy Families. What do you think?'

'Can you call these bloody animals off?'

Lottie laughed and shouted at the dogs. Reluctantly they backed away, snarling a reminder of what would happen if Bos made one false move. 'Don't panic. They won't check up. What if they do?'

'Lottie, please. Why risk it?'

Darren put a proprietorial hand on Lottie's neck and caressed it with condescending ease. Bos marvelled at his nerve. At his age – thirty-something – he would be assumed to be not only a gold-digger but a child molester as well. If Jermigan ever found out, Darren would be dropped at various locations all over the Continent. Bos remembered his mother's observation that whoever got Lottie got Sloping. He did not necessarily think that Darren was plotting a coup but, as with justice, appearances were everything. Darren could not possibly be in love with Lottie, it went against nature. 'He's right, babe. You'd better go. I don't want no trouble.'

'Then you shouldn't have started, should you?' Lottie was scathing. It was a far cry from *Romeo and Juliet*. Bos noted that despite her defiance she did get out of the cab. 'See you on Friday, okay?'

'Yeah.'

Lottie walked off quickly towards the Hall. Bos started to run after her. Without turning round, she told him to piss off.

'Bitch!'

Lottie just waved. Well, she *would* take it as a compliment.

Bos winced at the thought of Jermigan and Miss Tree blithely watching the end of Newsnight secure in the belief that she was tucked up in bed after a blameless evening spent listening to pop music with a suitable youth. Although Jermigan must now suspect that Bos and Lottie had got up to that which called for a shower afterwards, he did not seem to think it blameworthy. But it would make it that much more awkward to dump her. Bos gnashed his teeth in frustration. Perhaps this was what mums were for – sorting things out. He might have a word with Arden about it. Somebody should do something about Lottie.

When he got back to the cottage his mother was pacing up and down the forecourt. 'There you are! What on earth kept you, darling? I was imagining all sorts of terrible things.'

'Honestly, Mum. Like what? How could anything possibly happen to me walking over here?'

'I don't know. Burglars? Debris from outer space? You don't understand, Bos. Mothers panic first and ask questions afterwards. It's the protective instinct.'

'I'd have thought yours was a bit rusty.'

'That's not very nice, Bos. It takes more than a few years out of practice to wipe out millenniums of evolution. I was really worried. I even rang the Hall again.'

'What did you do that for? That was well stupid, Mum.'

'Oh, *sorry*. They said you'd left as soon as Uncle Tim called the first time so naturally I was worried. Where have you been, anyway?'

'I bumped into Darren. We were just chatting.'

'Bos, didn't they tell you it was urgent? It may be too late to phone back now.'

'Who was it anyhow?'

'He didn't give a name, just left the number.'

'Did he sound Russian?'

'I don't think so. More like the Wirral. You don't think they've tracked you down, do you?'

'Dunno. You're not in the phone book, are you?'

'Not yet, no.'

'That's all right then. Where did you leave the number?'

'By the phone. You can't ring now, it's twenty to twelve.'

'Mum, they're vampires, all right? Early nights aren't their thing.'

Arden hovered while Bos rang the number. Her anxiety had not been exaggerated. She had been close to tears as the conviction took hold of her that her son's battered body would be found in the undergrowth. And that was before she knew that the Russians were on to him. The downside of Sloping's charms struck her for the first time. There were just too many places where a garotte-wielding assassin could hide. The tower of rubble for a start. She bolted the doors. What a time to fall out with Jermigan. If they had still been on terms she could have appealed for his protection, which he revelled in dispensing. Especially as Bos and his beloved Lottie were now an item. The only way they could appease him would be to leave Sloping. Anything would be better than that, provided it did not involve human sacrifice. She went and sat on the sofa and studied Bos's face anxiously. He put down the receiver.

'No reply. I'll try again tomorrow.'

'Don't sleep with the window open, darling.'

'I'll sit up all night if you like.'

'I feel *I* should.'

'Ah – that's cute, Mum. You old she-tiger. Don't worry. I'll be all right.'

Quite ironic really, thought Arden, that the bonding tentacles should be closing round her at a time when most parents were lopping them off.

If only they could get the inheritance sorted out, some money might be found to pay off his debt and enable him to go back to university. Thank goodness for modular courses and all things multiple and flexible. She would have to nag Mr Gordon again and find out how he had got on with the statue of St Louis; she made a note to call him in the morning. For now, a bit of escapism was indicated. Arden was both appalled and tempted by the spate of medieval thrillers spawned by Brother Cadfael. She told herself she only read them for the fun of spotting anachronisms and had found one in the library that looked very promising, although evidence that the quest for original sleuths had gone too far. *The Strumpet's Inheritance: The Third Chronicle of Mother Slopladle* looked like a happy hunting ground for gaffes. Tim was already asleep. He had to take so many painkillers he fell into a coma as soon as he got into bed so Arden was happily able to spot gaffes until two in the morning without disturbing him.

He woke her at nine-thirty with a cup of tea and bad news. Interest rates had gone up again, her appointment in Loddon had cancelled – items that were probably no coincidence – and Mr Gordon had phoned to say he had serious news about the statue of St Louis and could they set up a meeting with him and Mrs Sewell as soon as possible?

10

Why Mr Gordon could not reveal the secret of the statue over the phone was the subject of much high-spirited speculation over the next few days. Arden was relatively light-hearted anyway since Bos had discovered that the urgent phone call had in fact been from a girl he had met at a club who could only pluck up the courage to call him when she was drunk.

Arden's favourite theory was that the piece was a peculiarly fine example of a seventeenth-century salt-cellar, of which the matching sugar sprinkler was in the Louvre, which would therefore be willing to pay at least half a million pounds for it. Tim thought it was more likely to be a fake, and that Mr Gordon wanted to break the news personally.

'Hardly, darling. We're not going to slit our throats over it, are we?' She knew his caution was just his way of trying to spare her disappointment. He did not have the air of someone about to be disappointed as he dressed for the meeting. It was getting difficult to remain entirely nonchalant about Tim's attraction to Thalia Sewell, particularly when he put on the mycelium mould singlet that Arden had had made for him by a New Age artisan in Wales, which had involved taking a papier mâché cast of his torso. This was its first outing. The first tentative stage of a relationship was very trying for bystanders. Arden was convinced she would be much happier if they got on with it. Of one thing she was certain. The words 'How about a spot of lunch?' were on the cards.

As they drove out through the gatehouse, Arden noticed that their wheelie bin had not been interfered with. This was sinister in itself. It was a reminder that the harassment had stopped. There had not been an incident for more than a week. Of course it was likely to be temporary. Another perverse psychological tweak. But knowing Jermigan it could not be mere oversight.

This time Thalia was not wearing the red suit but an identical model in green. It was such a pity she was hard up. She could do with a *Suitables* makeover. Mr Gordon was all smiles but appeared ill at ease nonetheless. Arden prepared to hear that the statue was a fake. He chatted with Tim about the rise in the stock market while Arden enquired of Thalia about her father and Gavin. There was instant hush when Mr Gordon finally called them to order.

'As you all know, I took the statue up to Sotheby's on your behalf.' And how much would that cost them? thought Arden. 'I spoke to several experts in the European Art department and they were indeed very excited about it. It is a very fine piece.' He referred to his notes. 'A silver gilt reliquary approximately forty centimetres high. Probably made in Bruges in the latter half of the fifteenth century or early sixteenth.'

'Not contemporary with the saint, then,' said Arden.

'No, indeed. I'll come to the history of the piece in a moment.'

'A reliquary normally has a relic in it. Are you saying this statue actually contains a piece of St Louis?'

'No, no. Have you ever seen the item?' He looked from one to the other like a teacher eliciting interaction. They shook their heads. 'The saint is represented in, shall we say, civilian clothes of the period—'

'He always wore crap clothes as a mark of piety,' said Arden. 'Not that he wished to draw attention to himself, of course.'

'Indeed.' Mr Gordon was annoyed at having his momentum interrupted. 'As I was saying, he is depicted holding a lance in one hand and a replica of what is believed to be the Abbey of St Denis in the other. Now, this is the crux of the matter. This replica is supposed to contain, not a piece of St Louis, but, almost as desirable in some quarters, a sizeable smidgeon of the Oriflamme, the sacred banner of the Kings of France!' He looked to them for some serious gob-smacking, but Tim and Thalia were only politely bored. Arden was sceptical.

'Rubbish! The original was lost at the Battle of Agincourt.' Nonetheless, she saw before her not Mr Gordon but the pious saint, taking the banner from behind the altar before setting out on his last fatal, or rather farcical, crusade. 'How do they know? There might be enough smidgeons of the Oriflamme around to make up a circus tent.'

'I couldn't say, Mrs Fairbrother. As it happens the provenance of this piece is well known. It has been in the possession of one family since it was made – the Comtes d'Y les Vignottes. The keepers of the flame, if you like.' As this sally went unremarked, he grew sober. 'The reason it came to public attention is that it was, sadly, stolen. In 1955. From the family home in Normandy.' He looked gravely at them, hoping they would draw their own conclusion.

'Oh. You mean, Dad had bought stolen property, so it didn't rightfully belong to him? Wait a minute. Isn't there some law on the Continent that if you sell stolen goods before lunch the following day it's counted as bona fide?'

Mr Gordon held up one hand in a supplicatory gesture. 'Do I have to spell it out, Mrs Fairbrother? The chances are your father stole it. You see, the culprit was an Englishman. It was in all the papers. This expert chap – Mr Franklin – made a note of the details, naturally, being in the business. In case the stolen item was ever presented for sale in London. But it never was. Of course, Mr Franklin is retired now, but we were fortunately able to confirm the details with him.'

They were silenced. There was a delay while the information went in, as on satellite interviews. Thalia rummaged for a hankie.

'I can see why you wanted to tell us personally, Mr Gordon,' said Tim. 'Thank you.'

'Now hold on a minute,' said Arden. 'It can't be true. Dad left that thing to Thalia. He would never have done that if he'd known it was stolen.'

Mr Gordon shrugged. 'As to that, who can say? It may not have occurred to him that she would sell it. That way it would never have come to light. And Mr Mason probably thought he would live longer than he did. He might have intended to give Mrs Sewell some instructions about the item.'

'How did they know it was an Englishman?'

'He was caught in the grounds. Badly beaten up, I gather, but later escaped.'

'If he was caught, why didn't they recover the statue?'

'They assumed he must have hidden it somewhere on the way out and recovered it when he escaped. Just as well he did. The Maquis was mentioned. They would have 'persuaded' him to reveal its whereabouts, I'm sure. At any rate, it was never found. And it has never shown up in a sale room. They rather assumed it had been destroyed.'

Thalia was crying openly. 'Poor Humph. Fancy beating h-him up. He never t-told me.' Tim put his arm round her.

'Not something he was proud of, I suppose,' said Arden. She too felt slightly queasy at the idea. On the other hand, it was rough justice. He had been caught in the act. More worrying was the fact that Humph could do such a thing. Admittedly he had been very young. Probably drunk.

'What was he doing in Normandy, anyway?'

'He used to work the ferries when there was nothing else on offer,' said Tim. 'Was the place it was stolen from near the coast?'

'That I would have to check.'

'He was still doing it when I started school. He took me with him to Dieppe once, when I was off sick with tonsillitis. The only time he ever took me anywhere, as it happens.'

'Well, thank you for that heart-rending reminiscence, Tim. Does that mean you accept this unlikely tale?'

'It does look bad, Ard.'

'That's not the same as proof, is it, Mr Gordon? It's still possible Dad might have bought the thing in good faith? So – he might have suspected it was stolen, but that's not nearly as bad.'

'True. True. It would be hard to prove one way or the other after all this time.'

'And these – Maquis – they didn't identify the man, did they?'

'No. Otherwise they could have pursued him over here, of course.'

'There you are then.'

'Where, Ard?'

'Well, it's all circumstantial. That's the word, isn't it, Mr Gordon?'

'It is.'

'So all we have to do is – nothing, really. We can't sell it, of course. You don't suppose this Mr Franklin would grass to the owners, do you?'

'Ah – I must admit I hadn't thought of that. Let's hope not. A fanatical partisan would have a long memory, I fear. Of course, I didn't mention your names, so it can't be traced.'

'Except to you, Mr Gordon. You'd better be prepared for that midnight caller.'

The solicitor evidently had not thought of that. He dismissed the idea as fanciful, without total conviction.

'The upshot is,' said Tim, 'that there'll be no benefit to the estate from that source.'

'Precisely so. In the circumstances, as executor, I could not possibly countenance a sale.'

'Where is it now?'

'In our safe in the office.'

'Here?' Arden's blood ran cold, as though the statue were a phial of bubonic plague.

'Yes. Would you like to see it?'

'I suppose we might as well.'

When Mr Gordon was out of the room, Thalia blew her nose and braced herself. She had a look of stoical determination that would have suited The Boy on the Burning Deck. 'All I know is, Humph didn't do it. There wasn't a mean bone in his body.'

'Is that a fact?' said Arden.

'Yes. Not the Humph I knew. I'm sure he didn't know it was stolen or he would never have dumped me in it. You were right there, Arden. Either way, we have to give it back. I won't sleep in my bed else.'

'What – publicly? Are you mad? We don't even know he stole it, but if we give it back everyone will assume he did. You can't want to blacken his name like that after all this time. What's the point? Nobody knows we have it at the moment.'

'Except that Sotheby's know Mr Gordon has it, as you pointed out, Ard.' Tim, sitting between the Alpha and Omega of female temperament, loosened his collar. 'They might be obliged to inform the owners.'

'So? They're not going to come over here and hold Mr

Gordon's head down the loo until he talks, are they? Humph's dead. We're totally innocent parties.'

'Unless we hang on to it,' said Thalia. 'That would make us accomplices, wouldn't it?'

'For God's sake,' growled Arden, 'why should we be dragged into this? What on earth was Humph thinking about?'

'Please,' said Tim, 'we can't discuss this here. How about a spot of lunch afterwards?'

Mr Gordon came in carrying a bulging black bin liner. He carefully unwrapped several layers of bubble plastic and reverently placed the statue on the desk. It was tarnished. The saint's broad, bland face smiled at them as though having a well-earned laugh at their expense. 'There we are. All in one piece. Well, two pieces, if you count the lance. See, it's removable.' He jiggled the lance with an insouciance that Arden found quite inappropriate. 'If only he could speak, eh?'

'Yes,' she said. 'Then he could tell us who nicked him.' The presence of the object raised no feeling of awe in Arden. She had never been keen on pious monarchs. A smidgeon of Simon de Montfort's hair shirt – now that would be a souvenir to make her bend the knee. Perhaps it was the connection with Humph that neutralized the thrill she would normally have felt in the presence of a medieval object. It was a curious item for her father to have possessed. He had not been interested in the Middle Ages at all. She had not inherited her enthusiasm from him, or anyone else in the family that she knew of.

'It's in very good condition,' said Thalia.

'It hasn't actually been used for anything. Apparently it was kept under lock and key in the family chapel in France continuously until the war when it was hidden for safe keeping. Well, have you seen enough?' Mr Gordon was disappointed by their reaction after the extraordinary trouble he had gone to. He was sorry, in fact, that he had tried to share his excitement with people of such mundane tastes. The statue was wrapped up quickly and returned to the bin bag. 'I shall keep it in the safe until such time as you decide between you what to do with it. I hope you will do so as soon as possible. Being in de facto possession of such a thing puts me in a very invidious position.'

'Does your secretary know about it? Can she be trusted?'

'Really, Mrs Fairbrother, I'm surprised you feel the need to ask. All our clients' affairs are completely confidential.'

'Good. Then unless there's anything else, we'll be on our way, Mr Gordon.'

'There's only one more thing: Barnacle Cottage will have to be valued for probate purposes. Unless you have any objection, I'll make the arrangements.'

'Please do.' This was an unwelcome reminder to Arden of the outstanding mortgage. With the reliquary out of the frame, the only hope of paying it off would be to sell the house in Chiswick. Trust them to be lumbered with tenants who paid the rent on time and maintained the fabric. There was no possibility of turfing them out ahead of the lease's end.

They were scarcely out of the building before she sensed the disposition of the parties in the argument that was to ensue. She would be on her own. Tim's body language was written in large print. He stayed close to Thalia and avoided looking Arden in the eye. They went to The Copper Bottom, a heritage cafe that served heart-warming soups and rolls covered in cracked wheat and Poacher's Pie with salad from the bar. Arden normally felt warmly enveloped by the ambience of cosy tradition. Today she was not in the mood for carbohydrate comfort and ordered kipper pâté with a bad grace.

'So. What are we to do? I suggest we demand that Mr Gordon hands it over and then get rid of it.'

'Ard! That would be vandalism. And may I remind you that it was left to Thalia? It's up to her what becomes of it.'

'I know that. But it's our responsibility, isn't it? Humph was our parent. Of course, Thalia, if you'd rather we stayed out of it—'

'No! I'm completely confused by all this. Besides, there's no one else I can talk to about it. I just want to give it back. What's the Maquis anyway? What did he mean by that?'

'They were just bands of guerrilla fighters in the war, my dear. Nothing to worry about. They're probably all dead by now.' Tim patted her arm. Arden was unconvinced by his reassuring tone. His trembling hand and starting eyes told another story.

Thalia looked strangely uncomforted. 'Supposing they aren't?

Supposing that man from Sotheby's lets them know about us?'

'Oh, blow the Maquis. They won't *know*.' Arden jabbed her fork into the checked tablecloth. 'You heard Mr Gordon: clients' affairs are *utterly* confidential. Look, Thalia, this idea of returning it is totally impractical. How would we find out where to take it? How would we explain where it had been for the last forty odd years without incriminating Humph? Think of the scandal if the papers got hold of the story. Think of Gavin. Is it fair to burden him with this sort of information when he has such a positive image of Humph? Think of the teasing he'd get at school.'

'Then we must return it anonymously.' Thalia looked to Tim for support. Arden groaned and covered her face in her hands. 'It's no good. I can't live with any other solution. It's the *right thing*. I know what, I'll ask my uncle. He'll know what to do.'

'Your uncle? Thalia, this must be kept to ourselves.'

'It's all right, he's a priest. Well, a monk. He won't tell anyone. Don't you think I'm right, Tim?'

'In principle, yes, I do. But Arden does have a point as to the practical difficulties—'

'A *point*! For God's sake, do we look like refugees from *Mission Impossible*?'

'I'm only thinking of Thalia's peace of mind, Ard. And morally there's no question but that we should return it.'

'*Morally?* Since *when* have you given a toss about *morals*, my *petit choux?*' He glowered at her. Arden was unbowed. What wimps they both were! They deserved each other. 'And it's all very well for you two to say what's *right*, but I know perfectly well who'd end up organizing it and doing the dirty work – me!'

'That's not fair, Ard. I'd – help.'

'You won't have to. I want nothing to do with it. If *you* want help, why don't you try Surprise, Surprise? Now if you'll excuse me, I've got a business to run. I'll see you later, Tim.'

In the circumstances it was hard to concentrate on *Suitables* solutions. Arden was exhausted and frozen after having to walk three miles from the town, although fuming within. As she trudged up the road towards the gatehouse she was distracted by the sight of a group of people, mostly with clipboards, standing outside looking intently at the towers and making notes. Jermigan was addressing them in the manner of a tour guide. On either side of him were the two men in suits she had seen on their frequent visits to the Hall. This had to be the official inspection of the district council planning committee.

Her first thought was to shove Jermigan aside and address the councillors herself. What better opportunity to register her objections? Then she remembered that until probate went through she and Tim were probably not the legal owners of the cottage and their opinions would therefore carry no weight. Even if they did it would mean applications in triplicate which would in due course be binned by the Department of the Environment. From the way Jermigan smiled and waved at her as she approached it was clear that he certainly thought so.

She would phone Laurence and Shara. They would know the legal position, she decided. That would mean another hour or so away from *Suitables*. Why was everything always up to her? Tim would no doubt use his hip as an excuse, and that was understandable, but even if he were fully fit it was always she who took the initiative and the burdens of leadership were assuming Sisyphean proportions. One essential difference between them was clear: she enjoyed a fight, while Tim did not. When there was nothing to fight about it was no matter. But if she could not carry him with her, perhaps he really would be better off with a comforting soul like Thalia.

Bos was asleep on the sofa. He seemed to need more sleep than a new-born baby. She looked fondly at his slumped body, the *Radio Times* open on his chest like a bib. He woke up, yawning.

'Hi, Mum. We got the day off.'

'And I think I know why. The powers that be are snooping round today. Jermigan wouldn't want them asking awkward questions of his moonlighting workers, now would he?'

'Oh, 'spose so. It'll be too cold to work outside when it's snowing and that anyway. Jermigan said I can help out on the trucks so's I don't have to come off the payroll. Maybe he'll even help me get an HGV licence.'

'That's nice of him. Why is he being so helpful? Do you think it's just because you're going out with Lottie?'

'Dunno. P'raps he fancies me. Mum, have you got a minute? I wanted a word about Lottie.'

'Darling, of course. Can I make some urgent phone calls first? Then I'll put my Dear Marge hat on, okay?'

'Great.'

Laurence and Shara were unobtainable. Their phone had been cut off. Arden was puzzled. She knew they had financial problems, but surely in such a case incoming calls would continue? Her sympathy for their plight was profound, matched only by her irritation that she would have to go round there personally and find out what was going on. More time away from *Suitables*. To make up for it she phoned a couple of her more lackadaisical ladies who were due for some major chivvying. If they fell by the wayside they would have to be replaced and her aim of making Group Co-ordinator by Easter would be threatened.

As expected, family crises were involved. Families! One lady was going through a difficult divorce. Arden was appalled that she could think of taking her eye off the ball at such a time, and besides, if her monthly sales points went down she would lose her chance to claim the complimentary ankle bracelet. Arden left her with this thought and moved on to another lady, an older person whose house had been partly demolished by a rogue lorry. This was indeed a bit of a facer and the lure of an ankle bracelet was unlikely to get her back on track. Arden was understanding, but pointed out that the more she got out of the house the better and urged her to sign up for the spring conference in Bournemouth so that she would have something really exciting to look forward to.

By the time she had finished motivating Arden was exhausted. It was all very well rallying the troups, but she had to keep her own presentations rolling too. Bookings for January were thin. Why had she not nobbled the manageress of The Copper Bottom? A perfect opportunity missed. It was all Thalia and Tim's fault, with their stupid plan for returning the statue. Tim had come back while she was on the phone and gone to lie down. Of course he was in pain, but the harsh truth was that afternoon naps would not butter any parsnips.

Bos was watching Ready, Steady, Cook! Arden was not in the mood to talk about Lottie, but she did offer. He said he would just watch the end of the programme so, grateful for the respite, she went to sit down with him. There was a knock on the door. It was Jermigan. Arden sagged against the lintel.

'I thought you had visitors.'

'They're gone. Can I step inside then? It's started snowing, case you 'adn't noticed.

'I had, actually. Come in.'

She did not offer him a seat. Bos smiled nervously at his boss.

'You recall me telling y' about Hempknott Hall and that?'

'Yes. What of it?'

'They's having one of them open days, special for Christmas. Said I'd ask you, didna? Well, now I am.'

Arden did not answer for a moment. 'Yes, but that was when ... Never mind. Excuse me for being a bit slow, but I rather thought we weren't – you know – communicating at the moment. Not through the normal channels, anyway.'

'Don't know what y're on about. You coming or not? Saturday week.'

'I'm usually busy on Saturdays.'

'Oh, go on, Mum,' said Bos. 'You know you're dying to. You love that sort of thing.'

Arse-licker, thought Arden. She could have crowned him. Obviously Jermigan was hoping to work her round under the influence of amateur wassailing and free mince pies. He did not stand a chance. On the other hand, it would be inadvisable to annoy him by an outright refusal. 'I'll think about it.'

'I'll take that as a yes. Regards to yer brother.' He gave her the odious wink.

Arden slammed the door and turned on Bos. 'What did you say that for? I could hardly give you an argument in front of him, could I?'

'Back off, Mum. I was only trying to be helpful. I thought you really wanted to go but didn't want to look too keen, sort of thing.'

'Well, if you know so much about female psychology I can't see that you need my advice about Lottie.'

'What are you so mad about? It's no big deal. What have I done?'

He looked wounded. Arden could see he was alarmed that she had gone for him. It was the first time, after all. She felt remorseful. 'You just said the wrong thing at the wrong time, darling. You're right, it's no big deal. But I can't go pussy-footing around you all the time, you know. If we're going to live together we've both got to feel free to be ourselves, haven't we?'

'Is that what you call accepting my good faith – pussy-footing?'

Arden felt absurdly reprimanded. That was the downside of taking delivery of an adult child: he came with an adult's point of view. 'No. It just means I can't go on treating you like a visitor. I'm not perfect, Bos. You musn't take it personally if I fly off the handle sometimes. I've got a lot on my mind.'

'Fair enough. I think I'll go out for a while.'

'I thought you wanted to talk about Lottie?'

'Another time. It's not urgent.'

This was her punishment then. Suspension of confidences. 'All right, darling. Love you. Honestly.'

'Yeah. Okay.'

He set off into the slushy swirls of ice, feeling that he might be some time. Yes, he had got the hump, but it was a righteous hump. Mums were a mixed blessing, it seemed. She had been all right up to now. Quite good, in fact. Not that he had given much thought to how she would be. But blowing up like that was well out of order. As though he were being blamed for stepping on a landmine. He hoped things were not falling apart. Perhaps his presence was proving a bit of a strain? He was beginning to feel her pain at having to share a room with Uncle Tim. It was pretty gross to be deprived of the comfort of familiar things. Bos missed his study bedroom at college. He missed his mates and Nathalie. He even missed his dad occasionally. On reflection, doing a runner was not the best idea he had ever had. The lights from the Hall beckoned. The pathetic truth was, there was nowhere else to go apart from slogging into town to the pub. At least Jermigan and that lot were a proper family, sort of. And Jermigan had taken more of an interest in him than sad Uncle Tim.

Miss Tree was in the kitchen preparing dinner. It was dead cosy in there, with the logs glowing in the massive fireplace and Miss Tree stirring a pot which gave off well decent food smells.

His mum did not cook proper food. Her idea of dinner was a grilled chicken breast and frozen peas. Still, it was better than when she went mad on her medieval gunk and forced them to eat parsnip, almond and cinnamon mousse followed by giblet custard pie. That even made him long for his dad's bulghur wheat casseroles. Miss Tree was pleased to see him.

'Hello, dear. I'm afraid Lottie's out. She stayed in Norwich to do some late-night shopping.'

'That's okay.' More than that, it was bliss. Except that now he had no excuse to linger. 'How's she getting home?'

'I'll have to pick her up later. Mr Jermigan's got a parish council meeting.'

'Ah-ha. Spreading his power base, eh?'

'I don't think you can assume that everyone on the parish council is empire-building, dear. Me, for instance.'

'Nah. Only kidding. Tell you what, I'll pick Lottie up if you like. Then you can go to the meeting as well.'

'Would you really? That's very thoughtful.' Miss Tree smiled, basking in the assumption that Bos could not wait to see Lottie. 'Sit down, dear. You can try my goulash first.'

Lottie was waiting outside Pizza Hut. She was not best pleased to see Bos. 'What's happened to Miss Tree?'

'Oh, you care, do you? You're getting soft.'

'Shut up. You know nothing about either of us. Miss Tree's all right. That's the only thing I agree with Jermigan about.'

'Very formal, you lot, aren't you? Why do you call her Miss Tree and not – I dunno – Auntie something? What is her first name?'

'Ivy, believe it or not. And I don't call her "Auntie" because—'

'—she's not your fucking auntie, I know. Ivy Tree. Are you sure? What were her parents thinking of?'

'You can talk.'

'Bosworth Fairbrother, my girl, is a moniker to be reckoned with. You don't find many blokes with names like Bosworth Fairbrother sleeping in doorways, I'll bet.'

'They'd keep pretty quiet about it. That is *so* stupid. Anyone can fall on hard times. How do you think you're going to hit the big-time with a degree in Welsh Women's Studies then?'

'Dunno. Don't matter what your degree's in, does it? I might become an entrepreneur like your Uncle Jermigan. Start me own business.'

'Not organizing gigs presumably.'

'Maybe. I learned a lot from that cock-up. Creative failure's a great incentive to success.'

'You're so eighties, Bos. How come? Just another kid who wants to be Richard Branson. That is *so* sad.'

'Shut up. I'm not stupid. What's wrong with making money? It's all very well for you, you'll get all Jermigan's dosh.'

'I don't want it. Anyway, you don't need much money to live, and I certainly wouldn't want to inherit Hideous Hall. There's this girl in my class, her sister's had two babies. She doesn't work, nor does her boyfriend, but they do all right. Everything in their house is nicked. It's brilliant. They've got a car and nice stuff for the kids and they go out to the pub every week. You've just got to know the system.'

'Eh? That system's on its last legs, mate. Don't you read the papers? New Labour, new workhouses. I thought you were supposed to be intelligent.'

'How would you know? How can someone your age be so reactionary? God, you've been brainwashed. They couldn't let people starve, could they? The EU would have them by the goolies. And they can't create jobs because that would rig the market. They can crack the whip as much as they like to impress the shires, there's always going to be benefits. You're going to work your whole life – for what? What's the point?'

Bos had to think. He knew there was something wrong with Lottie's argument but he needed a few hours alone to work it out. 'The point is, if you don't work, you don't live. That is going to be the motto of the twenty-first century. Why are you working for your GCSEs if you think like that? You're full of crap, Lottie.'

'I'm not working, if you must know. I've seen the light. You don't need GCSEs to get a job. Darren gets a hundred and eighty pounds a week.'

'Wow. Well, I can understand not wanting to work your whole life for that. You're showing your age, Lottie. You have no idea, do you? You couldn't live on twice that, not the way you're used to.'

'Then I'll have to get *unused* to it, won't I? It's not as if I had any choice in the way I live.'

'Lottie, I don't like the sound of this. Your shagging Darren is bad enough. You aren't thinking of moving in with him, are you? Right under Jermigan's nose!'

'Of course not. And don't talk like that about Darren. You've no idea what he's really like. He's the only person who accepts me the way I am.'

'Yeah. The boss's daughter.'

'Will you shut it! He doesn't care about that. I've told you, I don't want Jermigan's fucking money and neither does Darren.'

'What are you planning, you stupid cow? What are you up to?'

'Nothing.'

'You'd better not be.'

'Or *what?* You are ridiculous. Don't talk to me like you've got some influence, like you were my grandfather or something. It's nothing to do with you.'

'I'm only supposed to be your boyfriend, that's what. How's it going to make me look if you run off with Darren?'

'Who said I was? It's time that charade was called off anyhow. I'll tell them we had a row when I get home. That honest enough for you?'

'It's a start. But if you don't tell me what's going on, I'll have to find out from Darren.'

'You *dare*. If you so much as go near him, I'll – I'll torch your fucking house.'

'Yeah. Sure.

Lottie put the radio on with a furious gesture and turned it up so loud further conversation was impossible. Bos could not stand indie music, but it suited him not to talk. Lottie was a ticking bomb. It would take all his powers of concentration to work out what should be done about her.

The sleet battered at the bedroom window most of the night. Normally Arden loved to drift off to sleep to the sound of the elements in full throttle. It was sexy, and cosy too. This time they failed to soothe. Bos had come home in a foul mood and refused to talk. It was unlike him to hold grudges. She had not thought he would be so upset by their spat. Being a man, he would probably not know how to make it up so it would be up to her to proffer the olive branch. Something else to be done. There were already more lists in the house than betting slips at the Derby. Tim's hip was playing up. Aggravated by the weather, he said. He got up several times in the night, trying to be quiet, but he managed to trip over something in the dark and screamed in agony. Arden added to the list by her bed a note to call the hospital and find out how the waiting list was progressing.

Then there was Laurence and Shara to worry about. It was not exactly hurtful that they had not told her they were in such deep financial trouble, if that was what the problem was. They did not know each other well enough, and nor would they if the couple's reluctance to come to Sloping continued. They had invited Tim and Arden to a party, as a result of which Arden had made four bookings for *Suitables* presentations, and as she and Tim were still in their debt for taking them in after the quiz night the weight of obligation was already lopsided. It was not Arden's fault but it did make her feel she should at least find out what had happened to them. She had a full programme the following day but she decided to get up extra early and call on them before setting out on her rounds.

Contrary to the dictum about red skies at morning – it had actually been a nacreous flamingo pink – the weather had lifted and the sun filtered through a duvet of cloud balls. Waking up to see the towers of Sloping against that pink sky, driving through the gatehouse into the frosted landscape – Psalter Winter, as Arden thought of it – revitalized her allegiance to Sloping. Her head was full of snow scenes of well-wrapped peasants, and sheep, and wattle fences, and fesses, and snow-capped beehives ... and, in a cut-away hovel in the background, figures who held their feet out to the fire, frozen in time, with their heads to one side and an expression of profound puzzlement on their faces. It was unusual to find a picture of a medieval person who did not look worried. Such images revived envy for the simplicity of their lives – one room, one pot and plenty of wood for the fire, and an ennobling battle with nature for survival. Of course, she and Tim would both have died of childhood illnesses but at least while they were alive they would never have seen a pile-up on the M4 or the hellish view from the Dartford toll bridge. It was sad that medieval people never knew how lucky they were.

There was no one at home at Laurence and Shara's cottage. It was only twenty to nine and Arden was disappointed not to have caught them before they went to work. Their workshops were in a rural enterprise cluster about a mile away. Just to make sure they were not in she went round the back and looked through the kitchen window. The room was empty of clutter. There was only a pile of papers by the phone. She went to the front and looked into the living room. Ditto. Gone were the ethnic wall hangings and posters of French art exhibitions, the Moroccan floor cushions and banana plants. Arden was shocked, angry and then very worried. From next door she could hear the high-pitched yells of children late for school. A young woman pulled the door open and hurried out towards her car.

'Excuse me!' The woman stopped short and looked round. 'Do you know if Laurence and Shara have moved? I'm sorry to bother you but I'm rather concerned. They didn't tell me they were going.'

The young woman snorted. 'Me neither. They left a couple of days ago.'

'Do you know why?'

'No. But I can guess. They'd had enough. See over there.' She nodded her head towards the parking lot. 'Their car was burnt out. It's still warm.'

Arden squinted against the sun. She could see the blackened wreck of a station wagon. 'I don't understand. How do you know it wasn't an accident? Who would do such a thing anyway?'

'Don't ask me. I'd rather not know.' Two young boys ran out of the house and got into the car. 'Sorry, I'm off now, I am an' all. Back to Lowestoft. Gives me the creeps, things like that.'

'And you've no idea where they've gone?'

'Not the foggiest. Sorry.'

She drove off. Arden walked over to the wreck. It still smelled of burnt rubber and vinyl. Her anger had subsided into cold fury. Jermigan was the only person who could have had a motive for this. Getting rid of Laurence and Shara, *pour encourager les autres*. She scoffed at the notion that the ploy would even work.

Or would it? Laurence had been the driving force behind the

protest group, but there would surely be others? It would depend on just how passionate they were. She could imagine that at first they would be hotly indignant and determined not to be put off. Then they would talk to their partners, who would point out that, yes, it was outrageous that Jermigan should get away with it, but the pressure group was very time-consuming, wasn't it, and after all it was not as if the scheme actually affected them personally. One by one they would drift away. Voluntarily, of course. Not having been remotely intimidated. Intimidation was so easy, the amazing thing was that more people did not try it. She even felt a warped respect for Jermigan's nerve. And her own, as it seemed she was the only person who was prepared to stand up to him. But then his plans did affect her personally.

It was a lonely mission. And frightening. But the fear was delicious. Not for her to be counted among the lily-livered hordes. With amazement Arden remembered the years she had wasted on the vicarious thrills to be had from reading in the estate agent's lavatory. She could not wait for Yuletide at Hempknott.

11

Thanks to a concentrated blitz of advertising in the Great Yarmouth press, Tim's clientele in the area had increased to the point where, should he need an excuse to visit it, he was never short of one. His ability to simulate fascination, on tap, in anything from the heating bills of boarding kennels to the capital investment of Dyno-rod operatives eased his path. Arden was fond of saying that he would have been an invaluable royal personage, at his best hosting luncheons for those in all walks of life. Like many things that Arden said there was an implied criticism here which niggled but was not worth challenging. That was one thing about Thalia, she was uncomplicated. There was no side to her – unlike the Alpine range of Arden's personality. It would naturally be discourteous not to see Thalia while he was in the environs of Great Yarmouth. Fortunately there was a congenial pub near her place of work and Thalia was so distressed about the Oriflamme problem that she was more than willing to meet Tim at lunchtime or after work to discuss it. Less fortunately, she was under the impression that he had sufficient influence on Arden to persuade her that the statue must be returned.

'No, my dear, I'm afraid our only hope is to go behind her back.' They were settled at a table in the bay window before matching oval platters of scampi and salad – limp lettuce and raw onion rings like deck quoits that they both shifted on to their side plates. 'You have to understand that there is a reckless streak in her that's not amenable to argument. She made a very foolish marriage, you know, to someone who played on her susceptibility to fantasy. She got used to not having electricity but when Garth joined the Third Order of the Knights of St

Thurketyl and took a vow of celibacy it was the last straw. There's a very practical side to my sister as well. The two are always in conflict, I'm afraid.'

'Humph told me about that. So you decided to set up home together?' Thalia coloured slightly and kept her eyes down. Tim found it touching that the most oblique allusion to somebody else's sex life could produce such pretty confusion in this day and age – forgetting that Thalia knew nothing about his sex life.

'Yes. Well. It seemed like a sensible solution. I'd had a failed marriage myself, you see, which involved certain – well – financial losses. We decided to pool our resources, as it were.'

Thalia pursed her lips. 'I don't mean to pry, Tim, but did you ever discuss what would happen if either of you wanted to marry again? You must have been quite young to settle down like an old married couple.'

'Ha – yes.' He took a soothing swig of the house white. 'It just hasn't happened, that's all. Would you like my tartare sauce? I'm afraid it doesn't agree with me.'

'Thank you.'

'Now, to get back to the statue business, strictly speaking you don't need Arden's co-operation. It was left to you. I'm sure that's right.'

'I would like it, though. To be honest, I feel quite out of my depth in this business. The Humph I knew couldn't have done such a thing. He wouldn't have wanted to cause me all this worry.'

'Then my guess is he didn't realize its significance.'

'But Mr Gordon said it was in the papers at the time.'

'Perhaps my father didn't read them. He was away at sea most of the time.'

'Did you miss him lots?'

'Oh, not really. Arden and I were – very good companions.'

'I admire her. She's so plucky, isn't she? And she has got a point about bringing "shame" on the family and all that. Oh, dear.'

'Is something the matter? You've gone a bit pale.'

'It's nothing. I have to talk to Arden. I really do. Don't you think we could return it anonymously? I haven't been able to sleep since I found out.'

'Nor I. Poor Arden, I'm afraid I keep her awake.'

'How's that?'

'Well – we, ah, have to share a room at the moment. Since Bos has been with us. It's a bit awkward.' Tim marvelled at his own boldness. But putting an innocent gloss on the arrangement created a comfortable obfuscation in his own mind also. Besides, it was better that Thalia was primed in case she found out.

'It must be.' She put down her knife and fork and frowned at the plate.

Tim was afraid his bluff had misfired. 'Are you shocked, my dear?'

She looked up and smiled. Her clear blue eyes were as trusting as a child's in Santa's grotto. Tim's stomach lurched gently, like seaweed on the swell of the tide. 'Why should I be?'

'Oh – well – you know.' He forced a chortle. 'These things might be open to misinterpretation. Ha, ha.'

Thalia blushed. 'That's ridiculous. Nobody would think that unless it was on the television all the time. If writers can't think of anything else to make a story exciting than having – you know – brothers and sisters doing it, then they should get a proper job.'

'Quite. Quite.' Tim certainly did not want to see the subject aired on television, he had enough of it at home. 'Absolutely. However, I'm sure I can count on your discretion? In general, I mean. I don't like talking about Arden behind her back, you know. It makes me feel very disloyal.'

'I understand. And don't worry, I'll observe the secrecy of the confessional.'

'Thank you.' Tim fanned himself with the menu card. He needed a moment to settle his agitated heartbeat. Knowing where one stood with Thalia had its drawbacks. He had never come across an unashamedly Good Woman before. It was proving to be something of a minefield. 'Talking of confessionals and so forth, do you know why Humph – Dad – converted to the True Faith, as I believe you call it?'

'He didn't talk about it much. For spiritual reasons, I suppose. I think Mum had a lot to do with it, though. She was very pious. Very old-fashioned. She honestly thought Humph would go to hell if he didn't convert.'

'A saintly role model, then?'

'Saintly? Not in the least. She was a bad-tempered old biddy,
I always thought. Sorry. I shouldn't talk like that about her. We
didn't get on.'

'I'm glad you feel you can be so honest with me, my dear.'
In fact the glimpse of this bitchy streak in Thalia had made
Tim's day. It made her more accessible somehow. He had been
beginning to wonder if she even had bodily functions.

'Why do you call me "my dear", Tim? It's rather condescending. You can't be that much older than me.'

'What? Oh. Sorry, my – Just a habit.' Perhaps it was not just
a streak, more of a full-blown mural.

'I've offended you.'

'No, no. Not at all.'

'Yes, I have. It's just that Humph used to call me that. So it
makes me a bit sad.'

'Oh, I see. Funny little thing to be in the genes, isn't it? I didn't
think I had anything in common with Dad except a craving for
gherkins.'

Thalia smiled wanly, and Tim turned the conversation to
offshore trusts.

The Co-op was in a frenzy. With the prospect of the shops being
closed for two days homemakers were stocking up as if for a
nuclear holocaust. Arden was in a hurry and cursed the crowds
and the towering columns of seasonal biscuit tins that made
progress round the aisles such an obstacle course. It seemed that
her entire acquaintance was in the shop too, each requiring a
festive chat. Among them was Miss Tree. Arden could not but
admire her chic co-ordinated appearance – forest green suit with
velvet revers, matching tights and a silk foulard. All without the
aid of *Suitables*. But Miss Tree's expression was troubled as she
stood before the nibbles selection and it did not lift when Arden
greeted her with assumed gaiety. Miss Tree's own absence of
artifice as usual made Arden feel like a gallumphing twat.

'I'd give the Marmite Cheddaries a wide berth, Miss Tree. They
taste like Dettol.'

'Oh, I won't be eating them. Mr Jermigan's having his staff
party tonight. It's catered, of course, but we need some nuts and

bolts. It was all Twiglets and olives in my day. Life was simpler then. Look at that – curry-flavoured mini-chips. Really!'

'Cheese balls are always popular.'

'Are they? Thank you. Anything else?'

'Pringles. Try the Cheese 'n' onion. Ambrosia, I assure you. And maybe some prawn Skips. I'm told they taste like communion wafers.'

'Jolly good. Thank you.' She piled ten packets of each into her trolley and they ambled off towards tinned vegetables. 'Well, thank goodness I ran into you. I would have been here all day.'

'You do look a bit fraught, Miss Tree. Is it the party, or the prospect of Christmas cooking? I suppose Mr Jermigan likes the boat pushed out at Yuletide. Boars' heads and all that.'

'It's not as bad as that. We settle for goose and flummeries. No, it's not the cooking that bothers me, although it is getting a bit much.' She sighed. 'We'll be on our own this year, and Lottie's being so – moody. There'll be a distinct shortfall in good cheer, I'm afraid. And Mr Jermigan sets such store by these things. He wants everything to be ideal – for Lottie, really. But I don't know. She always withholds herself. I'm afraid it's going to be rather painful.'

Arden could feel the harrowing pitifulness of the scene as Jermigan and Miss Tree tried in vain to create a riot of family fun for their petulant charge. She could picture them in paper hats, bravely donned as a mute gesture of love, locked in bonds of misery across the ironic remains of a feast prepared in doomed hope. She could almost feel sorry for Jermigan. 'Couldn't you invite some relatives? There's safety in numbers at Christmas, I always think. If things are likely to be sticky.'

'I'm afraid Mr Jermigan has quarrelled with most of his family. Or they with him, I should say. You'd be surprised how insatiable some poor relations can be. To tell you the truth, I had hoped to invite you and yours, what with Lottie and Bos going out together. But now—'

'Now what? You mean, they aren't?'

'So Lottie tells me. Didn't you know?'

'No. But he has been rather grumpy lately. And it's not like him. That could explain it.'

'Bos is such a charming young man. You're so lucky.'

'I know. But don't worry, Lottie will come round. Perhaps you've both indulged her rather, because of her mother dying like that, but it's perfectly understandable. Example's the great thing with child-rearing, isn't it? You've given her so much love and attention, I'm sure it will work in the end.' On the other hand, Bos had grown up largely without the benefit of Arden's attention, and had turned into one of the nicest people she knew. But there was no place for scientific method in moral support.

'I'm not so concerned for myself. Lottie and I get on quite well in a non-communicative sort of way. It's Mr Jermigan who bears the brunt of it. He tries so hard with her and she's so ungrateful.' Miss Tree lowered her voice. 'Lottie has been playing truant from school.'

'Oh, dear. Does he regard it as a badge of shame?'

'Not so much that. He just doesn't know how to deal with it. He's not accustomed to failure, I'm afraid.'

'No. He can't burn Lottie out, can he?'

'What do you mean, dear?'

Time for a hasty exit. 'Nothing. Do excuse me, I've forgotten the custard.'

Brother Sebastian's thoughts were less than avuncular as he prepared for his niece's visit. He found her worshipful respect embarrassing. She made him feel like a piece of the True Cross. His previous career as a Lada dealer had not prepared him for life on a pedestal. The Abbot, however, seemed to think it had prepared him to take charge of the monastery's five-year development plan. The Conversion of England was still some way off and if the community was to keep going in the meantime its finances were in need of radical realignment.

It was a challenge. The market was already saturated with easy-listening plain chant – joints for the soul, as the envious Abbot scoffed. Foulbrood had wiped out the honey crop and the application for charitable status for Holidays in Retreat was not going well. Brother Sebastian's suggestion for Murder at the Monastery weekend breaks had gone down like a dose of cascara. He had little hope that Thalia's visit would provide either inspiration or welcome distraction, and prayed for charitable thoughts as his bleeper went off and he made his way to the visitors' lounge.

It was quite a relief to find that she looked, if not sore afraid, certainly troubled. Her expression held the prospect of a serious conversation rather than the usual monologue on the doings of Gavin since they'd last met and the touching, though tedious, report on her father's mood swings. He was dying for a fag, and suggested they walk in the grounds.

'But it's raining, Uncle.'

'Just a drizzle, pet. Good for the complexion.' He felt a twinge of meanness. Thalia spent her life on her feet and could probably do with a sit-down. Still, it would be easier for her to confide in him if they were on the move.

The monastery was not an ancient foundation but had been an unstately home of the Lutyens era. Its grounds had mutated to the conventual norm of laurels and lawns and gravel paths leading nowhere, with a former rose garden that they could not afford to keep up. The empty beds were piled with manure, donated by a devout riding school proprietor with a storage problem, and wafts of noxious steam drifted into the drizzle, creating the melancholy ambience of a battlefield.

'It's the feast of St Dominic of Silos today, isn't it, Uncle?'

'So it is.' Sweet. She had been doing her homework, like Cilla Black on Blind Date, one of his favourite shows. He did not actually have a clue whose feast day it was. 'What's troubling you, pet? You're not yourself, now are you?'

Thalia sighed on a smile, crediting him with supernatural insights into the human soul. 'You are amazing, Uncle.'

'So I am. Come on now, spit it out.'

If he had been obliged to hazard a guess as to the nature of Thalia's troubles, they would have been of the order of Gavin coming out as gay, or indeed Thalia herself. Or perhaps her father had completely lost his marbles and was trying to get into her knickers. Something predictable and everyday, well within the scope of the problem page at any rate. His role as the senior male in the family *with* all his marbles accentuated the protective distance he felt between them, as did the privileged insight he had of the goings-on within the family – knowledge of which she had to be spared.

It was not that long ago when it was his sister Monica, Thalia's mother, who had regularly cornered him for therapeutic chats. He had not been a monk then, although he would have become one much earlier if he had not known how much pleasure it would give her. His sister was not the sort of person who had wanted advice, just constant endorsement. And, of course, the chance to unburden herself of guilt. Not about her chaste affair with Humphrey Mason, but because she could not bring herself to sleep with him.

Wilf, as Brother Sebastian then was, could not see the problem. Humph was not even pressing her to sleep with him. But his sister felt guilty about it anyway. Was it unreasonable, she had worried, to expect Humph not to consummate their love, which went back to primary school at least? Wilf thought it was as reasonable as expecting a terrier to help a rabbit across the road, but if Humph had been prepared to accept those terms that was his problem and no reason for Monica to get her spiritual knickers in a twist. He had advised her to end the relationship if it gave her so much grief but she could never bring herself to renounce the comfort of Humph's inexplicable devotion. He wondered if her state of perpetual torment on the subject had not contributed to her relatively early death. It had certainly solved the problem.

When Thalia had taken up with Humph, while her mother dwindled towards her end, Brother Sebastian, as he was by then, had been uneasy. He could understand the attraction from Humph's point of view – a sentimental concern for the child of his beloved was a natural thing in the circumstances. Like many natural things, however, it was a potential disaster area, as Thalia was unaware of Humph's motive. As their friendship developed Brother Sebastian's unease had grown to the point where his conscience dictated that he have a word with Humph, more as an uncle than a moral policeman. Humph had been indignant, tearful, and had demanded to know what possible harm it could do to befriend Thalia, who had such a hard life? Brother Sebastian had ended up feeling like an evil-minded voyeur, and when Humph himself died the following day could not rest until he had assured himself it was not suicide. Even so it had given him a nasty turn, somewhat assuaged by the thought that Humph and Monica were united at last. Not exactly the Cathy and Heathcliff *de nos jours*, but an awesome example of the irrational power of love.

The provisions of Humph's will, with which Thalia began her tale, revived his alarm, as did the fact of her contact with Arden and Tim. It seemed perverse that the connection should be passed on to the next generation, and Thalia's encomiums to Tim in particular were worrying. Supposing she fell in love with him? Her own husband was still alive, and she would never countenance divorce, so history would repeat itself like cucumber. He dragged hard on his cigarette, tossed it into the compost and lit another. Impatience with the endless cavortings of the human heart was one of the things that had driven him into the monastery and he prayed for the strength not to advise Thalia to get a dog, a life, anything – but to leave him out of it.

His attention was drifting when she came to the matter of the statue of St Louis and the sizeable smidgeon of the Oriflamme. They had left the former rose garden and were approaching the empty swimming pool, which was inadequately covered with a torn tarpaulin that sagged under puddles and soggy leaves. He stopped and asked her to repeat that section. 'Are you sure, Thalia? That's a very unusual thing, you know.' He had to haul in his wandering mind like a kite. Even so, the part of his brain that usually handled such bizarre scenarios was reluctant to become activated.

'Mr Gordon, the solicitor, had it checked out at Sotheby's. The thing is, it's not just any old statue of St Louis. It's a particular one. The awful thing is, Uncle, it's – it's stolen. It was stolen in the fifties, from a house in Normandy. In France,' she added, hoping this *aide memoire* would shift his expression of total incomprehension.

'What? So it is.'

'There's worse, Uncle. Mr Gordon reckons Humph stole it himself. When he was working the ferries. He was beaten up.'

'Good Lord!'

'By the Maquis.'

'Good grief!'

'I don't believe it. I don't *want* to believe it. But that's beside the point. It's my feeling it has to be returned. Apart from the fact that it's stolen, it's a holy relic, isn't it? It's a nightmare, Uncle. I'm in illegal possession of a holy relic!'

'Well now, that's debatable.'

'What is?'

'The "holy" thing. It's not like, say, the metatarsal of Simeon the Stylite, for example. It's more of a national treasure, sort of thing, I would think.'

'How do you mean?'

'Well – it's a bit like if some Frenchman stole King Harold's eye with the arrow still in it. Provocative, yes. That would certainly rouse passion in some quarters.'

'Particularly the owners.'

'Undoubtedly. I think I'd better sit down, pet. Over here.' He led her to the ruined pergola overlooking the swimming pool and they sat at either end of the rusty bench. Thalia was concerned. He was clearly in shock and deeply preoccupied. Of course it was gratifying that he regarded her predicament as seriously as she herself did. She would have been less pleased if she had known that he was fighting visions of Oriflamme teashops, T-shirts, mugs and bumper stickers.

'You do think it should be returned, don't you, Uncle? Because Arden thinks it's better to keep quiet about it. If we were found out it would be awful for the family. What do you think?'

'Well, you're both right.'

'Oh, Uncle, that's not very helpful. Surely you think it should be returned?

'So I do. In principle. The logistics would be tricky, though. Arden's right there.'

'Uncle, you go on holiday to France, don't you?'

'What? No, no, I can't get involved in that sort of caper, pet. I've the reputation of the community to consider here.'

'Of course. Sorry. It was just a thought. Oh, I wish I could dump it at the bottom of a lake. I couldn't, could I?'

'If you've got nightmares now, pet, imagine what it would be like if you'd to imagine the spirit of St Louis rising up out of the mire hell-bent on revenge.'

'True enough.'

'No, no, you're right. It must be returned. I'll pray about it. If anything comes up I'll let you know right away. Now, they'll be serving tea any minute. Shall we go?' He stood up.

'Before we do, there is just one other thing that's bothering me, Uncle.'

'Ah. Fire away.' He sat down again and lit another fag. Given the order of business he anticipated an item of lesser rather than greater magnitude.

'This is a more personal matter.'

'Well, you know you can tell me anything, pet. It will go no further.' So, perhaps Gavin was gay after all. He swiftly rehearsed the peculiarly unhelpful message about hating the sin but loving the sinner. At least Thalia was unlikely to take him to task about homosexual popes and priestly child abusers.

'I know. It's such a luxury having you in the family, Uncle.'

'That's kind of you, pet. Some people might prefer Bill Gates or someone of that sort.'

'Not me. This is a real moral dilemma. I don't think Bill Gates would be much help. You know Arden and Tim, Humph's children?'

'Yes, of course. We've just been talking about them.'

'Oh, dear. This is so difficult. You see, at Mum's funeral Humph got terribly drunk. He was so upset about it.' She sighed and waggled the finger ends of her gloves, reluctant to go on.

'Yes, I remember. What is it? My lord, he didn't make a pass at you, did he?'

'*No!* Honestly, Uncle, that's not a very nice thing to say.'

'Sorry, sorry. In this job you hear such terrible things, you know.' He would have to be careful or Thalia would be converting to the Bahais in disgust.

'He did start talking, though. He didn't know what he was saying. Going on about everything he held dear being lost and all that. I didn't understand him really. I tried to say, of course it wasn't, he had his wife and children. As one does.'

'Indeed.'

'And then he said some not very nice things about Arden and – and that Tim wasn't his son anyway.'

'What? Good lord. What a shocking thing. And does Tim not know about it?'

'No, he doesn't. He's such a nice man, Uncle. I'm sure it would upset him terribly if he found out, but – I'm wondering if he has the right to know.'

'I see. Did Humph say who the father was then?'

'Unfortunately not. He was pretty incoherent anyway. And when he sobered up he never mentioned it again. He probably didn't realise he'd told me. I rather thought I wasn't supposed to know.'

'So why do you think Tim should be told, pet? It would leave him not knowing who his father was. That would be cruel.'

'Yes. And it would disinherit him as well, I suppose.'

'Not necessarily. Not if he'd been brought up thinking Humph was his father and been named in the will.'

'Really? That's good. The thing is, Uncle – this is the embarrassing bit – you know he lives with Arden?'

'I didn't.'

'Well, he does. They're both divorced. What made me think about things is, he happened to mention that he and Arden have to share a bedroom at the moment.' The very word brought a blush to her cheek. 'While Arden's son is living with them. The point is, wouldn't it be awful if they were innocently sharing a room like that thinking they were brother and sister when actually they were no relation at all? Wouldn't you want to know that you were – well – at risk? I mean, living with someone who wasn't your sister. Technically a stranger. I would.'

Brother Sebastian stared at her. He suddenly realized that Thalia was living in a parallel universe. How could he put it to her that most people would be relieved to know that they were not sharing a bedroom with their sister? 'Thalia, pet, if they think they're brother and sister then presumably they aren't "at risk" as you put it anyway. Or is it that you think they're already having a sexual relationship?'

'*Of course not!* It never crossed my mind.'

'If that were the case, I could see that it would make sense to inform them.'

'No, Uncle, it's not that. It's just that they're co-habiting without realizing it. Isn't that bad?'

'Look, pet, we're not their moral guardians, you know. And I honestly don't see what good would come of upsetting that particular apple cart.'

'Don't you? I'm a bit surprised at that, Uncle. I thought you might take a stronger moral line.'

'I'm sorry to disappoint you. If they were even Catholics now, I might take a different view. Well, maybe. We musn't be judgmental, you know. It's not everyone who has your delicate conscience. And we've all done things we could be sorry for. Even you, I daresay.'

'Yes, I certainly have. And I'm not being judgmental, Uncle. It's just that if it were me I'd want to know. Besides, if they're so fond of one another, they'd be free to marry, wouldn't they? Isn't that a good reason for telling them?'

Brother Sebastian exhaled powerfully. He had a strong intuition that a couple who had been living innocently as siblings would be unlikely to jump at the chance to leap into bed. On the other hand, marriage to an adopted sibling was not unknown. That was the only argument likely to sway him in favour of revelation. On reflection it might be a relief to the couple, in more senses than one, if they were able to marry. And in general he was against deception as it was never of more than short-term benefit. Poor Thalia had been put into the position of unwillingly being obliged to maintain one if she did not reveal what she knew. What with that and inheriting the sizeable smidgeon of the Oriflamme, he was surprised that she had not had a nervous breakdown. Remembering the tortuous confidences of her mother, he guessed that Thalia's psyche was too delicate a vessel for such weighty contents.

'It would be a terrible responsibility for you, pet, if things fell apart between them as a result of this information.'

'It's a terrible responsibility knowing and not telling.'

'So it is. You must do what you think is right. No one can be blamed for that.'

'Thank you, Uncle. That's what I hoped you'd say.'

12

From the way Tim fussed, anyone would think Arden was going undercover to flush out a serial killer rather than on a day trip to a living heritage experience. She dressed with *Suitables* care in layers of flowing co-ordinated Bilberry garments, and a dramatic swirl of a hat with integrated scarf pennants ideal for throwing over the shoulder and knocking someone's eye out. Slender black handmade boots, now ten years old but conserved like antiques, completed the protective clothing. Arden knew she was going into battle and that it was not only the assertive flamboyance of her dress that would give her strength in the struggle with Jermigan, but the fact that she was prepared to stand out like the Lighthouse of Alexandria in a sea of anoraks and scruffy jeans. Jermigan would not know that he was influenced by such messages but Arden had no doubt that he was as susceptible as the next man.

One of the joys of the *Suitables* calling, and the aspect that had overcome her own scepticism, was seeing the confidence which radiated from so many newly co-ordinated converts, women who had had no perceptible image at all up to that point. She always encouraged them to add a *gamine* wash-'n'-go hairstyle that said, 'This is me!' as the training manual put it, to women who had been wondering who they were. No more hiding behind flopsy hair and anodyne tracksuits. It worked so well with some women that they had consequently divorced their husbands. Mrs Brady was now an inspiration to her customers as well. Arden had met her in Norwich – radiant in a Racing Green car coat and matching leggings, and with a new partner already.

'At least take a pepper spray,' Tim urged. He brushed non-existent fluff from her Bilberry shoulders.

Arden laughed. 'Don't be silly. He doesn't rape women, just places. There'll be crowds of people there anyhow.'

'You're going in his car, though. He could take you anywhere. There are so many remote spots round here, he's spoilt for choice.'

'It's very sweet and protective of you, darling, but I really don't think Jermigan is interested in anything but my bricks and mortar. Anyway, why would he bother with K2 when there are so many handy hummocks around?'

'Are there?'

'So I gather. Don't worry. Everyone will know I've gone with him.'

'I'm not really worried that he'll rape you, Ard. But he can get violent when he's in a mood and you can be – you know – provocative.'

'*Honest*, Tim, that's all. If he finds it provocative that's his problem. Besides, he's trying to soften me up, isn't he? That's the whole object of the exercise, so he'll be trying very hard not to put me in hospital, I should think.'

'You've got your mobile phone, just in case?'

'*Yes*. Look, I won't wait for him to come and pick me up. I'll walk over there. See you later. And don't forget to do the tax returns. It would be so ironic if you did everyone's except ours. I still don't understand why you shouldn't claim the married man's allowance. It's so unfair.'

They met halfway, hard by the tower of rubble. Jermigan had trimmed his beard and looked incongruously natty in a new sheepskin jacket and Tyrolean hat. He did not flinch as the booted Bilberry vision approached.

'You look fine, gal.'

'Please, Mr Jermigan, spare me the compliments. This is a formal occasion as far as I'm concerned.'

'Don't see that. I just thought as you'd enjoy the outing.'

'I daresay I shall. But I'm well aware of your motives so don't let's waste time on pointless pleasantries.'

He shrugged. 'Fall in be'ind then, gal.' He strode back towards the Frontera which was parked outside the Hall. Miss Tree came to the front door and he went to speak to her, brushing aside whatever concern she had with an impatient gesture. When he joined Arden in the vehicle she said she hoped the jaunt was not taking him away from some critical business problem.

'Nah. It's only the Grand Duchess Lottie up to 'er tricks. She didn't come 'ome last night, see. Miss Tree worries, like, but I told 'er Lottie'd be with 'er friends in the city right enough. She done it before. You knows how thoughtless young folk is when they's enjoying themselves.'

'Still, I'd be worried too. Why don't you ground her when she does that?'

'Ground 'er? You don't know my Lottie. She'd shin down a drainpipe and away.'

'Huh. Some use having a castle and not being able to lock up one small maiden in it.'

He found this idea hilarious.

'Seriously, though, speaking as a mother, I don't think it's always a good idea to give teenagers too much freedom. They think that's what they want, but they don't really. It makes them insecure. What they really want is to make their parents look like monsters and if you're too nice to them they can't.'

'Mebbe. But as Lottie would be the first to tell you, I ain't her parent, is I?'

'Of course you are. She just uses that technicality as an excuse.'

Arden could see that the subject caused him real pain. She thought about Laurence and Shara's burnt-out car to stop herself from becoming too sympathetic.

Yuletide fun had been the last thing on Arden's mind in recent weeks. It usually was, even without the distraction of the Oriflamme, Jermigan's harassment and the pre-Christmas rush to provide *Suitables* clients with versatile garments for that unexpected invitation. The visit to Hempknott might at least fan the dormant embers of seasonal excitement. She and Tim had always spent a quiet, sophisticated Christmas: braised pheasant and celeriac puree, medieval carols and a bracing walk by the river, before an evening spent in front of the fire playing the mint chocolate edition of Pictogram. No tree or presents. There was nothing to celebrate with no children in the house.

Bos always stayed at home with his father, who favoured the winter solstice interpretation of the festivities. Arden had recently learned, to her horror, that these involved a barrel of homemade ale and group sex under a magic oak at dawn while Bos shivered in the car with a thermos of nettle tea and an environmentally correct stocking filled with things like painted pebbles and bead necklace kits. She was particularly outraged by the group sex. How could her ex square that with a vow of celibacy? It was a further tribute to Bos's innate niceness that he had survived such corrupting hogwash unscathed. This Christmas he would be with them, of course, which called for a modest flurry of traditional touches. Arden had offered to release him to go to his father, but Bos did not think it would be right to desert them at this time after he had descended on them for his own convenience. What a contrast he was to the wretched Lottie.

Yuletide at Hempknott had featured in the November issue of *Country Matters* magazine, and boasted of attracting visitors from as far away as Birmingham and Basingstoke, all hoping to have their souls stamped with a little *joie de* Merrie England *vivre*. Arden felt her own soul contract with apprehension as they joined the queue of cars crawling through the stately gates. To speed things up medieval jesters had been dispatched along the queue to collect the entrance fees. She shuddered as a young man with bells on his headdress approached the car.

'*Waes hael*, your worships! I commend me to your worships and wish you good tidings of the season and right welcome to Hempknott. And here's a nosegay for your lady.'

'Oh, my *God*,' muttered Arden. She had reckoned without the humiliations of the day being added to by the assumption that she was Jermigan's moll.

'How much, lad?'

'Ten sovereigns apiece, an' it please your worship. Would your worship and your good lady be interested in trying their luck at the Shove-Groat competition? One sovereign a go. Proceeds to the needy of this parish and a firkin of malmsey to the winner.'

'You fancy a firkin o' malmsey, gal?'

'*No*. Thank you. I'd as soon have a firkin of dropsy.'

'We'll just have the entry tickets.'

'As your worship pleases. Here they be. Would your worships be so kind as to take direction from the Master of Parking yonder.'

The jester moved on to the next car.

'What's he directing traffic with – a pig's bladder? Is it going to be like this all day? I don't know if I can stand it.'

Jermigan was struggling with irritation, whether at the incompetence of the traffic management or Arden's open resistance she could not tell. 'You got no sense of humour, gal.'

'I just lost it.'

Entertainment for those in the traffic queue was provided in the form of hoppesteres, that is women dancing on one leg to the rackety accompaniment of shaum and tabor, and men balancing cartwheels on their noses. A tumbler vaulted over the bonnet of the car. Arden was gratified when he landed face down in the mud. 'And is this what you have in mind for Sloping, Mr Jermigan? A haven for sad individuals and frustrated gymnasts?'

''Course not. This lot be special for Christmas, don't they? Got their eye on the coach parties, like. Sloping's going to be some'at different. I told you, real authentic. Like going back in time.'

'But the overheads will be enormous. How many people would be prepared to pay what it would cost even to get your money back, never mind make a profit?'

'Americans. Japs. Get a spot on the Internet. You try finding some'at like that on offer. There ain't nothin'. You think I ain't done no market research? It's a gap in the market, gal.'

'Perhaps because all the others have fallen through it.' But still, accessing potential customers through the Internet would certainly maximize the world-wide market.

'Then there's film and TV. Locations, like. They wouldn't have to go to Eastern Europe to make no Brother Cadfaels. They could do it right 'ere.'

'I see. What a pity they've already made them.'

'Look, I ain't going to fuck around with you. You knows

you and your *half*-brother could hold the whole operation up, doesn't you?'

He clearly did not realize that probate had not yet been granted. From a strategic point of view, if he burnt them out now he would stand a very good chance of getting away with it. However, Arden had not thought of the situation in quite such bald terms, in that their refusal to sell was the one obstacle in his path. Why not she could not think, as it was patently obvious now.

'I suppose plans for our cottage are included in your application?'

'That's right.'

'What! I wasn't serious. You can't do that – apply for permission to develop a property that isn't even yours.'

'Yes, I can. Check with the council an' you don't believe me.'

'That's outrageous! I certainly will check it.' But she had a grim feeling that with Scylla and Charybdis in tow, as she thought of his navy blue-suited lawyers, he was probably right. 'Tell me, Mr Jermigan, if this project has always been so close to your heart, why didn't you work on Humph? Wouldn't he have been more sympathetic than we are, being such an old friend and all that?'

'What do you take me for? I wouldn't hound 'm out his 'ome after I gave it to 'im, now would I? 'Sides, I owed him a favour.'

'And what would that be?'

'None of your business.'

'So, if Humph hadn't died, the whole thing would have remained a pipe dream? You didn't help him on his way, did you?'

'No, I did not. May you be forgiven, woman.'

'It's all very well your getting pious about Humph. Don't pretend you aren't capable of it. I know what you did to Laurence and Shara.'

'What – snuff 'em?'

'Well, no. But you scared them off, didn't you? Burnt out their car.'

He shrugged. 'Don't know what you're talking about.'

'No, of course not.' But his smug expression was a blatant contradiction. Arden's blood ran cold at this virtual admission of guilt, and then strangely fizzy.

It seemed like several weeks since they had set out from Sloping by the time they were parked. Arden was starving but did not like to admit to such weakness. She suspected that Jermigan, like his fellow predators in the animal kingdom, went for days without eating and then gorged himself into a stupor. They joined the trail of visitors heading for the manor house. Arden was impressed with the building which was an enchanting jumble of mellow brick façades and turrets and gatehouses, with a thicket of twisted chimneys, all surrounded by a moat. Jermigan contained his impatience when she had to return to the car to fetch her *Companion Guide to the Smaller Medieval House*, without which the visit would be virtually pointless.

At the main entrance they were given some lukewarm punch in a paper cup and a plan of the house and outbuildings which detailed the various historical re-enactments they could enjoy. Arden felt a reluctant curiosity to see the flax-treading demonstration and leper house, while Jermigan was naturally more drawn to the torture chambers and cannonball foundry. As a compromise she suggested they start in the kitchen. At least there might be free samples.

The passage to the kitchen led past small rooms dedicated to the preparation of game, cheese, herbs and spices. *Nature morte* tableaux of dead ducks, geese, rabbits, hand-thrown Hempknott Cheddar, gizzards and entrails excited a lively reaction from the punters shuffling past. A couple of middle-aged women in front of Arden and Jermigan cast a cursory glance at the exhibits.

'Very constipating, poultry,' observed one.

'Ooh, tell me about it! I'm in agony for weeks after Christmas. We don't have the pudding, see, and that gets the turkey moving so to speak. The kids won't eat it and Dan's allergic to sultanas so I don't bother with it.'

'You don't have Christmas pudding? Well, I never. What do you have then?'

'Profit rolls usually. Marks and Sparks. They're absolutely delicious.'

'Are they really? I must try them. Mind you, you expect quality from Marks.'

'Well, you say that, but they only got four out of ten for their brandy butter in my magazine.'

'Never?'

'They did. I was very surprised . . .'

The whole pig rotating over the roaring fire brought forth a mixed reaction, mostly 'yuks' and 'urghs'. One small boy asked his mum if the eyes melted. 'Shut up, Ryan. That's disgusting.' The kitchen was a large, vaulted room set up with several tables at which volunteers in dun-coloured clothing were making bread, gutting fish, gilding marzipan and stuffing chickens. Arden's critical eye was in overdrive as she scrutinized the demonstrations for inaccuracies. She worked her way to the front of the crowd and asked the man stuffing chickens what he was using. 'Why, lady, this 'ere be farsed, with a mixture of oats and ale and ripe cheese made in the dairy and lentils and fine cherries from my lord's orchard right here at Hempknott.'

'Where do you get cherries in December?'

He glanced at her, recognizing a troublemaker.

'Israel?' said Jermigan helpfully.

'Why, gentles, it be not my place to ask wherefrom the makings come. Do thou ask the steward yonder. He has charge of the providing.'

'Hmm. 'Thou' is a bit familiar, isn't it? I thought that was reserved for intimates.'

The servitor screwed up his eyes and whacked the chicken menacingly on the chopping board. 'I meant no disrespect, lady. An' you have a grievance of my behaviour, pray mention same to the steward while you're enquiring about the cherries.' Another very large man in a leather jerkin who had been lolling against the wall stepped up to stand beside him.

'Trouble, friend?'

The chicken stuffer made a face of the 'There's-always-one-clever-dick' variety. Jermigan grasped Arden by the elbow and steered her away. 'Give them a break, gal. I told you, they pays to do this.'

'If they're that keen, they should be grateful to have mistakes pointed out.'

It was impossible to get near the popular marzipan and pastry table. Hordes of children were crowded round it squawking with delight at a living pie. When the lid was removed a frog tethered with a piece of tinsel leaped on to the table. 'It's worth the money just for that,' said one satisfied dad as he beamed at his hysterical son. On the way out Arden took a proffered piece of fried orange from a young woman with her jaw wrapped up in a white scarf, and a faraway look in her eye.

'Umm, that's delicious,' said Arden. 'Do you use yeast in the batter?'

'East, ma'am? Why, the sun he rises in the East.'

'Yes, I'm aware of that. I said *yeast*. Is this a yeast batter or not?'

'They come from the East, ma'am, that do tell their numbers with a piggin's ladle.'

'What is this – *King Lear*? Are you the token half-wit or what?'

'I wot thou'rt witted like a nakers drum, ma'am, and God grant 'ee a good ling for thy coffyn.'

'*Jesus*!'

They went out of the kitchen into the courtyard, where fire-eaters were performing in one corner and stilt dancers in another. 'Someone should tell that girl she'll never make it to the RSC and put her out of her misery. *Honestly*. Do you still not understand my objections to this sort of thing, Mr Jermigan?'

'You made yourself clear enough, gal. What you 'aven't made clear to me is why I should give a toss. You ain't no professor or expert type. You're just an opinionated amateur. Why should you get away with stuffin' my plans? You're doin' people out of jobs, you know that.'

'So you've said. You'd use the same argument if you were planning to build a cattle incinerator on the site. And I may be an opinionated amateur, I don't deny it. But why should I apologize for it? Are you saying you aren't? And as for stuffing your plans, you forget that you're talking about our home. If it weren't for that you could build all the historical theme parks you like.'

'Your home? Huh! It's only been your home five minutes. And that's only 'cause I gave it to your dad in the first place. And I've offered to buy it back! Beats me why you can't see 'ow selfish you's being.'

'It's my spiritual home, Mr Jermigan. It didn't take me long to recognize that. And don't pretend you wouldn't do the same in my place. You're the arch-priest of self-interest.'

'I'm wasting my time then?'

'Yes, I'm afraid so.'

'We'll see about that. Well, might as well go 'ome, then. You obviously ain't enjoying it.'

'No, no. Not after we've come all this way. I'm thriving on it, actually. It's so *appalling*.'

'I don't understand you, gal. Or do I? Mebbe you're just a common or garden snob.'

'No, I'm *not*. Well, only when it comes to heritage pantomimes, anyway. We'll never see eye to eye on this one, Mr Jermigan. Your mission was doomed from the start, I'm afraid. Look, why don't we split up? We won't get round everything if we stay together. You can go and inspect the dungeons and whatnot and I'll meet you later.'

He shrugged. 'If you want.' There was an expression of genuine disappointment under the Tyrolean hat, which suddenly gave him the air of being all dressed up with nowhere to go. He must honestly have thought she would be enchanted by the *Carry On Up The Middle Ages* cavortings at Hempknott. It was his own fault for not believing her in the first place. However, the visit might serve a useful purpose if it persuaded him that her opposition to his plans for Sloping was implacable. He would then either have to give them up or assassinate herself and Tim. Even Jermigan would not go that far, surely? She was glad that the inevitable argument had come up so soon. It had provided a timely excuse to go their separate ways. Her heart pounding noisily with triumph and stress, Arden gathered her Bilberry robes about her and headed off for the Painted Solar alone.

The room was one of the oldest in the manor, an octagonal chamber with a graceful vaulted ceiling painted green with gold stars. Mullioned oriels to either side created an atmosphere of airy spaciousness. Unfortunately, the afternoon sun streamed through them on to yet more volunteers in dun garments, in this case pounding herbs and mucking about with coloured powders and egg yolk. Few visitors had made this trek to the art department so Arden was able to enjoy the room at her leisure, in particular what appeared to be fourteenth-century wall paintings so charming and well preserved that she was astonished she had not been aware of them previously. Between the graceful pilasters were scenes of Judith beheading Holofernes, hounds tearing a stag limb from limb, the Blessed Virgin weeping at the foot of the Cross, and Satan being expelled from an enchanting Gothic palace at the end of St Michael's sword. They looked genuine enough, even on close inspection. Nicely distressed and faded. No tell-tale 'McDonald's *Hoc Saxum Posuit*' inscribed over the palace portals.

There was something about the style of the figure painting, though, which made her question their authenticity, something fluid and sensuous, but the kind of sensuality that ultimately runs to fat. She was rather cross with herself for her inability to be sure that they were genuine, especially so soon after Jermigan's swipe at her amateurism. He could talk! At least she was not trying to impose her private fantasies on an indifferent world. On the whole, she felt she had dealt with him very effectively, and gave credit where it was due – to *Suitables* – for lending her the courage to go that extra mile of self-assertion.

The woman mixing paints had several customers so Arden waited at the herbal distillery table. The young girl so dextrously mashing Old Man and sheep's fat to a fine paste had a beautiful, delicate face and lithe figure. The glossy hair was crowned with a garland of chortleberries. Only her air of fanatical concentration suggested why she was spending Saturday in this penitential way and not shopping with some besotted boyfriend as nature intended. She was explaining, in the Chaucerese which apparently went with the uniform, that the mulch was meant to ease women's pains. Her customer was a young man, possibly a doctor as he pressed her – unfairly, Arden thought – for more precise pharmaceutical data. She decided to intervene, as the girl was getting flustered and had failed to put the young man off the scent with the fascinating information that childbirth was much assisted if the cupboard doors be open. Arden elbowed the young man aside.

'Aren't you afraid of catching something from that fat?' she said, in what she hoped was a kindly way.

The girl smiled gratefully. 'What could I catch, ma'am? I be no sheep.'

'No. All right.' Arden was not sure when Scrapie had started so there was no point in pursuing the matter. 'Look, I'm very interested in these wall paintings. Would you happen to know if they're authentic? As old as the room that is, or reproductions?'

'Your long words confuse me, ma'am. I know only they were first painted in my grandfather's time, under the old King Edward, God assoil him, he that claimed the Kingdom of France.'

'Yes, but have they been restored? They have that droopy-drawers look of the pre-Raphaelites to me.'

'Pray, ma'am, what is a drawer?'

'For God's sake, can't you come out of character for a minute? I only want to know if the bloody things have been touched up.'

The girl looked offended. Arden was pretty sure that when not demonstrating medieval medicines she was a pillar of the Young Conservatives. 'I take not your meaning, ma'am. I know only that they were painted in my grandfather's time under the old King Edward, he that—'

'Yes, yes, claimed the Kingdom of France. *Honestly*.' Arden turned to see if the queue for the pigment expert had gone down at all. If anything there were more people waiting for a word with her. Arden flounced out of the room in despair.

Back in the courtyard she consulted the programme of attractions. She was already so frustrated that if she harangued any more volunteers it would only be a matter of time before she thumped one. What was the point of educational displays if the presenters spoke in impenetrable tropes that were a combination of Middle English and The Archers? There was an hour to go before she was due to rendezvous with Jermigan in the gift shop. She decided to get something to eat and then park herself in the Great Hall, where seats were provided for those interested in a non-stop performance of Wassailing the Milly.

In contrast to the raw cold outside, the Great Hall was a haven of heat and light. There was a huge fire in the grate. Candelabra – electric, admittedly – swung from iron chains. Huddled bodies in steaming puffa jackets filled the benches and clusters of children sat on the floor. The minstrels' gallery was full of minstrels, and a group of dancers, their assorted shapes and sizes inadequately disguised by matching green garments, jiggled and swayed in the middle of the hall. Arden felt a wayward response to the atmosphere. She supposed that her critical faculties had been wrung dry, because she had to admit that the seething jollity in the hall came closer to an approximation of the Real Thing than anything else she had seen so far.

The only vacant seat was over by the fireplace, a huge wooden carver adorned with episcopal devices. She picked her way through the bodies and squashed mince pies and settled down to enjoy the performance. After a while her eyelids began to droop. The warmth, mulled wine and the exhausting effects of stress were an irresistible narcotic. Before drifting off she had enough presence of mind to draw the folds of her scarf across that side of her face visible to the public.

The hall was nearly empty when she came out of her snooze with a jerk. The fire had died down, the entertainers and most of the audience departed. A few people sat in huddles chatting and some children were running amok among the debris. Worse, it was quarter to five and she had promised to meet Jermigan in the gift shop at three-thirty. She was shivering as she stood up, and not just from the drop in the temperature. Her mind scampered for plausible excuses. Jermigan was the sort of irrascible male who would fail to see that it was really his impatience that was to blame for the row that would ensue, and not her very human error in falling asleep because he had upset her so much. Furthermore, he must have deliberately failed to look for her in the Great Hall when she did not turn up, as it was the obvious place.

The gift shop was a longish walk down the main drive to the entrance. It was closing up when she got there. Jermigan was not among the few customers still deliberating between traditionally baked biscuits and floral stationery. The assistants remembered him, though, as he had asked if they had seen Arden. No, they had no idea where he had gone.

'Mind you,' said one of the ladies, 'there's been an accident. Perhaps you should check with the ambulance? It must still be here, mustn't it, Iris, because it would come out this way.'

'Oh, no. An accident? What happened?'

'I think someone fell down the Priest's Hole. Isn't that right, Iris?'

'So far as I know, yes. We always said it was dangerous, didn't we, Fran? One of these days, I said, someone's going to lean over a bit too far and go down head first. Of course, I don't know as that's what happened. I do hope it wasn't your friend, dear.'

'So do I. He wasn't in a very good mood anyway.'

'Oops! Did you get lost, dear? Lots of people do.'

'Do they?'

'You'd be surprised. It's the corridors, you see. Like in a forest. You're going one way and you think you'd know it again, but when you turn round and look back it's a totally different landscape, isn't it, Iris?'

'That's right. We've had grown men in tears because they couldn't find the exit.'

'Or the tea room.'

'Thanks. That's a useful tip. I'd better go. Where did this accident happen?'

'North end of Lady Wilhelmina's Chamber. Between there and the Knights' Robing Room. Here, give me your plan and I'll show you.'

Arden ran back up the main drive, clutching at her voluminous clothes as best she could. She was in two minds as to whether to make a diversion to see if the car was still in the car park but it was already pitch dark and she was not sure if she could find it. If Jermigan had had an accident, how on earth was she going to get home? Following the plan she ran through the main courtyard and across the famous knot garden to the chapel and Olde Halle wing. An ambulance was drawn up outside and a stretcher was being loaded into it. Jermigan's unmistakably baronial head was visible above the scarlet blanket. At least it was not under it. Arden slowed down and tried to control her breathing. Her chest was raw. He saw her coming and pointed at her.

'This be all your fault, woman. Where the fuck was you?'

The ambulance men urged him not to move and to calm down.

'Are you his wife, madam?'

'God forbid!' yelled Jermigan, up to that moment an atheist. He was now safely inside the ambulance.

'No, but we did come together. Is he going to be all right? What happened?'

'I gather he was trying to look down into the Priest's Hole and lost his balance. Toppled over the rope. Bloody death trap. He's lucky he didn't break his neck.'

'I was lookin' for you, y'bitch!'

'Mr Jermigan, *please*. May I go inside?'

'Of course, madam. But don't be long. Possible leg fracture. He's in a lot of pain.'

Arden climbed into the ambulance and leaned over Jermigan, hoping she looked amazed, concerned and innocent. He lay as stiff as an effigy on the narrow cot. Only his face was animated. With fury. What a relief he was immobilized. She had never seen his eyes so fully open. They were almost black, but lit up like sparklers. 'I'm very sorry about this, Mr Jermigan. But why on earth did you think I would be down the Priest's Hole?'

'I can't remember. It be just the thing you'd do, innit? Go poking your nose in where it ain't allowed. I dunno. I was that panicked, I did'n' know what I was doing.'

'Well, I'm flattered you think I'm the kind of person who goes into roped-off areas. And I'm sorry you were worried about me. I – I got lost. We must have just missed each other.'

'I weren't worried about *you*. You'd got the fuckin' car keys, 'adn't you? For when you went back to fetch that book.'

'Of *course*. What do you want me to do about the car?'

'Drive it 'ome, what d'you think? You wanna stay here the night?'

'No. Is it insured for other drivers?'

'Fuck me, what a question for a time like this! 'Course it is. Ain't you gonna ask me how I feel?'

'Sorry. Yes. How are you?'

'Fucking shattered. And it be all your fault. I won't forget that. Don't think I'm out of action just 'cause I'm on my back. Now, you get that car home and tell Miss Tree as how I'm sorry I won't be able to take her to church in the morning. Your lad can do it.'

'Certainly. He'd be pleased to help. Poor Miss Tree. I suppose she'll have to take over the business again?'

'Not for long. I'll give 'er a call just as soon as I can. In the meantime, ask 'er if she's 'eard anything of Jake yet and to let me know. He's got a load o' batteries for Romania. If he ain't called by Monday morning ask her to get in touch with the car factory. There's a lot gone down with these storms they're havin' over there and that truck ain't fitted with a satellite tracker yet.'

'Excuse me, madam. We've got to get going.'

'Yes, I'm coming. Is he going to the Norfolk and Norwich?'

'That's right.'

'Goodbye then, Mr Jermigan. Honestly, I'm really sorry about all this. By the way, is the car automatic?'

'You'll fucking find out, won't you?'

There was a gloss of sheer gloat on Tim's expression of concern when Arden phoned to say she would be late back and why. Not because Jermigan might have broken his leg, but because the outing had ended in disaster as he had predicted. Arden was irritated that he did not fully appreciate the ordeal she was faced with, of driving a strange car in the dark through unknown territory. That night in the Saints had given her a healthy respect for the lethal by-ways of the area. 'You'll be all right, Ard,' was the jovial assurance. There were times when she got fed up with her own competence.

At least the dark spared Arden the embarrassment she felt at sitting at the wheel of a Landrover-type vehicle while dressed up as Lawrence of Arabia. There were no maps in the car, which was infuriating. As a consequence she drove all the way round the Norwich ring road and made a side trip to Dereham before finding the correct route. At one point she was close to tears and was convinced that she would never see Tim or Bos again. The towers of Sloping had never been a more welcome sight.

Miss Tree had a reviving malt whisky at hand. Arden had not eaten since the parsnip burgers she had had for lunch at Hempknott and the whisky flamed through her body like a fireball. She was glad she would not be entirely sober when facing Tim's self-satisfied recriminations. Miss Tree sat her down by the fire in the kitchen. It was nice to be looked after. Even nicer in this orgasmically medieval room and in the certain knowledge that Jermigan was stranded in Norwich with his leg in traction. Miss Tree had been informed by phone of the accident and now had the look of a broken-backed camel. There was no way she would complain but Arden could tell that her resources, extensive though they were, had reached their limits. The only concern she expressed was for Jermigan's welfare. Arden told her what had happened as fairly as she could, only omitting the part where she fell asleep. When she passed on Jermigan's message about Jake and the batteries, Miss Tree's reserve faltered.

'Mr Jermigan puts too much faith in me, I'm afraid. And it was such a comfort to have him back at home. Now he'll be away again for weeks. Oh, dear. This isn't good for Lottie.'

'Blow Lottie! It's you he should be worried about. Don't think me rude, but you're too old to assume such responsibilities. Why doesn't he have an under manager or something, who can take over when he's not here?'

'We've managed so far. It was my idea. All the data is on the Nobo board in the office. It's not *difficult* work but . . . Oh, I don't know. It's drumming up freight contracts that I'm not so good at. You're right, I'm getting too old.'

'I hope he doesn't expect you to be a general factotum for his bloody theme park too? Sorry.'

'No. I've told him I can't have anything to do with that. I support him in it in every other way, but my practical involvement is not in question.'

'Don't you think he's rather old to start such a project?' Arden was disappointed that Miss Tree backed the Sloping Experience. Her manner gave no indication that she was aware of Arden and Tim's opposition to it.

'That was my only reservation. But he's very fit. He must have at least ten more years of active working life. Long enough to get it off the ground.'

'And then what, though? Lottie won't want to take it over, will she?'

'I'd really rather not get into this argument, Arden. Sufficient unto the day are the evils thereof.'

'How true. Like today, for example. And it's not over yet. Well, thank you for the drink. I'd better be going. Tim will be anxious. But if there's anything I can do, just ask. One of us will take you to church in the morning.'

'Don't worry, I'll have to give it a miss. I'll be too busy trying to locate Jake and his batteries.'

The walk back to the cottage was a winding one. Arden could scarcely believe such a small drink could have such a powerful effect. She was scarcely aware of the head-on encounter with the tower of rubble and very surprised when Tim exclaimed at the blood on her face. Bos was out, fortunately. Arden thought she might sober up if she had something to eat and went into the kitchen, ate a large piece of red Leicester straight from the fridge and shortly afterwards threw it up again on the living-room carpet. Tim was beside himself and wanted to call the doctor.

'Don't be soft.' Arden had fallen back on to the sofa, still in her Bilberry garments. 'It's only stress. What a day! Were there any calls for me?'

'Several. Mostly *Suitables* stuff. That doctor in Wenham wants a presentation.'

'Oh, good. Anything else?'

'Nothing important.' He decided this was not the moment to tell her that Thalia had called, to ask for a meeting with both of them as soon as possible.

13

It was with many a rueful reflection on the conflicting demands of work and family that Arden set off for the Christmas visit to Mattie the following day. Draped over the back seat of the car were Bos, snoring off a good night at 'Tipples', and plastic-wrapped bundles of clothes for delivery on the way home. She reminded herself that she had had time-off-in-lieu in advance and was due for a stint of caring, but even so the timing was unfortunate. Starting a business was stressful enough without the distraction of dependants, however fond of them one was, and never mind the sideshow with Jermigan. It was certainly his fault that she had bumped into the tower of rubble. And if he had not been so short-tempered he would not have thrown himself down the Priest's Hole. The swelling on her forehead had spread to her eyelids and she peered out with difficulty, from under matching buns of flesh. What effect her appearance would have on Mattie's confused mind she dreaded to think.

The Ashes was an even more melancholy place decked overall with foil streamers and fold-out Father Christmases with bulbous red stomachs. The decorations created an air of still-born expectancy. Everyone knew that nothing would happen here except death. The prospect of a Christmas party featuring gluten-free mince pies, diabetic biscuits and a magician all the way from Ipswich was not in the same league. Arden supposed that the celebrations were at least good for staff morale, which was just as well as they would have to spend half the time explaining to patients what the fuss was about and those who understood would be even more depressed than those who did not. It would take a forklift truck to raise the patients' spirits on New Year's Eve.

Arden tried not to add to what she perceived as the general gloom. They had brought wine and chocolates for the staff, which injected real warmth into their welcome. The manager was making an effort to be cheerful. She wore a twist of tinsel on her watch, and had good news for them.

'You'll find your mother much improved, I'm glad to say. The doctor's had her on a new drug, Trydopamide. It's done wonders. She even knew the girl had brought her the wrong thermal undies from the chemist. Now isn't that progress?'

They agreed that it was. She wheeled Mattie into the dining room so that they could have more privacy and sent an assistant to bring coffee, both seasonal concessions. Mattie was bright-eyed and pert. Her baby-fine skin was again suffused with the healthy tones of Max Factor Creme Puff and she wore bright red lipstick, more or less on her mouth. She recognized Tim and Arden immediately and only needed reminding who Bos was once. They all complimented her in astonished delight on her improved condition. Bos, who had not seen his grand-mother *compos mentis* since he was twelve, was particularly impressed.

'You look dead pretty, Gran. I had no idea you were such a corker.'

She smacked him lightly on the hand. 'Cheeky boy. I'm not dead yet. Come and sit by me. Tim, you go over there. I like this one.'

Arden glowed with pride at Bos's generous frankness. She was slightly perturbed that Mattie had not so far noticed any alteration in her own appearance and told her about Jermigan's accident. Mattie chuckled in undisguised *schadenfreude*.

'About time he was brought down a peg. I pity the nurses, mind. They'd ought to nail their skirts down while he's around.'

'Really, Mum. "Forbear the ren child," as you used to tell me.' She indicated Bos. Jermigan was still his boss and it was not appropriate that his sex life should be brought to Bos's attention. There were clear disadvantages to Mattie's coherence. Her mother looked crestfallen. She put a hand on Bos's arm and leaned towards him in conspiratorial mode.

'Your mum's a proper bossy boots, isn't she? Just like her father.'

He laughed and agreed. 'Who's Uncle Tim like, Nan?'

Mattie glanced at Tim then looked away. 'That's harder to say, my love. Where is Humph? Why didn't he come?'

'Ah, well . . .' Arden had forgotten that Mattie did not yet know about his death. If her improvement was sustained it would not be possible, even if desirable, to keep it from her.

'He had to go to a reunion service, Mum.' Tim, as ever, was first into the conversational breach. 'He's sorry he couldn't come. Sends his love and so on.'

Arden raised a congratulatory eyebrow. Mattie did not seem unduly upset. 'That's a pity. Perhaps he'll come later in the week, will he?'

'Possibly.' Up to that point Arden had been wondering if their mother would be well enough to come home for Christmas Day. But that would mean telling her about Humph. They could not possibly pretend he was in the loo all day.

'I've got some presents for you all,' said Mattie. 'Just bits of rubbish I made but you might as well have them. Arden, my love, would you mind fetching them? They're in my room. Do you know where that is? If not just ask the nurse.'

'Of course.' In fact she was glad of the chance to snoop round the home.

Mattie made sure she had gone before turning to Tim with a grave face. 'Have you been knocking her about, dearest?'

'No, Mum, of course not. As if I would! No, she bumped into a wall in the dark outside.'

'Phew! You hear such awful things. You make sure she gets her eyes tested. She might have damaged them. It won't improve her chances if she has to wear glasses like Billy Blizzard, now will it?'

'Who's Billy Blizzard?' asked Bos.

'Your memory going?' laughed Mattie. 'He's a character in the Rupert Bear stories, my love. I think.'

'It's amazing that you can remember things like that, Mum. Well done.'

'Are you pleased with me then, son?' She winked at Bos.

'Very. But what did you mean by Arden improving her chances?'

'Why, getting a fella, of course. She's no oil painting even without her face bashed in. She ought to think of the future while she's got the chance.'

'I always thought Arden was a rather fine-looking woman, Mum. I'm sure she could get a fella, as you put it, but the truth is the only man in her life is Simon de Montfort. Always was.'

'Do I know him?'

'No, Mum. He's a person in history. He's dead.'

'Oh, I'm sorry.'

Perhaps, thought Tim, they had rejoiced too soon at the extent of Mattie's recovery.

Many of the bedroom doors stood open as the cleaners were busy in them. Arden lingered on the landings before finding Mattie's room, so that she could take in as much as possible. The decor was fresh and light – wipe-down magnolia surfaces for the most part. Sunflower patterns were favoured for bedspreads and curtains. No doubt a clinical psychologist had been paid a great deal to come up with this suggestion. As in a hospital, these attempts to brighten the atmosphere had ambiguous results. They worked, and one could not help but respond to the caring ethos they represented. At another level, the life-enhancing touches were a painful counterpoint to the business in hand, particularly here in the queue for life's exit. No sunflower could alleviate Arden's depression as she observed the bundles of balding patients shrunk into vinyl armchairs while their beds were made, the spitoons and kidney dishes and wheelchairs with potties in. While Mattie was confused it would not matter so much, but if she were fully conscious it must surely be unendurable for her?

Mattie's current room-mate, Muriel, was a big woman who sat in an upright chair by the window, in a man's dressing-gown and ruffled pink nightie. She had been a distinguished criminal lawyer in her day. Her large, horsey face did not flicker as Arden came in. Arden had been upset to learn that Mattie had to share a room again, and had taken some convincing that the company was good for her, particularly in the form of Muriel. She had since come to appreciate that Muriel's outward appearance concealed a humorous and kindly nature. They talked for a while, about Muriel's family and Mattie's startling improvement.

Muriel asked after Tim, Arden's facial injuries and the progress of *Suitables*.

'Why don't you bring some samples next time?' she said in her deep, slow voice. 'Some of these old girls have got loads of money and nothing to spend it on. We're not all on the DSS, you know.'

'Oh, no, I couldn't. That would be exploitation. Anyway, I doubt if it would be allowed.'

'Nonsense. Ask the manager. They're always looking for events to stimulate our brain cells.'

'Well – trying things on might be a bit of a problem. Labour intensive, shall we say. But still, perhaps some of the simpler designs might be of interest. Actually, now I come to think of it, there's a gap in the market there. I mean, clothes for people who are semi-invalid. Sort of halfway between night clothes and regular clothes. You know, I think *Suitables* might be interested in that.'

'You could call it the Walking Wounded Collection.'

Arden laughed. 'Muriel, I know you won't mind me speaking frankly, but what are you doing in this place? You're much too alert.'

'Dying, dearie, that's what I'm doing. About a month, the doctors reckon. Stomach cancer.'

'Oh. Oh, God. Sorry.' Arden felt as though she had stopped short at the edge of a cliff: Muriel's announcement was so unexpected. And yet, of course, hardly news. 'I really am very sorry. Are they sure? You know doctors—'

'I'm not. Sorry, that is. I've been ready for years. Don't upset yourself about me, dearie. It'll be a shock for Mattie, though. We're a good team. Hadn't you better be getting back to her? No offence, but I'm a bit tired.'

'Yes. Well, all the best, Muriel. I hope I see you before—'

'I expect so, dearie. And don't forget those samples.'

'Right.'

Relativity was a real bugger. Only moments before Arden had had only a superficial, easy-care liking for Muriel. Now that she knew the woman was dying she realized that she had fairly harrowing feelings about it, that in fact she cared about Muriel. It was one of those complications that Arden had been studying her whole life to avoid, without success. On a practical level, it presented problems for Mattie. It was a good thing that she was *compos mentis* again, but that would be a mixed blessing if it meant she would suffer all the confusion and pain of losing her room-mate. Coming on top of the news about Humph, she could well be back in ga-ga land by February.

Monday's post brought an invitation to view the plans for Jermigan's Sloping Experience. It was a circular letter that was supposedly being sent to all the affected householders. Apart from themselves, Arden could not think of any. The nearest farm and the village of Sloping were both more than a mile away. There was little chance that the villagers would object. They had been popping corks already because the plan involved the HGVs moving elsewhere. In fact, anyone who opposed the scheme risked death, and not just from Jermigan. And of those who did, not many would have time off during the day to go to the district council offices to view the plans. Fortunately, Arden and Tim's role in holding up the scheme was not public knowledge. They had few contacts in the village anyway, but it might be a good idea to steer clear of it altogether until the fuss had died down. Arden had every faith in the ability of local residents to understand her point of view eventually.

With Jermigan in hospital, the outlook for Christmas at the Hall was grimmer than ever. The stuffing had certainly gone out of Miss Tree for the time being. Arden was concerned. She encouraged Bos to make himself useful. Jermigan would be grateful, and he would have a much better chance of picking up information relating to their cause at the heart of power, as it were, than washing trucks in the yard.

'I am not spying for you, Mum. No way.'

'I'm not asking you to, darling. That wouldn't be the purpose of your helping Miss Tree. But you're good with computers and things, and I'm sure you could easily work out how to operate this satellite link thing. And if you did hear anything of interest – well, you could use your discretion about whether to pass it on.'

Bos still looked dubious. To reassure him of her motives further, Arden said she would invite Miss Tree and Lottie for

Christmas Day as they would otherwise be alone. Bos groaned. 'Can you see Lottie pulling crackers and playing charades, Mum? It'll be like having the ghost of Savonarola at the table.'

Arden was impressed. 'How do you know about Savonarola?'

'Contextual Studies.'

'Ah. But you surely can't think it would be right to leave them on their own?'

'No. 'spose not.' After Christmas Eve on the tiles there was a good chance that he and Lottie would be unconscious until well after the Queen's speech anyhow. 'I still don't see why it has to be us, though. Don't they have family they can go to?'

'Miss Tree wouldn't want to leave Sloping at the moment. And I can't see Lottie volunteering to stay with uncles and aunties.'

'It's disgusting what she gets away with.' Bos had decided, after deep thought, that there was no point in raising the alarm about Lottie. Her puerile philosophy might well not lead to action. Darren would have to be a complete idiot to encourage her to run away with him. The most likely danger was that she would get pregnant, and there was not much anybody could do to stop her short of enforced sterilization.

In the event Bos was spared the factious young philosopher's presence at the feast. Lottie was indisposed on Christmas Day and Miss Tree came alone. He felt curiously disappointed. Bodies were the essence of the celebration. That was widely accepted, and not only because his expectations had been influenced by the group sex under the sacred oak that had been the defining feature of his dad's social season. It bothered him to think of Lottie by herself. She was a sad kid. And it bothered him that it bothered him. He asked Arden if she would mind him taking Lottie some pudding. She would not eat it, but it was a good excuse to go over to the Hall. Conversation with Miss Tree in her present state was heavy going, and best left to Uncle Tim. Arden was surprised but pleased by his thoughtfulness, and having successfully dished up roast goose with raisin and quince sauce and ten vegetables, and drunk a couple of pints of Chardonnay since breakfast, she would have agreed to anything. Miss Tree went into transports of gratitude.

Bos let himself in at the kitchen. In contrast to the cheerful mess at the cottage, it was soullessly tidy. There was no fire in the grate and the house felt cold. He went through to the Great Room. There was a large tree and the usual slew of cards on every flat surface. He wondered who had decorated the tree. Not Lottie, for sure. No doubt poor Miss Tree had made the effort. Even Bos could sense that there was something very wrong about the emptiness of this house that had been wont to reverberate with noise and people and warmth at this time of year. He was surprised that it was not even pulsating to Lottie's music. Perhaps she was genuinely unwell and not just being a dog in the manager as he had assumed.

He put the pudding down on the floor outside her room and listened. If she were asleep he would not wake her. There was a sound, though, and one with which Bos was not unfamiliar. A moaning, groaning, panting sound which, assuming Lottie was not in the throes of childbirth, suggested that she was pleasuring herself, as masturbation was quaintly referred to in a monograph he had read – *Mental Illnesses Resulting From Sexual Repression in the Vale of Glamorgan 1850–1914*. Acting on an impulse that he could later explain only by the amount of alcohol in his system from the night before, he opened the door. Through a smog of marijuana fumes he could see Lottie in bed, the covers thrown back over her knees so that he could not see exactly what she was doing, which was probably just as well. She smiled, unperturbed.

'Hi, Bos. You're just in time.'

'Sorry. I – er – I've brought you some pudding.'

Lottie giggled. 'Shall I tell you where you can put it?'

'No, thanks. Well. See you later, then.'

He ran back down the stairs. He was in shock, reeling from the image of Lottie in lascivious disarray. If it had been anyone else he would have been in there like the proverbial rat up a drainpipe.

Miss Tree was disappointed that he came back so soon. 'Is Lottie all right?'

'Yeah. Fine. Tired. She didn't feel like chatting.'

'Thank you for trying, Bos. It's such a shame she's unwell. She's been in a much better mood for the last few days.'

'Since Mr Jermigan went into hospital?' said Arden, with a

rueful expression meant to signal sympathy with Miss Tree's anxiety.

'Oh. Yes. I suppose that's right. Oh, dear. She went to see him, you know. I thought that was a good sign.'

Arden nodded in agreement. Privately she thought it likely that Lottie had been checking to make sure he really was out of action.

Despite the fact that Miss Tree went home after tea, and Tim and Bos did the washing-up, Arden was still tired the following Sunday morning so she stayed in bed late. It was ever thus at Christmas, she reflected. With preparations starting in August, it was no wonder women in particular were too tired to enjoy it. But there was satisfaction to be had from such an organizational triumph, even if it had laid her low for several days. Lunch had been served before the sun went down, cards, gifts and *Suitables* orders all got off on time, and Jermigan was, perhaps, permanently disabled. All good reasons for self-congratulation and letting Tim pamper her a little.

She sipped the cappuccino he had brought her on to which, in festive mood, he had sprinkled toasted marshmallow cubes. Bos had gone to watch the meet of the local hunt, from the comfort of a pub. It was a sunny, warm day. Arden luxuriated in the cocoon of well-being created by her cosy bed, Tim's TLC, enforced leisure and the completion of so many jobs well done. This part of Christmas she had always loved. The work was over, the rewards of relaxation and a well-stocked fridge were now to be enjoyed. Best of all she could start on the pile of books Tim had given her, and opened *Monastic Drainage Systems* with a feeling of near perfect contentment.

So absorbing were the diagrams of pipes and drainage channels that she did not hear a car drive up to the cottage, and only became conscious that they had a visitor when she heard Tim's voice, and could tell from it that the person was an agreeable surprise but one that he would have appreciated more at another time. Arden was irritated. She had assumed that their limited social life would at least have the consolation that they could count on some peace and quiet over the holiday. She hoped he would get rid of the visitor as soon as possible but feared the worst when she heard him coming upstairs. He looked flustered, but pleased.

'It's Thalia, Ard. Do you want to come down?'

'*Thalia!* What does she want? Hasn't she got some family binge to go to?'

'Shhh. She'll hear you. She thought as it was our first Christmas here she'd come and – you know – make a social call. I think it's very nice of her, don't you? She's brought us some presents. Have we got anything for her?'

'No, of course not. How annoying. Now we'll have to get her something every year till the end of time as well. And Gavin. And her dad. Honestly, how thoughtless.'

'That's a bit hard. I'm sure she doesn't see it like that.'

'I daresay not. But people should *think* more, shouldn't they? Oh, bring her up here. I really don't see why I should get up.'

'But Ard—'

'Don't fuss. Your bed's made. She's far too unworldly to suspect anything. And what if she does? Who cares?' She sat up. 'Thalia! Come on up. I'm too lazy to come down.'

'Ard!'

'Oh, shhh. Go and get her, go on. And you'd better make some more coffee. No, I've got a better idea. Open that champagne Miss Tree brought us. Why not? It's Christmas.'

'She's driving.'

'Yes, but we're not. I'll need a drink if she's going to go on about the blasted Oriflamme again.'

While Tim, ashen-faced, went down to fetch Thalia, Arden got up and brushed her hair, powdered her nose and liberally sprayed herself with some old Bal á Versailles. She got back into bed and composed herself as though reading her book. Thalia put her head round the door.

'Are you sure this is all right, Arden?' Her eyes were stretched to the limit, and strayed immediately to Tim's bed.

'Of course, come in. Sorry to be such a slug, but I was so tired. What time is it?'

'Quarter to twelve. I'd hoped it wasn't too early.'

'It isn't, if you don't mind the informality. It's very good of you to come out. Most people have engagements today, don't they? Christmas Sunday, as it were.'

'Well, I had to bring Gavin over this way for a football match so I thought I'd pop in. What's wrong with your face?'

'I had a close encounter with a brick wall. The bruise is coming out. It isn't as bad as it looks.'

'That's good. No wonder you're tired. Here, these are for you.' She handed Arden two parcels wrapped in brown paper covered with potato prints.

'How kind. You shouldn't have, really. I'll wait for Tim before we open them. What – original paper.'

'The old people where I work do it in occupational therapy. Bless them. They're so happy to save us a few pence.'

Arden forced a smile, but felt slightly nauseous at the thought of Mattie or Muriel getting their kicks in this way. 'Are you feeling okay, Thalia? You're shivering.'

'I'm fine. I just feel a bit – strange.'

'You're embarrassed. There's no need to be. In the Middle Ages people received visitors in their bedrooms all the time. Even royalty. There wasn't much option.'

'Really?'

Arden was amused. Thalia was probably reacting to the feral odour of Tim's pheromones that hung about the bedroom air. The idea of him as predatory animal was a joke only she could appreciate. At that moment she felt rather proprietorial about Tim, he was being so attentive. If anyone craved the comfort of familiar things it was Tim. Even if he did fancy Thalia, Arden was sure it would pass. She and Tim were so enmeshed with each other after all this time, no other relationship could come close. 'Sit on that bed, Thalia. Don't be shy.'

'All right.' She perched on the side, her hands firmly gripping the edge.

'Well.' Arden yearned for Tim to reappear. Thalia was awed into conversational paralysis by the unconventional venue, though goodness knows she should have been used to talking to people in bed. 'Did you have a nice Christmas?'

'Yes, thank you. Yes. Very nice.'

'Just the three of you, was it?'

'No. My auntie and uncle are staying with us. They came down from Derby.'

'Goodness, they must be – devoted to you.' She was going to

say 'desperate'. 'That's a bit of a bore for Gavin, though, isn't it? If the party's so top-heavy with OAPs.'

'He doesn't mind. It's only for one day.'

'Right.' Arden was already so strapped for topics she could see the danger of bringing up the Oriflamme herself. After all, it was almost the only thing they had in common. Except Humph, of course. Arden had almost forgotten about him, but she had not been as close to him as Thalia. Perhaps coming to the cottage – to the bedroom – was painful for her. Arden was annoyed that she had not thought of this complication before, even as she cursed the fate that cast such obstacles in the path of the advancement of – well, *Suitables* for starters.

Other people's emotional lives were so draining, so time-consuming. Especially grief. Why could not everyone, herself included, have Muriel's stoical indifference to death? What on earth was the evolutionary purpose of minding about it? Her favourite role model after Simon de Montfort was Mr Spock. How much easier life would be if it was logic driven. When Thalia arrived Arden had been enjoying a much-needed restorative break. Now she felt obliged to offer comfort to her. Encourage her to display her feelings, as the trend would have it. Honestly.

'Is it difficult for you to come to Humph's home, Thalia? Does it bring back – memories?'

'Yes, but not really sad ones. Not sad at all.'

'Oh. Sorry to be nosy, but I thought that was maybe why you seem upset?'

Thalia shook her head. 'May I have a drink of water?'

'Certainly. Here. Are you going to be sick?'

Again she shook her head. 'It's just over-indulgence, I think.'

'Well, Tim will be here in a minute with the hair of the dog.' Thalia looked puzzled. 'Alcohol. The homeopathic cure for a hangover.'

'Oh, I don't think I'd better.'

'Nonsense. A glass or two won't hurt.' If Thalia did not loosen up there was no point in her staying. Arden wondered at her making a social call uninvited when it was so obviously not her thing.

Arden blustered bravely on about Bos, the hunt and the

warped logic of saboteurs who, if they wished to do some good in the world, should try throwing themselves in the path of Serbian tanks or Algerian massacre merchants. Thalia agreed, but had nothing to add, so Arden tried the hot topic of President Clinton's penis and how *utterly* irrelevant its activities were to the conduct of government, it would be far more serious if he had stolen a five shilling postal order like the The Winslow Boy – and at this point, thank heavens, Tim arrived with the champagne.

Thalia had gone green and sweaty at the mention of the word 'penis' and Tim had no trouble persuading her to drink up. She gulped two glasses and then asked if she could lie down for a minute. Tim, who was on autopilot describing the difficulties he had had extracting ice cubes from the special freezer bags, snapped into action. He removed Thalia's shoes and laid her out. She shut her eyes and clasped her hands on her chest as if in prayer. For Arden, this was the last straw. Over-sensitivity was one thing, but wasting champagne was unforgivable.

'Open the window, Tim. And you'd better get a plastic bag and put some of that ice in to rest on her head.'

'Are you sure, Ard? Won't the cold contract the blood vessels even more?'

'Well, what do you suggest? Do people normally apply hot water bottles to the head in these situations?'

Tim glowered at Arden, and gave her the coded signal for *'Shut up, she is not dead but sleeping'*. Thalia raised a hand without opening her eyes. 'I'm all right, Arden.'

'You don't *look* it. Honestly, I don't want to be rude but why did you come out if you weren't feeling well?'

Thalia opened her eyes and sat up. 'Give me another drink and I'll tell you.'

'Are you sure that's wise?'

'Please.' She tossed off the champagne and again clasped her hands and bowed her head as if in prayer. They stared at her, now completely baffled by her behaviour.

'Should we all join in?' said Arden. 'Perhaps we should hold hands and sing Amazing Grace?'

'You're talking nonsense, Ard.'

'I know. It seemed appropriate.'

Thalia composed herself. An air of quiet resolution had settled on her. Arden prepared to hear that she had had an affair with President Clinton.

'Why don't you sit down, Tim? I'm fine. Thanks.'

'If you're sure.' He sat at the end of Arden's bed, wondering what evil demon had made him decline to accompany Bos to the meet.

'The trouble is,' said Thalia, 'I don't know whether what I have to tell you is good news or bad. For you two. And I can't find out without telling you what it is.'

'Then why don't you get to the point?'

'I will.' She drew a deep breath. 'Do you remember, Tim, telling me that you and Arden had to share a bedroom? It started me thinking.'

'Never a risk-free activity.' Arden bristled. If Thalia was going to announce that she had reported them to the Vice Squad, or voice any opinion whatsoever on their personal lives, she would brain her with the Heidsieck Reserve.

'It's very difficult. You see, Humph told me something that I believe he didn't really want me to know. Or anyone, probably. It was at Mum's funeral. Well, afterwards, at the reception. He was drunk, I'm afraid. It wasn't his fault. He was very upset. He didn't drink normally, so it went to his head. And he – he let something out.'

'Not the cat, presumably. What?'

'It was about Tim.' Thalia looked fixedly at the duvet cover.

'*What* about Tim?'

'Humph said Tim wasn't his son, that's all. Then he started crying.' She glanced at Arden, hoping to see an eruption of repressed emotion but prepared for something more ambiguous. Arden's face was locked into a facsimile of rigor mortis, with her glass halfway to her lips. Tim, too, appeared to have stopped breathing.

'You see, I couldn't ask him any more about it, he wasn't in a fit state. And anyway, I didn't know Tim then, so I wasn't that interested to be honest. And I was pretty upset too.

'It was only after Humph himself died, and I met you two, that I remembered him saying that. I didn't know if I should mention it. But then, when Tim said about your – arrangements here – well, I thought you had the right to know. So that you could –

regularize your position, as it were. And people do want to know the truth about their parents these days, don't they? Except, of course, Humph didn't say who Tim's father really was. Which is a shame. Roots and so on. Self-knowledge. It's the modern way, isn't it? Mind you, I've always thought it was a bit of a dead-end. Not useful, like knowing how to bleed a radiator, but still.

Well, looks like it's bad news, then. Oh, dear. I'd hoped you'd be pleased. It's come as a shock, of course. Perhaps you'll be pleased when you've had time to think about it.'

She was still faced with two waxen images. For once Tim was unable to bring forth an irrelevant but diverting comment. Thalia started to feel hot and fidgety. The possibility that they might have heart attacks or hysterics now occurred to her. She offered Arden a glass of water, but Arden still did not move. She tried standing up and looking brisk and positive, then sat down again.

It was Tim who made the first move. He spoke to Arden. 'I think I'll just go and top up the battery.'

When he had gone Arden slowly came back to life. She buried her face in her hands for about ten minutes, waving away Thalia's concerned enquiries but accepting more champagne. Thalia was getting worried. She was due to pick Gavin up at three. They heard the car start up. Thalia went to the window. 'Tim's gone for a drive. That's best. Men always feel better when they're controlling something, don't they?'

Arden spoke through her hands. 'Strange you should use that word – control. Who's controlling who, here?'

'What do you mean?'

'What I mean is, what do you get out of this?' Arden looked at her fiercely, her face white as bone.

'Me? Why, nothing. What could I get out of it?'

'Tim, perhaps?'

Thalia gawped. 'How could you think that? I'm very *fond* of Tim, but no, not in that way. Besides, if I was after him, surely I'd have a better chance if he thought you were his sister? This way, you two could get married if you want. Well, it's a bit soon to think about that, I know, but that's what *I* was thinking. That proves I wasn't after Tim, doesn't it?'

'*Married?*' For a moment Arden stared at Thalia as if trying to frizzle her up. Then she crumpled. Thalia stepped back in horror as Arden collapsed sideways into the foetal position and broke into bellowing sobs. 'Huh – it's all been a – huh – lie – our whole relation-huh-ship—'

'Yes, but – dear Arden – you're still the same people. You can still care for each other.'

'Oh sh-sh-shut up. You d-don't understand – huh – he d-doesn't belong to *m-me* – not to – huh – *me*.'

'There, there. I'm terribly sorry you feel like this, Arden. Truly.' Thalia was indeed aghast at this torrential passion. She thought she had witnessed the apotheosis of irrational feeling in Humph's attachment to her mother. But then Thalia was an only child. Obviously the bond between siblings was stronger than she had realized. Or perhaps it was true what people said after the reaction to Princess Diana's death, that thanks to global communication the British were all turning into South Americans.

She patted Arden's quivering body ineffectually for a while, keeping an eye on the time. She was mortified to have caused so much pain. It was mystifying. But there was still hope that after the shock had worn off Arden would realize that nothing need change, except perhaps her bedroom. She felt an urgent need to communicate the result of her mission to Uncle Sebastian. 'I have to go, Arden. Will you be all right?'

The answer was a strangulated growl. 'T-Tim's p-probably g-going to kill – huh – himself in the c-car and it'll all be y-your fault—'

'Of course he won't. Why should he? I wish I could stay till he gets back, but Gavin will be waiting. Goodbye then. And I'm really sorry.'

She left Arden howling and chewing the pillow. It was awful to abandon her in such a state but there was no help for it. As she let herself out of the front door Thalia was glad to see a woman approaching the cottage whom she guessed from Tim's description was Miss Tree.

'Hello there. Is Mrs Fairbrother at home?'

'Yes, but she's not feeling very well.'

'Mr Mason?'

'No. He and Bos are both out. Can I help?'

'I don't think so. My – well, I never know what she is really – Lottie, that is. She hasn't come home from her friend's house and I can't get past their answering machine.'

'Mr Jermigan's niece? She isn't here, I'm sure of that.' Thalia moved towards her car. Miss Tree lingered outside the cottage, attracted by the noise from Arden's bedroom. 'It's the Curse,' said Thalia in a stage whisper. 'Best not disturb her.'

'Dear me. Poor woman. I thought it wasn't so bad after one had a child.'

'Stress, that's what it is. Excuse me, I have to go. I hope you find Lottie. How old is she?'

'Sixteen.'

'She'll be all right. She's old enough to get married after all.'

'Or murdered.'

'Surely not? How long has she been missing?'

'She was supposed to come home late last night.'

'Perhaps you should call the police?'

'Not yet. I'll wait until Bos gets back. He might have some idea where she is.'

14

Bos was surprised to find his mother sprawled face down across the bed clutching an empty champagne bottle. It was cool. He checked her pulse and heaved her back into bed, in the recovery position in case she threw up. Feeling slightly the worse for a skinful of Adnams himself, he decided that a nap was in order before he went out again for the evening. When Tim returned the cottage was gloomy and silent. He went upstairs and listened outside their bedroom, then looked in and saw that Arden was still asleep.

In fact she was pretending, and when he had gone downstairs again she opened her eyes and hot tears rolled into the pillow. So this is what loneliness feels like, she thought, before drifting back to sleep. Tim, casting budgetary caution to the winds, turned on the gas fire in his study and sat staring into its inscrutable jets.

After some time he crept downstairs – painfully, as the shock had gone to his hip – and rummaged in the bureau for his birth certificate. That was no help. Humph was given as the father. Well, he would be. It must be one of the most common lies in the history of registration. Though not without noble precedent. Joseph, for example.

What bothered him was not who his father actually was, but why Humph had done it, and the dawning of a realization, of crushing immensity, that what Tim had always regarded as Humph's inadequacies as a father were actually evidence of heroic virtue. How different now that day-trip to Dieppe appeared. Tim had never even taken another man's child to the cinema, never mind a foreign port. What Humph's motives had been he could not begin to guess.

And Mattie! Of course, Tim had always loved her and appreciated her care, but how much deeper his gratitude should be knowing that he was neither her son nor Humph's. Perhaps she had not been told. Tim wondered if she was now well enough to talk about it, if she remembered, or whether it would be unwise to bother her about the past. There was always the chance that his mother could be traced in Canada. He had started the process once, after his divorce, but it was so complicated he could not stick at it. When Arden moved in it no longer seemed important. And it would be galling to go to all that trouble to discover that she did not even know who his father was.

His ruminations were interrupted by Bos clattering downstairs. Tim was about to tell him off for making a noise while Arden was asleep, then thought better of it. He smiled, tentatively.

'Have a good sleep, Bos?'

'What? Oh. Yeah. Thanks. Where's Mum?'

'She's still in bed. You'd better have something to eat before you go out. Shall I – er – make you a ham sandwich?'

Bos looked puzzled. He had always got on well enough with Uncle Tim, but the idea of being waited on by him was extremely weird. Bos put it down to the Christmas spirit. 'I'll do it myself, thanks.' He walked off to the kitchen, then thought he had better reciprocate. 'Would you like one?'

'No. But thank you for asking. By the way, there's a new jar of pickled walnuts in the larder.'

'Pickled walnuts. Right. What's wrong with Mum?'

'Nothing. I'll go and see if she wants anything.'

Monastic Drainage Systems had lost its charm. Arden was flicking through the photographs with the lack of enthusiasm she normally reserved for crocheted egg-cosy patterns. She did not look up when Tim came in.

'All right, Ard?'

'No.' She continued to feign nonchalance, but could not stop her mouth from trembling.

He sat on his bed. 'Look, it may not be true, you know.'

'Of course it is. Why would Humph say that otherwise? You don't deny your own son for nothing. There's truth in the cup, as they say.'

'Don't take it out on me, Ard. I can't help it.'

She threw the book down. 'I know. Sorry. It's worse for you. You don't even know if you're an orphan or not.'

'That doesn't matter. All I can think about is Humph. How – kind he was, actually. Considering. I mean, including me in the will as his own. He didn't have to do that.'

'It would rather blow his cover if he didn't. Though why it should matter after he was dead, God knows. Don't you *care*, Tim? Doesn't it mean anything to you that we're complete *strangers?*'

'Don't talk nonsense, woman. Of course we're not complete strangers. It's a technical detail, that's all.'

She began to sniff and pulled the duvet cover to her face in the absence of a handkerchief. 'How can you say that? I feel awful. Guilty. *Dirty.* Don't you understand? What we had was unique to us. I never felt it was wrong or anything because it was just – our thing. It didn't bear comparison with anything else. And it was all a – huh – lie.'

'I really don't understand that, Ard. On balance, I think I'm rather relieved. But there's no reason to think anything will be different because of it.'

'We're just common or garden fornicators, that's what's different.' She started to cry.

'That's a terrible thing to say, love. It won't change the way I feel about you.' He went and sat beside her and tried to put his arm around her but she pushed him away.

'No. That's finished. Sorry, I just can't.'

'What? What do you mean? You're not going to throw me out!'

'No. I'll sleep on the sofa.'

'Ard, don't be stupid. What will Bos think? You're in shock. You're being totally irrational.'

'No, I'm not. *You're* being totally obtuse.'

Tim had to agree. A thicket of impenetrable density had grown up around Arden's thought processes, preventing comprehension. Her reaction seemed perverse. True, the news had been a facer at first, bringing on blinding confusion. He should not have bolted. Thalia must have thought him very rude and he must call her to apologize. But after a pensive drive – to Ipswich – the energy needed to fuel a major personal crisis had petered out. He could understand that it was a little sad that he and Arden were not related as they had always thought. It must be similar when a child discovers that he or she is adopted. But what it had to do with their sex life, if you could call it that, was a bafflement. Thalia had a point. They could get married. They would have some explaining to do, especially, if she was ignorant of the truth, to Mattie. Also the registrar. Changing a birth certificate was so difficult it would require the services of an alchemist. Perhaps that might be too complicated. The simplest thing would be to carry on as if nothing had happened.

It was Arden who was always moaning about life's complications, and yet here she was positively inventing one. It was lucky that he had a great deal of work into which to retreat until she adjusted to their modest change in status. Thank God for self-assessment. He was turning panic-stricken tax-payers away.

Twixsteads was an isolated ranch-style home of fashionably non-matching bricks, customized with interesting round-topped windows. Miss Tree felt like Scott of the Antartic by the time she located it – two miles off a B road that cut through the brown, watery flatlands near Mautby. She was nervous, wanting yet not wanting to find out if Lottie was really there, but she spared a thought to wonder how on earth the children got to school in Norwich. The mother must be a slave to the four-wheel drive. There were three of the vehicles parked on the vast gravelled forecourt, around the edge of which young Leylandii struggled for survival in the flattening wind.

There was a long wait before the door was opened, by an anorexically thin blonde woman in her forties, dressed in jeans and a lace top.

'Mrs Willoughby? I'm so sorry to disturb you. Miss Tree – Mr Jermigan's housekeeper.'

After a nano-second's hesitation, Mrs Willoughby smiled as though the visit was the most natural occurrence. 'Of course. Sorry, I didn't recognize you. But then, we've only spoken on the phone!' She laughed and grasped Miss Tree's arm for support. 'Come on through and meet my husband. He loves old people.'

Miss Tree sighed. Happy hour evidently started in this household at eleven o'clock in the morning. She stepped into a marble-floored atrium set about with dusty date palms. The temperature must have been in the nineties and she loosened her woolly scarf. 'No, please, I don't want to bother you. I was just looking for Lottie. Is she still here?'

'Lottie?' Mrs Willoughby thought for a moment. 'No, I don't think so. Not since Christmas. She was here for the weekend before. Hang on, I'll call Doe. The kids have their own annexe, see. Their friends come and go all the time and we don't even know they're there. Hang on.'

'Oh, I see.' This offered some hope.

'Have a seat, Miss Tree. I won't be a jiffy.'

Mrs Willoughby disappeared through a black glass door and Miss Tree sat down on the leather Chesterfield. There were magazines on the coffee table in front of it. It was like waiting to see the dentist, only more nerve-racking. If Lottie was not here, there was no escaping the fact that she was missing. Mr Jermigan would have to be informed. The first thing he would want to know would be why Miss Tree took Lottie's word for it that she was staying with Doe and had not personally checked with the parents. Useless to point out at this stage that Lottie had often stayed with Doe without anyone checking up on her, and it was Mr Jermigan who indulgently allowed her to go where she liked on the assumption that she was old enough to be trusted.

The sound of two female voices approaching the door set Miss Tree's heart a-flutter. Pray God the second one was Lottie's.

It was Doe's. To judge by the undies and T-shirt she had just got out of bed, although beside her mother she looked quite uncrumpled. They both wore an expression of guilty concern. Doe sucked a strand of her thin brown hair which was streaked with glittery red. 'I'm sorry, Miss Tree. Lottie isn't here.'

'But, Doe – look, I don't want to indulge in recriminations at this point, but – well you did say she *was* when I phoned the other day.'

'Yeah. Well. I'm really sorry. It was Lottie's idea.'

'That I can believe.'

'Honestly, Miss Tree, I didn't know she was going to stay out more than one night. I thought she'd have gone home Saturday night, like she said.'

Mrs Willoughby looked from one to the other, trying to focus and work out what was going on. 'You covered up for Lottie, Doe? Stupid girl. What d'you do that for? It's dangerous.'

'Let's hope not.' Miss Tree suspected that the show of indignation was for her benefit. 'This note arrived from her this morning.' She handed it to Doe. 'It was posted in Stowmarket. It just says she's staying with friends for a while, to dry out her soul whatever that means. But she doesn't have any friends in Stowmarket. That's why I hoped she might still be here. I knew it was an outside chance. The point is, do you have any idea where she is?'

'I'm not absolutely sure. But I'd guess she's with Darren. 'Cos, you know, that's where she usually is.'

'Usually? With Darren? Our Darren? Mr Jermigan's driver?' Doe nodded. 'Are you telling me that Lottie has been having an affair with Darren? I must sit down.'

'Well, the little slag,' said Mrs Willoughby. 'I am surprised.'

'Oh, shut up, Mum. Lottie isn't a *slag*. She's in love. I wouldn't have helped her otherwise, Miss Tree, d'you know what I mean?'

Hearing Lottie described as a slag was the last straw for Miss Tree. The date palms dissolved into each other before her eyes and she sank her head on to her knees. Mrs Willoughby panicked. She sent Doe to fetch some water and fanned Miss Tree with a copy of *Hello*. In a short time, she had recovered herself. 'What you are telling me is, this was a regular habit?'

'Yeah. Well. Sort of. I've never covered for her before, but—'

'Stop mucking Miss Tree about, Doe,' said her mother. 'You've caused enough trouble.'

The girl looked embarrassed. 'Lottie'll kill me.'

'Lottie may be dead already, Doe. Please tell me everything you know.'

She shook her head vigorously. 'No, don't worry. She'll be with Darren all right.'

'But where?'

'Well, she used to stay at his place. You know.'

'What – at Sloping? At his cottage? Right under our noses?'

Doe nodded. 'I don't believe it! How could she do that without our knowing?'

'It was only for the night. She'd go in and out her back stairs. She thought it was a laugh. She said she always jogged back, so if she met anyone they wouldn't suspect anything. I wouldn't have told you except to convince you she's okay. With Darren, I mean.'

'I'm afraid I regard that as a contradiction in terms. So that's it.' Miss Tree faced a fact she had always feared: that she and Mr Jermigan had been guilty of criminal negligence where Lottie was concerned.

'Why did you let her talk you into it, you silly girl?' demanded Mrs Willoughby. 'You wait till your dad hears about this.'

'Shut up, Mum. I feel let down too, y'know. Lottie's my best friend. I didn't think she'd land me in the shit. She's very – I dunno – heavy, when she wants something. She'd have cut me right out if I didn't go along with it, d'you know what I mean?'

'Don't blame yourself too much, Doe. We all allowed ourselves to be bullied by Lottie against our better judgment. However, there are more than usually powerful reasons to hope she is *not* with Darren. He is currently en route to eastern Russia with a consignment of sardines.'

The disappearance of Lottie was a welcome distraction for Arden and Tim. They heard about it through Bos, to whom Miss Tree had appealed for help. Bos was stupefied. The silly cow had gone and done it! He felt bad that he had kept quiet about Lottie and Darren, and some fancy footwork was required when Miss Tree asked him reproachful questions about his putative relationship with the girl. To compensate, he put himself out to help her manage the crisis. Darren's truck was not yet fitted for satellite tracking and his mobile was not responding; neither had he checked in for the last couple of days. This was at least encouraging in the sense that he was behaving strangely, and made it more likely that Lottie was with him. They managed to fool Vera, who ran the office, that they were concerned only about Darren's axle load.

Doe had provided a list of telephone numbers of all their

mutual friends, and Bos personally called them as a first step. None admitted to knowing anything about it. He swore them to secrecy. If the school got to know about it Lottie would be excluded automatically. The next step would be more of a problem. Miss Tree was adamant that as few people as possible at Sloping should know what had happened, and would not agree, as yet, to Bos's questioning the other drivers. Consequently, he was the only person on site in whom she could confide.

'We don't know for sure,' explained Miss Tree, 'that Darren is to blame. Lottie may have stowed away and he panicked.'

'I certainly would!'

'If that's the case, it wouldn't be fair to penalize him unduly. Knowing Lottie, the whole affair may have been driven by her. Men think with their willies, as you probably know, Bos.'

He laughed, gaining time while he adjusted to Miss Tree's language.

'If and when we have to tell Mr Jermigan, we shouldn't mention Darren's role in all this. Not until we know the whole story. Mr Jermigan might jump to the wrong conclusion and then Darren would be—'

'Mincemeat?'

'Slurry.'

'Right. Problem is, what do we do now?'

'Wait another day and see if he calls in. There is another odd thing. Lottie's cat is missing too. It could be a coincidence, but my guess is that she may have put him in a cattery. She's so neurotic about that animal, she's afraid he will run off if she's not here. She did that once before when she went on a school trip. Would you mind ringing round the catteries and seeing if you can trace him? If she did do that we'll know she means to come back.'

Less diverting, from Arden's point of view, was Mr Gordon. The probate of the will was almost completed, and he was becoming increasingly importunate on the subject of the reliquary and telephoned her every few days. This annoyance quite cancelled out the *schadenfreude* of Lottie's disappearance. Mr Gordon was insistent that the beneficiaries should come to a decision and became uncharacteristically assertive.

'You must understand, Mrs Fairbrother, that the possession of stolen goods puts me in an untenable position. It compromises my professional integrity. The item must be removed from my premises immediately.'

'But why do you keep going on at me about it, Mr Gordon? The blasted thing was left to Mrs Sewell. She must remove it.'

'I can never get hold of her. And, with respect, I think you are being somewhat disingenuous. Legally the item may be the responsibility of Mrs Sewell, but morally, shall we say, I don't think you and your brother can eschew involvement in the matter. It was your father who created this situation.'

'Yes. Our *father*. Not *us*. Who's being unprofessional now, Mr Gordon?' Hysterical was more like it. 'I suggest you confine yourself to legal commentary.'

There was a pause. 'You're right. I withdraw the remark. Nonetheless, if the item is not removed shortly I shall have to take matters into my own hands. Please use your influence with Mrs Sewell to conclude this business.'

It took all Arden's willpower not to chuck the telephone through the window after this conversation. She could not explain that one did not have influence over a person before whom one had broken down like a wino in the last stages of delirium tremens. She had avoided thinking about Thalia and the horrible news she had brought. Our Lady of Interfering Busybodies. How could she have imagined that they would be pleased? How would Thalia like it if they told *her* that her beloved but mysteriously unmeetable dad was not her real father?

Admittedly she did not understand the true nature of the relationship between Arden and Tim. At least, she had not done before she broke the news. Arden had been so upset she could not now remember if she had said anything that might have enlightened Thalia. Despite her professed defiant attitude on the subject, Arden did not particularly want Thalia dragging them off to confession or perhaps informing the *Suitables* hierarchy that Arden was an unsuitable person to sell mix-'n'-match garments. In fact, she did not want it at all.

Thalia was a do-gooding loose cannon. There was no knowing where she might explode. It would be advisable to get her on board, find out how much she knew or suspected, and persuade her if necessary to be discreet. It was a pity that Arden did not know any juicy blackmailing titbits about her as back-up in case persuasion failed. Although Thalia's addiction to doing the right thing might well be proof even against blackmail. Not for the first time, Arden felt envious of the Jermigans of this world, who would have no hesitation in using illegal methods to achieve their ends. Not violence, of course, but a little arm-twisting in a good cause was a real temptation.

The disposal of the reliquary was a convenient pretext on which to contact Thalia. Arden had a presentation in Kessingland and offered to call at the house. Once again Thalia hedged. This time her father had been exhausted after the third disability assessment review in two months. A likely story, Arden thought. They arranged to meet on the coast road at Great Yarmouth. It occurred to Arden as she put the phone down that she never had much trouble contacting Thalia, so why did Mr Gordon? Perhaps he was uncomfortable with Thalia's 'otherness' and had not really tried?

Arden drove through the funfair jungle of the seafront to a quiet cul-de-sac behind the dunes. There was a field of beige mobile homes on the land side, and on the other the sea could be glimpsed through a gap in the scrub-covered dunes. It stretched away wide and featureless, greyish-green with dubious dark shadows beneath the surface near the shore. A tiny ship appeared motionless on the horizon, as if held up on a stick by an unseen hand. With a yoga-like stretch of the imagination one could just about conjure up The Death of Steerforth, the reading of which had provided one of the more salacious experiences of Arden's schooldays. How she had thrilled to the image of his evil beauty justly destroyed by the raging seas. Steerforth was such a bracing antidote to David Copperfield's wimpish charms and the puke-making cuteness of the Peggottys' upturned boat. And the name – *Steer-forth*. Phallic or what? Who would not run away with Steerforth, given the alternative of a fresh-faced goody-goody called Ham?

The other goody-goody of her acquaintance parked further down the row of cars. Arden made a show of getting out, but Thalia hurried towards her and got in the car.

'I'm on duty at one, Arden. I'm afraid I can't stay long.'

'Well, I'm sorry to have to go through all this again. It's Mr Gordon. He's in a flap about the reliquary. Threatening to take matters into his own hands, whatever that means. He can hardly go public without risking his own reputation. Anyway, I said I'd talk to you. You must make a decision.'

'You know my view, Arden. It should be returned.'

'I notice you always use the passive tense in this regard. You don't fancy a trip to France yourself?'

Thalia looked away. 'Dad relies on me, Arden. It would be difficult to get someone to take over, especially at short notice. He can just about manage while I'm at work. Gavin's very helpful too. But I couldn't go away overnight, I'm afraid. Besides, I've never been abroad. I don't know the ropes.'

'*Never?* Not even a day trip?'

'No.'

'Do you have a passport?'

'No.'

'That's sad. I'm sorry. I hope you'll be able to when you're – freed up.'

Thalia shrugged. 'Can't say I mind. I can use my imagination, and watch *Wish You Were Here*.'

'But still, life's so short. To die and never to have seen – I don't know – Venice, say, it's *appallingly* sad.'

'And it doesn't help to rub it in.' There was a directness in the way Thalia delivered this remark that made Arden realize they had never seen her with her gloves off, but that the opportunity might be at hand. 'Anyway, never mind my holiday arrangements, how are we going to take the statue back?'

'"We" as in "me and Tim"? It may surprise you to learn that we can't afford holidays at the moment either. If it was up to me I'd dump it in the sea. Or leave it outside the French Embassy. Would your honour be served by that?'

'Wouldn't it be guarded all the time? And there's no need to be sarcastic, Arden. We're talking about a sacred relic. People don't care any the less about these things with time. Look at the Elgin Marbles.'

'Hardly in the same league as a scrap of flag, probably phoney.'

'I'm surprised at you, Arden. With your interest in the Middle

Ages and that, I'd have thought you'd be keen to see it go back to its rightful home.'

'That's because, like lots of people, you don't understand me very well. Yes, I'm besotted with the Middle Ages. But I'm not *crazy*. A, I know enough to be virtually certain the thing isn't genuine. B, it's been officially missing now for years and I don't see the point of going on some hare-brained mission to return it which could result in our arrest, assassination by the Maquis, or provoke the people of France to rise up with one voice demanding the exhumation of Humph so that they can give him an appropriate send-off.'

'What a *horrible* idea. Why did you have to say that?'

'You think I'm joking? Relations with our European partners are extremely delicate, Thalia. A PR cock-up like this could delay our entry into the single currency for years.'

'You're right. I don't understand you very well. You shouldn't have said that about Humph, even as a joke.' Thalia's mouth trembled. 'Is this your way of paying me out for telling you about Tim?'

'Please, don't even mention it. I've been trying to forget what you told us and so has Tim. And, no, I'm not paying you out, as you call it. Just trying to get you to see reason.' And doing a less than brilliant job at getting Thalia on board, co-operative and eager to help Arden in any way she could. They sat for a while staring out to sea, their hearts pounding in unison with furious indignation. Arden struggled with the murderous urges that always gripped her when an outsider even strayed near the boundaries of her relationship with Tim. 'The point is, Thalia, you and I approach things from very different angles. Now, I wouldn't say I was amoral. Certainly not the way Jermigan is. In fact, *I* think I'm a highly moral person. In that I examine the morality of my actions all the time. But without reference to any outside agency.'

'God, you mean?'

'If you like. Examine my cheque stubs. I believe I'm as generous to my fellow man as anyone. But, unlike you, I don't think it's necessary to refer to abstract notions of what's right.'

'Yes, yes. I know. So long as it doesn't hurt anyone else, it's okay.'

'What's wrong with that?'

'Loads. For one thing, you can never be sure that it won't hurt someone else, in a roundabout way. Even if you only hurt yourself that could be true. I suppose you could justify having sex with animals according to your theory.' Thalia blushed as she spoke, but exasperation had released her inhibitions.

'Why not, if the animals enjoy it?'

'Oh, Arden—'

'Look, all I'm trying to say is, while I respect your opinion – no, I do, honestly – there's no way I'd agree to do something silly and dangerous because of a moral theory.'

Thalia smiled and leaned her head back against the seat. 'It's quite funny, actually. You think I'm so "good", don't you? Just because I want to do the right thing by that statue.'

'Yes. Aren't you?' Arden sat up, all ears.

'Shall I tell you something that might change your mind? In confidence.'

'*Please* do.'

'Well. You know how fond I was of Humph. I've never tried to hide it.'

'Yes. Is that it?'

'Not exactly. The truth is, I fell in love with him. Completely, utterly – shamelessly.'

'With *Humph?* You actually fell in love with *him*? Are you sure?

'Yes. I'd known him for years, as a friend of the family. Well, of my mother, really. I never thought about him in that way because – I had my own life. You know, I got married, had Gavin, got separated, all that. I always liked Humph, but it wasn't until Mum became ill and had to go into the nursing home that I fell in love with him. I saw a lot more of him on his own. He was so worried about Mum, so kind and concerned. You'll groan, but I've always found good men terribly sexy. If I see a bloke helping an old lady who's fallen over or something, I go all weak at the knees.'

'Really.'

'Anyhow, I can see now that it may have had something to do with me being at a very low ebb after my husband ran off. I was probably influenced by the fact that Humph was older and so reliable and that. And I must have been depressed. Not that I'm making excuses, but I behaved in a way I never would normally.'

'Like what?'

Thalia pursed her lips and looked far out to sea. 'I begged him to have sex with me. Yes, you may well gasp. You can imagine how Humph felt. And I'm not talking once or twice. All the time. Every time I saw him. I rang him up at home. I wrote letters. I went to the cottage many times. At night, so no one would see me, of course. It was awful. I was completely deranged. I'd have raped him if I could and I told him so. Poor Humph. How could I have treated him like that?'

Arden grasped the steering wheel for support. 'What did he – do?'

'He was brilliant. Very patient. But he refused absolutely to oblige. He was horrified, I could see that. Most men would have either taken advantage, or refused to have anything to do with me. He actually spent *more* time with me. Just talking. Therapy type stuff, you know. Then when Mum died and I could see how heartbroken he was, it sort of broke the spell. I was upset as well, and I had Dad to think about. It just ran its course, and we stayed friends. I'll always be grateful to him for the way he handled it. Just imagine if he'd agreed—'

'I'd rather not.'

'Well, have I shocked you now?'

'A little. It's an unusual story.'

'It's odd, isn't it? I was so ashamed of myself afterwards I kept trying to think how it could have happened. I suppose I was lonely, and he was there. The chemistry seems to operate on its own, doesn't it? When you're with someone a lot, you can't control it. You must have felt that.'

'Yes, but then Tim and I had to share a bedroom so it was almost inevitable.'

There was a long pause. Arden realized that she had been talking to herself, or had intended to. Thalia did not move a muscle. Eventually she said, 'Pardon?'

'Nothing. Forget it.'

'Are you saying – you and Tim—'

'*Forget it*. You can't handle it.'

'Dream *on*. I feel faint. I can't believe this, I'm going to be sick . . .'

'Oh, don't be so melodramatic, Thalia. These things happen. We're only half – But then, we aren't even that, are we? You saw to that. So there's nothing to get excited about.'

'But you *thought* you were. That's just as bad!'

'Is it? Well, I'll leave that to your moralometer to work out. I thought you'd realized? Actually I wasn't sure. Afterwards I thought you must have guessed because I was so – gutted.'

'That doesn't follow. If you and Tim – well, I'd have thought you'd have been delighted.'

'Tim was. That was quite a shock. Quite upsetting. I can't explain the way I feel about it. It's too private. The point is, I'm sure you'll find it within your ethical framework to be discreet, Thalia. That would be the "right thing", wouldn't it? Can I count on you not to mention this to anyone? After all, we now both know things about the other that we wouldn't want spread around.'

'You're mistaken. I don't mind who knows about what I did. It makes me a witness to Humph's good character.'

'So. What does that mean? Will you go straight to the *Sun*?'

'No, of course not. But I shall have to tell Uncle Sebastian at least. I'll *have* to, Arden. I feel I need some sort of absolution. I feel almost defiled, just knowing about it.'

'For fuck's sake—' Arden strained every muscle not to throttle her. This was precisely the sort of ignorant bigotry that made her blood vessels burst. 'How can you be such a hypocrite when you've just admitted you tried to seduce my father!'

'I'm not *proud* of it. I don't try to *justify* it.'

'Well, good for you. Just keep your trap shut and forget about it.'

Thalia looked hard at the dashboard. 'But, you know, there is something you can do for me. If you want to be sure of my discretion.'

'What?'

'You know what. Return the Oriflamme.'

'For God's sake!'

'You don't believe in God.' She opened the car door. 'Let me know when you've done it.'

'What do you want – a receipt?'

15

There was no communication from Darren and Miss Tree reluctantly decided that Mr Jermigan must be told about Lottie's disappearance. She asked Arden to go with her to the hospital, so as to put off spreading the news.

'I may need to be carried out,' she explained. Miss Tree was experiencing a new range of emotions. Fear of the unknown, certainly. The awesome gamble of assuming Lottie was with Darren and had not been abducted by a psychopath. And then, just as bad, fear of the known. It was true that Mr Jermigan had always caused her a great deal of anxiety. His incarceration in HMP Durham had brought shame, sadness and the sickening feeling of being touched by undeserved squalor. Undeserved by Mr Jermigan. The revolting man he had beaten up should have been dealt with by the law. Mr Jermigan had performed a public duty. The incident had turned Miss Tree temporarily into a raving anarchist who fantasized about bombing the Crown Court. There were few outward signs of this conversion, except a persistent vibration of the head whenever she thought about it. Mr Jermigan had recognized the signal, and it was he who had persuaded her to adjust to the unfairness of the verdict. Life was a game. He had drawn a joker for once. So what?

But at least, despite what she had suffered on his behalf, they had been on the same side. In the matter of Lottie, she was afraid he would fail to see the disappearance as just another move on the board. There would be rending of temple curtains, grapes of wrath exploding all over the place – some of which were bound to land on Miss Tree. Justifiably, in her opinion. She had been responsible for Lottie while Mr Jermigan was in hospital. For the first time she was afraid of him, and it showed in her expression and the way she revolved the rings on her fingers, now thinner than ever.

To Arden Miss Tree cut a nobly pathetic figure. She was the kind of woman who would have been a distinguished Abbess or, at worst, have made an art form of genteel desperation in a mansion flat. The circumstances that had brought her into Jermigan's milieu were still a mystery, but it was apparent that her refined nature was not up to dealing with its more brutish aspects. It made Arden feel protective towards her, and she was perfectly willing, in principle, to accompany her to the hospital as bodyguard. Miss Tree was not to know that Arden had just recruited three *Suitables* ladies who needed training, and was overwhelmed with requests for presentations from homes for the elderly after the success of the experimental show at The Ashes. Secretly she was also working on some ideas for a collection of all-purpose garments that did up at the back with Velcro. The organization encouraged creative input, and there was no reason why old ladies should not know the joy of co-ordinated colourways.

This exciting new development had helped Arden recover from her initial shock over Tim. Or at least to put off thinking about it. Likewise Thalia's attempt to blackmail her into returning the Oriflamme. Arden had still not got over that. What a ruthless little madam she had turned out to be! The fact that Simon de Montfort would doubtless have approved of her methods was strangely unconsoling.

Miss Tree led the search for Mr Jermigan down the cavernous corridors of the hospital. The many paintings and collages of butterflies were all very well as an earnest of welcome, but Arden would have preferred a map. It reminded her of the London Underground and seemed to be similarly populated by strangers. A total of thirteen doctors, porters and others were stopped and questioned before they found Jermigan's ward. It was unexpectedly cosy, and cluttered with equipment on wheels and bins of used linen. The ward was in cruciform layout and three nurses sat at the desk in the centre. When Miss Tree asked to see Mr Jermigan their faces locked into expressions of prim distaste.

'Is he expecting you?'

'Yes.'

'That's good. It's down that bit, at the end on the right.'

'Thank you.' Miss Tree turned to Arden. 'Perhaps you'd better wait outside the room, at least until I see how the land lies.'

'I'd planned to. He wouldn't want to see me anyhow. He still blames me for the accident, I expect. Take your time – and good luck.'

It was a blessing that Jermigan was in a room on his own. At least the painful scene would not be played out in front of an audience. Unlike the larger rooms, which had a half-glazed wall on to the corridor allowing a full view from outside, his only had a glass panel in the door, so that Arden could not keep an eye on Miss Tree without deliberately peering in. She lolled against the wall in the corridor, studying a poster of instructions for use of the bathroom. The door was well soundproofed. The alternating deep and delicate fuzz of voices suggested a normal conversation to start with. She wished Miss Tree would get on with it. Arden was not nervous – her sweaty palms were due entirely to the overheated atmosphere – but there was no point in lulling Jermigan into a false sense of well-being.

An entire fifteen minutes passed before the balance of the conversation changed and Miss Tree spoke, hesitantly, for some time uninterrupted. Silence. Jermigan made one or two remarks, answered by Miss Tree at length. More silence. Then a log-splitting cry from Jermigan in which the words 'fucking' and 'kill' could be clearly distinguished. He went on shouting. An object hit a wall. Arden became concerned for Miss Tree's safety and peeped into the room. Miss Tree sat beside the bed, facing the door. She held her hand to her mouth and was crying, or trying not to. Jermigan was stranded like a huge bearded baby in his white cotton gown, purple-faced and dribbling with rage.

If he had not been so unfairly castigating Miss Tree for what were essentially his own failures as a parent Arden would have allowed herself to be quite touched. Jermigan's weatherbeaten face and hands were in marked contrast to the white, crêpey skin of his upper arms and sad wisps of grey hair that curled against the neck of the hospital gown. He looked much older than when swaggering around in a puffa jerkin. Too old to be coping with teenagers, still less launching Sloping Medieval Enterprises, a project that would daunt much younger men, if not actually kill them. Perhaps the council would take his age into consideration when assessing the viability of the project. It would be a nightmare if he died before it was finished and the site was littered with half-finished banqueting halls and Charnel House Cafes.

Arden wondered at the origin of his passion – a passion they could have shared had it not taken such very different forms. But then, she could not exactly locate the origin of hers, unless it had been an early love affair with an illustration in a book of fairy stories – of a perfectly formed young prince in a fur-trimmed cote-hardie and matching liripipe, feeding a swan. Which would not be Jermigan's excuse presumably.

A patient in the room next to his summoned a nurse to alert her to the racket next door. She hurried in to investigate before Arden could stop her. Arden was impressed by the air of authority the slight young woman assumed. Having established that nothing was wrong she reprimanded Jermigan for disturbing the other patients. He told her to fuck off. Miss Tree apologized for him and explained that she had brought bad news. Reluctantly the nurse accepted that Miss Tree would keep him quiet. Without thinking, Arden peered curiously over the nurse's shoulder into the room, so that Jermigan had a clear view of her. He shot up in bed, wincing with pain, and she quickly retreated.

The nurse looked Arden up and down, implying guilt by association. 'Are you a relative?'

'No. Just a friend.'

'I'm surprised he's got any.'

Arden considered this a rather unprofessional remark and was about to say so when Miss Tree came out. She looked ten years older than when she went in.

'He wants to speak to you, Arden.'

'Oh, no.'

'Please.'

'Very well. But only because *you* asked.'

'Understood.'

'Ah, well, the innocent have nothing to fear, do they?' Miss

Tree only smiled, leaving the question open. 'Does he think we should notify the police?'

'No. That's not Mr Jermigan's style. Besides, he's satisfied that she has gone off with Darren. He's in shock, Arden. You must make allowances.'

'Huh. He sounded in pretty good form to me. Right. Here goes.'

She put her hand to the door handle and then paused and looked at Miss Tree for guidance. The unmistakable sound of a choking sob could be heard, like the snort of water from a tap when an air lock is released. Miss Tree put her ear to the door. She pursed her lips and wiped away a tear.

'Poor Mr Jermigan. He's had such a tragic life.'

That was putting it rather strongly, thought Arden. He had an Achilles heel, true, but the rest of him was pure Saddam Hussein. They listened a while longer for the stutters of after-shock, and when there was silence again Miss Tree signalled that she should go in.

Jermigan was blowing his nose on the bed sheet. Arden handed him a tissue, avoiding eye contact. Thus obliged to look round the room her eye fell on the object that had hit the wall. It was a leatherette photograph folder. She picked it up. It showed a collage of Lottie, as a baby, a toddler, in her first school uniform. The latest one must have been taken when she was eleven or twelve, just before she turned pubescent and self-conscious and went into parent-as-vile-jailer mode. No wonder the photographs had upset Jermigan. Even if Lottie had not bolted, the contrast between the happy, smiling child here and the vituperative adolescent female that Arden knew was enough to break anyone's heart.

'Chuck it in the bin. I won't look on her face no more. Never.'

'Now, now, Mr Jermigan, that's rather melodramatic. You're hurt. That's understandable. But you can't mean to abandon Lottie forever. You're reacting like a Victorian patriarch. You won't be able to keep it up, you know. I know how fond you are of her.'

'Do you? Well, mebbe I won't abandon her, but that don't mean I've got to see her. She's made her choice. She'll have to stick by it.'

'That's very hard, Mr Jermigan. Lottie is only sixteen. The choices children make at that age are fuelled by hormones and self-loathing and peer pressure and all sorts of things. Didn't you do anything when you were young that you regret? No. Silly question. You never regret anything, do you? A regular Edith Piaf. May I sit down?'

'If you want. I can't take it in. I just can't. Where is she? What's she doing? That young swine Darren'd better look after her or – or—' His voice was choked with emotion.

'As I said to Miss Tree, you shouldn't jump to conclusions about Darren. She might have stowed away.'

'Why ain't he called in, then? He's got fifty thousand quids' worth of truck and forty tons o' sardines under 'im. Don't tell me he just "forgot" to check in like normal.'

'I wonder how much that lot is worth in roubles?' said Arden, to herself more than him. 'If the worst came to the worst they could live on the proceeds for a while.' Bos's brush with the Moscow mafia, Newton le Willows branch, had made her aware of the possibilities of free enterprise in that part of the world.

'You trying to give me a heart attack on top of everything?'

'Would you mind, then? What happened to your *laissez-faire* attitude to crime and punishment?'

He looked at her through narrowed eyelids. 'You smug bitch. You're enjoying this, ain't ya?'

'*Of course not.* I'm far too busy for one thing. But, let's face it, Mr Jermigan, it is *your* problem, isn't it?'

'Bitch. I wouldn't be stuck in here like a carcass if it weren't for you. I could've gone after her.'

Arden groaned. It was back to Great Yarmouth. Shades of Mr Peggotty and his insufferable Little Emily. 'That's ridiculous. It was an accident. Anyway, I thought you just said you didn't want to see her again? Look, why exactly did you want to speak to me?'

'You've got to go after her. Like I said, it's your fault I'm in 'ere.'

'*What?* Are you out of your mind?'

'Mebbe. We've got to find her. He won't stick with her. He'll dump her out some place where she don't know where she is, don't know the language, nothing. You know what happens to girls in that set-up. We got to get her back. Darren don't read the papers. He'd like as not head right for that Chechnya. It's like the fucking Wild West out there. They could both be kidnapped. And s'pose he does chuck her out? S'pose they make him hand her over? Even if she got away she'd have to hitch a ride and then she'd be as good as dead.'

'Honestly, I do think you're exaggerating. There's no reason to suppose Darren would dump her.'

'No? Not greed? You said yourself he could likely make off with the truck. He wouldn't want to be lumbered with Lottie, would 'e?'

'Even so – how would one start to look for her? She could be anywhere in Europe!'

'Take Miss Tree with you. She knows all the routes like the veins on 'er hands. Speaks French and German and that an' all. She used to teach languages. You didn't know that?'

'No. But I'm not surprised. Even so, you're deranged. I'm sorry. Miss Tree is a frail elderly lady. I couldn't drag her round the transport caffs of Europe on such a wild goose chase. It would kill her.'

'Take the Audi. You'll catch 'em up in no time.'

'Stop!' Arden put her hands to her head. She got up and walked to the window. 'You've got me talking as if I've agreed to do it. I haven't. It's insane. This is a job for Interpol, not a ladies' fashion agency.'

'It wouldn't be a goose chase, any road. I've got contacts. Friend of mine – a lady – she's got a trucking outfit runs out of Beccles. Owes me a favour, an' all. Took a load o' hot lawn mowers off of me one time. She can contact her lads out there. They can look out for us. Spread the word, like. Someone'll have seen them.'

'Why don't you send one of your drivers then? They'd be in the best position to work the grapevine.'

'You think I'd trust one o' them after what Darren done? Besides, they got work to do.'

'And I haven't? Just how much do you want Lottie back?'

'You know how much. I can't let the contractors down, I'd lose the business and my lads'd be out of a job.' He swallowed hard and clenched his fists. 'Please. You won't be out of pocket, I'll see to that.'

Arden leaned her head against the window and sought an explanation for this turn of events in the jumbled roofscape of Norwich. It yielded only the thought that clay tiles were a remarkably flimsy way of protecting a house from the elements. She suppressed the thought that life had been much less complicated in Chiswick because, if she were honest, it would involve admitting that simplicity had lost much of its charm. This volte-face was too earth-shattering to deal with at the moment. But she did recognize that there was a part of her that was tempted to jump into a car and chase Lottie – anybody – across the Continent. To leave *Suitables* and Thalia and even Tim behind for a while and have an adventure. Perhaps it was a latent upsurge of inherited wanderlust. Thinking of Thalia proved productive.

'Mr Jermigan, you say you want Lottie back. What would you be prepared to do if I agreed to go? Do for me, I mean.'

For a split second his face registered relief that she had agreed to the plan. It was followed by a cynical smile of something like admiration. 'I get it. You think you've got me where you want me, eh? Spit it out, gal. You're learning.'

'Yes. And not just from you.' Her arm was still sore from Thalia's twist, and if Thalia could do it she, Arden, would not be found wanting. As Tim always said, fate did not play into one's hands, one had to go after it with a butterfly net. 'Put it this way. The thing you most want in the world is to get Lottie back. The thing I most want is for you to drop your plans to turn Sloping into a theme park. Are you with me?'

A monumental stillness came over him. It went on so long she eventually turned to face him and check that he was still breathing. The chest hairs registered slight movement, but otherwise he was as still as stone.

'Mr Jermigan? I know it's a lot to ask. I know how long you've planned to do it and all that. But, honestly, it might be a blessing in disguise. I'm sure you don't know what you're taking on. I was an estate agent, and believe me, builders' estimates can safely be doubled, if not trebled. And that's before interest rates are taken into account. If you have to borrow, you should consider that if we stay out of the single currency they'll have to rise even more to keep up the pound. Which will be very inflationary in the long run and lead to a recession which will leave a lot of regular businesses up the spout, never mind fledgling theme parks.' Tim's strictures had not gone to waste.

'And as for relying on Japanese tourists and the like, that may have been all very well before the Far Eastern markets collapsed but it looks like very dodgy speculation now.' Still he did not even blink. 'And the hassle. I daresay you think you can cope with that with all your business experience, but – well – look at your mead hall. You wanted it finished by Christmas but it hasn't even got the roof on yet. Even if the builders do stick to schedule they'll probably dig up the remains of a Neolithic burial site or something and English Heritage will put the boot in and hold up the project for years.

'If you don't like being in hospital now, wait till you're in intensive care with the mother and father of nervous breakdowns. I've known people who've committed suicide because they couldn't cope with subsidence on a semi-detached Edwardian villa. So, you see, it's really in your own best interests to stop now, before you're in it too far to turn back. Mr Jermigan?' She went nearer to the bed and frowned at him. 'Are you all right?'

He spoke in a deep monotone. 'You'd bargain with my Lottie's life?'

'There you go, being melodramatic again. I'm telling you, it's in both our best interests. Of course I wouldn't hold you to it if we didn't get her back. You couldn't put a price on Lottie's life anyway, could you? I'd feel the same way about Bos.'

'You don't feel nothing.'

'Oh, nonsense. You don't know me at all. What do you say then?'

He held her gaze for some moments. On the whole, Arden was glad she could not read his mind. 'Very well.'

'Right. Good. Well. In that case, if you want to get on with contacting your friend with the hot lawn mowers, I'll go home and start making arrangements. What do you suggest – Harwich to the Hook of Holland?'

He nodded. 'Ask Miss Tree. And don't forget to take your mobile.'

'Of course. Okay. We'll be in touch, then. Before we go.'

Miss Tree was astonished by Arden's change of mood. She attributed her evident excitement to the prospect of action; the hope, at last, of tracing Lottie. Arden did not disillusion her. There was no point in telling Miss Tree about the deal she had struck with Jermigan. It would only confuse her, and Miss Tree might share his hurt that Arden was not prepared to drop everything and chase after Lottie for purely altruistic motives. But it was hard to keep it to herself. Her achievement in getting Jermigan to give up the Sloping Experience was dizzying. She could hardly believe it. Well, that was love for you. And as she was perfectly sincere in her belief that she was doing him a favour, there was no accompanying guilt. All they had to do was find Lottie. She could not wait to inform Tim of this amazing coup.

On the way home they discussed ferry crossings and Euro trunk routes in earnest.

'You won't believe this, Miss Tree, but Mr Jermigan actually suggested that you should come as well. I told him it was out of the question.'

'Why? Would I be a nuisance?'

'No, it's not that. I just thought it would be too much for you.'

'I don't see why. I assumed that I would go with you. It can't be worse than staying at home. Pithead syndrome, I call it – helpless waiting. I've had enough of that already.'

'Are you serious? It will be very tiring, you know. We won't get much sleep.'

'I can sleep standing up. It's one of the perks of old age. But you can't be thinking of doing all the driving yourself. Surely Tim will want to go too? And Bos. He's young. He'll enjoy the challenge.'

'There won't be room for Lottie at this rate. Tim's got too much work at the moment. Self-assessment deadlines and all that.'

But Tim was absolutely adamant that he would make up the party.

'Bugger the deadlines,' was his verdict. 'I've completed most of the cases, and if the others are late I'll pay the fines myself. You are *not* going on your own. *No.'*

There was no arguing with Tim when he was being masterful. Arden was amused by the feebleness of his protest at the plan, which no amount of blustering could conceal. In fact he saw it as a solidarity exercise, which would go some way to healing the rift that had arisen between them since finding out they were not related. His main objection was the dubious value of rescuing Lottie. Despite his willingness to go, he could not understand why Jermigan was not cheerfully changing the locks and planning how to spend the money he would save. Arden had to spin Jermigan's own lurid scenario of Lottie's possible fate before Tim could accept that there might be a case for preventing it.

And he was more restrained in his reaction to the promise Arden had extracted from Jermigan – to drop the Sloping Experience – than she had anticipated. According to him, the chances of finding Lottie were not high enough to justify the assumption that they would be able to claim the reward. He thought it more likely that Jermigan knew the planning application would be turned down, so would not be making the ultimate sacrifice that Arden had imagined. She was rather put out by this suggestion. It cast doubt on her powers as ruthless negotiator.

They stopped off in the city to get foreign currency and ferry schedules. Arden remarked on the fortuitous strength of sterling. Miss Tree grew nostalgic for a time when the Deutschmark had been twelve to the pound. It led to further reminiscences of her travels in Europe when young. Arden realised that Miss Tree was not just energized by the prospect of recovering Lottie, but, like herself, by the unexpected release from routine. In Miss Tree's case it was also a chance to revisit a continent of which she had been a virtual habitue for many years. 'Mother and I went touring twice a year at least. We had a Lagonda. I sold it after she died.'

'And did you not go so much after that?'

'No. Package tours had come in by then. And it was no longer safe for a woman to travel on her own. Or much fun, frankly.'

'Didn't you have any friends to go with?' Like boyfriends. But

Arden did not like to appear prurient. She could pretend to be a lady with Miss Tree and did not want to sully the image.

'Yes. But you know what holidays are like. One may start out friends but one is often enemies for life afterwards.'

'I hope that doesn't happen to us.'

'It won't. This isn't a holiday.'

'True. Still, I hope you managed to get some diversion. Teaching is a stressful occupation, I should imagine.'

'Not for me. I taught in a very respectable girls' school. But I gave it up after Mother died. Retired sick. Couldn't cope. With the loneliness.'

'Ah.' Arden felt honoured to receive such a confidence. It was a clear hint that Miss Tree had had a nervous breakdown after her mother's death. If it had been anyone else, Arden might have thought it pretty sad for an adult to be so close to a parent that they could not deal with life without them. It was so very different from her own experience. But Miss Tree had pulled herself together, made a new life, albeit as dogsbody to a despot. And she had won his respect and that of all who knew her. No mean feat these days. Even Arden, coper extraordinary, felt that much more confident with Miss Tree on board.

When Bos heard they were to take the Audi he insisted on accompanying them. While Arden hogged the telephone cancelling appointments and enquiring into ferry sailings, he badgered her to agree.

'Don't be silly, Bos. I don't expect your passport's even up to date.'

'Yes, it is. I had to do it last year to go to Ibiza with the lads. Oh, please, Mum. This is partly my fault anyway.'

'You can't just walk out on your job, Bos. Mr Jermigan would take a very dim view of that. Besides, I'm sure he would rather you were here to help out in his absence.'

'They can manage for a while. Shall I ask him? He'll well think I should go if he knows that whole thing with Lottie was a front to cover up for her carry-on with Darren.'

'Are you suicidal? You can't tell him that. He'd never forgive you.'

'At least let me ask him for the time off to go. Unpaid leave.

Honestly, Mum, I feel responsible. If I'd warned them earlier this might never have happened.'

'Oh, very well. I suppose it can't do your position at Sloping any harm to appear keen to get Lottie back.'

'You are incredible, Mum. Do you never take your eye off the main chance? This has nothing to do with my position at Sloping. I don't have one. I'm just a casual employee.'

'Then there's plenty of scope for improvement. Mr Jermigan has no sons, and the way things are going no daughter either. If this wretched theme park does go through, perhaps you should consider transferring to Events Management?'

'Mum, shut it. Still, I suppose I should be grateful you've dumped the fantasy about me taking Lottie to the altar.'

'What a quaint expression, darling. Stranger things have happened.'

'You're crazy. Hasn't Lottie done enough to give me the message she's not interested?'

'Just because she's run off with Darren? Rubbish. She's only sixteen. She'll get over him. And there'll be plenty of time for your many virtues to make a suitable impression.'

'What are you *like*? I don't even want to sha—' But then, that was not entirely true. At least, it had not been true for that brief sticky moment on Christmas Day when he had taken her the piece of pudding. 'Never mind. Just give me the phone.'

As Bos predicted, Jermigan was in favour of his going with them. More, he was emotional with gratitude. Bos kept this embarrassing side-effect from his mother as it would only fuel her dick-headed ambitions.

Over supper they went over the check-lists of items to take and the re-scheduling. They were interrupted by a phone call from Mr Gordon, which Tim dealt with. He rejoined them at the table looking quite put out.

'That man's getting very stroppy. But I was firm, Ard. I told him we were going away and would be in touch when we got back.'

'Good. What a nerve, calling at this time in the evening.'

'He was working late. Besides, it's a well-known harassment technique. He'll be getting us up in the wee hours soon. Tax inspectors do it all the time.'

'I've told him to harass Thalia but he seems to think we'd be better at it. Now, let's think. Luggage, money, passports, Immodium, wet-wipes, toilet paper, credit cards. Miss Tree's bringing the food. There must be something we've forgotten. I know I'm well organized but I can't believe we've done it all so quickly.'

Tim struck his forehead. 'Mattie! We won't be back by Sunday, I don't suppose. Now she's so much better she'll miss us when all the other visitors arrive.'

'What's the time?'

'Half-past seven. Why?'

'Let's go now. It only takes half an hour to get there. I think we should.'

'Oh, I don't know, Ard. I've still got some paperwork to do.'

'We needn't be long. Just for luck. Supposing we had an accident? Her whole family wiped out.'

'Look on the bright side.'

'I'm only being realistic. Those autobahns are bloody dangerous. I'd feel much better if we saw her before we go. And we can explain why we won't be there on Sunday.'

Bos stayed behind, to liaise with Miss Tree if necessary. Arden hoped that Jermigan's contact with his hot lawn mower friend would already have produced a lead. It would give the expedition a much-needed action plan.

They had never seen The Ashes after dark. There were a couple of visitors besides themselves, their presence much more obtrusive than during the daytime. Lights were dimmed; half the residents had already gone to bed, although it was only quarter past eight. 'I feel like Burglar Bill in the night nursery,' Arden whispered to Tim as they followed a nurse through the quiet rooms looking for Mattie. The silence was disturbed only by the muffled rattle of stainless steel trolleys and the cries of patients resisting their medication.

Mattie was in the far corner of the day lounge, in a distressing pose with a bespectacled woman carer who appeared to be pulling her out of the chair by her arm. Mattie cried and protested, the woman insisted she come along, and as they got nearer they could see that she too was almost in tears.

She let go of Mattie's arm and shrugged. 'What can I do? I'm off duty at nine. She won't budge.'

The nurse discreetly checked Mattie's arm for bruising. 'Don't worry. I'll see to her. These people are Mrs Mason's children. You'll let them persuade you into bed, won't you, Mattie love?'

'Why can't I stay here? I don't want to go to bed.'

'Sure you do. You'll freeze if you stay here, pet. The central heating down here goes off at ten.'

'I'll freeze then. What does it matter?' She turned to Tim and Arden. 'What are you two doing here? Is anything wrong? Can I come home with you?'

Tim took her hand and sat beside her. 'Sorry, Mum, that's not possible. We have to go away for a week or so and we wanted to see you quickly before we left.'

The nurse took Arden aside. 'She's a bit down at the minute. On account of Muriel, you know. Her room-mate.'

'Is she worse?'

'Very much so. She died on Tuesday. Mattie hasn't got over it.'

'I'm not surprised. Oh, dear. I'm really very sorry. For Mum, anyway. Muriel must be delighted. She couldn't wait. Is that why Mum doesn't want to go to bed – because she misses Muriel?'

The nurse nodded. 'She doesn't like the lady we've put in with her. Unfortunately there aren't any other beds free at the moment or we'd move her to another room. Mind you, there's not much point if she's going to Felixstowe.'

'Felixstowe? What are you talking about?'

'Have you not heard from social services? They should be writing to you shortly.'

'No. Perhaps they wrote to our old address? But the mail should be forwarded. What about Felixstowe anyway? They can't be thinking of moving her. It's miles away and she's too distressed.'

'Actually I agree with you. In an ideal world, Mrs Fairbrother – you know how it goes. I was talking to our manager about it just yesterday. The fact is your mum's so much better since she's been on the Trydopamide she doesn't need the kind of nursing care we provide here anymore. So they're moving her to a residential home. Or that's the suggestion at least.'

'It's outrageous! She's not a dog. She can't just be kennelled wherever there's a space. It'll kill her. I don't believe this.'

'I understand how you feel. Truly. But the fact is, there's someone else in a worse state than your mum who needs the bed. They can't release her from the hospital until there's a vacancy here. And the place at Felixstowe is lovely. Purpose-built, you know. Specially adapted bathrooms. The doors are wide enough for two wheelchairs! And she'd have her own room with a little balcony overlooking the garden. Right near the sea as well. When you see it, I'm sure you'll come round.'

'I won't see it very often, will I? It'll take hours to drive there and back. Sorry, I know it's not your fault.'

'That's all right. But no decision's been made yet, so keep it under your hat for the minute.'

This was easier said than done. Mattie was now weeping quietly on Tim's shoulder. Arden boiled with indignation. As if a minuscule balcony and specially adapted bathrooms could compensate for the disruption and confusion entailed in moving her mother in her condition. It was enough to bring on a relapse. Another battle to fight. Perhaps there was a private home in the neighbourhood she could move to? Arden could see the point of making room for someone worse off. But then there would be a ding-dong with social services about the fees. There was no room on the timetable for this sort of campaign. *Suitables* was already sliding further and further down the list of priorities. Arden could not wait to sound off to Tim about this development. He managed to calm Mattie down with his trusty patter, this time about the new Individual Savings Plans that were to replace TESSAs. It was not long before she decided she would go to bed after all.

Tim was appropriately upset at the suggestion that she should be moved but he admitted that his brain was not functioning properly, what with all the excitement. He wondered if Arden should pull out of the quest for Lottie and stay at home to pursue the matter with social services. It was not until he said this that she realized just how much she was looking forward to the trip.

'I would – of course. But the decision hasn't been made yet. Let's hope there'll be time enough when we're officially informed. Besides, you couldn't go traipsing round Europe with Miss Tree and only Bos to chaperone you. She would think it most improper.'

He chortled. 'Afraid I'll lift my leg, are you?'

'Tim. That is not funny. You've got so lewd since we found out we're not related.'

'Sorry.'

The scene in the cottage kitchen smacked of a war cabinet. Miss Tree had come round to go over the route with Bos and the table was covered with maps. She looked tired but indomitable, and had changed into Calvin Klein jeans and a sweat shirt. Arden could barely contain her astonishment. Miss Tree looked like one of those perennially glamorous grannies in catalogues who push lightweight lawn mowers or smile with relief from constipation. Thinking of lawn mowers prompted Arden to inquire if there had been any news from Jermigan's contact.

'Not yet, dear. We'll keep in touch, hourly if necessary. Mr Jermigan has been greatly energized by the need to mastermind all this. In a perverse way it will be good for him. Give him something to occupy himself.'

'I would have thought running a business from a hospital bed was enough for that. Still, you know him best. What is the plan, then? Where are we heading?'

'Our furthest destination is probably Linz over here in Austria. If indeed we get so far. The round trip would take too long otherwise and I know you don't want to be away for more than about ten days. I've got a map marked with all the TIR routes and lorry parks. All we can do is stop and ask in all the ones our men usually frequent. Of course, if they're well on their way to Russia, we've lost them.'

They looked hard at the map, each hoping that one of the others would say something to counteract the doubts that set in as they contemplated the vast tracts of Central Europe. Tim spoke for all of them.

'You know, Miss Tree, it is a bit of a long shot.'

'Yes, I'm not optimistic. But at least if we do get some information on their whereabouts we'll be on the spot.' Again they looked dubiously at the map. 'The spot' seemed a bit of an understatement. 'If you want to pull out, please say so. I understand. I'll go by myself, if necessary. I simply cannot sit around waiting. Not in that empty house. It's too awful.'

They were clamorous in their insistence that of course they had not changed their minds and there was no question of their pulling out. Miss Tree wept with gratitude, then pulled herself together. 'Now, if you'll excuse me, I really must get some sleep. Bos, you will come over first thing and check the tyres and so forth?'

'Sure.'

As she gathered up the maps there was a repeated ringing on the doorbell. They looked at each other, disconcerted.

'The Traveller,' said Miss Tree drily. 'Knocking on the moonlit door.'

Arden and Tim went together to answer it, knowing it could not be good news at this time of night. In fact it was almost bound to be the police, probably with a request that one of them accompany him to the station in Dnipropetrovsk to identify the body of a young girl. It was a relief to find Mr Gordon, carrying a crate with a lot of bubble wrap sticking out of it. He brushed past them and dumped it on the coffee table. The fumes of Drambuie hung in the air.

'There! It's your problem now. I'm sorry but it really was the last straw, your going away and leaving no instructions about this bloody object. I understand you don't even know when you'll be back. It is beyond my comprehension how you can be so irresponsible. I have co-operated with you in every way in this matter and got nothing but prevarication. That's all I have to say. When the estate business is completed you will be receiving my account and then I must ask you to find another solicitor. Oh – Miss Tree. Good evening.'

'Good evening, Mr Gordon. This is rather a late hour for a house call.'

'Yes. Well. I was just on my way home.'

'Arden dear, perhaps Mr Gordon would like some coffee. Shall I put the kettle on?'

'Oh. All right. Thank you. Honestly, Mr Gordon, don't you think you're over-reacting? Nobody even knows you've got the stupid thing. And I've told you, legally it has nothing to do with us.'

'Sotheby's know I've got it – as a result of inquiries undertaken on your behalf for which you will be invoiced in due course. And I've told *you*, Mrs Fairbrother, that legally I think it has, considering your father stole it.'

'That is unproven. I could sue you for libel.'

'Slander, actually. I don't think your legal nous is quite up to it, do you? And perhaps you've forgotten that your father is dead.'

'Now steady on,' said Tim. 'That was uncalled for.'

'Yes, yes, all right. I apologize. Put it down to the state this business has got me in. Can you not appreciate the frustration that your lackadaisical attitude has produced in me? Speaking for myself, I'm not accustomed to being in possession of stolen goods.'

'Stolen goods?' Bos had come in and started to unpack the box and take out the bubble wrap. 'What's all this about, Mum? Can I have a look?'

'I'll explain later, darling. It's just something that belonged to Humph. Mr Gordon reckons he stole it. Ages ago.'

'Cool. I wish I'd known him better.'

'You'll find enclosed a dossier with all the known facts about the piece, including the address of the *Société de l'Oriflamme*, should you wish to explain yourselves to them.'

Bos carefully lifted out the tarnished figure and placed it on the table. He pulled a face. 'Who's this geezer, then – Braveliver? Ooh, look, moving parts.' He wiggled the lance. 'What's in the box – lunch?'

'Don't touch it, Bos. It's fragile.'

'I see your son shows the same level of seriousness as yourselves in this matter, Mrs Fairbrother.'

'Oh, leave us alone, can't you? We've got *far* more important things to worry about at the moment.'

'Indeed. In that case I won't take up anymore of your time. Be so kind as to make my excuses to Miss Tree. I'll not be wanting that coffee. Good evening.'

Tim showed him out. Arden collapsed on the sofa. Bos announced he was going to bed.

'Put that thing back in its box first, darling. I can't bear to look at it.'

But before he could do so Miss Tree came into the room, took one look at the statue and passed out.

16

The first scale to fall from Lottie's eye did so before they reached the coast. She had assumed they would travel via the Channel Tunnel which was the in thing to do. Half her classmates had already been through it. There was a stigma attached to the prehistoric use of ships for the purpose which Lottie felt keenly. Worse, she had got her period. Not only was there to be no sex for a week, but she was accustomed to changing her tampons every two hours and Darren proved singularly obtuse about the necessity to do so. He was like some kind of camel that had the ability to retain fluid for days at a time and, were it not for the tachometer, would have taken a pit stop only every five hundred miles. As they drove off the ferry and set off for Frankfurt, Lottie took one look at the scenery and rummaged in her holdall for a book. Darren gawped.

'What are you doing?'

'Reading. What does it look like?'

'Oh, that's nice. I thought you came on this trip to be with me.'

'I am. With you. We can't talk all day. It's not natural.'

'Oh. Great. Can't talk, can't fuck. Great.'

'It's not my fault I've got my period.'

'No, I know. I'm not bothered, actually. But if you're going to sit there reading all the time, it's going to be a right pisser.'

'Sorry. I've got cramps. I might be feeling more sociable this afternoon. Turn the music up. It helps with the pain.'

'Great. What are you reading?'

'*The Pope's Rhinoceros*. It was the longest book I could find. It's all right, I don't get sick from reading in the car.'

'Great. Lottie—'

'What?'

'Are you sure your folks know about this?' Now they were actually on the road Darren had to admit he had taken the easy option in not checking out her story. The truth was he had not wanted to deal with her wrath if she'd found out.

'Of course.'

'Then why did you want me to pick you up in town?'

'I told you, Jermigan thought it would spare you the hassle if the other guys got to know about it. Staff morale and all that.'

'Didn't they worry about your – you know?'

'Virginity? Of course not. They're really cool about that sort of thing, d'you know what I mean? It's surprising, considering Miss Tree's so old. We had a long woman-to-woman thing about contraception and cervical cancer and stuff before I left. She's well sweet. Dead embarrassed but determined to do her duty sort of thing.'

'Yeah. She's a darlin'. Do her and Jermigan – you know—'

'*Please!* What a revolting idea. He really respects her. It's the only good thing I've got to say for him. No, I reckon she was a right little raver when she was young. Now do shut up, Darren. I really hurt. How long before we stop?'

'Three hours forty-two minutes. We should make the German border by then. Here, take the TachTrak.' He handed her a calculator. 'It'll beep a warning.'

'Can't you go any faster?'

'No, stupid. She's got a speed limiter. We're stuck at fifty-six. Do you wonder I don't want to keep stopping? God, you're like a little kid. I'll tell you when we get there, all right?'

Lottie resumed reading, her teeth clenched in fury. How dare Darren patronize her? Why had she not realized that once away from the hierarchical set-up at Sloping, in which she had the advantage, he would start behaving like a run-of-the-mill arrogant prat? Him and his forty tons of penis extension. It was really pathetic.

Darren was basically a no-hoper with a good body. He made Bos look like an intellectual. Of course, Bos should not have tried to interfere. The fact that he was right made her angry rather than repentant. She was quite prepared to take responsibility for her own mistakes. But how could she have been so blinded by Darren's sex appeal? And how boring northern Europe was to look at. Two weeks of Darren's farts and *The Pope's Rhinoceros* for entertainment . . . she would have to endure it. Nobody need ever know what a let-down it was. She closed the book and leaned her head back, her eyes tightly shut to keep in the tears.

When Miss Tree came round from her faint she apologized. They laid her on the sofa until she felt better, instantly refuting all suggestions that she was not well enough to travel.

'It was just the shock of seeing that – object.' She indicated the statue. 'I'm all right, truly.'

Arden was riveted. Had Miss Tree been Humph's accomplice? No. If she had known him that well she was not the type who would have been able to simulate the symptoms of a kindly but distant friendship. Now was not the moment to press for details, but if Miss Tree knew the truth about the statue's origins they might be able to clear Humph's name. What a ridiculously dramatic notion that was, reeking of the Guildford Four and James Hanratty. Arden could not quite account for the fact that she felt so keen to pursue the matter. 'I'm surprised you recognize it, Miss Tree. It hasn't seen the light of day for years.'

'I've never actually seen it. But I know what it is, all right. I'm sorry, I can't talk about it now. Did Mr Mason have it? Has it been in this house all the time?'

'He left it to – a friend. I don't think he realized what it was. He kept it at the bank.'

'If only he'd mentioned it! So that's what happened. Oh, dear. Oh, dear. I can't think about this now. I must get home.'

Arden saw her to the door. 'There is just one thing I must ask you, Miss Tree. Do you know where the statue comes from? Where it belongs, I mean?'

'Yes, I certainly do. If it weren't for that thing I wouldn't be here now.'

Arden regretted that she could not put a gun to Miss Tree's head and force her to explain this intriguing remark. Instead she wrapped up the statue in the box and fetched a blanket to put on top for extra protection. 'Stick this in the boot, darling,' she said to Bos. 'I think we can kill two birds with one stone.'

By the morning Miss Tree had fully recovered her composure. She sat in the front of the Audi, with Tim at the wheel, armed with a full complement of maps, computer print-outs of alternative routes, lists of all known truck parks, customs stations and compounds, CB bands and mobile phone numbers. Arden and Bos looked at each other in a mute conspiracy of amusement tinged with despair. The thoroughness of Miss Tree's preparations at such short notice bore witness to the depth of her hope, and mocked it in equal measure. There was an unspoken agreement among the cottage party that the expedition was a token of solidarity rather than an undertaking with any real hope of success.

Bos, knowing Lottie as even Miss Tree did not, was the most gloomy of all about the outcome. Even if they managed to locate her, he could not see Lottie succumbing to the temptation of coming home quietly, with only the prospect of life at Sloping and returning to school with her tail between her legs to tempt her. He imagined a ghastly tug-of-love in a lay-by off some hellish autobahn, during which he intended to keep a very low profile.

'We can start on the ferry,' said Miss Tree.

'Start what?'

'Inquiries. I daresay there'll be plenty of drivers going to the Continent. Somebody might have heard something. We should take advantage of every opportunity, otherwise there's no point. Don't you agree?'

They reassured her warmly. Tim caught Arden's eye in the rearview mirror. 'Perhaps you should let Bos and me take care of that side of things? It might be rather upsetting for you.'

'No, no. We should maximize our resources.'

Arden smiled. Miss Tree had never had children but her ferocious devotion to Lottie would knock spots off many a natural mother. At least, she assumed Miss Tree had never had children. Her involvement with the blasted Oriflamme hinted at a past that might contain all sorts of skulduggery.

A gloopy helping of celeriac salad on the ferry put paid to

Arden's good intention to help with inquiries. It took a while for the Immodium to work and by that time she was too exhausted to do anything but retire to an extremely uncomfortable recliner in the dozing lounge. Tim and Bos started with a will, but quickly gave up. Contrary to Miss Tree's expectations, it was almost impossible to find a truck driver, although they approached dozens of the most crumpled-looking men in lumber jackets. Miss Tree had no luck either, and when they rendezvoused with Arden she pluckily admitted defeat.

'It will be more efficient if we just ask at the truck stops. I'm not disheartened. Not at all. But I will call Mr Jermigan. You never know.'

Arden and Bos went up on deck and stood in the stern to watch the churning wake. Whenever she went across the Channel she always thought, dolefully, of the wreck of the White Ship, when the son of Henry I was drowned after lingering too long at a drunken party in Calais. Some things never change. No doubt young William thought he was immortal, as adolescents always do. She could just imagine Henry bewailing the fact that if he had come home when he was told he would be alive today, etc. Bos yawned, revealing a set of strong white teeth, like a dog's.

'Bos, put your hand over your *mouth*. How many times do I have to tell you?' At the same time she put her arm through his and gave it a squeeze.

They stopped at a promisingly busy lorry park near Brussels airport. Apart from quizzing truckies of many nations, of which there seemed to be about five thousand in the steamy self-service cafe, they had to study the map and decide where to spend the night. Their party attracted curious glances. A man with bulbous eyes under an Iveco baseball cap leaned over from the next table and asked them, in a heavy Platt-Deutsch, if they were lost. Miss Tree explained their mission to him in German. He was so delighted by her fluency in his language he brought his chair over to their table and started telling her about his delivery problems with a well-known supermarket chain in the north-east. But even Miss Tree's skills faltered before the German for palleted potatoes and tipping times and when she excused herself to go to the toilet he moved off. They went back to studying the map when Miss Tree returned.

'I don't suppose we could make a detour to Bruges?' said Arden, resigning herself to more personal sacrifice. 'There would be masses of hotels.' Bruges was stiff with medieval tenements, and the very house to which William Hastings – later dragged to his death from the bed of the strumpet Jane Shore – had been exiled in 1470. The thought of treading the same boards as that unfortunate but 'loving and passing well-beloved man' was ravishing. But she suspected that in the circumstances sight-seeing was out of the question.

Miss Tree looked guilty. 'It's too far out of the way, dear. But I tell you what, when we get Lottie back and all this is over, why don't you and I go together? My treat. I know Bruges well. I'd be delighted to show you round.'

'Oh, yes, *please*. Now that *is* something to look forward to.'

Arden did not notice the pensive look on Tim's face. He wondered if Arden would have so readily agreed to go off on a jaunt with someone else before Thalia's revelations. She was starting to behave like an unattached person, and yet it had always been she who urged him to feel free, not realizing that she was an impossible act to follow. He hoped she would notice his dejected air, but Arden was too interested in helping Miss Tree plot the route. Bos went off to play the fruit machines.

As a big concession Darren stopped in a parking lot beside a railway station. 'There'll be a washroom or something. You can freshen up.'

'What – strip off in front of other people? Are you mad? I might be arrested.'

'This is Germany, not Saudi Arabia. What's the problem? I would.'

'You're a *bloke*, Darren. I need a shower.'

'Well, you'll have to wait a couple of days. Jesus, Lottie, this was your idea, y'know.'

'Tell me about it.' She clambered down from the cab and was almost felled by a wind which whammed straight through her and out the other side, as though she were made of wire netting. She shouted to Darren and he came round and they staggered like three-legged racers towards the station, a town hall replica that thoughtfully labelled itself '*Bahnhof*'. Once inside Darren tried to help her untangle her hair. She pushed him away. 'I'm frozen. Where's the Ladies, then?'

'Down the hallway there. It says *Damen*.' Darren put his hands in his pockets and stared purposefully at the small crowd milling about the concourse.

'Yes, I know that. Where shall I meet you?' Lottie noticed that he looked blatantly fed up. 'You aren't going to run away, are you?'

'What? 'Course not. Are you?'

'No. Unless you want me to. If I'm such a pain. There are trains here.'

He pulled her towards him by her lapels and kissed her on the nose. His rough-hewn cherubic features were softened into an expression of condescending concern. 'Stuff this dog-in-the-manger act, love, eh? It's just the curse talking. I understand, honest. How about a beer? It'll warm you up.'

'Okay. Thanks.' Lottie thought how unfair it was that men's faces stood up so much better to the weather. Darren's thick, perfectly formed eyelashes were edged with becoming raindrops, whereas her eyes must now look like a toddler's art work.

'Meet you in the bar. Don't be long.'

At least there were plenty of paper towels and hot water in the toilets. Watched with clear disapproval by a middle-aged woman with a feather in her hat, Lottie ripped off several hundred yards of towel and divided it into two, soaked them both in hot water and applied liquid soap to one of the wads. The woman spoke to her. Despite four years in the top group for German Lottie was annoyed to realize that she could understand the sarcastic tone, but not a word that the woman said apart from 'forest'. She could have said with confidence that she had a cat but no brothers and sisters, or from which platform departed the train for Mainz, but for a moment was stuck for the vocabulary for: 'Don't give *me* lectures on the rain forest, you old trout.' Then she remembered the word for hospital, courtesy of 'The hospital is situated on the outskirts of the town.' '*Krank*,' she explained, gesturing to her stomach with her elbow.

The woman raised her eyebrows. '*Ja, klar.*'

So much for European unity, thought Lottie as she locked herself in the toilet. Tears coursed on to the rapidly cooling wads of towel. She had thought she was being pretty resourceful, all things considered. Only the fact that she had the curse could explain how the censure of a complete stranger produced such feelings of shame and humiliation. She waited until she was sure the woman had gone, but when she joined Darren in the bar the interfering busybody was at a table with her husband, giving him the low-down on Lottie's anti-social vices by the looks of it. She pointed Lottie out to him and their indignation went up a notch. The beer was very welcome. Darren looked disappointed that her mood had not improved and asked if she wanted anything to eat. She did not, but he brought her some soup and a roll anyway. The soup appeared to be watered down Bovril with a shoal of maggots floating in it. Darren tucked in to schnitzel and chips.

'Sure you don't want some of this? We'll have to cook on the diesel from now on. The budget don't run to restaurants.'

'You're joking?'

'No, I'm not, Lottie. I did warn you.'

'I thought you were joking. I'll pay. I've got five hundred Deutschmarks.'

He shrugged. 'If you want. I'd hang on to it, for emergencies.'

'Where are we going to stop tonight? Or does that count as nagging? No chance of a motel, I suppose. I'm black and blue from last night.'

'Didn't used to be.' He kept his eye on his plate.

'Well, I never spent the whole night in the truck before.' She was silent for a while as she watched him eat. His jaws pulsated under the skin of his cheeks as though trying to get out. She had never watched him eat before either. Once was enough. It was sad in a way. Darren was all right. He would make some slapper very happy. In fact, he would probably makes hundreds of slappers happy with a face like that.

'What's up? You bored? Get your book out, I'm not bothered.'

'Bored? You're projecting, Darren. Be honest, you'd be having more fun on your own, wouldn't you?'

He rolled his eyes. 'Stuff it, Lottie.' He finished eating and took out a cigarette. 'Look, if you want to go home that badly, I can drop you off at Berlin airport. It's a bit out the way, but I'd do it. It's fuckin' miles where we're going. Think you can organize your own ticket and that? You should have enough money. When I call in I'll tell Miss Tree what you're doing and she can have someone meet you in London.'

'*No.*'

'No what?'

'You mustn't call in.'

'Why not?'

Lottie sighed angrily. 'Why do you think?'

'Think? What should I – Hang on. You're not saying—'

'Yes. They don't know. I lied. So what? I posted a note to Miss Tree when we stopped in Stowmarket. They won't worry. Anyway, Jermigan's in hospital. They probably won't even notice I'm not there.'

He sank his head into his hands. 'Je-sus. You stupid, *stupid* bitch! I can't believe this. Where do they think you are?'

'I didn't say. Just that I needed some space and not to worry. Corny, but true. It's what they'd expect. And don't slag *me* off, Darren. It's your own fault for not checking, isn't it?'

He shook his head slowly, stunned.

'What's the problem? They don't know I'm with *you*. And if you don't call in you needn't find out. It's okay.'

'No, it *isn't*, you stupid cow. They'll be shitting themselves with worry.'

'It's Jermigan who'll be shitting himself if he finds out I was with you. Which he will, if you call in and tell them.'

'But they've got to know. They might have the police out looking for you by now.'

'Of course they won't. I'm not a missing person, I left a note making it quite clear I'd be back. They're not going to waste their time on a case like that.'

'Don't you have *any* idea what grief you'll be giving them? Miss Tree especially. I thought you cared for her?'

'I do. What's that got to do with anything? I've often stayed out without telling them. It's okay.'

'Not for weeks at a time, I'll bet. You've got to call them.'

'All right. If you want to implicate yourself, fine. You know how Jermigan deals with people who upset him.'

'Shit. Don't mention me then. Just say you're okay and where you are and give them an idea when you'll be back.'

'I hardly think it will set their minds at rest if they think I'm bumming round Europe on my own.'

He thumped his forehead with his fist. 'Shit, shit, *shit*! What are we going to do? I could kill you, you stupid bitch.'

'Go ahead. Want a spliff first?'

'You can't smoke that in here, you'll be arrested. And I won't hang around to bail you out.'

'No. I can see you're a fucking brilliant port in a storm, Darren. I'll call them if you want. But don't blame me if Jermigan's waiting for you with his friends from the Duck 'n' Barrel. Shall we go?'

17

They settled for the first small concrete hotel they came across, in the suburbs of Cologne. Arden longed to have some time alone with Tim for that cosy review of the day that serves as emotional Horlicks for couples, but as Miss Tree could hardly be expected to share with Bos, Arden suggested that they pair off. Neither of them felt like dinner so Tim and Bos went off for a bonding session over *bratwurst* and potato salad, Miss Tree went to bed and Arden dozed off in the TV lounge. When the men returned they were the worse for drink. Arden was angry. Their compliance with the cliche that wherever two or more men are gathered together alcohol must surely lubricate the proceedings was bad enough, but she did not want Tim and Bos getting too matey and forming a power bloc. It would cause a shift in the domestic dynamic that would not work in the long run, but she did not know if she was more jealous of Bos's affections or Tim's.

'Neither of you will be fit to drive in the morning,' she chided. 'You're being totally irresponsible.'

'Yes, Mum,' hiccupped Tim. Bos cracked up.

'I knew we shouldn't have let you come along. You're supposed to be *helping*, and look at you.'

He collapsed in a chair. 'It's a shtupid idea anyhow. Lottie'll be a shex shlave in Oman by now.'

'Don't you dare say that to Miss Tree. You admitted yourself all this is partly your fault.'

'Well, I've changed me mind. I blame the parentsh.'

'Parentsh are a bugger,' said Tim.

'Yeah.'

Arden growled and marched upstairs, trying to keep her anger on top of her misery. Tim had betrayed her. He had ganged up with someone else to make fun of her. If this development continued at home the situation would become intolerable. And what might he not confide in Bos while they were sharing a room and his tongue was loosened by drink? She was so angry and anxious it was difficult to creep soundlessly around the bedroom and stop the curses as she bumped into the furniture. Miss Tree woke up and put on the light.

'It's all right, dear, I wasn't properly asleep.'

'Sorry. Tim and Bos have been drinking. They'll be useless tomorrow. I'd better drive. God, I wish we were on our own.' She avoided looking at Miss Tree, but noted how chic she looked in her navy blue sleep shirt and rumple-resistant haircut.

'It's all a bit of a lark so far as they're concerned, I'm afraid. I can't blame them. I know what the odds are. In fact, I've been thinking. Unless we get any hard information via Mr Jermigan I suggest we press on to Geiselwind. It's the truckers' mecca. If we don't pick up any clues there we can call it a day.'

'That sounds like a good idea. You'll have done all you can then. If it were up to me I'd be quite willing to go on but the men are bound to get restless.' Besides, Arden wanted to leave time for her own mission. 'Don't worry, Miss Tree. I'm sure Lottie will be all right. Who knows? She may be back before us.'

'Wouldn't that be wonderful?'

'Why don't you turn the light out? I can manage from the light in the bathroom.'

But after Arden was showered and in bed Miss Tree was still not asleep. The glow from the street through the orange hessian curtains showed up her slight, motionless form, hands folded on her chest, eyes fixed thoughtfully on the polystyrene tiles on the ceiling.

'There is one thing, Miss Tree. It's just a suggestion – you don't have to agree – I won't mind.' She would, but everything depended on Miss Tree's co-operation.

'What is it, dear? I wouldn't like to think you couldn't speak frankly to me. Do you know something about Lottie you haven't told me?'

'No, it's nothing to do with her. It's that statue. Don't worry,

I'm not asking you to talk about it but – well, I promised the owner I'd try and return it. The wrongful owner, that is. I never thought the opportunity would arise, quite frankly, but – well, it has. In a way. And when I realized you knew where it belonged, I thought – maybe on the way back through France . . . Sounds very blase, doesn't it? "Oh, I just thought we'd pop into France and restore the Oriflamme to its rightful owners." Honestly, the things one finds oneself doing for other people – Oh, sorry, I didn't mean it like that.'

'I know.' Miss Tree sighed and wiggled her toes. 'You deserve an explanation after all this. But you must promise not to breathe a word to anyone. Not Tim, Bos – anyone.'

'On the soul of Simon de Montfort, I promise.'

'Simon de Montfort was an avaricious thug, you know. His rule in Gascony was an abomination.'

'Steady on, Miss Tree. They wouldn't have asked him to be Constable of France if he was that bad. We'd better not start arguing about him. I take no prisoners on that subject. People argued about him at dinner parties even at the time. I like that idea. People don't change, do they?'

'They stop hacking each other to pieces with poleaxes anyway. In some places.'

'I wonder if Simon de Montfort ever saw the Oriflamme? I wonder if he ever touched it? I hadn't thought of that. Just think, if there *is* a smidgeon of the Oriflamme in that reliquary, I could touch it myself. If it weren't soldered shut. Our fingerprints could mingle. Oh, joy.' This was said not entirely to indulge an erotic fantasy, but also to bring Miss Tree back to the subject. 'Sorry. I'll think about that when I'm on my own.'

'Yes. Oh, dear, this is going to sound like an episode in a Bunuel film.' Arden felt unable to comment. 'I think I've told you that my mother and I used to go on motoring holidays on the Continent. That word "motoring" dates me, doesn't it? It reeks of hand-cranked engines.

'We were quite daring, I suppose. People thought they were well-travelled if they'd been to the Isle of Wight in those days. My mother's grandmother was French, though, so she always prided herself on what she called her cosmopolitan background. I doubt if the French would see things like that in similar circumstances.

However, she thought it entitled her to be more adventurous than the average inhabitant of Nuneaton at that time, and when my father died she decided to "go for it", as they say.

'It had always been a bone of contention between them because he refused to set foot in France. He thought they all wore hairnets in bed – the men, anyhow. And then my brother was killed in the war. In Normandy. He was shot down near Alençon in 1943 and hidden by the Resistance. Then the following year he was killed in an American air raid just before the Liberation. Ironic, but there you are. I never got over it, really. I think that's why I never married. I was just too sad. And then I was too old. You probably can't understand that.'

'Oh, yes, I can.'

'In 1955 she decided to go to Normandy and visit the people who had helped my brother during the war. She couldn't face it until then. It was a very moving experience. I was so glad I could understand the language, they told us so many incredible stories. It was utterly humbling to hear what ordinary people went through, and if they were taken prisoner, well . . . There was a group of men taken to prison in Paris. One of them had scabies, and the only way they could relieve it was by piddling on him. Imagine that. It makes one feel one should never complain of anything again.'

'I know what you mean. And it must make it hard for you to put up with spoilt br—children like Lottie.'

'Yes, it does sometimes. But then I'm sure that if Lottie were put to such a test she would come through with flying colours. Anyhow, the main thing was, we learned that the escapees had kept their spirits up. Well, you'd expect that of Englishmen, wouldn't you? One of my brother's friends got away, and guess what was the one thing he managed to carry all the way home to Carlisle?'

'What?'

'A sack of millet for the budgerigar. In the last letter he had from his wife she'd complained about the shortage.'

'How *terribly* English.'

'Quite. Well, one evening we were driving from Camembert to Le Havre, on our way home. We were hoping to find a *pension* in Lisieux for the night as we'd stayed too long at one of those wonderful French Sunday lunches. Everything cooked in cream, including the sausages, but you know how dreadful food was in England then. We couldn't resist. I actually felt quite ill – thought I was going to be sick. I think my liver had collapsed under the strain. Mother turned off down a side road and we were looking for a suitable place to stop, but I couldn't wait so we stopped by a field gate.

'I was just getting out of the car when we saw a young man running towards us. He stopped when he saw us, and was about to jump into the field when he must have noticed the car was English. And I suppose –' she sighed '– with two women in it he had nothing to fear. He ran up and asked us to help him. He said he was being chased by some people who thought he'd stolen something. Naturally he didn't go into details. He was in an awful state. Blood all over him and a cut over his eye, but still – god-like. Handsome. Amazing physique. I forgot to mention he was stripped to the waist.'

'And that was Humph, was it?' Although 'god-like' was a bit wide of the mark.

'No, that was Mr Jermigan.'

'Oh, I *see*. I think.'

'He was twenty-one. I was thirty-two. Still quite a young woman, you see. Young enough to appreciate Mr Jermigan at any rate. Well, we had to make up our minds very quickly, but it wasn't difficult. Apart from one's obvious instinct to help a fellow patriot, we were feeling pretty emotional about all the people who had helped my brother. So we bundled him on to the floor of the car, and when we had gone what we thought was a safe distance we stopped and took the luggage out and made him comfortable in the boot. When we got to Lisieux we booked two rooms and smuggled him upstairs. I suppose if all this had happened in Nuneaton things would have turned out very differently, but you know what it's like when one is abroad. Everything is rather surreal anyway. So . . . oh, dear, what will you think of me, Arden?'

'What? You can trust me, Miss Tree, honestly.'

'I hope so. At first Mother and I decided to let him have one of the rooms and we'd share the other. But then, that wouldn't work, because if someone knocked at his door expecting to hear a woman's voice – so Mother persuaded me to stay in his room. Oh, dear. She was feeling so sentimental and Gallic. She'd seen at once that I – I thought he was extremely attractive. And she said, this was my chance. I was a virgin, you see. We discussed these things very freely when she was in her Colette-ish mood. I suppose I was infected by the spirit of doomed youth, though my brother would have had a fit if he'd known.

'I needn't go into details. The point is, I'm sure Mr Jermigan did not realize what had happened, or else instantly forgot. He had a head injury, for one thing, and he had also drunk quite a lot of brandy and – how can I put this? – so far as sex is concerned, Mr Jermigan is on auto-pilot. At least he was then. In the morning he behaved as if nothing had happened. And so did I. By then I felt rather foolish, to say the least. It had finally dawned on me that I might become pregnant. Fortunately I didn't. And I was immediately distracted by the business of getting him back to Dieppe. I don't know how he explained himself to his employers.

'There. A Jezebel's story. I don't suppose it strikes you as much to get worked up about by today's standards, but Nuneaton in the nineteen-fifties – well, it was like Iran under the ayatollahs. Mother was thrilled. I think she quite fancied him herself.'

Arden stared, speechless, at Miss Tree's prim face.

'Have I shocked you, dear?'

'No. *Yes. Wonderfully.* You're *amazing*, Miss Tree.' Arden was equally staggered at this further evidence that the most unlikely women could turn out to be ball-breaking predators. Well, that was perhaps putting it too strongly in Miss Tree's case. She could not understand it. Sex was all right. It was necessary, and often quite relaxing, but her lust for it had never equalled her passion for the Middle Ages. 'I just can't get over you and Jermigan—'

'I know. I'm so old and dried up now it must seem like quite an obscenity to you.'

'Not at all. It's just so odd when I think of the relationship between you. What I've seen of it, anyway. You're both so respectful – formal. It's really strange to think—'

'But I told you, Mr Jermigan didn't know. And you must never tell him, Arden, or I will kill you. I mean it.'

'I believe you. I won't. He'd probably kill me as well. He

wouldn't believe it either. Were there others? Did it get you going, as it were?'

'My dear, there was nowhere to go. One simply didn't do it. There were a couple of divorced civil servants later on, when I was past caring. Pathetic, don't you think?'

'That's the last word I would use to describe you, Miss Tree.'

'Thank you, dear.'

'So how did you end up at Sloping?'

'Ah. Mr Jermigan was, naturally, extremely grateful to Mother and me for saving his life, as he always put it – rather exaggerating the case, I always thought. As one does, he said if there was ever anything he could do, and so forth. We kept in touch, at Christmas mainly. Then, when his wife and his sister died in that giant teacup tragedy, he wrote and asked me if I would be his housekeeper. I'd retired early from teaching. I missed Mother so much after she died, I had a nervous collapse. It was a wonderful opportunity to start a new life. With little Lottie as well. Never having had children, I thought it was a miracle. You can't imagine what an enchanting child she was.'

'That's true.' There was a smile in Arden's voice as she said, 'You weren't hoping to get back into Mr Jermigan's bed, were you? Good Lord, fancy me asking you such a thing. We have come a long way.'

'Certainly not. No, I had long since come to the conclusion, like Bernard Shaw, that mathematics was far more interesting. And I wasn't even interested in mathematics! Mr Jermigan had married a rich widow and made a fortune on the strength of it – mainly in the Far East, I believe. Sloping belonged to his wife. Her family had lived there for over four hundred years. He was very much the seigneur when I arrived. But once again he felt obliged to me, and he's always treated me accordingly.'

'But where does the Oriflamme come into all this? Was it Mr Jermigan who stole it?'

'And your father. I felt rather bad about that, I must admit. But, well, they were young. Mr Jermigan had had a terrible childhood, you know. His mother left him when he was six years old.'

'Huh! That's no excuse.'

'But his father – we won't go into that. He and Humph had

taken some leave in Paris and were hitch-hiking home. A farmer had picked them up and then left them on the road near Livarot. They were rather put out because he hadn't offered them a bed for the night. It was getting dark and there was very little traffic. And then they were hungry. They had a bottle of whisky with them so I'm afraid they were drinking on empty stomachs. They noticed a large car drive up a long avenue of lime trees so they followed it and came to a small château where there was a party going on.

'Mr Jermigan decided to ask if they could spend the night in an outhouse or equivalent, but thought it would be as well to reconnoitre the place first. They managed to approach without being noticed and saw that most of the guests were in one of the ground-floor rooms – the library, I think. It was summer and the windows were open so they went up to the room and watched what was going on. They saw that statue on a table. It was obviously being shown off to the guests by the owner. I read about it later in the papers. The man was the Comte d'Y les Vignottes – unfortunately for Mr Jermigan the head of the local cell of the Maquis during the war.

'When the guests began moving out of the room, Mr Jermigan thought he and Humph ought to make themselves known before they all sat down to dinner. They went round to the kitchens but got a rather dusty answer, I'm afraid. With dinner about to be served, one can imagine that the timing was unfortunate, and the arrival of two slightly drunk foreigners alarmed them. The chef sent a boy out of the room, presumably to fetch someone to throw them out – or that was the impression they got. So they agreed to go, but by then Mr Jermigan was so incensed he had decided to pay them out if he could. The sight of all that food must have been very provoking.'

'Was the entire nation obsessed by food?'

'Yes. We'd only just given up ration books. But it wasn't only that. Remember, they'd been drinking as well. They made off down the drive, but then came back and hid in the garden until they were sure the library was empty and Mr Jermigan climbed in and took the statue.'

'Why on earth was it left unguarded?'

'I suppose they never thought about it. This Comte was a very

influential person, apart from his Maquis connections. No one in
the neighbourhood would have dared steal anything from him.
Besides, not many people had cars then. There wasn't the kind of
itinerant burglary you get these days. And perhaps they thought
it was under some kind of divine protection. Their family legend
maintains that an ancestor had cut the fringe from the Oriflamme
after Agincourt and guarded it as a relic ever since.

'As you probably know, valuables were taken away and
hidden during the Occupation. The party they were having
that night was to celebrate the tenth anniversary of the day
the statue was returned to the family. They were going to have
a special service the next day when it was installed in a new –
secure – monument in the family chapel.'

'Oh, my lord.'

'Precisely. Humph and Mr Jermigan had no idea about all this,
of course. They ran off into the wood around the garden. I gather
there was a harvest moon, but still visibility wasn't that good. Mr
Jermigan tripped – over a body. Two bodies, actually. Two young
men in evening dress, asleep in each other's arms.'

'Oops!'

'They'd taken their cocktails with them, supposedly to inspect
the pheasant covers, and passed out. One of them was the
Comte's eldest son. He was the one who realized what was
going on when he recognized the statue that Mr Jermigan was
still holding. He went for Mr Jermigan but he threw the statue
to Humph and told him to get away. Humph had the presence
of mind to take Mr Jermigan's bag as well. His passport was in it,
so they couldn't identify him afterwards. If Mr Jermigan hadn't
been drinking he could have dealt with both those young men,
I'm sure, but he wasn't up to it and he fell and hit his head. By
that time the dogs had raised the alarm. Mr Jermigan was taken
back to the house but Humph escaped, although they searched
for him all night.'

'How did Mr Jermigan get out of that one?'

'By exercising his lack of scruples, I'm afraid. He was surprised
that the police were not called straight away. They locked him
up in a real dungeon and the Comte's son, who spoke English,
offered to stand guard over him for the night. There was a lot
of arguing. The son explained to Mr Jermigan that his father

wanted to interrogate him personally; that if the police took over they wouldn't have the chance to get any information out of him.'

'Yuk.'

'The young man had offered to guard Mr Jermigan because he didn't want anyone else talking to him. He was terrified that Mr Jermigan would tell his father what he had seen. Whether he hoped to appeal to Mr Jermigan's better nature, I don't know.'

'He hit a brick wall there.'

'Obviously, Mr Jermigan was not feeling particularly magnanimous. He said he would tell the Comte unless the son helped him escape. The young man couldn't make up his mind. You can imagine what a thing it would be for him to assist in the escape of the man who stole the Oriflamme.'

'Certain death.'

'Precisely. The next day the interrogation began. Mr Jermigan wouldn't tell me the details, thank goodness. He says now that he had no intention of telling the Comte about his son, but that threat was his only hope. Well, it seems the son had no stomach for that sort of thing. He was exhausted from lack of sleep anyway. Perhaps it made him more queasy.'

'And Mr Jermigan was of god-like appearance after all, stripped to the waist . . .'

'Yes. I never thought of that aspect. Whatever his motives, he could not face seeing Mr Jermigan beaten up again. Between them they faked a fight and Mr Jermigan escaped, but not before the son had warned him never to set foot in France again.'

'And that was when he ran into you and your mother?'

'That's right.'

'No wonder he didn't know what he was doing that night. He must have been so tired he slept right through his – encounter with you.'

'Quite possibly. The amazing thing is, he doesn't bear a grudge against the men who assaulted him.'

'Yes, I'm aware of Mr Jermigan's moral philosophy. "Don't get caught" about sums it up, doesn't it?'

'There's rather more to it than that. Some people have one law for themselves and another for everybody else. Mr Jermigan believes in moral autonomy and personal responsibility. He rejects authority, that's all.'

'A mere irritant, I agree. I suppose that's why he was so hands-off with Lottie.'

'I suppose it is. I should have stood up to him where she was concerned. Children should be protected from the consequences of their own ignorance.'

'And so should other people.'

'You're quite right.'

'Sorry, I didn't mean to sound censorious.'

'No, no. You're absolutely right. I only hope it's not too late.' Miss Tree yawned delicately, rolled over and lay with her back to Arden. 'I'm glad I've told you, dear. You're the only other person I have told apart from Mother.'

'I'm glad too. Mind you, I don't think I've quite taken it in yet. As you said, being abroad is all a bit surreal. I won't abuse your confidence, honestly.' Only with Tim anyway. 'What happened to the Comte's son? Did he get into trouble?'

'I've no idea. I shouldn't think so. No one would have suspected him of such treachery. He's succeeded his father now. I read an article about him in *Paris Match*.'

'This article – it didn't mention the Oriflamme, did it?'

'Yes, it did as a matter of fact. Gave me quite a turn.'

'Hell! So it's still a sore point.'

'That's not surprising, dear. People will die for symbols sooner than they would for their own children.'

'So what do you think about making a detour to return the statue?'

'Yes, I think we should. It would be a great blessing for me to expiate Mr Jermigan's sin, as it were.'

'And Humph's. Is that why Mr Jermigan gave him the cottage? Hush money?'

But Miss Tree had slipped into unconsciousness.

Ignoring Darren's fulminations, Lottie curled up on the bunk as they approached the border with Poland. As he ranted on about her stupidity, childish ignorance and what the fuck he was going to do with her, her mind wandered. On to the economics of sardine haulage. She tried to work out the profit on forty tons of sardines once diesel costs and Darren's wages had been deducted. Also road tolls, taxes, administration costs and truck maintenance. The only data she could be sure of was the price of sardines, which she bought for the cat. Even so, the results of her calculations made her thoughtful. Was it possible that they could be carrying a more sinister cargo? Or more expensive at least. She shut her eyes and tried to purge her thoughts of the influence of road movies and TV thrillers. On the other hand, sardines came from Portugal, surely? Not Suffolk. Perhaps they were ex-army surplus. Best before 2020.

'Are we going through Turkey, Darren?'

'Does this look like Turkey? We are on the way back. I've got to pick up some furniture.'

'I don't want to go through Turkey.'

'Oh, don't you? Well, you should have thought of that before, shouldn't you?'

'Sanctimonious git,' she muttered. 'How long before we stop?'

'Couple of hours. Maybe sooner. I'm worried about the suspension.'

'How big is Poland?'

'Shit, I don't know. Huge.'

'Darren?'

'What?'

'Will I be questioned at the border?'

'Shouldn't think so. If you are, say we're on our honeymoon, ha ha.'

'Yeah, right. Still, I think it's a shame the Cold War ended. It would have been much more exciting then. Being able to drive all over the place without visas and crap like that is a good thing, I suppose, but rather boring.'

Darren did not reply. He opened and closed his mouth a few times and made a small squawking sound.

'What's the matter? You look as if you've swallowed a fly.'

'Nothing.' He drove on for a while. Lottie resumed reading. 'Actually, Lottie—'

'What?'

'I've just thought. You *do* need a visa. For Russia. Fuck. Fuck, fuck, fuck.'

'*What?* What a time to tell me! Have you got one?'

'Yeah. 'Course. For me.'

'Why didn't you *think* of that? How could you be so *thick?*'

'All right, all right. I dunno. I can't think of everything. Fuck.'

'Great. What do we do now then? Well?'

'It's not *my* fault. This was all your idea. Why didn't you think of it?'

'How should I know? You're the experienced traveller. Great. Well, what are we going to do?'

'I dunno. We'll have to dump some sardines and hide you in the back, I s'pose, and just hope they don't have their heat detectors going.'

'You can't be serious. There is no *way* I am going to stow away disguised as a carton of sardines.'

'Fuck.'

The transit park at the border crossing was full. Darren cursed, worried that officials would decide to probe his tilt. 'Perhaps you'd better take a walk, Lottie. Till we've got clearance. Jesus, suppose they're looking for the truck?'

'I've told you, they won't be. But I'll certainly go for a walk.' She took up her holdall.

'What d'you want that for?'

'It's incriminating evidence, isn't it? If you'd rather no one knows I'm with you.'

'Oh. Right.'

'How long will you be, d'you think?'

'Hard to say. Couple of hours maybe.'

'Well, thanks!'

'It's boring for me too, Lottie.'

'Yeah, yeah. Look, there's some Russian truckers over there, aren't there? Why don't you go and chat them up about the best route to smuggle nice white girls into the country?'

'Sarky cow.'

'See you, Darren.'

18

Lottie took up a position where she had a good view of cars coming through into Germany. From the disapproving glares of the drivers it occurred to her that she might be doing something illegal and it would be as well not to hang about. There was a notable absence of British cars with grannies at the wheel, but Lottie by now recognized German number plates, and when a Dortmund-reg Renault covered in decals of elephants and driven by a blonde woman in sunglasses hove into view she flagged it down frantically. The car lurched to a halt. The blonde turned out to be a young man with long hair. Still, young men who sported decals of elephants were bound to be okay.

'*Entschuldigen Sie – sprechen Sie English?*'

'Certainly I am speaking it. What are you doing? This is not good. It is dangerous. The police are not liking this.'

'Can you give me a lift? Please. My boyfriend dumped me. I'm desperate. *Please*. I can pay for the petrol.'

He looked dubious. 'Very well. Get in, please.'

'*Thanks.*'

Lottie realized that the young man, who introduced himself with a handshake as Axel Klonne, might be more nervous of her than she of him. But by the time she had explained to him that her boyfriend, a thirty-five-year-old doctor, had turned really nasty once they left England on a mercy mission delivering children's clothes to Romania, that he had demanded anal sex and stolen her money, Axel was a pulp of indignant sympathy and gratified that Fate had allowed him to rescue her from such a fiend.

'This man must be arrested, Lottie. This is terrible. You must be telling the police of these things.'

'I know I should. But – that would be rather hard on those children. I'll do something about it when he's back in England.'

'Promise me?'

'Sure.'

Slightly mollified, Axel relaxed. They exchanged personal data. He was a student of molecular biology and would very much like to do a doctorate at Cambridge. He was returning to his home in Dortmund after visiting his girlfriend in Warsaw. Lottie experienced a twinge of disappointment at the mention of a girlfriend. He was extremely interested in politics and successfully conducted a one-sided conversation about the expansion of the European Union for a good hour or so. She had never realized it was such a stimulating topic. At the end she felt qualified to hold a seminar on the GDP of Greece or the natural resources of Latvia. Furthermore, unlike Darren, Axel was quite willing to stop for refreshment whenever she wished. And not just at a caff in a lorry park. He turned off the main road to seek out a *Gasthof* creaking with black-beamed Fatherlandish charm. He ordered her a huge salad platter of freshly grated, chopped and corrugated vegetables. Lottie found herself salivating for several reasons. She let Axel talk on, about integrated interest rates and the likely successor to Chancellor Kohl, until her hunger was sated.

'Am I boring to you, Lottie? Please stop me if this is the case.'

'Oh, no. It's fascinating. In fact, I belong to a political party myself.'

'Really? Which one?'

'Er – the Young Liberals. Liberal Democrats, that is.'

'Really? This is strange. I am understanding that they are abolished since—'

'Well, I'm trying to get a new group going at school.'

'Ah. Excellent. So, you are still at school? I thought maybe you are – excuse me – a little young to be finished with the school. I am wondering, should you not be at school right now? What is the story with this?'

'I had special leave to go to Romania for my Duke of

Edinburgh's Award scheme. That's like, you get medals for doing stuff – surviving in the wild, knitting baby clothes – anything really. It's supposed to impress employers that you're a serious person, but personally I just think it's meant to make low achievers feel good about themselves.'

'But you are not a low achiever, I think. What are you going to become, Lottie?'

'Actually, I'm hoping to go to medical school.'

'Excellent. I wish you very much luck with your studies. It is much work.'

'I know. I think now this trip was a big mistake altogether. I should be revising.'

'And not only have you missed much time, but the trauma also will give you problems, no?'

'The trauma. Yes. It hasn't really hit me yet.'

'Of course. But you know, you took a very big chance to hitchhike. I would not like my sister to do this.'

'I had no choice.'

'I understand. You will wish to telephone your parents, I think.'

'No. It would only worry them.'

'But I insist. This you must do, Lottie. Come, when you are finished I will help you with the dialling.'

'Oh – all right.' It was not that she had any real objections to phoning home at this stage, but her brain needed a rest from churning out porkies.

The call went through to Vera in the office. Miss Tree had been obliged to inform her of Lottie's disappearance so that she could act as their reference point. Lottie was surprised when she broke down in tears, and concluded that Vera was getting menopausal. When she had recovered they agreed that Lottie would call again in an hour to give Vera time to liaise with Mr Jermigan. Fortunately she was too emotional to ask any awkward questions. In the excitement, she almost forgot to mention the search party. Lottie thought it was quite funny, until she learned that Bos was with them. He was really stupid about telling the truth and stuff like that. She did not like the idea of his being in close contact with Miss Tree for long periods. He might just get it into his sanctimonious head that he should tell

Miss Tree all he knew about her and Darren. Lottie was perfectly justified in having sex with Darren – she was over sixteen and in control of her own sexuality – but Miss Tree was old-fashioned and should be protected from her own ignorance.

Axel could tell that Lottie was preoccupied after the phone call. He respected her mood and they drove on in companionable silence. Vera had said that Miss Tree called in morning, afternoon and evening and Lottie imagined her understated relief on being told that Lottie had been located. She liked Miss Tree for her classy restraint. It was an antidote to Jermigan's intrusive so-called affection. She had still not forgiven him for going to parents' evening and warning her English teacher that he knew where she lived just because Lottie had been given a C for her course work on *Troilus and Cressida*.

When they made contact with Vera again, she had instructions from Jermigan that they should make their way to the Hotel Sonnenhof, Auffahrtstrasse 10, off the E35 towards Leverkusen. Mr Jermigan had told Miss Tree to return there and wait for Lottie. Axel took the phone and had a business-like conversation with Vera about map references. Lottie was struck by the wonderfully normal oddity of the situation. Vera had never met Axel and yet Lottie could hear her chatting away as though they were old friends, bonding in the wonderfulness of Lottie's imminent return to the family. Yet neither Vera nor Axel had anything to do with Lottie really. It confirmed her opinion that human affairs were oiled by repulsive quantities of glib emotion. Nonetheless, she could appreciate that Axel's generosity was genuine enough.

'Are you sure it's not too far out of your way?'

'No, that's okay. I cannot abandon you anyhow. How are you finding this hotel without me, Lottie?'

She was glad that he did not pretend there was no element of inconvenience in the arrangement.

It was four o'clock in the morning when they arrived at the Sonnenhof. Both fell asleep in their seats. They were woken up before seven when cars began revving up all around them.

'I need the lav,' said Lottie. 'How about you?'

'I also. I will ask to use in the hotel. Then I must be going.'

'Don't you want to meet them – my – I don't know what to call them. Emergency service, I suppose. I'm sure they'd like to thank you.'

'There is no need. Also they are maybe not out of bed already. It is too early for English people, no?'

'Miss Tree would probably say that it's never too early for good manners. But I understand if you want to be off. Give me your address so that they can say it with flowers.'

He laughed. 'And yours also.' He took some pages from his filofax. 'For what stands "C.E."?'

Lottie screwed up her face. 'Must you know? Charlotte Elizabeth. It's so naff. I'm going to change it by deed poll when I'm older.'

'But why? Charlotte Elizabeth Makepeace. This is a beautiful name. It is suiting you.'

'*Please.*' Lottie looked thoughtfully at his address. 'You will get in touch if you come to Cambridge, won't you, Axel?'

'Of course.'

'Then I have to tell you something. You know all that crap about my boyfriend demanding anal sex and that? It was bullshit. Not true. I don't know why I said it, really. Oh, yes, I do. It was to make you feel sorry for me. The truth is, I bunked off with one of my father's drivers. It didn't work out, that's all. Sorry.'

'Bunked?' Axel was afraid this was also some perverse sexual practice.

'Ran away.'

'Ah.' He looked at her with exasperation, but more indulgence. 'I am glad. I am thinking perhaps you are a little too cool about this.' He smiled and stroked her hair. 'Lottie, Lottie – you are a very brave girl, you know. Foolish but brave, I think. You go home now and work hard and become a good doctor. Then you can really help the children of Romania.'

Lottie choked back a rogue lump in her throat. Why was it that instead of dismissing Axel as a condescending wanker she was trying to decide between ophthalmology and paediatrics?

After they had been to the lavatory in the hotel Lottie came out with him to say goodbye. He kissed her in the Continental fashion. His stubble brushed sharp and soft against her cheek.

'Please say my apologies to your family. I hope to meet them also in the future.'

'I will. And thank you *very* much, Axel. You really saved my bacon.'

'Your bacon?'

'Sausage, then. Thanks, anyway.'

'Okay.'

She waved until his car disappeared into the traffic.

As far as the desk clerk was concerned seven-thirty was mid-morning and he had no hesitation in calling Miss Tree's room to inform her of Lottie's arrival. Arden groaned and pulled up the duvet. She had been driving for most of the previous day thanks to the chaps' hangovers. Now Tim's hip had seized up as well, so she and Bos would have to share the driving all the way home and Arden had not slept well. Miss Tree was restless and had kept getting up to go to the bathroom, producing a token tinkle in the pan and getting back into bed with much sighing and sucking of teeth. Arden knew she was emotional about getting Lottie back and only wished she could share Miss Tree's joy. But now that this unusual interlude of close companionship was nearly over, Arden suspected that it would have no lasting effect. They would each retreat to her own domain at Sloping. Miss Tree would always be grateful to Arden for her help in the crisis and would step up the gifts of homemade pickle to reflect that, but in effect everything would be back to normal.

It was a wicked thought, but Arden could not help reflecting that she would have got a more useful foot in the door of Sloping if Lottie had *not* been recovered. Not that she wished that the girl had been swallowed up by the Steppes. It was more that befriending Miss Tree was Arden's only untried ploy in her resistance to Jermigan's plan. Once he had got Lottie back he would start to think that the deal had been too generous. It had been a relief to get away from all that for a while.

Miss Tree sat up in bed and put on her dressing-gown: a heavy pistachio silk number embroidered with pale pink lilies that Arden deeply envied. She patted her hair. 'Do I look all right, Arden?'

'Of course. But does it matter?'

'Oh, dear, I haven't time to take a shower. What will Lottie think?'

Arden was totally bemused. 'She should think it's her fault for getting you up early. This whole thing is her fault. Why should you dress up for her?'

Miss Tree was not listening. 'I don't know if I can do this. What shall I say?'

'I'm the wrong person to ask. If it were me I'd tear her to shreds and flush the bits down the loo.'

'Oh, please don't say anything like that, Arden. I'm not very good at scenes.'

'Of course I won't.' There was a confident knock on the door. 'That must be her. I'll go in the bathroom.'

Lottie put her head round the door and then came in. 'Hi, Miss Tree. Sorry it's a bit early. Where's that dreadful woman?'

'Lottie, shh! Don't speak like that. Mrs Fairbrother is in there.'

'Oh. Sorry. Well, here I am. You weren't worried, were you?'

Instead of replying Miss Tree gave a quivering sigh and fluttered her hands. Then she put her fist in her mouth and began to heave with silent sobs. Lottie was taken aback. First Vera, now Miss Tree. Perhaps she was cracking up, as anyone associated with Jermigan was entitled to do. It was surprising that she had come on this jaunt if she was not feeling well. Lottie did not know what to do. She thought some sort of apology might be expected. 'Look, I'm really sorry, Miss Tree. But I was quite okay, you know. It's all right.'

Arden was listening behind the louvred door of the bathroom – with difficulty as she had put the shower on to give the impression that she was not. She became worried by the long silence between them and thought Lottie might have left, so she opened the door to look. Lottie sat on the end of Miss Tree's bed, frowning at her. Miss Tree hugged her knees, eyes closed, shuddering out of control like an over-heated car engine. Lottie looked at Arden with a helpless shrug. Arden rolled her eyes and made a hugging gesture. Eventually Lottie logged on. She sat gingerly beside Miss Tree and put an arm round her, pulling the crumpled figure to her confused bosom. As the moments went by and Miss Tree's sobs became more graphic, Lottie turned a rather sickly shade of pale.

'Who's this Axel geezer then?' Bos was squashed in the back seat with Lottie and Miss Tree. He was in a mood with his mother because she would not let him drive, as a punishment for getting drunk. 'Stupid name.'

'You can talk.'

'Yeah, yeah. Well, who is he?'

'Is that a philosophical question? I've told you, his name is Axel Klonne. He's a student. He gave me a lift. That's it.'

'He must be a poof with a name like that.'

'Don't be stupid. You didn't even meet him!'

Miss Tree held Lottie's hand. 'We must invite him to Sloping. I'm sure Mr Jermigan will want to thank him personally.'

'Yeah, great. I haven't noticed gratitude clogging *your* airways, Lottie.'

'Shut up. Mind your own business. I never wanted you to come and fetch me. It's nothing to do with you.'

'There, there.' Miss Tree turned a tremulous smile on Bos. 'Lottie has had quite an ordeal. It's best we don't talk about it just now, dear.'

Arden was depressed. The chances of Lottie and Bos uniting the factions at Sloping looked increasingly remote.

'How long before we're home, Mum?'

'A couple of days, I hope. Don't forget we've got to go via Normandy.'

'Oh, shit. I had forgotten. Do we have to?'

'Your mother and I have decided it's best, dear,' said Miss Tree. 'Be patient.' She outlined the situation to Lottie, saying only that the object was known to be stolen, but not by whom. Lottie was unconvinced.

'Why don't you post it?'

'It's too valuable, dear. And too fragile.'

'Even with loads of bubble wrap?' Arden thought Lottie had got a point. Why *couldn't* they post it? It could be done anonymously, if rubber gloves were worn. But Miss Tree was now fixated on seeing justice done personally. The safe return of the prodigal was a clear sign to her to make a reciprocal gesture.

'It would be a terrible shame if we didn't seize this opportunity, Arden. I'd rather set my heart on it.'

Lottie was as unenthusiastic about the detour as Bos, but did not want to appear to agree with him. Having witnessed Miss Tree's hysterics she was worried about her reception by Jermigan. If he was going to go to pieces as well it was something to be got over as soon as possible. But she did not want to argue with Miss Tree in her present volatile state. 'I'm surprised you left the cottage unattended, Mrs Fairbrother. Aren't you afraid Jermigan will accidentally back a tanker into it or something?'

'What? What do you mean?'

'Well – I just thought you might want to get home as soon as poss, to be on the safe side. I know he's got his sights on it. It's a perfect opportunity for him to get careless with a fag end and a can of petrol.'

'But he's in hospital.' Arden's mind thrashed around like a haddock on deck.

'So? He wouldn't do it personally, anyway.'

'That's a terrible thing to say, Lottie.' Miss Tree spoke by rote, not taking the suggestion seriously. She was used to Lottie's theatrical hostility to Mr Jermigan.

But Arden remembered Laurence and Shara's burnt-out car. Jermigan's inprisonment for GBH. He was perfectly capable of it. Her temperature dropped several degrees. He might even have persuaded them to go chasing after Lottie to get them out of the way. His derangement might have been a complete sham. 'Are you sure, Miss Tree? I suddenly don't feel very well.'

'I know Mr Jermigan, Arden. He would never do such a thing. Put it right out of your mind.'

Lottie shrugged. 'Normandy it is then.'

Arden put her foot down.

The Comte d'Y les Vignottes was on the Internet, having a conversation with a wind farmer in Ohio. It was in the nature of homework for his role as chairman of a committee looking into the least politically damaging way of achieving France's reduction in greenhouse gas emissions. The Comte sat on twenty-three committees and this was one of the more tedious. He much preferred the committee for scuppering the compensation of

British truck drivers caught in road blocks, but, alas, into each life some rain must fall. The farmer in Ohio was reluctant to stick to statistical information and thought the Comte would rather hear the latest jokes about President Clinton's penis. The Comte did not give a monkey's about le Big One's penis and was thankful when his housekeeper, a former Moroccan army officer, announced that there was a young Englishman to see him. The Comte was startled. 'At this hour?' It was ten-thirty.

'He says he is in the neighbourhood and cannot come another time, Monsieur.'

'I see. What's he like?'

The man shrugged. 'Okay. He could lose a few pounds.'

'No, no, I mean do you think he looks suspicious? It's a bit odd, isn't it? What can he want with me?'

'I don't know, Monsieur. He has a large parcel with him and insists on speaking to you personally.'

'Show him in, Ahmed. But wait outside the door in case there's any trouble.'

When Bos entered the Comte deduced at once that he was not a deranged representative of the British Road Haulage Association. He was bedraggled by the rain and smiled in a timid, nervous manner that was utterly enchanting. Bos put the box on the floor and shook himself like a dog, casting pernicious water spots on to an inlaid chiffonier. The Comte moved discreetly to remove them with the sleeve of his jumper while directing Bos to sit down by the fire. Bos looked round with polite interest at the unframed modern art, of the 'Surely they're upside down?' school that adorned the faded panelling and held out his hand to the Comte.

'Bosworth Fairbrother – m'lord.'

The Comte smiled. ' "Sir" will do. Zis is 'ow you are called?'

'That's right. You don't know me or nuffing.'

'Correct. Zen 'ow can I 'elp you, Monsieur Fairbruzzer? I am intrigued.'

Bos scratched his head. 'Actually – sir – this has got nuffing to do with me. My mum made me do it.'

'Your mum? Excuse me, I am not acquainted wiz your mum eizer, I tink.'

'No. It's a bit complicated. The fact is, her dad – my grandfather

– stole something from this house years and years ago. Well, he's dead now, and she wanted to return it. It was on her conscience, like, and we was coming this way so—'

The Comte had gone pale. He sat motionless with his fingers steepled. 'What did the dad of your mum steal exactly?'

'A statue thing – with a bit of some flag in it. Anyhow, they were well worried about it. My mum made me come because she says I look the most gormless. Thanks, Mum. The thing is, they wanted me to spin you this wad of porkies about how some bloke I met on the train said if I brought it back I'd get a reward and that, but that's just so stupid.'

'Excuse me, what is a "wad of porkies"?'

'Sorry. Lies, basically. They was afraid of getting into trouble for having it. Something about your dad being in the Maquis and you'd have us all shot and buried in a mass grave in the forest. As if! Well, I thought it was stupid. My grandad's dead now, anyhow, as I said. I reckoned you'd be okay about it. I would.' The Comte continued sitting motionless. He stared at Bos, unblinking. 'Er – shall I open it for you? I expect you'd like to see it.'

'Please.'

Bos was glad of something to do. The Comte's deathly stillness was unnerving. He tossed the bubble wrap on to the floor and carefully drew out the statue and put it on the desk. 'There. That is yours, isn't it? I'd piss meself if I'd got the wrong house.' He laughed, but quickly sobered. The Comte was now as pale as a ciggie paper and crossed himself repeatedly, murmuring in his native tongue. Bos was reassured. 'Right. That's it then. Mission accomplished. I'll be off, if it's all the same to you. We're going to try and hit the coast tonight.' He moved towards the door.

'*Non!*' The Comte had come to life. He jumped up and ran to the desk, from which he took out a gun.

'*Jesus!* What d'you think you're doing, you tosser? That's gratitude.'

'Ahmed!' In a flash Bos was in a stranglehold. The Comte was now flushed right over his bald head. 'Your *Mum*? You expect me to believe zis? You are liar, like your *grandpère*. Zis time I call ze police for sure. I 'ave dreamed for years of zis. You 'ave stolen zis also.'

'No! Please! Why the fuck would I bring it back if I'd stolen it?'

The logic of this argument struck the Comte against his better judgment. He lowered the gun. 'Maybe you do tink zere is a reward. Maybe you are as stoopeed as you look.'

'Thanks! Jesus, Mum was right. You're a nutter.'

'Stop zis talk of your mum. Zis I do not believe.'

'See for yourself. She's here.'

'Where?'

'In the car up on the road. And my uncle, and – Oh, never mind. Check it out.'

The Comte hesitated. 'If you are lying . . .' He drew his hand across his throat. 'Zat grave in ze forest is ready.'

'Oh, *yeah*. I *don't* think.'

'Correct.' He spoke to Ahmed, who released Bos and prepared to follow them out of the room.

'You're not going to leave that thing unguarded, are you? You don't want it nicked again, do you?'

Again the Comte hesitated then told Ahmed, despite his violent protests, to stay. He ordered Bos to walk ahead and they went down to a lobby at the rear of the chateau. 'Wait! I need a *parapluie*.'

'Don't put it up in the house, it's bad luck.'

'From you I do not need ze advice.' Once outside, Bos watched with some amusement as the Comte tried to put up the umbrella without shooting himself in the elbow.

'Ready?'

'*Oui*.'

They walked briskly down the long avenue of lime trees and the quarter of a mile to the farm gate where the car was parked. Bos shivered, not just from the freezing rain. It was dead isolated out here. This nutter could shoot them all and no one the wiser. Old Ahmed wouldn't let on. When they reached the car he looked in anxiously. They were all asleep. Unless someone else had shot them already. He knocked on the driver's window. 'Mum! Wake up! Mum!'

Arden opened her eyes a fraction, convinced she was in a diving bell. She wound the window down. 'Bos?' Her speech was slurred. 'Are you all right?' The others snoozed on.

'Yeah, fine. Mum, that Comte thingy's here. He wants a word with you.'

'What?' The Comte had come up close behind Bos, so that they were both under the umbrella, and he peered curiously into the car. 'This is my mum – Mrs Fairbrother. And that's my Uncle Tim, and that's our neighbour Miss Tree, and Lottie my girlfriend. Former girlfriend.'

The Comte could not believe what he saw. 'What are you doing 'ere? You are on vacation?'

'Yeah, right. Well, sort of. See, Lottie was with this trucker going to Russia and she got in a spot of bother, like, and we had to come and get her.'

'I am not understanding.'

'Yeah, well, it's complicated.'

'Good evening, Madame.'

'Oh. Good evening.' Arden and he shook hands.

'Your son tells me zat it was your father who took *ze Saint Louis de l'Oriflamme*. Is zis true?'

'Yes.' She looked daggers at Bos. 'It is. I'm terribly sorry. We didn't know about it until he died and we've brought it back as soon as we could. I really am sorry. Dad can't have realized how important it was to you, but I knew at once. Sorry.'

The Comte's anger had evaporated. He took it for granted that Arden's knowledge of French art history was comprehensive. 'Very well. Tank you. Also from my family and ze people of France.'

'There's no need.'

'You are cold, I think. Will you come into ze 'ouse? You cannot drive longer tonight.'

'No – no, thank you. That's very kind, but I'm in a terrible hurry to get home.'

'But we cannot be leaving it like zis. I must know all zat 'as 'appened.'

'Oh, Monsieur, I don't really know anything. It was all such a long time ago, I was hoping we could just – you know – let bygones be bygones, as we say.'

'Zis is very 'ard for me, but – I believe zat you are sincere. Boswort, I apologize.' He put a hand on Bos's shoulder and then leaned his head on it. To their consternation he began to cry.

Bos was wet enough already. 'Hey, it's all right. But is it okay if we go now? I'm soaked.'

The Comte nodded. He embraced Bos with his free arm and kissed him several times on both cheeks. 'Tank you. Tank you. Saint Denis will lead you personally to your trone in paradise.'

'Right. Great. Ta ta, then.'

19

'Phew! He changed his tune a bit smartish. He actually pulled a gun on me, Mum. I was shit scared.'

'He didn't!'

'Now would I make that up? He ought to get out more, the nutter. When I was taking the fucking thing back! If you've got any other missions of mercy planned, Mum, call out the fucking Three Musketeers – count me out of it.'

'Well, it just shows I was right – it *was* dangerous. Poor you, darling. I am sorry. Didn't he believe your story, then?'

'No. *And* it was the truth. I couldn't stick to that crap about a bloke on a train, Mum.'

'Oh, Bos, you didn't mention any names, did you?'

'Only my own. It'll be okay. He seemed like quite a decent bloke, really. Bit excitable. But he was all right about it in the end, wasn't he? When he thinks about it, I'm sure he'll decide to let sleeping dogs lie and all that.'

'On the contrary. He was in shock – highly emotional shock. When he calms down he may get extremely irrational about it. And he's unlikely to forget a name like yours.'

'You've only got yourself to thank for that, Mum.'

'All right, don't rub it in. Oh, *God*. Now we'll have to worry about it for the rest of our lives. It'll be like living under the threat of a bloody fatwa. Don't tell Miss Tree about the gun – or the fact that you introduced yourself. I don't want her worried. Honestly, Bos, why didn't you give a false name?'

'Why should I? You've got to trust people, Mum. Give them a chance to rise to your expectations.'

'Jermigan is a person, Bos. Am I supposed to trust him? Even as we speak he might be burning our house down.'

'Oh, that's bollocks. What evidence have you got that he'd do a thing like that?' She told him, but he was still unconvinced. 'You've no proof about that car.'

'He didn't deny it. And *you* can't deny that he's been to prison.'

'So? I expect he did loads of basket weaving and found inner peace. Mr Jermigan's been good to me, Mum.'

'Yes, I know. I can understand that you don't want to think badly of him. That does you credit, Bos. But I won't have a moment's peace until I've seen that the cottage is still standing. I feel sick. So sick. Like I'm going to be executed in the morning, or something.'

'Why – aren't you insured?'

'Yes. That's not the point. Where would we go? How would we work? All my records – and Uncle Tim's – are in there. It would be utterly horrendous.'

'You'd better let me drive, then. You're in no fit state.' He glanced over his shoulder. Miss Tree sat upright in the middle of the back seat, eyes shut, Tim and Lottie lolling on her shoulders. 'Do you think this lot will sleep till we get home?'

'Possibly. But I certainly won't.'

The prospect of homelessness and the destruction of their work was only the practical side of the nightmare that haunted Arden, and that Bos might be expected to appreciate. She could not explain to him what would sound like sentimental guff: that Sloping was where she belonged, that anywhere else would now be exile. Admittedly, Barnacle Cottage was not the executive hovel of her dreams. But to wake up within the womb-like circle of Sloping's flinty walls, to see the playful swoop and flutter of doves over the tower of rubble, to feel the presence of doughty ancestors who might just have caught a glimpse of Henry V from a distance – this benison must not be snatched away so soon. Fate had sent her to Sloping to save it from Jermigan's sacrilegious schemes. She would endure any amount of turds through the letterbox, if it came to that, to do her duty. The thought of him lying smugly in his hospital bed ordering the destruction of Barnacle Cottage on his mobile phone brought tears of rage to her eyes. As did the possibility that he had outwitted her. If the cottage were struck by lightning it would be bad enough, but the idea that he could get his way by trickery and brute force was insufferable.

The fact that no one shared her anxiety made it harder to bear. Revived by their slumbers, Lottie, Tim and Miss Tree were irritatingly perky. It was all right for them. They could relax with a sense of mission accomplished. Bos had only come along for the ride anyway and he was more than happy to align himself with the majority. Even Lottie was being quite pleasant, no doubt to consolidate the care and concern they had shown her in the face of the imminent show-down with Jermigan. On the ferry Arden left them to their fun and wandered off on her own, pacing the decks, too punch drunk with tiredness and worry to think about trivia like eating or duty-free goods. She ended up in a packed, smoke-filled bar and sat at a table by the porthole with a couple of Australian youths and a swarthy man in a long sheepskin coat and too much gold jewellery. He tried to chat her up but she pretended not to understand and kept her gaze on the rain-lashed sea.

The return to British terra firma had a sobering effect on them all. On the drive back to Sloping Tim instinctively chipped in the occasional remark in a vain attempt to revive the bonhomie of the voyage. Post holiday stress disorder set in as soon as they were on the open road, in tune with their individual reasons for introspection.

Miss Tree had been turned inside out emotionally, what with the worry over Lottie and thankfulness for her return. But revisiting the scene of her first meeting with Mr Jermigan had revived memories painful in their pleasantness, and led to the rueful reflection that the role of best friend had never been filled since the death of her mother.

Bos was bored, and depressed at returning to his exile at Sloping. The trip had been a welcome diversion, but the rest of his sentence appeared interminable.

Tim was in agony with his hip. The portfolio of small business accounts that awaited him cast him into a deep funk. He rehearsed in his mind a scene with Arden which he would never have the bottle to enact, in which he pointed out that if they had never come here and had to economize they could have kept up their BUPA payments and he would have had the operation by now.

Lottie was trying to psych herself out of the dread of explaining herself to Jermigan. Miss Tree's over-reaction had been sobering, and by now even Lottie could dimly appreciate that she had taken a potentially terminal risk. The gently ordered English landscape reproached her hot-headed ways. It seemed to say, One simply doesn't, and although Lottie knew that one simply did, the opprobrium that one rejects intellectually can still seep into the bone. Besides which, whatever Jermigan might think of her caper, he would go ballistic if he knew how much it had upset Miss Tree.

Arden was simply dissolving in dread.

The rain had stopped and a rippled blanket of cloud stretched to the horizon. Arden was teased with hope when she saw that it had been raining. Arson would not be the chosen method. That just left the rogue tanker. It would have difficulty reversing at speed round the bend in the drive. But all such comforting thoughts evaporated as the towers of Sloping came into view. The pounding of her heart seemed to have expanded it to bullock-sized proportions. She dabbed her sweaty face with a hankie.

They drove through the gatehouse past Jake and his girlfriend, hand-in-hand. Jake waved to Miss Tree. His expression gave no sign that there was anything amiss, but Jermigan's minions would not bat an eyelid if the cottage were flattened with Arden and Tim in it, if that was what the boss wanted. Bos stopped the car at the end of their drive. Without a thought for goodbyes Arden shot out of the car, leaving Tim to struggle out with Lottie's help.

It was still standing, just as they had left it, only with ten bottles of milk on the step. The tatty rhododendrons gleamed wet from the rain. A piece of gutter hung down, and there were signs that a sluice had emptied on to their bedroom window. Fresh dog turds lay on the flagstones. Arden wept for joy. She sank to the ground clutching her knees. Tim hobbled down the drive with Lottie.

'Ard! What's the matter?'

'Nothing,' she mumbled into her knees. 'Precisely nothing. Thank God.'

Lottie gawped. 'You didn't really think Jermigan would demolish it, did you? I only said that because I thought it might get you to come home directly.'

'I dare say.' Arden wiped her eyes and stood up. 'However, it didn't strike me as that fanciful. It still doesn't. I mean, tell me, who would care – apart from us?'

'I see what you mean.'

'Oh, dear, Miss Tree will think me rude. I didn't say goodbye.'

She ran back down the drive, but the car had gone. The luggage stood on the grass. Bos could bring it in. Arden had to lie down. They let themselves into the cottage and she helped Tim up to their bedroom. He took some painkillers from the bedside table and sat on the bed wondering whether it would help the pain if he stood on his head. Arden stared at the ceiling, every muscle sagging.

'I couldn't go through that again, Tim.'

'What – chase after Lottie?'

'No, of course not. Though that's also true. I actually think she's grown up a bit. Did you hear her say she was going to be a doctor?'

'Just in time to perform my operation, the way things are going.'

'Is it bad? I'm sorry, darling. No, I meant I couldn't go through a panic attack like that again. I feel as if every cell in my body is black and blue. I know you all thought I was paranoid, but *I* know I wasn't. Jermigan is unscrupulous and proud of it. He'll keep trying.'

'Then you'd better get used to panic attacks, hadn't you? Why don't we just let him have it? Is it worth it, to live in fear the whole time?'

'No.'

'You mean, you agree? You'll go back to Chiswick?'

'Not exactly. But – I wouldn't try to stop *you* going, Tim, if that's what you really want.'

'What – split up? Is that what *you* want?'

'Of course not. I'm only being realistic. Perhaps we want

different things now, that's all. And – well – things aren't the same since Thalia dropped her little bombshell, are they?'

'Well, I'm buggered. After all this time. I never thought I'd see the day.'

'Don't be like that. I *don't* want you to go. I'm trying to be unselfish.'

'Why don't you just shoot me in the head, then, if you want to do me a favour? What would I do on my own?'

'Oh, Tim, don't. Look, things haven't worked out down here as far as you're concerned. It's my fault, I know. I take full responsibility.'

'Easily said, Ard. What does it amount to in practice?'

'I'll think of something.' In fact she already had. An obvious, if extreme, solution had occurred to her while under the influence of panic. A solution long since in desuetude, but due for a revival in these days of hard choices and personal pension plans. Tim was not in a suitable mood to discuss it. Besides, he would have to be sedated before she told him.

There were twenty-one messages on the answering machine. Some were from frantic tax-payers. There was a request for an urgent meeting from Mattie's nursing home. Most of the others were from *Suitables* clients demanding advance viewings of the Spring Collection or complaining that their shoulder pads had become deformed in the wash. There was an encouraging number of requests for presentations, several from residential care homes. The post contained an invitation from the district council to register their comments prior to the planning meeting with regard to the developments at Sloping. To Tim's surprise Arden said she could not be bothered. As long as they continued with their resistance the plans could not go ahead anyway. He took this disinterest as a further sign that she was considering giving up the cottage to Jermigan. The suspicion was reinforced by the air of brisk stoicism that she adopted, as though resigned to the inevitable.

The weather was unseasonably warm and Bos was ordered back to work on the mead hall. He was disgruntled. It was much more to his liking to work on truck maintenance and help out in the office with traffic planning and load allocation and the like.

And in view of his involvement with Operation Black Sheep, he felt he deserved more than demotion to the building site. Tim, as a fellow displaced person, was more sympathetic than his mum. By way of reward, Bos sometimes asked Tim to go with him to the pub. Tim rather enjoyed going. He needed male company and was amused by the detached way Bos showed him off, as though he were a very bright terrapin. And he had no difficulty in talking to Bos's young friends on a wide range of topics of interest to them.

As expected, the urgent meeting at The Ashes concerned Mattie's move to Felixstowe. She was distraught at the idea and articulate enough to mount a reasoned objection, namely that the disruption would kill her. She had also become insistent that Humph should be told and asked repeatedly why he never came to see her any more. Humph would never allow it. Moreover, he should not be expected to drive all the way to Felixstowe every week.

While their mother was engrossed in decapitating an iced fancy, Arden and Tim went for a tête-à-tête with the matron. They agreed that Mattie must now be told of Humph's death, as her agitation about his absence could be worse than the distress of knowing he was dead. Arden volunteered to come in the following morning when there would be few visitors and impart the news in a quiet, woman-to-woman situation. Tim questioned that his presence would add to Mattie's trauma, but the manager pointed out that, however fond she was of him, at times of great distress it was almost always better for women to be attended by their own sex. Tim could be of greater service to his mother after she had got over the initial shock.

This attention to the details of Mattie's care impressed Arden. It confirmed her opinion that their mother should not have to leave The Ashes. The new home might well have an air filtration system and Sky TV, but it would also have a lower ratio of staff to patients, therefore less individual care of this sort. She asked the manager, in a casual way, what the fees would be in the event that they took over responsibility for Mattie from the local authority, and, if that were the case, whether she would be able to stay. The manager was almost sure that she could as Mattie was a long-term resident, although it was not her decision, and she gave them a brochure with the slate of charges, advising them not to open it until they had had a drink.

They could see why. Five hundred pounds a week, plus extras for laundry and special diets. Arden opened a bottle of Cava while Tim got busy with columns of figures in an attempt to squeeze this money out of their current income. As things were they could spare at most eighty pounds a week. This sum was approximate as their income varied so much.

If they sold either the cottage or the house in Chiswick the money could be invested and the interest used for the fees. Tim was obliged to admit that the Chiswick house would fetch more and that the cottage was virtually unsaleable with the planning application outstanding. On the other hand, they had to pay back a mortgage on the Chiswick house. And they would have to pay tax on the interest, and there was a strong possibility that interest rates would come down to converge with European rates in the future.

Arden almost nodded off. All she wanted to know was, could it be managed? In a word, thought Tim, no. There was a shortfall of approximately three hundred pounds a month. Even if the figures added up, the move was planned for two months' time and the Chiswick house could not be sold so soon, particularly with tenants in it. Strangely Arden did not seem as depressed as she might have been to hear this.

Lottie put off going to see Jermigan for as long as possible. They spoke on the phone but Miss Tree became increasingly concerned that Lottie should visit him in person. He would be coming home soon, and he would be extremely offended if she had never been to see him. Lottie asked Arden to go with her. The 'dreadful woman' had her uses. Lottie had a childish dread of finding her way around strange places and at least Arden was of approximately motherish age.

On the way into Norwich she took the opportunity to sound Lottie out on her state of mind. The girl certainly needed distraction. She was pale and twitchy and asked if she could smoke in the car. Lottie did not mind confiding in Arden to some extent. Her assistance to Miss Tree had earned her brownie points. She went on at length about how insufferably cloying she found Jermigan's affection. It was so phoney, and could not be sincere because Lottie knew perfectly well that it was she who was insufferable. She blamed him for adopting her. Just because he had no children of his own that was no excuse for using her as compensation. He had always been too busy with work to spend much time with her, while the fact that she was clever gave him unearned gratification. If she had been thick and dead ugly his attitude would have been vastly different. She was just a trophy child.

'That's rather unfair, Lottie. It's an added bonus for him, naturally, but that doesn't mean he wouldn't have thought the world of you anyway.'

'You think so? I take a more jaundiced view of human nature. Isn't it true that men have a hard time being proper fathers in general, never mind if the kid isn't theirs *and* isn't worth showing off? I should have gone to one of my mother's sisters. They've both got big families. I'd have had much more fun.'

'The grass is always greener, Lottie. Children from large families often long to be only children. Besides, if your aunts already had a lot of children they didn't need another one. Presumably they could have fought for custody if they'd really wanted you. Did they?'

'Don't know. I expect Jermigan just told them to push off.'

'Have they kept in touch? Are you close to them?'

Lottie was silent for a while. 'Sure. Anyhow, Jermigan doesn't get on with them. He wouldn't let me have contact with them, I expect.'

'But they send you birthday cards and so on, do they?'

She shrugged. 'No. I dare say it's too painful for them.'

Arden shook her head and changed the subject. They agreed that Lottie would tell Jermigan that she had come alone. Arden was not ready for another confrontation just yet.

Considering her intention to become a doctor, the girl showed remarkably little interest in the hospital. She walked close behind Arden, looking straight ahead. When they reached the ward Arden checked with the nurses that Jermigan was still in the same room and directed Lottie towards it. 'Are you sure you're all right?'

'Yeah.'

'I'll wait outside where he can't see me.'

'Okay.' Lottie's eyes were wide. With the air of a defiant rabbit she entered Jermigan's room.

While she waited Arden rehearsed a few tactics for dealing with the aftermath. It was likely to be an emotional scene. She just hoped that Lottie would have the maturity to show patience with the blubbering bully and accept responsibility for all the upset she had caused. He would surely be mollified by her decision to become a doctor, if she remembered to tell him. Privately Arden doubted that Lottie would follow through. It was an obvious, off-the-shelf choice for someone in need of a cloak of sanctity to conceal their faults. But, being a parent, Jermigan would probably choose to believe her and gladly accept such a prop for his delusions.

It was bed-making time and Arden felt in the way, so she went out and explored the possibilities of the landing. After a quarter of an hour she went back in and furtively hung about near the door of Jermigan's room. The noise from the vacuum cleaner made it impossible to hear anything except the pitch of raised voices. It sounded like a row. Perhaps it had not been such a good idea to get Lottie to articulate her resentment of Jermigan. With it fresh in her mind the stress of the moment might make her blurt it out. The woman with the vacuum cleaner drew nearer. She might go into Jermigan's room, at which point Lottie would probably leave, so Arden nipped back on to the landing. As usual she had a busy schedule of *Suitables* appointments and hoped Lottie would not be long.

It was another ten minutes before she emerged, slamming through the doors with considerable violence. Her eyes brimmed with tears and her face was white except for a bright red mark.

'Lottie! Did he hit you? Lottie!' Arden chased after her down the stairs, losing ground. She got into a lift, hoping to cut Lottie off, but could not see her and ran in panic up and down the corridors. The girl had disappeared. 'Not again!' cursed Arden. 'She can bloody well find her own way home this time.' It was with mixed feelings that she saw Lottie waiting by the car, her arms tightly folded, her face averted.

'What happened?'

Lottie said nothing but got into the car in one swift movement.

Arden decided to let her take her time. Lottie was so pent up the pressure was bound to tell sooner or later and Arden was not surprised when she burst into tears as they turned on to the by-pass.

'Did he hit you?' Arden pressed. The girl nodded. 'Well, I don't blame you for being upset. That's outrageous. I don't care what you've done, he had no right to do that.'

Arden was shivering herself. It was another manifestation of Jermigan's violent methods. She consoled herself with the thought that it was the first time, and excusable to some extent in view of his strength of feeling. At least he was not in the habit of bashing his loved ones. On the other hand, habits have to start somewhere. 'Of course, you could say it shows how much he cares for you, in a perverted sort of way. It must have been awful for him to be lying there helpless, not knowing what had happened to you.'

'Th-that's what he said. And I s-sort of had a go at him – you know.'

'Not the old what-do-you-care-you're-not-my-real-parent cart-horse? Honestly, Lottie, you don't do justice to your own intelligence by persisting with that attitude.'

'It wasn't th-that. You know wh-what we were talking about before – I h-hadn't thought about it. Why I d-didn't g-go to my aunties. How th-thick can you get?'

'That's understandable. Children don't usually question their domestic circumstances until they're older. Thank goodness.'

'It made me s-so mad I asked him and he s-said they w-wouldn't have me. Th-that's why he q-quarrelled with them. They thought I'd be b-better off with him b-because he had money.' Her voice rose to a scream. 'He's a fucking liar and I told him so!' Her sobs became hysterical.

Arden put a hand on her arm but was shaken off. 'And that's when he hit you?' Lottie nodded. 'This is my fault. I should never have put the idea into your head. Don't hit me yourself, Lottie, but there could be some truth in it. But that doesn't mean your aunts didn't want what was best for you.'

'Then w-why don't they s-send me cards and stuff?'

'Now you're arguing Jermigan's case. People have such busy lives, it's easy to overlook these things.'

'If th-they'd loved my m-mother they w-wouldn't.'

'I'm afraid that simply isn't true. This will sound patronizing, Lottie, but children sometimes set impossibly high standards for adult behaviour.'

'That wouldn't be *impossible* – sending a card?'

'Perhaps not. But believe me, it is possible to be careless without being malicious. You can get in touch with them yourself, you know. Jermigan can't stop you.'

Arden was rather pleased with her sallies into child psychology. It was satisfying to give one's accumulated wisdom an airing occasionally. Lottie had clearly suffered from the lack of a mother. Miss Tree's affection, however deep, was no substitute. A girl needed a punchbag in adolescence. 'Are you going to tell Miss Tree that he hit you?'

'I suppose I'll have to. I don't give a shit. At least he was behaving like a proper parent.'

Thalia was so ecstatic that they had returned the Oriflamme she insisted that Arden and Tim should come to Gavin's confirmation party by way of celebration. 'I don't entertain as a rule,' she explained. 'Do say you'll come?'

Arden was caught off guard. Parties where one knew absolutely no one except the host were not her idea of fun. They were too much like *Suitables* presentations. But she felt a residual wariness of Thalia. Nothing was said about lifting the threat of scandal. She would have to trust Thalia on that score. It still seemed prudent to accept the invitation. She managed to get them out of going to the church service on account of Tim's hip. His rapture, when told about the party, was also muted. Not because he did not want to go. He had missed Thalia. She was a hot-water bottle of a person, exactly what he needed in his condition. Which was exactly why meeting her with Arden in tow was a mixed blessing.

20 ∫

They delayed their arrival to the point where there was a good chance that half the guests would have left. Thalia had hired the upstairs room of a pub in Great Yarmouth. The exterior was promising – heavily beamed, with a projecting upper storey like a ship's poop, the window dark with ancient leaded lights. The room itself was in similar style. A log fire and red-shaded wall lights created an unexpectedly cosy fug in the gloom of the lengthening afternoon. Around forty people were enjoying the last, stay-loosening phase of the event, relaxed by booze and the satisfactory conclusion of tribal ritual. The buffet was savaged, and dirty wine glasses stood on every flat surface.

Thalia, who had given them up, hurried towards them, smiling broadly. She was the better for drink, eyes lit up and her fair skin a flushed raspberry sorbet. She wore a black mini-dress with a velvet yoke of such impressive style that Arden tried to get a look at the label as Thalia kissed them repeatedly and with all the appearance of equal warmth.

'There you are. I was worried.'

'Sorry. We had some urgent work to finish.'

'Never mind, you're here now. Come and get a drink and I'll introduce you to everyone.'

'This is quite a production, Thalia. Is it normal to have a do like this for a confirmation?' The thought crossed her mind that Thalia's expectation of Humph's money might have been the inspiration, not that there was anything wrong with that.

Her face fell. 'Do you think I've overdone it?'

'Not at all. *We* haven't even been christened. I know nothing about these bar mitzvah type things.'

Thalia smiled, but more guardedly than before. 'I'll go and get Gavin. Then you'll understand why I like to make a fuss of him!' She ploughed back through the bodies.

'Why did you have to say that, Ard?'

'What?'

'Implying that Thalia had ideas above her station. That was very hurtful.'

'I did not! I meant it as a compliment.'

'In your *dreams.*'

'That's Bos-speak, Tim. It sounds perfectly ridiculous coming from you.'

'Don't change the subject.'

'Well, stop policing my every utterance! I'm fed up with it.' They quickly composed their features to meet Gavin, whom Thalia proudly presented. He was quite a surprise: tall and slim, his hair slicked into spidery crescents like a *Monarda didyma*, and with an earring through one eyebrow. He looked whacked-out with meeting relations, but answered the customary queries about his GCSEs with great politeness. 'What a charming boy,' said Arden, when they had released him. 'He must be such a comfort. Is your father here?'

'No. I'm afraid it would have been too much for him. A neighbour is baby-sitting. But you must meet my uncle, Brother Sebastian. He knows – knew – Humph.' She had been going to say 'all about you' but thought better of it. Her uncle did not know the worst – yet. Thalia still had difficulty believing that people she liked as much as Arden and Tim could behave so badly. She had prayed for them, and hoped that their role in returning the Oriflamme would bring them forgiveness.

'Give me a moment, Thalia. I have to go to the bathroom.'

'That's fine. He isn't here just now. He's gone to take someone home.'

When Arden came back, Tim was surrounded by a group of women, entertaining them to some effect by the looks of things. Thalia had an arm round his back in proprietorial fashion. It was a curiously liberating sight, and for that reason a sad one. There was no point in pretending that she and Tim were not 'drifting apart', as the language of marriage guidance would have it. But Arden did not intend to drift for long. She would paddle for dear life. Several guests smiled at her from their conversational clusters, implying an invitation for her to join them. To procrastinate she went to fill her glass and inspect the display of family photo albums, recording Gavin's progress to this point, that had been set out on a table with his souvenir candle and presents. Arden flipped through them looking for pictures of Gavin's father and Thalia's parents.

She was fascinated to find several of Humph in family groups: at the seaside, at Christmas, Humph holding Gavin as a baby, Humph at a wedding kissing the bride. No sign of Mattie. Arden turned to the front of the album. There were black and white studio portraits of Thalia's parents, taken at the time of their engagement in the early-fifties. Her mother's beauty triumphed over the hideous roll-mop curls, boomerang eyebrows and dark greasy lipstick that were the fashion of the time. She looked at the camera with the hint of a self-satisfied smile. The photo-graph of her fiance showed a presentable, sandy-haired young man, uncomfortable in a suit. A man's hairy hand tapped the page.

'That's my sister. Lovely girl. I'm Thalia's uncle. Sebastian.' He held out his hand.

'How d'you do? Arden Fairbrother.'

'Ah!' And then again, 'Ah, I thought so.'

Arden laughed. 'Was it the whiff of sulphur that gave me away?'

'Sulphur? I could swear it was Tweed.'

This so-called monk was all right, Arden decided. She had been prepared for a Savonarola look-alike who would see straight into her soul and escort her to the nearest bonfire, but he was dressed in a blue grandad shirt and jeans, which helped. 'Do you think we could find a seat? I'm rather tired.'

'Surely. Come.' He went and drew up some chairs by the fire. Arden took the photo album with her. 'Can I get you a cup of tea?'

'Yes, please. That would be lovely.' She noticed Tim looking at Brother Sebastian with interest, but he was securely locked in to the huddle of women. 'Perhaps you can enlighten me?' she said, when Sebastian had returned with two cups of tea and some sugary cake.

'That's my job, ma'am.'

She giggled. Arden liked talking to men, as opposed to potential customers. 'No, I mean about the people in these photos. This is your sister?'

'Elder sister.'

'And that's Thalia's father. It is her own father, isn't it? I mean, her mother didn't remarry or anything?'

'Definitely not. I'm positive she'd have told me.'

'We've never met him. Is he in a very bad way?'

'I'm not a doctor, Mrs Fairbrother, but I would say yes. He'd have been long gone without Thalia to look after him, in my opinion. It was a blessing in disguise for him when her husband buggered off.'

'Not the Church's official view, I take it?'

'I'm off duty. Cake?'

'No, thank you. It seems very hard that she can't get divorced. Or won't. Do you think she'll ever change her mind?'

'I really couldn't tell you. She could get a civil divorce all right. But if she wanted an annulment she'd have a hard job explaining Gavin away. She's not royalty, you know. Why are you so interested anyhow?'

'No reason. Just nosey. My father seems to have spent so much time with this family and I know hardly anything about them.' She noted that he shifted in his seat.

'Did you find a parking space all right?'

'What? Yes. Do you know how the connection began?'

'That's an easy one. Your dad and my sister were at school together. Primary school. And all the others.'

'Oh, I see. Childhood sweethearts. But if they were just old friends, why did he never talk about her? And why isn't my mother in any of these photos? Were they lovers? There's no harm in telling me now they're both dead, is there?'

Sebastian had taken out his tobacco and now fumbled nervously with a roll-up. 'What is this – the Spanish Inquisition? How would I know if they were lovers? I'm not a priest. I couldn't threaten him with eternal damnation, you know.'

'Then why are you so jumpy about it?'

'I'm a monk! I'm not supposed to know about these things. It's embarrassing. Do you want a rollie?'

'No, thanks. If it's so embarrassing, I presume you know they were lovers?'

'No. They weren't. You shouldn't think that.'

'How can you be sure?'

'She told me. Monica – my sister.'

'Ah-ha. So there was a suspicion? Or did she just come out with it? "By the way, Humph and I aren't lovers"?'

'I wish you wouldn't keep using that word. My tobacco's all steamed up.' He sucked furiously on the fragile cigarette while holding a match to the tip so that there was every chance it would go up in flames before he got a draw.

'Was he in love with her, though? He was my father. Don't you think I have the right to know?'

'No, I don't. It was his life. And hers. Not yours. Sorry, but that's what I think. Bugger this thing.' He threw the stub into the fire.

Arden blushed and busily stirred her tea. She could see why Brother Sebastian was not assigned to pastoral work. But she respected his bluntness. 'All right. Can you tell me one thing, though? Do you remember the date she died?'

'The date? Of course. September the third. Why?'

'Never mind. I think that tells me all I need to know.'

'Thank God for that. Now can we talk about something else? I gather you're in line for the *Légion d'Honneur*?'

No amount of earlobe tugging on Arden's part got the message through to Tim that she wanted to go home. The line had gone dead. Arden was frustrated. Tim probably thought she wished to tear him from Thalia's side and was deliberately ignoring her. In fact she was only eager to share with him her deductions about Humph and Thalia's mother as a result of the conversation with Brother Sebastian. However, even when she did manage to get him away, his disinclination to talk about it almost matched the monk's. Tim had been zapped to the spot by Thalia in her little black dress, which clung to her curvaceous figure – or some of it – like skin to a seal. She was a completely different woman – a real one. His thoughts had carried him no further at this stage. He was so much in the habit of sharing them with Arden it was better not to have any that he could not share. She tried to arouse his interest.

'If Humph was in love with her, it explains so much. She had married somebody else, so Humph didn't care who *he* married. The fact that your mum was pregnant by another man does rather suggest that, doesn't it?'

'No. Why would he bother to get married at all?'

'Oh, I don't know. Perhaps he wanted to show this Monica he didn't care. Make her jealous? Who knows? Perhaps he was bribed by your mum's father. Do you think it's worth trying to trace her, to find out?'

'No! Why should I go crawling after parents who didn't want me?'

'And then Mattie – well, after your mum went off he had to have a wife to look after you. Mattie's an angel, but no match for a Beatrice Portinari. And the calendar – don't you remember, it was left at September the third? Time stopped for him and all that. And then he went and died himself. Of a broken heart, obviously. People do, you know. Their immune systems break down. And they weren't even lovers, that's the incredible thing. You see, he married rather than burn. Poor old Humph.'

'I don't know how you can talk so glibly about all this. If you're right it's very sad.'

'Well, of course it is. But how come you're so sentimental about Humph now? Especially as you know he wasn't really your father.'

'But he was. Precisely because he wasn't.'

'Fuck me, what *are* you talking about? You mean, he was a better father for not being one?'

'Relatively speaking, yes.'

'Well, I can't say that, can I? The reverse is true for me.'

'Yes. That's why you're always so angry about him.'

'Angry? Of course I'm not *angry*. I was only curious as to why he was such an inadequate father. Now I know. Those letters must have been from Thalia's mother.'

'What letters?'

'The letters in the coffin. Don't you remember?'

'I suppose so. But, Arden, I don't care.'

*　　*　　*

Jermigan came home from hospital and took up headquarters in the library, where a bed had been installed. Arden noted a resumption of visits from his navy blue-suited familiars, with increased frequency. She kept away from the Hall. Fortunately he would be immobile for some time so she could be sure not to encounter him until she was ready. It was disappointing that he had not felt the need to thank her for her part in Lottie's rescue. Presumably Miss Tree siphoned off his limited store of finer feeling in that respect. And it was quite possible that he had convinced himself that Arden owed him a favour after causing him to fall down the Priest's Hole. No man would let slip an opportunity to blame a woman for his misfortunes.

Jake had a call from Darren, who was too scared of Jermigan to come home. He had been offered a brilliant job in Azerbaijan and wanted to know if Jake would be able to come and pick up the truck. As an afterthought, he asked if Lottie had got home all right. Jake put these items in reverse order when he informed Miss Tree. She went pale and put her hand to her brow. 'Mr Jermigan isn't going to like this, Jake.'

'Right. Thing is, will 'e like it more or less than what he likes Darren at the moment, type o' thing?'

'I haven't discussed Darren's – behaviour – with Mr Jermigan. But I'm certain he will want the truck back. Oh, dear, we are becoming a regular breakdown service. For people, anyway.' She promised to have a look at the schedules and see if Jake could double up with someone on the outward journey.

Lottie was amused to learn that Darren had gone into voluntary exile. She told Arden about it on one of the now regular calls at Barnacle Cottage bearing gifts of homemade produce from Miss Tree.

'What's Azerbaijani for bonk, I wonder? Darren's so naive, Mrs Fairbrother. He'll never stick it.'

'Umm. I hope he's considered the effect on his personal pension plan.' Arden had been giving much thought to her own. 'Likewise his National Insurance contributions.'

'Get *real* Mrs F. Darren would no more organize a pension plan than he would an – I don't know – eisteddfod.'

'Lottie, don't you feel *any* responsibility for Darren's fate?'

'No. Well, okay, yes. When Uncle Harry's calmed down a bit I'll get him to issue a pardon.'

'So Darren's right, Mr Jermigan *is* angry with him?'

'Probably. I wouldn't know. We're not speaking at the moment.'

'Oh, good. That sounds very healthy.'

The crucial meeting of the district council planning committee, at which the Sloping Experience would be discussed, was set for 14 March. Tim was astounded that Arden did not intend to go. He found her change of attitude quite mysterious. 'Don't you care anymore, Ard? You used to be so passionate about it.'

'Passion is a high-maintenance self-indulgence, Tim. I'm just being realistic. Anyway, even if the plans are approved Jermigan can't proceed without this place, you know that.' She noticed his look of disappointment. 'I know you want me not to care, but don't think I've given up. I'm just doing some creative thinking.'

'Like what?'

'I'll tell you if it works out. By the way, don't you think we should get Mum over here soon, if we're going to at all? While it's still as she remembers it. It's going to be difficult enough now she knows Humph is dead. It would be too upsetting for her if the place was a building site.'

'I thought you said he couldn't proceed without our consent?'

'Yes. Well. You know Jermigan. He may yet succeed in exterminating us. Besides we can't bring her back and forth from Felixstowe, it's too far. She might as well come when she can.'

'I don't see the point. Wouldn't it be better to let her remember it as it was when she and Humph lived here?'

'All right. If you think that's best.'

There was little pleasure to be had from Arden's acquiescence. It was eerie, the way she had suspended open conflict. Over the years that they had been together Tim's muscles had developed a Pavlovian tendency to seize up whenever she opened her mouth. It was a wonder he was not permanently deformed. Now he thought about it, his hip could well be a psychosomatic consequence of all this tension. Strange to think that all the time he had assumed that living with Arden was the only really life-enhancing experience he had known it was actually making him ill.

On the night of the planning committee meeting she took the unusual step of going to the cinema with Bos. She thought *Titanic* would match her mood, with its monumental symbols of unequal struggle. Bos could not understand why she had wanted to come. She could have stuffed her face with butterscotch popcorn in silence at home. There was a couple he knew sitting a few rows behind and he asked Arden if she would mind if he sat next to them. She told him to shhh, not listening to what he said, and did not seem to notice that he had gone.

The conditional approval of the development plan was published in the local paper. Arden knew she must act before she lost her nerve. Mr Gordon put up manful resistance to seeing her again. His dramatic appearance at the cottage door in the dead of night was now a matter of considerable regret to him. He was aware he had been drunk and disorderly and feared that the redoubtable Mrs Fairbrother would take him to task on that account. At the least she reminded him of his own unseemly behaviour and he dimly recalled that he had threatened to withdraw his services. That now seemed like one of his better ideas, but the woman was persistent, and as the execution of the will was not yet concluded he supposed he had to see her. He arranged the appointment for first thing in the morning. It was not something he wanted to look forward to all day. Before calling her into his office he combed his thick white hair and assumed an expression of, he hoped, judicious dignity.

'Mrs Fairbrother?' As if he did not know. 'Come in, please.'

'Thank you.' Arden stood up and smoothed the folds of her magenta and white ensemble. She knew the colours to be a stunning contrast with her black hair, and stunning people always gave one confidence. She kept on her goatskin driving gloves to shake hands with Mr Gordon because she knew her palms were sweaty. The gleam of appreciation in his eye as he discreetly looked her up and down was an encouraging sign. 'Thank you for agreeing to see me. Before I forget – my brother, Mr Mason, doesn't know I'm here, so I'd be obliged if you wouldn't mention it.'

'As you wish. Please sit down. This isn't a family matter, then?'

'Yes and no.'

'Oh. That's a pity. Your family's affairs are far too exciting for my nerves.'

'I trust you won't be demanding damages.' He laughed, unsure if she was joking. 'You'll be pleased to know the Oriflamme is back in its rightful home.'

'Indeed. Good. Good.'

'Talking of rightful homes – Mr Gordon, bear with me. The matter I've come about is also not your average conveyancing quibble. It's certainly a test of nerves. Mine, anyway. The thing is, I'd like you to write a letter for me. That's what solicitors do, isn't it?'

'If there are legal implications, certainly.'

'Well, there are.'

'And to whom is this letter to be written?'

'Mr Harry Jermigan.'

'Ah, the laird of Sloping. As it happens I've written several letters to that gentleman in my time. Most of them concerned with DNA testing, I regret to say. I trust that's not the case on this occasion?'

'No. You're probably aware that Mr Jermigan wants to turn Sloping Castle into a medieval theme park. He thinks it's going to be frightfully up market and attract lots of rich twats who – well, never mind that. The plans have been approved, conditionally, but as our cottage is on the site he can't do anything unless we sell it to him. He made us an offer, but for reasons I won't bore you with, we didn't feel able to accept it. He has promised me that he will drop the plans, but I don't trust him. I didn't get it in writing, like a fool.'

'Have you changed your mind?'

'Yes. But – I have a proposal I would like to put to him.'

'A proposal. Not of marriage, I presume?'

'Yes, as a matter of fact.'

'I beg your pardon?'

'A conditional proposal.'

'Mrs Fairbrother, you take my breath away. This isn't my line of country at all. If you want to marry Mr Jermigan, why don't you simply ask him?'

'We're not talking about a love match, Mr Gordon. It's a business proposition. I don't want anyone, including Mr Jermigan, to be in any doubt about that. I couldn't live it down if there were the faintest suggestion that I was in love with him or anything stupid like that. If I applied to him directly he'd be bound to think that, or at least would feel free to spread it around in those terms, and there would be no proof to the contrary. Whereas I wouldn't mind people knowing that I considered an arranged marriage for business reasons. Actually I don't think Mr Jermigan likes me very much, so it will save us both a lot of awkwardness if he doesn't accept my terms.'

'But, my dear woman, if he doesn't like you and you are not in love with him, what sort of marriage could you possibly have?'

'The same as half the marriages in the country, I should think. It could only get better, let's put it that way.'

Mr Gordon shook his head. 'I knew I shouldn't have got out of bed this morning. Very well, Mrs Fairbrother, what are these terms?'

'First of all, please make it clear that everything depends on my brother's agreement. I haven't told him yet. I thought it was better to sound out Mr Jermigan first.'

'I can't agree with you there. I think you know your brother will be horrified at his sister's engaging in such a bargain. What brother wouldn't? Are you sure you're not just avoiding the inevitable?'

'Possibly. It's true Tim will be apopleptic. But I don't see what difference the timing makes.'

'Very well.' He began to make notes. 'Go on.'

'I propose that we cede the cottage to Mr Jermigan in exchange for certain – disbursements.'

'Is that how you would describe marriage, Mrs Fairbrother, as a disbursement?'

'That's a very cynical interpretation.'

'Oh, I beg your pardon.'

'But it is one of the conditions, yes. There are others. My brother is in urgent need of a hip replacement. I would like

Mr Jermigan to pay for immediate treatment.' She waited while Mr Gordon wrote. 'Also our mother, Mrs Matilda Mason, of The Ashes, Lower Upton, needs funding at her nursing home. The council want to move her to a place in Felixstowe, but you needn't put that in. We have a property in London that's currently rented. When it's sold the proceeds can be invested to provide fees for our mother's home, but I would like Mr Jermigan to guarantee to top up any shortfall, at present estimated at three to four hundred pounds a month.'

'Anything else?'

'Yes. I would like a controlling share in Sloping Enterprises.'

'What? Oh, come now, Mrs Fairbrother, he's hardly going to give you that. It would make a nonsense of the whole project from his point of view. Besides, I hardly think this junket is going to be floated on the stock market.'

'Oh. Well, how can I make him consult me about the arrangements?'

'You could simply make it a condition of the contract. Hard to enforce – but if you have, shall we say, permanent access to Mr Jermigan, I'm sure you'll be able to make your influence felt.'

'All right. There's only one other thing. Rent-free accommodation on or near the site for my brother, Mr Timothy Mason, for life. Also the right of abode at the same accommodation for my son, Bosworth Fairbrother, as long as Mr Timothy Mason resides there. I thought it was too much to expect that Mr Jermigan should have Bos living with us, you see. I don't want to overdo it.'

'That's the spirit.'

'I couldn't expect to move my whole family in with me.'

'Not at first.' His ironic intonation was lost on her. 'If this contract is going to take the form of a pre-nuptial agreement, Mrs Fairbrother, are there no terms you would wish to include to cover a possible breakdown of the marriage?'

'Good thinking, Mr Gordon. In that case I would expect a reimbursement of the full market value of the cottage, adjusted to take account of inflation in the property market – but not less than the current market value in the event that the market had gone down.' The cottage would be a thatched stew by that time anyway. And if the marriage broke down she would be unlikely to stay on in its shadow.

'That's a prudent proviso. You should have been an estate agent, Mrs Fairbrother.'

'I was. Also, a proportion of Mr Jermigan's pension amounting to £500 per annum for each year of the marriage up to a maximum of £8000 per annum. That's not too greedy, is it?'

'Very modest, when one considers his resources.'

'Quite. How long will it take you to draw up the letter?'

'It can be done this afternoon. I have to ask you, are you absolutely sure this is what you want?'

'Yes. I've given it a lot of thought. Can your secretary be trusted?'

'Of course. She may fall off her chair, but she will be discreet.'

'Right. I think that's everything.'

'I shall look forward eagerly to Mr Jermigan's reply.'

'So shall I. It will be a test of how much he wants his Sloping Experience, won't it?'

In this context, thought Arden, it was an advantage that Mr Gordon was such a conservative old stick. His reaction to her proposal was a severe test of its credibility and she had expected him to be shocked. But he had adapted to the idea remarkably fast. Jermigan was much more of a free thinker than Mr Gordon. She did not expect him to be particularly shocked. She would have to brace herself for a fair amount of yokelish ridicule from him if he rejected her, but then, she had been a martyr to misunderstanding all her life.

On the other hand, Jermigan was someone who respected honest greed, and her suggestion fell far short of that, so perhaps he would not find it risible at all. She would even be prepared to admit to him, as she had not to Mr Gordon, that the gloss on the arrangement – that she would be mistress of Sloping – had been one factor in her decision. Theme park it might be, but she could at least ensure that it was in the best possible taste. And it would certainly not do her *Suitables* career any harm to operate out of such a spacious facility. There might even be sales opportunities from the clientele, if they could be torn away from the joys of cavorting to the reebeck and wiping their bottoms with dock leaves.

For the next few days Arden kept herself busy. Fortunately it was high season for *Suitables* and the warm weather induced a spate of manic spring cleaning. When that was done she started on the garden, lifted half the paving stones in the back and planted the gaps with medicinal herbs. After ten days without a word from Mr Gordon she began to wonder if she had hallucinated the incident. The tension ebbed out of her as if by force of gravity but when, finally, a letter from the solicitor arrived, it gushed back into every fibre. She could not possibly open the letter with Tim in the house. Whatever Jermigan had decided she would need to calm down in private. The day's schedule was for the Cromer area so she set off towards Norwich and stopped in the carpark of McDonald's on the Beccles by-pass. At least there would be a toilet handy.

Dear Mrs Fairbrother,
Further to our meeting of 25 March, I have written to Mr Harry Jermigan setting out your proposal as discussed. I have now received a reply. Mr Jermigan is in principle disposed to accept your offer subject to further negotiation. His comments on the conditions proposed can be summarized as follows:
1. Privately funded hip replacement operation for your brother, Mr Timothy Mason, will be funded in full, providing the venue and choice of consultant are at Mr Jermigan's discretion. No further related treatment, however, will be guaranteed.
2. Top-up funding for the residential accommodation for your mother, Mrs Matilda Mason, will be capped at £300 per month, plus inflation. The sum to be paid only in the event that proceeds from the investment devoted to this purpose fall below the average market return for the preceding twelve months and that the sum constitutes no more than 15% of the overall fee.
3. Accommodation, with life-time residential rights, will be provided for Mr Timothy Mason at the market rate less 25% discount. Mrs Fairbrother will agree to cede her rights in the investment fund ring-fenced for the provision of Mrs Matilda Mason's residential fees to her brother, Mr Timothy Mason, after the decease of the said Mrs Matilda Mason.

4. In the event of a breakdown of the proposed marriage between Mr Harry Jermigan and Mrs Arden Fairbrother, Mr Harry Jermigan will pay to the said Mrs Arden Fairbrother (Mrs Arden Jermigan/Fairbrother) a sum equal to 60% of the current market value of Barnacle Cottage, plus the sum of £500 per annum for each year of the marriage up to a maximum of £6000 per annum adjusted to base rate inflation excluding mortgage costs, to be paid on the issue of a decree absolute of divorce between the said Mr Harry Jermigan and Mrs Arden Fairbrother (Mrs Arden Jermigan/Fairbrother.) These conditions will only apply in the case that the divorce is by mutual agreement.

5. The contract between Mr Harry Jermigan and Mrs Arden Fairbrother will be put into effect only on the following conditions:

    a) The written consent to the contract of Mr Timothy Mason.

    b) The successful outcome of a compatibility trial between the proponents, Mr Harry Jermigan and Mrs Arden Fairbrother.

Mr Jermigan is anxious to arrange a meeting with you in regard to 5b. Should you wish to discuss this, or any other aspect of the matter, please contact me at your earliest convenience.

Yours sincerely,

Abel Gordon

The terms swam before Arden's eyes. The only one that registered was 5b. What did he mean by a 'compatibility trial'? Not – sex? What had that got to do with anything? There did not seem to be any other interpretation. She had accepted that it was inevitable once the marriage took place, on the lie-still-and-think-of-Sloping principle. But could she go through with the humiliation of *failing* such a test? Rage bubbled up to quash the satisfaction she ought to feel at the potential success of the scheme. Jermigan was not going to give up his manipulative games. The carrot was held out on the other side of a chasm in which her pride, at least, could crash to extinction. The cunning bastard. He probably planned to get a free bonk and then renege on the contract.

Depressing doubts set in. Did this amount to prostitution? But then, prostitution had become quite respectable. It was axiomatic these days that a woman had the right to do what she liked with her own body. Prostitutes argued their case on Heart of the Matter, formed unions and sent their children to private schools. It was not as if she was proposing to sell herself to the highest bidder. At the very least a counter-condition was indicated. Jermigan would not get his free bonk if she had anything to do with it. She got out a pen and drafted a reply on the back of the letter.

> *Dear Mr Gordon,*
> *Subject to my brother's agreement, I accept conditions 1–4 stipu-*
> *lated by Mr Jermigan as stated in yours of 5 April. With regard*
> *to 5b, I feel some compensation should be due to me in the event*
> *that Mr Jermigan considers the 'compatibility trial' a failure.*
> *Should I agree to go through with this trial, I would like Mr*
> *Jermigan's agreement in advance that Condition 1, relating to*
> *my brother's hip replacement operation, should be implemented*
> *regardless of the outcome. This would be not only in respect of*
> *any indignity I might suffer as a result of the 'failure' of the said*
> *trial, but also in recognition of the stress caused to my brother and*
> *myself as a result of Mr Jermigan's harassment with regard to the*
> *purchase of our home.*
> *I would also request that the said trial should be deferred until*
> *Mr Jermigan's plaster has come off, as I would prefer the trial to*
> *be conducted at a neutral location and he would otherwise have*
> *difficulty travelling.*
> *Yours sincerely,*
> *Arden Fairbrother.*

There was no question of telling Tim about this particular aspect of the arrangement. He would suffer till the cows came home rather than let her sleep her way to his private operation. But there was no escaping the fact that it was time to sound him out as to the overall plan.

Privacy would be essential. Arden lay awake in bed, listening to Bos's muffled snores from the next room and trying to think of the most suitable venue for what was bound to be a trying occasion. It would be a good idea to get Tim away from home, which was subject to constant interruptions, but where could they go to be private in public? A pensive stroll on the beach, or anywhere else, was impossible because of Tim's hip. It was rather early in the year for a picnic although the weather was unseasonably warm. Arden was sweating and threw her covers off. It was like July in the Deep South. She crept out of bed and as quietly as possible opened the window. Tip-toeing back to bed she noticed that Tim was also wide awake.

'You should turn the central heating off if you're going to open the windows, Ard.'

'We're not that hard up that we can't afford to let a bit of air in, surely?'

'There's no point in wasting money.'

'Fine. I'll go and adjust the programmer.'

'Don't be daft. It can wait till morning.'

'Did you wake up because your hip hurts or were you just too hot?'

'Both. Your thrashing around like a beached whale doesn't help.'

'Sorry. Bos won't be here for much longer then I can move into his room. He's almost saved up enough to pay off his debt. I'm afraid he won't stay around long once that's done. There's nothing much for him here.'

'That's gratitude. Aren't *you* something?'

'You know what I mean. He'll come and go, but he can't wait to get back to his friends at university.'

'I thought he'd given that up? He told me he was thinking of working full-time for Jermigan once he'd got his HGV licence.'

'You must have misunderstood. Perhaps he meant full-time as long as he's here.'

'I don't think so. I hope Jermigan isn't under a misconception. I thought it was rather generous of him to pay for it considering Bos is only going to be around for a few months. Still, I'm going to see him in the morning. I'll ask him about it.'

'What? Why are you going to see him?'

'Because he asked me to.'

'What about?'

'I've no idea. Perhaps now the plans have been approved he's going to up his offer?'

'Why didn't you tell me?'

'No reason. I forgot. You've been in a trance the last few weeks anyhow. Why should I deliberately conceal it?'

'You can't.'

'Can't what?'

'Go and see Jermigan.'

'Why not?' Tim raised himself on one elbow and peered at her.

'Well, not before – Oh, Tim, you know I love you, don't you?'

'Eh? I suppose so. It sounds a bit ominous, though. What have you done now? Are we moving to the Far East? I thought this *was* the Far East.'

'No, we're not moving. At least, I don't think so. But there's something I have to tell you.' Which she did, omitting only the side issue of the compatibility trial. Tim lay open-mouthed, staring at the ceiling. 'He hasn't made a final decision yet. The thing is, it all depends on you, Tim. You have a half share in the cottage. You can't be forced to give it up.'

He rolled his head from side to side. 'Did you hear yourself, Ard? I can't be *forced*? That must mean you have considered it. What's happened to you?'

'Nothing. You know I've always been a pragmatist. It wasn't an easy decision, Tim. The thing is, the way I see it, life here would be intolerable if we held out against Jermigan now the plans have gone through. I know I said I could take it, and I can, but I don't think *you* can. You must admit it would make life less complicated if we came to a compromise with him?'

'But *marriage!* What kind of compromise is that? You despise him. And after all you had to say about his appalling schemes for Sloping, how *can* you—'

'Think the unthinkable? It's all the rage, darling. I know it must seem like a bit of a volte-face, worthy of our esteemed Front Bench, indeed. But this way I will at least have some influence on how it's done. He does have a point about the employment opportunities, you know. And it's a lonely job, manning the altars of aesthetic purity. But it was really Mum's having to move that tipped the balance. How else could we manage to keep her at The Ashes? The margins are too tight. Aren't you even pleased that she'll be able to stay where she is?'

'I don't know. I can't think. So that's why you didn't put up more of a fight against the plans? If they hadn't gone through you wouldn't have had your bargaining chip.'

'If they hadn't gone through, Jermigan would have blamed us. Life would have been intolerable anyway.'

'We could have left. We could have gone away somewhere else.'

'If we did that he would be the only person who'd buy the place even so. If we sold it to someone else he'd just smoke them out too. Not that anyone round here would walk into his cage. It would probably be some innocent old pensioners from Essex who'd give in as soon as he set the dogs on them. This way he gets what he wants but so do we.'

'*We?* What's this got to do with *me*? I'm just an obstacle in your path.'

'That's not fair, Tim. I'll always be close by. I'll always look after you. But, well, things have changed between us, haven't they? And, be honest, you're not the sort of person who does want anything in particular.'

'Did you ever ask?'

'Well, do you?'

'I can't be expected to think of something straight off.'

'In other words, no. What do you think, then? Do you agree?'

'I suppose if I don't you'll make Jermigan's methods look like a gentle nudge.'

'That's a horrible thing to say. But I'll take it as a yes.'

Tim did not say anything. Despite the heat he put his head under the pillow. Arden was hurt that his only reaction to the idea of her marrying Jermigan was incredulity.

The condition regarding the plaster cast was not accepted. Jermigan joked to Mr Gordon that he had two legs left, but this comment was not passed on to Arden. She objected that as Mr Jermigan was temporarily disabled it would hardly be a fair test of his capabilities. He sent back a terse reminder that marriage was in sickness or in health and she could take it or leave it. Arden was momentarily tempted to leave it. But with Tim behaving as though the arrangement were a fait accompli, and spending conspicuous amounts of time with Thalia, she had too much to lose by withdrawing at this stage. At least Tim would get his operation. All she would have to do was come up with some story as to how she got the money. That was solved while she was at the newsagent's. The lottery – of course. Before breakfast on the day of the dreaded tryst she asked Bos if he could roll her a couple of spliffs.

Jermigan, with his greater local knowledge, had been allowed the choice of hotel. Arden was curious to see how far away they would have to go to get to an area where his writ did not run. Always assuming he wished to keep their meeting secret. In the event she only had to go to the London side of Bury St Edmunds, to a country house hotel newly built to be indistinguishable from a pretentious supermarket. She had to admit that the dimensions and luxury of the fittings were awe-inspiring. The flower arrangements in the foyer were of ecclesiastical splendour. On enquiry she was told that Jermigan had not arrived. They were registered in the name of Sewell, at Arden's suggestion. The desk clerk was distressingly breezy. Arden would have preferred a bit of old-fashioned collusion, which at least maintained the pretence that this sort of thing was not a commonplace.

There was nothing for it but to go up to the room. She did not want to meet him under the public gaze. More flower arrangements, precisely scaled to suit the room, were disposed on the dressing table and other furnitures. It looked like a Las Vegas funeral parlour. More to the point, a bottle of champagne substitute stood in a gilt bucket by the bed. She thought at least two would be needed. It was still half an hour before the appointed time so she went out and found a window over looking the entrance so that she could see Jermigan arrive.

He was late. The first thing to emerge was his plastered foot. The taxi driver went round with the crutches and helped him out. By some miracle of tailoring he had got himself into a grey pin-stripe suit, one leg cut off at the crutch to accommodate the plaster. Arden wondered if Miss Tree had been involved in this feat and if so what he had told her. She was quite confident that Miss Tree would be the least of her worries. It was she who had waxed lyrical about Jermigan's 'god-like' appeal but as she had long since retired from the field she would be gracious enough not to object if Arden stepped in. Lottie was another matter. She might well be hostile. Having disowned Jermigan for years it was almost inevitable that she would now decide she did not want to share him. Arden told herself not to jump the gun. She would be ordering new curtains for the Great Room before the sun went down at this rate.

There was a clunk against the door as Jermigan thwacked it with his crutch. He hobbled in without looking at her.

'Couldn't wait, eh, gal? That's the ticket.' He headed for the armchair closest to the champagne. 'I damn' near sent you the bill, gal, but I s'ppose you'd want that written off an' all?'

'Too right. Why do men always have to blame someone for every little thing.'

'It ain't just men, gal. You never blame nobody for nothin'? My arse.'

'All right, we won't argue about that. But I think you could have waited until your leg was better.'

'Waited? I been shut up in a bleedin' nunnery for weeks. Ain't you got no pity?'

'Yes, but I'm not a contortionist. How is this going to work?'

'No problem. You get on top back to front, like, it'll work a treat. Pass me that bottle and let's get crackin.''

'This is ridiculous. I demand an independent arbitrator. Send for Ofsex.'

'Off what? Ain't you going to get your kit off?'

'All in good time. I think we'd better get yours off first. You're going to need some help.'

'That'll be a first. Drink up, gal. I'll 'ave to order another one of these before we gets down to business.'

'This isn't a trial of compatibility, Mr Jermigan, is it? It's just a laugh so far as you're concerned. A very expensive laugh.'

''Course not. You can't expect me to marry you on spec, like. Got to inspect the goods, don't I?'

Arden forced a grin. 'I know you mean that in the nicest possible way.'

'Right.' He downed another glass and asked her to put the radio on and tune it to Classic FM.

'Well, there's a surprise,' muttered Arden. When she turned back to him he had taken off his jacket and shirt. He had lost weight since she had seen him in the hospital and the roll of flesh that splayed over his trousers was not as extensive as she had feared.

'Here, help me on the bed, gal.'

She put his arm around her shoulders and heaved. He unzipped his trousers and tried to wriggle them off but they got stuck at the top of the plaster. 'You shouldn't have rolled them down, like that. You should have pulled them off from underneath.'

'Fuck. Fuck. Fuck. Ain't you got no scissors? Just cut 'em off.'

'You can't do that. How will you get home?' Arden started to laugh and rolled on to the bed beside him. He smacked her thigh.

'Ain't no laughin' matter. What am I going to do?'

'Start again. Roll them up again and then do what I said – pull them from the bottom.'

He tried to balance on his free leg to achieve this manoeuvre but fell back on the bed, cursing. 'You do it! That's what a wife's for, ain't it?'

'God, you're romantic. Lie down then.'

It was dark when she woke up. The room was lit only from the lamps outside and the safety lights on the skirting board. She was fairly confident that she had passed the test – four times – in various positions reminiscent of the logo of the Isle of Man. Jermigan was still fast asleep, his plastered leg outside the sheet, his arm heavy across her stomach. Oh, well, if this was a taste of things to come she should lengthen her life expectancy by several decades, if statistics were to be believed. She propped herself on her elbow and took a swig of the bubbly left in her glass. Hair of the dog and all that. She examined Jermigan's body, from the tight grey curls on his head and chest to the toe sticking out of the cast. A very long toe. Like Lottie's, as she had observed that time that she had gone over to the Hall to fetch Bos. Like Tim's too. She recalled thinking that Lottie would have trouble getting up on points.

She put the glass down carefully and lay back, suddenly feeling rather weak. Could it just be coincidence or could Jermigan be Tim's father? Her mind scrambled after the evidence. It would explain the favour that he had owed Humph. She had assumed it was Humph's co-operation in the affair of the Oriflamme. But if he had bribed Humph to marry Tim's mother that would be a much more weighty obligation. She knew Humph and Jermigan had married at about the same time. Jermigan's wife was the one with the money. If he had got some other girl pregnant he would have had a lot to lose. But how could he have persuaded Tim's mother to co-operate? Quite easily, knowing him. No wonder the marriage didn't last. On the other hand, Jermigan had never shown any interest in Tim. There could be two reasons for that. One – Tim did not interest him. Two – he might have deliberately ignored the fact out of consideration for Humph. And Lottie had long since been the only child he cared about.

The possibility was too appalling. Arden did not want to know. For one thing, it would mean she was marrying Tim's father and she had been looking forward to an incest-free relationship. A clean slate and all that. It would be less complicated. Of course, she was not technically related to Tim, but she still felt as though she was. And if he were the son, he would also be the heir. These days, it could be proved one way or the other and Tim could sue for a share of the inheritance: Sloping.

By failing to pursue the matter, would she be cheating him?

Not really. He had been brought up as Humph's son and treated as his heir. Which was decent of Humph, when one thought about it. Perhaps they had had unreasonable expectations of Humph's behaviour. Of course now Tim's share was to be traded in for a life policy as part of the marriage settlement. But he would get the proceeds of the house in Chiswick as well. She was sure that he would not want to know that Jermigan was his father. The shock might well kill him. The toes had to be coincidence. It would be impossible for the marriage to work if Tim started claiming his filial rights. He might expect to move into the Hall! It was all far too confusing. Lottie's nose would be put severely out of joint. She would probably leave as soon as she could. Arden still had hopes that Lottie and Bos would fall in love. After all, they would see a great deal of each other if they were practically brother and sister.